TOTH

TOTH

A Science Fiction Novel

by

JAMES C. GLASS

The Borgo Press
An Imprint of Wildside Press LLC

MMIX

CONTENTS

DEDICATION

For Gary

And the good folks who worked
for you at Books in Motion

We had a good ride

CHAPTER ONE

Rudy Hoffman stared with dismay at the graphics display overlapping his electromagnetic sensor data from IR to gamma. It was a ship, all right, trailing a plasma stream a mega meter long, and it had appeared suddenly like a new comet before disappearing over the eastern horizon. Now it was back again, the plasma plume gone, but a heavy hydrogen gamma signature clearly visible. A fusion drive now shut down with the ship inserted in a high, circular orbit. Rudy hesitated. He'd been trained for this moment since childhood, performing routine duties for twenty years and seeing nothing until this day. Nothing to indicate the arrival of visitors to the world of Toth. His orders were clear; he switched off all scanners and called the mainland, ordering them to maintain a scan and receive any radio transmission from the ship. Now it was time for his most difficult task.

It was time to inform his Master about the arrival of visitors.

The control room was at the top of the dome and he descended the helical staircase into the bowels of the temple, came out into a circular room lit dimly by the displays of the computer, his Master's extension in monitoring and controlling the life of the planet. It was a formality to give his report, for the scanner data was already absorbed, analyzed and coded.

Toth would know his report before it was made. He was all knowing.

Rudy went to a podium in the center of the room, the panel there giving him visual access to a Master he had never seen in person, a man transfigured yet still human, holding himself apart physically from His people while maintaining constant contact with them in their everyday lives. How would he take this news? Rudy took a deep breath and let it out slowly as his fingers played over the keys of the panel.

The space in front of him glowed suddenly green and a shimmering figure appeared there, a man, old beyond description, seated on a throne of stone. His face was thin and wrinkled, eyes blazing like twin emeralds. Rudy felt fear, then euphoria as his Lord smiled, and he felt The Pleasure in every part of his body. His Lord was pleased.

"You've done well, Rudy," said Toth. "Your quick action should divert the ship's attention to the mainland."

"I am your servant, Lord Toth. The ship is now in orbit and contact should be expected. Can this be the visitation you've prepared us for?"

"I'm afraid it is," said Toth. "I had hopes we'd been forgotten, but that is not to be. It was too much to expect for such a long time, and finally we must deal with it."

"Weapons control awaits your command, Lord. In four hours we'll have an exact calculation of the orbit, and all batteries are at full power."

Toth waved a hand gently and smiled again. "Fear is an enemy, Rudy. The Chosen do not quickly kill that which they fear, but look for alternatives. Those who come here are not of The Chosen, but are known to Me. I have dwelled in their midst and counseled them. The fact they've not chosen to follow our ways doesn't make them evil people, only ignorant. We'll deal with them, hear what they have to say and send them on their way. But you are correct in maintaining a full alert. If these people threaten our world in any way they must be dealt with harshly, even if it means others will come after them. For the moment, we'll wait. In the meantime you should calculate the exact Orbit of that ship and remain alert."

"Yes. My Lord." Toth looked away from him, nodded at someone outside the limits of the holographic image, and then turned back.

"There is someone else I must speak with. My blessings on you, Rudy." He waved his hand slowly and once again Rudy Hoffman felt the wave of Pleasure pass through his body from head to toe, quickening his heartbeat as the image of Toth flickered and disappeared.

Rudy climbed the stairs to the control room, nerve-endings still tingling from His Lord's Pleasure. He was relieved, for he'd not always received such reward for his deeds. There had been times, mostly in his youth, when his own desires had superseded those of Toth, and he had paid the necessary price.

He still remembered the pain.

CHAPTER TWO

Michael's first conscious thought was a desire to stay where he was, floating in a dream about the baths on Arkon. Waves of warm water surged against his chest, and Mira squeezed his hand. They were standing naked in roiling waters as Daniel paddled ahead of them towards a huge, marble fountain covered with screaming children in the center of the great pool. Daniel, now four years old, was a child of Arkon's elite, his father a captain over five hundred combat marines in Victoria's Legion. Daniel reached the fountain, clambered up onto it and waved to his parents.

When they were close he threw himself towards them, coming up sputtering, arms thrashing as he swam his first, tentative strokes without the support of the poly-board.

Mira gasped. Michael drew her close and smiled with pride s his son swam freely for the first time, and—

There was a stinging sensation in his body, the dream shattered. His mouth tasted like tarnished silver, and cold air was blowing on his face. He traced the pain to his arm now lying across his chest. There was a voice and flashing light as his eyelids fluttered.

"Major Queal? Rise and shine, sir. We've got a problem here."

Michael squeezed his eyes shut tightly, and caught a whiff of Oliazone, the stuff that dreams are made of, but it was too late. He was awake now, and the cocoon was open. He could feel his legs; hear the dull thud of his own heart beating, the click-click of a circulation pump, the distant growl of a fusion engine.

He was back on *Belsus* again.

"Please, sir. They're waiting for you on the bridge."

Michael opened his eyes, blinked twice at light first bright, then dull as an unfamiliar face blocked it. Someone leaned over to peer closely at him. "Private Osen, sir. They sent me to fetch you. The rest of the detachment has been up for several hours."

A boy, thought Michael. Every time I wake up, they get younger and younger. He moved his arms and grasped the edges of the

9

cocoon. Osen removed the stim-cuff and helped him sit up where he teetered for a moment. A wave of nausea passed quickly.

"Would you like some water, sir?"

"Anything to get this crummy taste out of my mouth, private." His voice was hoarse, and sounded foreign to him. How long since he'd last heard it? He really didn't want to know, but asked anyway.

"How long have I been under this time?" he asked, took a poly-bottle from Osen and sipped slowly.

The boy consulted a chart at the end of Michael's cocoon. "A little over fifteen years Arkon, sir. Three jumps since they put you in the cocoon, it says here. Colonel Mootry is expecting you right away, sir."

"Well, there's a familiar name. Help me out of this thing." Michael returned the poly-bottle after draining it, then held out his hands and Osen pulled him out of the cocoon and onto his feet where he stood swaying for a moment, the boy hanging onto him.

"Lead the way, private," said Michael. He took one uncertain step, then another, legs shaking. They walked the length of the long sleep bay past row upon row of Cocoons now empty. He'd been the last to be awakened, had missed at least two planet falls. *Why? I'm turning into a piece of old, frozen meat kept for emergencies,* he thought, *while my ex-wife's hair has turned gray or white and my son is nearly as old as his father. All of this for a generous pension and mustering out on some colonial planet hundreds of light-years from the hollowed-out asteroid I grew up on, the spaceship of The New Christians, a thousand years from Earth, when Victoria ruled supreme. What now?*

They reached the lift. Osen inserted the bridge security card as the door closed them in. Michael's stomach dropped away and he swallowed hard when the odors of oil and hot metal and his own sweat assailed him. They ascended four flights where two marines he didn't recognize were there to greet them, rigidly at attention, M34 assault rifles at port arms. Kids, both of them, probably recruits like Osen. How many had come aboard while he was in hibernation? He followed Osen and the marines along the long, featureless hall-way to the bridge, passed four techs that looked curiously at him as they snapped to attention. He didn't know any of them.

The double doors to the bridge hissed open as they arrived. Marines stepped aside and came to parade-rest. As he entered, someone called "Ten-hut!" and there was a scuffing of boots on the metal floor. The ceiling panels were off in the circular room, the only illumination coming from screens of four concentric circles of monitors, beside each of which a dark figure stood at attention. Michael descended four shallow flights of stairs to where two men in full dress uniform of blue and red stood hunched over the observation desk by the commander's chair. They looked up at his approach and he saluted smartly to the older of the two, a square-jawed man of fifty who smiled and saluted back. "Welcome back, Mike. Sorry to drag you here straight out of deep sleep. You look like hell."

"Feel like it too, sir. Good to see you again."

Colonel Floyd Mootry, commander of *HMS Belsus*, reached out a furry paw to grasp Michael's hand. "Fifteen years of easy pay, if you ask me," he said, "but something has come up that doesn't look routine and I need you here. If so, this could be your last planet fall. This could be the place, and there's a problem here, at least I think there is."

"Where's 'here', sir?"

Mootry's fingers played the controls of the observation desk, the screen there at first showing only stars until an emerald green planet slid into view.

"It's beautiful," said Michael.

"Emerson," said Mootry. "Class one—no terra-forming— agricultural base. The colony was established two hundred and fifty years ago with minimum-tech and a handful of bioengineers. Three hundred souls looking for land to farm and seas to fish after the flare forced everyone under quartz domes on Riga. They came seven hundred light years in deep sleep to populate this little gem and all you can see now is green, green, and green down there."

"And that's a problem?"

"Shouldn't be," said Mootry, "but it seems that the natives would prefer to be left alone, and I think you'll agree our first radio contact with them can only be classified as hostile. Lieutenant, set up that chip for the Major, please."

The young officer standing next to them disappeared into the surrounding gloom. "Nels Sadir," said Mootry. "He came aboard from Brown's planet about a year after we put you under and then went straight into hibernation. He's been up for three months now as my communications officer, one of the ninety-day wonders the colonies are growing for us these days, all proper and clean, full of loyalty for their queen. Hell, Victoria's probably dead twenty years by now. Sometimes I wonder why we're even out here."

"Yes, sir," said Michael.

Mootry smiled. "You telling me you don't wonder about it, too? I don't have anything to hide from you. You're my number one."

"I haven't done much thinking lately, sir. I've been asleep for fifteen years."

Mootry frowned, put a hand on Michael's shoulder. "Ah, well, let's talk about that after you've heard the recording. Maybe a couple of drinks will get you to use my first name again and—oh, here we are."

Lieutenant Sadir had returned, a recorder chip in one hand. He inserted it in a slot on the observation desk, and then stepped back. Mootry's hand moved over the desk controls, the image of Emerson suddenly filling the screen. Beneath scattered clouds, four land masses were visible, dark green splotches on an azure sea. Mootry pointed at a coastal spot on the largest mass. "When we made orbital insertion they were already scanning us, but the power level suddenly dropped before we got a fix, and is steady since then. It's coming from the coast, right there, and we called for over an hour before they finally acknowledged us. Here, see what you think." Mootry pressed a button, holding it down until there was a crackle from the desk. "Here's their first answer; no hello, kiss my ass or anything."

"I wish to inform you that your ship's orbit is inside our five hundred kilometer limit and is in violation of our free space laws. Please move yourself beyond the limit before initiating further communication." The voice was deep, hoarse—commanding.

"Emerson, this is *HMS Belsus*, a frigate of Her Majesty's survey fleet. We have arrived to take a census and record the progress of a colony established in Her name. Please acknowledge."

There was a long pause filled only with crackling static, and then, "There are no colonies on Tothwelt, and we are a native people. You have mistaken our planet for another. Please remove yourselves at once before we are forced to take protective action."

"Friendly," said Michael, as static resumed.

"We had a quick conference after that remark," said Mootry, and the next voice on the recording was his own. "Emerson, this is Colonel Floyd Mootry, commander of *HMS Belsus*. We come in the name of Queen Victoria, sovereign of Arkon and ruler of the Rubion Federation, of which you are a member. We're here to survey progress since your establishment and to provide you with contacts you might desire with the rest of the Federation. You have nothing to fear from us, and our stay will be brief if you cooperate. Please understand we are fully armed and capable of strong retaliation if attacked. Any hostile action on your part is ill advised. Respond immediately, please."

The voice, when it came again, seemed a bit more conciliatory. "Your engines are endangering our atmosphere, and we are not a space-faring people. We must rely on your good intentions. You can show this by moving your ship to the five hundred kilometer limit, at which time you may contact us again."

Mootry shut off the recording. "So we did it, buying some time for both of us to cool down. I'd already called battle-stations, all the panels were deployed and we had enough microwave energy to incinerate the source of that communication. Now listen."

He snapped the recording on again.

"Emerson, this is *HMS Belsus*. We are keeping station at five hundred nautical directly above your position. All fusion drives are shut down and residual radiation completely contained. There is no possible threat to your atmosphere. Come in, please."

The new voice that answered was soft, a monotone. "Thank you for your cooperation, Commander Mootry. There was a moment of concern for our safety here, but it has passed. Now, what can we do for you?"

"Who am I speaking to?" asked Mootry.

"I am Diego Segur, a Counselor to our people."

Mootry explained his mission: a census of the population, medical data, and statistics on agricultural production and environmental data for comparison with measurements taken at first planet fall, an offer to make contacts with suitable trading partners within a radius of a thousand light-years via federation-subsidized freighters equipped with hyper-drive.

"If you'll direct us to a suitable landing location I request permission to send a survey team in a flyer within the next two of your days."

"I see no need for that, Commander," said Diego. "There are only small farms here, and we take much of what we need from the sea. Our people are without illness, and our environment is pure. We have no desire or need for trade, but I can transmit our population data and estimates we have for the production of foodstuffs on Tothwelt."

"I'm sorry, Counselor, but we require a survey team to provide us with the necessary data to supplement your estimates," said Mootry, his words clipped short. "The team is self-contained, and we require no services. The flyer itself has simple reaction engines that will produce little or no measurable pollution to your environment. Now, please provide us with landing coordinates."

"We are a peaceful and secure people," returned Diego. "We have no desire to participate in the affairs of other worlds, or to have contact with them. You are not welcome here, Commander."

"I'm very sorry to hear that, Counselor," said Mootry, his voice tight with self-control, "but I must insist that we send a team down to conduct the survey. Landing coordinates, please."

"You have undoubtedly found the location of our transmission, and that is where we are. I feel no obligation to give you any further information. You have not been invited here, Commander, and I will assume no responsibility for the peril to those you send down to us."

Static returned.

"Definitely not friendly," said Mootry, snapping off the recording.

"And I guess I know why I'm out of deep sleep," said Michael, rubbing one hand over the long, black tangle of his beard.

"Right. Let's talk about that. Get yourself cleaned up and meet me in level-six-Mess room for some pabulum and weak booze. I'll try not to smirk while I eat my steak. Lieutenant Sadir will see you to your quarters."

"Yes, sir!" said Sadir. "Follow me, sir!"

Michael wearily followed the young man up the steps and out of the room, turning left and along the hall in a long, featureless curve to another lift which took them quickly to fifth level. Officers' quarters was directly above the command center, was bathed in soft, greenish light from ceiling panels, doors leading to living cubicles twenty by twenty feet, large by military standards.

Sadir stopped by a door marked 'Queal' on a plaque, beneath which was the four-bar with crossing thunderbolt insignia of a combat major. He took a plastic mag-card from his pocket and handed it to Michael. "Your key, sir. I've taken the liberty of arranging your things, and my video-code is marked above the screen in your room. Please call me at any time you require assistance; Colonel Mootry has placed me at your command until drop. A pleasure to serve you, sir!" Sadir saluted smartly, Michael returning it with a vague gesture, then inserting the card in the lock, the door hissing open. He stepped inside, turning, finding Sadir still standing there rigidly at attention. "I'll call you if I need something, Lieutenant," he said softly.

"Yes, sir!" said Sadir, turning sharply and marching away as the door hissed closed. All spit and polish, thought Michael. But would he have the balls for a firefight?

The room was Spartan and efficient. There was a writing table and small chair in one corner, a single bed along one wall opposite the videophone screen and intercom panel, and a standing dresser and closet along the third wall. Two ceiling panels filled the room with soft, green light. A full dress uniform had been laid out on the bed: blue jacket, matching pants with red stripe, belt with silver buckle, shirt, tie, socks, and on the floor black jump boots gleaming in the light. His beret, with insignia of rank, was on top of the dresser, next to the faded picture of a woman and young boy. Michael touched the frame of the picture, checked the contents of drawers, the clothing hanging in the closet. He sat down on the edge of the bed, and stared at the picture for a moment in the total silence of the room then removed his clothes and crammed them in the wall hamper. Naked, he opened the door to the shower stall in the corner next to the closet, set the control to warm, and stepped inside. As the door closed, six streams of warm water hit him from all sides for ten seconds, and shut off. He soaped his body and hair, rinsed with a one-minute blast from the showerheads, then rubbed depilatory into his beard and rinsed again, mind blank.

Back in the room, Michael toweled himself dry, went to the dresser and put the picture in the top drawer. He dressed, checked his reflection from the blank video-screen.

Still slim, cheeks a bit hollow, perhaps. Not bad for forty five—seventy-seven Arkon, that is. It was silent in the room. Horribly silent. He adjusted the beret on his head, the insignia gleaming. The combat marine in the video screen looked back at him sternly.

Welcome back, marine, it said. *You are Arkon's finest*. Michael sighed. This was what he had wanted—a long time ago.

Floyd Mootry was waiting alone for him in the sixth-level officers' mess when he arrived. The dim light came from two electric candles on a linen-covered table set with plates and silverware, Mootry came out from a darkened corner with a glass in each hand.

"That was quick," he said, smiling.

"It sounded urgent, sir," said Michael, saluting sharply. Mootry didn't return it.

"What's my name?"

"Floyd," said Michael uneasily. He took the glass offered to him.

"Some Chablis—for a special occasion," said Floyd. "The finest of Brown's planet. Seventeen years old. Sit."

They sat down at the table, facing each other. Michael sipped cautiously, and the wine burned a path into his stomach. "To the Corps," said Floyd, and their glasses clinked together. "I'm not kid-

15

ding when I say it's really good to have you back again, Mike. You're going to find out quick how much times have changed. And not for the better."

"How do you mean?"

Floyd drained half his glass in one gulp. "No sense of mission anymore—no wars to be fought—all this survey work on planets with aging histories, no cultural connection to the Federation, or Arkon, or a queen who's more myth than reality. Most colonies have strayed from their original goals, gone in their own directions, and with a few exceptions they have no feeling of connection with anything off world. We've expanded too far, Mike, and lost touch. We've reached the fringe of the Federation, both of us are close to mustering out, and these people basically don't want us here."

"Sure sounded like that on the recording I heard," said Michael.

A steward arrived and served their meal: a small steak for Floyd, three small mounds of mashed potatoes, a mystery vegetable and something reminding Michael of pork chops. "Want a bite of real food?" asked Floyd.

"Better not. My stomach is out of practice." They finished eating in silence, and then Floyd filled their glasses again.

"You're not going to recognize many people. Half the crew mustered out on Brown's planet. We're all getting old together, you and me especially. We're the oldest, now, two old girenes looking for a place to rest. Even *Belsus* is old, two hundred years overdue on retrofit. Survey ships are always last in line these days. No laser armor, hopper suits, IR glasses instead of night helmets, weaponry as old as the colony below us. Those bastards on Brown's planet wouldn't give me anything last time around. 'Finish the survey, then comes the retrofit', they said. Well, this drop finishes it."

"We still have some tread left," said Michael.

Floyd looked at him solemnly. "We might need it on this planet fall, Mike. We might need all of it."

"I'm leading the drop team?"

"Who else? Maybe half a dozen combat-experienced marines on board, the rest fresh out of basic with clean underwear, no scars, no nightmares, not one day of combat.

"How about Massey, or Underhill, or—"

"Gone—all the men from zee-squad. Massey used most of his pension for a deep-sleep birth on a freighter heading back to Arkon. Can't see doing that. Can't see it at all."

"Kari still here?"

Floyd smiled. "I was wondering when you'd ask that. Yeah, she's still here—but so's Krisha. When they're not making it in the cubicle they share, you can find them in the gym."

"So some things haven't changed."

"Yeah. But they're still good marines. Just don't turn your back on Krisha. She still remembers you and Kari."

"That was twenty years ago, Floyd."

"Most of it in deep sleep—for all of us. They're dropping with you, and I don't want you waking up with a live grenade in your sack. Behave yourself."

Michael took a long sip of wine. "You expecting bad things on this drop?"

"Maybe—maybe not. I've got a bad feeling about this one. That voice on the recording—no shouting or screaming—just a quiet threat, and it pisses me off. I've been thinking about Emerson for months, even looked up the founding history, the first survey. It sounds like a paradise down there, a good place to end it, and now...."

"...We get threats," said Michael. "We won't really know 'til we get down there, Floyd. When do I go?"

Floyd drained his glass, filled it again. "The team is assembled. I can give you another forty-eight hours Arkon to get ready."

"Forty-eight days is more like it. I can't even walk straight yet."

"The drop team hasn't been up much longer, and I think they're ready enough. The machines work you quick, Mike. You'll just have to hurt more than the others. Two days is what you've got, and two nights to go over what we know about Emerson. I want this survey done in a hurry."

"Tothwelt. That's what Diego Segur called it."

"Whatever. Get down there, get it done and then you and I— well—we stay, go back to Brown's planet to raise bees and grapes or we go our separate ways. It's mustering out time, for both of us. This is the last drop for you and I. Let's get it done. If there has to be a firefight, then—then maybe that's a good way to end it, too. I'm sure you don't feel like it, but I'm ready for some sleep. Breakfast here at oh-four-hundred, something light, and then you hit the gym. I'll have your team assembled in the drop bay at sixteen hundred to meet you. Okay?"

"Yes, sir," said Michael.

Floyd got up; looking tired, and leaned over to put a hand on Michael's shoulder.

"Oh-Four hundred, major. Just like the old days." Floyd lurched away from the table, and quickly left the room.

CHAPTER THREE

There was no sleep that first night, or what passed for night in the routine of *HMS Belsus*. For Michael Queal the concepts of day and night had long ceased to have meaning, replaced by a cycle of work and rest encouraged by programmed light intensities and colors in the work areas of the ship. Morning was a warm, orange glow, day brightening to flat white, evening following in deepening hues of red. The body responded with the memories of a yellow star that was Arkon's sun, though even on the hollow asteroid of Michael's birth interference filters had been used to achieve the same effects. Arkon, the spherically-domed city-ship within a planetoid shell, had been home to ten thousand souls whole ancestors had traveled a thousand years to escape the decay and religious wars of old Earth. A thousand year journey towards the galactic center to find an Earth-type planet had found nothing.

The yellow star had adopted them, and they had been content until Victoria the First had come to power. Her scientists had used the high star densities near the galactic core to develop a hyper drive that followed the changing patterns of folded space. She had built small ships to sail the folds of space-time and sent them out in all directions to find new worlds and new life forms, and to bring with them the doctrine of the New Christians to those who could understand.

There were none who could understand, but there *were* new worlds, three within ten light-years of Arkon. Victoria had lived long enough to hear about them, name them, follow the progress of the first small colonies of humanity spreading sentient life in a seemingly lifeless galaxy. These she named Blue Haven, Victoria and Israel. Together with the lonely, floating city of Arkon, three Earth-like planets became charter members of the Rubion Federation, the name coming from that of Victoria's lineage on her father's side.

In the darkness and silence of his cubicle, Michael thought about these things. He thought about five thousand years of human history since the exodus from Earth, the hundreds of Victoria's descendants who had kept the expansion going, fighting the first wars with dissident colonies refusing allegiance to a capital city that was not even a planet, a city of wealth and ease, safe from blazing sunlight and weather's violent moods. The tiny ships sailed away from Arkon, filled with adventurers, scientists, genetic engineers, those who simply yearned for open skies and wind and unlimited land on which to raise their children. Many of the ships had never been heard from again. And the first survey ships were sent out to find them.

All but three had never returned to Arkon.

Michael's father, grandfather and great-grandfather had all been marines before him, fighting the wars on Israel, Ceti, and Rubion, running down the renegade freighters that sprang up to sell the booty of devastated planets. He had joined the Corps at eighteen, continued a family tradition of nearly two hundred years. He'd been decorated for valor and wounds received on Israel and Rubion and a freighter they'd surprised a hundred light years from Arkon. Sharp pieces of metal had become a permanent part of his bones, the price paid for a battlefield commission received on Rubion. By age thirty, the fighting ended, he was a marine captain without a war to fight, chained to an Arkon desk, pushing paper. Mira had been happy, content with their elevated position in a bubble-encase society, had ignored her husband's misery with his job. His own attitude had been the problem, he realized. Why couldn't he have been content with the life he'd had, Mira there for him, loving him, his son arriving when they'd nearly given up hope of ever having a child?

Michael gave up on sleep, got up from his bed and went to the video console to punch out access to the ship's database on Emerson. It was a short file, and he read it quickly. A thousand light years from Arkon, he was at the Rubion Federation edge nearest the galactic core. A thousand light years away his former wife and son were—were even still alive? And what did it matter now? He'd made his decision, as Mira had made hers, and there'd been nobody there to see him off the day he'd shipped out on *Belsus*. His only reality, his only immediate future, was on an emerald planet spinning below him, a planet colonized by farmers and fishermen and a handful of agricultural genetic engineers.

It was a beautiful planet—but hostile to his presence.

He read the file through twice more, then shut down the terminal as the ceiling panels in his room began to glow a dim orange.

Morning was near. The silence was suffocating. In twenty minutes he showered and dressed and left the cubicle for his first full day after a long sleep.

The officers' mess was empty, but smelled wonderfully of fresh-baked bread from the adjacent galley when he arrived. The twenty-four hour tea urn steamed and grumbled as he poured himself a cup before sitting down at a bare table in dull, orange light, his mind unfocused.

An orderly came out of the galley, carrying a pan filled with fresh rolls. "Good morning, sir," he said brightly. "I thought only bakers got up this early. Fresh out of the oven, sir, and some of my own jams on the table here." He arranged the rolls on a platter, served two of them to Michael and started back to the galley when Michael didn't offer a reply.

For God's sake, be decent to the man. He served you breakfast.

"Smells delicious," he shouted after the man.

Michael ate quickly, drank a second cup of tea and left the mess, turning left and walking the gray, featureless curving passage halfway around the bow of *Belsus* to reach the gym. Bright lights came on as the door hissed open. No change, same Aeroflex machines of his memories, same pain, especially when you were fresh from deep-sleep. He stripped to shorts and shoes and went through the circuit slowly, cautiously, the machines' resistance responding to his stress levels as measured by the flex-cable monitor strapped across his chest. In ten minutes his legs and shoulders were aching. In twenty they were afire with pain. Tears were in his eyes as he finished the circuit and switched on the evaluation output screen. He stared at the readings in dismay. "Terrific," he said out loud, "I have the fitness of an eleven-year-old child."

The scientists had told him there was no deterioration of the body during deep sleep.

He didn't believe them.

Michael toweled down and sat on a bench to rest. Sweat glistened on his face again within seconds, a heart thump loud in his inner ears. Two days to get ready. No way.

He went through the circuit a second time, and was mid-way through it when the door hissed open and someone else came into the room. At the moment he was not free to look around, for he was locked in the grasp of a rope-net-climber sim, titalloy claws pulling on his arms and legs at a level only slightly below the threshold of dismemberment. A musky odor wafted over him as he struggled.

"Hi, Mike, I heard you were up again."

20

Kari.

"Up, but still half-awake," he growled, climbing another six feet on the shuddering, swaying machine.

"Nice view from down here," she said as he reached the top and began clambering down. "Deep sleep does good things for you." She was standing in front of him, a smirk on her face when he reached the floor and looked at her past the tangle of metal cables making up the machine.

The first thing he noticed was her hair. It framed her thin face in an auburn, billowy mass down to her shoulders. "What happened to the butch-cut?" he said sarcastically.

Kari's eyes narrowed. "Krisha likes it this way, so I let it grow. What do you think?"

"It makes you look like a woman," he said, then turned away from her to grab a towel, and wiped his face. Standing there in a shoulder to knee, spandex workout suit her body looked hard yet somehow soft in all the right places. It made him angry. "Still with Krisha, I hear. How's it going with you two?"

Kari's smirk broadened, and she put hands on hips, thrusting her breasts forward. "Oh, you know me, Mike. I'm always ready to go either way. You still have a nice ass, but I see some flab on the rest of you. Better work it out quick, 'cause I hear this drop might give us some trouble."

"Yeah—maybe," said Michael. He threw down his towel and saddled up on a leg-press machine, adjusted the hydraulics to a hundred kilos, and began pumping.

"Mind if I join you?" said Kari, but he didn't answer. She settled herself on the bench-press next to him, fiddled with the control unit until the monitor registered eighty kilos. She finished thirteen reps easily, long, smooth strokes while he struggled to finish ten. When they finished, his face was glistening with sweat and Kari wasn't even breathing hard. She looked at him, amused. "Don't worry about it, Mike. I've got a three day head-start on you."

It was said in a friendly way, and Michael smiled as they sat facing each other. "Am I getting that transparent in my old age?" he said. "Hey, you're looking good. Really."

Kari smiled, reached out a hand to touch his knee, and then drew back sharply. Her eyes shifted to the door behind him as it hissed open.

"Well, isn't this cozy," said Krisha Elg from the doorway. "Maybe I should come back later."

Michael sighed. Kari laughed, and slapped him on the knee. "Our major is definitely out of shape. He has a lot of work to do."

She stood up and went to the next machine without looking back at him. Krisha swaggered past him in spandex bra and knee-length pants, sat down on the bench press machine, dialed the control to a hundred kilos, and looked over to be sure Michael had seen it. Her hard, chiseled body already glistened with sweat, and he guessed she had warmed up by running the long corridors of *Belsus.*

Unlike Kari, there was no softness about Krisha Elg. She was as tall as Michael; black hair cut close, and had a pretty yet hawkish face with sharp features and thin lips. There were prominent veins on her forearms and shoulders. She glowered at him from deep-set eyes, looked him up and down appraisingly. "Yep, there's work to be done. You look tired, Major, and the day's hardly started." She lay back on the machine, did ten slow reps and sat up again, breathing deeply. "Ah, that works the kinks out. Ready for a firefight when you are, Major." She gave him a venomous look, hands on hips, and tensed her muscles in display.

"I'll be relying on that, Captain," said Michael. "You're the best marine I have in the drop team, and I'm putting you in charge of security. We're going to need experience on this one."

Her face showed surprise, and softened. For the moment, he had defused her. "I'll do the job, Major," she said.

"The situation sounds hostile, but might not be, and I'll need a cool head for security. No show of force; a couple of squads will do, and I don't want any trigger-jerkers with us. You don't have much to choose from with all these fuzzy-faced recruits, so go over their psych-profiles and weed out the heroes. I want a force ready for security action only on orders from you, but respectful of the natives and their customs. Everyone should be a diplomat on this drop. Okay?"

"Laser and jump suits, sir?"

"Negative. Assault rifles are lighter, more intimidating, but less vulnerable to defense hardware. Call me old-fashioned, Captain."

"Yes, Sir. How long have I got to do this?"

"Mootry wants the team assembled in the drop bay at sixteen-hundred today."

"We'll be there," she said, stood up and toweled her face. Michael stood, moved a step closer to her and spoke softly. "Krisha— one more thing. You'll be my number one down there, and I want to be able to depend on you a hundred percent as a professional marine. I don't want anything to get in the way of that. Do you understand?"

22

Krisha looked him square in the eye. "Yes, sir. I'll get the job done, sir."

"Good. Break time for me. I have to pick the rest of the team before I get back to this torture-pit. Carry on with your workout, Captain." He looked over at Kari, who was grinning at him from a quad machine. "Lieutenant," he said, then turned and left the room. The look on Kari's face stayed with him a moment and he could guess what she'd been thinking.

You always were a good talker, Mike.

* * * * * * *

Michael spent the rest of the morning in his cubicle, dialed up personnel records and selected a small group of scientists commissioned as marine lieutenants to accompany drops. He lunched alone in the officers' mess, forced down a carbohydrate porridge said to be easily digestible for stomachs fresh out of deep sleep. It was flat, grainy and tasteless, and he had a sudden yearning for real food. He spent an hour with the logistics officer to arrange for supplies, figured a one-week mission for twenty people without reliance on native help or foodstuffs, and then returned to the gym for another hour of sweat and pain. His legs were sore and wobbly when he returned to his cubicle, but he felt stronger, and his stomach had ceased its grumbling. He even felt pleasantly relaxed and caught himself nodding off as he studied the global map of Emerald on the video screen. The signal had come from the southern coastline of the greater landmass to the north, one long island and several smaller ones scattered offshore out to fifty kilometers. There were no details, and no topo maps to go by.

They would be landing blind.

At fifteen hundred he took a shower and got into full dress uniform for the meeting with the team. The walk to the drop bay on level one seemed like ten kilometers, and by the time he got there he was sweating again. Mootry had warned him about changing times on the ship, the fact that mustering out time was approaching for both of them. It had only been reinforced by what he's seen in personnel records that morning. Everyone was new, young, without experience, only a handful from the old crew, including Kari and Krisha. He'd had to use both of them, and knew it could possibly lead to trouble on the drop. All the young marines were untested in battle. Krisha could have whipped them into shape if they'd had the time, but they didn't.

Mootry was waiting for him at the door leading to drop bay one. "Well, how are the bones holding out?" he asked, smiling.

"Sore but secure, sir."

"Good. So, let's go in and meet some young people."

The big door hissed open and someone cried "TEN-HUT!" over a loud-speaker. The team was standing at attention in two rows on both sides of them along the flanks of two ungainly-looking entry sailing craft appropriately named Gull One and Two. Krisha had assembled her security force in full assault gear with helmet and rifle, an intimidating sight compared to the scientists in simple dress blues. Michael followed Mootry down the ranks and back again on inspection, past Kari in her blues, and Krisha's unfocused stare from under her helmet. He passed Hal Odin, who had fought with him on Rigal, and Nik Balestrieri, a civil engineer forever. Everyone else was a stranger.

A podium had been set up forward of the Gulls. Mootry called parade-rest, introduced Michael as drop commander, and stood away from the microphone. Michael stepped up to the podium and gazed silently for a long moment at the collection of bright faces looking up at him. A strange feeling passed over him, an alien thing, remoteness as if he didn't belong there, had somehow been thrown into a parallel world with history and culture unfamiliar to him. He was old, even by military standards on the survey ships, a relic of past wars the young people before him might not have read about in their classes. *Muster out time. The last drop. Time to hang it up.*

A last drop, with strangers now looking at him expectantly. He cleared his throat, and spoke.

"All of you have been hand-picked for this mission by me and Captain Elg. It is our expectation that all of you will uphold the traditions of The Corps and conduct yourselves with dignity and discipline during planet fall. We will tolerate nothing less." He stared at them; jaw set, a long pause for effect. Krisha seemed to stand taller than an instant before, and even Kari's expression was grim. "Now, here's our situation," he finally said.

The briefing was short, for there was little to say. They were going in without reconnaissance, and the welcome mat was not out for them. Resistance was a possibility, but not likelihood. Their behavior could earn them a welcome, and their mission was service, not hostility. They would assemble in the drop bay in full battle dress, all of them, at oh-four-hundred two mornings from now. In the meantime they would relax and study the briefing packets awaiting them on a table in aft bay. He looked forward to serving with them.

Mootry stepped forward, called the team to attention and dismissed them. There was a rush to the table, names called out, the sound of envelopes being opened. Mootry took Michael by the elbow. "Sounded good. Nice touch with Krisha, made her sound like co-commander. She'll like that."

But Krisha was waiting for them at the aft door. "Major, sir, may I have a word with you in private?"

"I'll meet you in the mess-room, Mike," said Mootry, and left them at the door.

"What is it, Captain?"

"It's Kari, sir. I don't understand why she's going on this drop."

"That's easy. She's the most experienced botanist we have, and this is a survey party."

"Lieutenant Ganeff has two drops, sir. Were you aware of that?"

"I was, yes. His specialty is grasses, and I don't think that's appropriate for Emerson. What are you getting at here, Captain?"

"I would prefer it if Kari did not accompany us, sir. It could be dangerous from the time we hit the ground."

"And for all of us, Captain. Why is it different for Kari? She has marine training."

Krisha swallowed hard, struggling to speak. "It—it's our relationship, sir. I don't want it to distract me from my responsibilities down there. If I'm watching out for her, I'll—"

"I wouldn't have chosen you as security officer unless I was convinced you're a total professional, Captain."

"Yes, sir. Thank you, sir."

Michael looked at her closely. "Kari will be under your protection along with all the other scientists, and you'll be billeted in the same compound, so what's the problem?"

"I just don't want her to get hurt, sir." Krisha was struggling for control. Gone, for the moment, was the strutting butch whose very presence often irritated him, a woman he didn't understand and, when he was able to admit it, a woman he saw as a competitor. And then it occurred to him what the real problem might be.

He leaned close to her and spoke softly. "I don't want anyone hurt, Captain, and that's why you're heading up security. Look, Krisha, what happened between Kari and me was a long time and lots of deep sleep ago when you two barely knew each other. She's made her choice, and I don't intend to do anything to mess it up. Okay?"

"Yes, sir," said Krisha, and for the first time since he'd known her the arrogant smirk was gone, replaced by something softer. She sniffed. "Thank you, sir." And then she turned from him, and walked quickly out the door.

Mootry was waiting for him in the officers' mess, sipping tea. "Well, what was that about?"

"Kari. She didn't want her on the drop."

"Doesn't want to share, huh?" Mootry smiled.

"There's nothing between me and Kari anymore," said Michael.

"Yeah? You tell that to Kari?"

"I think she gets the idea," said Michael, feeling a little defensive.

"Well I've got news for you, mister. I don't think that little girl believes it for a minute. You watch your ass down there. I don't need any love triangles on this drop, and neither do you. Jesus, Mike, why don't you and I just find some nice ladies on Emerson and hang it up here? That's assuming, of course, they don't shoot our butts off first."

They both laughed at that.

CHAPTER FOUR

The drop bay was bathed in deep red light, and there was the smell of machine oil and leather. Everyone moved quietly, for it was part of the drill. They formed two inspection lines along the flanks of the Gulls, and each figure leaned slightly forward with the burden of full pack and assault rifle. Krisha used hand signals to direct her flock into position while Michael watched from the door. Watching her work renewed his confidence in his decision to make her his number one on Emerson. He paced the ranks quickly, stopped only once before a tall man who gave him a wan grin. "How you doin', Nik? Here we go again, huh?"

"Yes, sir," said Nik Balestrieri, "just like the old days, and using the same old equipment."

Nik had saved Michael's ass on Rubion four deep-sleeps ago. He'd driven an earthmover over a laser emplacement that had just shot away part of Michael's elbow, and was preparing to do worse. A good engineer. A good marine.

Michael moved ahead, counting shadows in crimson gloom. The number was too high by one. The reason for this anomaly was standing at the forward-bay end of right rank, and came to a brace as Michael stepped up to him and growled softly.

"Osen, what the hell are you doing here? I didn't pick you for drop, and I'm sure Captain Elg didn't either."

Osen's eyes flicked left, past Michael's shoulder. "Orders, sir. Commander Mootry has assigned me as your orderly on the ground. I'm responsible for daily, private communication between yourself and the Commander, sir." He was whispering.

"Orders?"

"In my shirt pocket, sir."

"Let's see 'em."

Osen withdrew a tightly folded piece of flimsy from his shirt pocket, and handed it over. The statement was short, and Osen had repeated most of it. The supplies order had even been corrected for the addition to the drop team. An orderly? Why? He handed the re-folded flimsy back to Osen. "We'll talk about this later, private," he whispered.

Metal groaned. The maws of the two Gulls opened simultane-ously to receive their human cargo. Mootry's voice blared from a loudspeaker; "The drop will commence in ten minutes." Krisha barked an order, and her security force of fourteen trotted quickly up the loading ramp of Gull One. Michael moved his crew of scientists, and Osen, into Gull Two. The two flyers, though heavily armed with laser cannon, guided bombs, and two twenty-millimeter Gatlings were mostly hollow shells with benches along the fuselage and a closed-in supplies bay aft. Michael got his people strapped in. Their faces were grim. For everyone in Gull Two, except Michael, Kari and Nik, it was a first drop.

A moment later their stomachs lurched with the impulse of thrusters pushing them out of the bowels of *Belsus* and into the vac-uum above Emerson. Leaving their rotating home after days in orbit, they were suddenly weightless again, and there was a muffled groan from one of the scientists. There were no portholes to give them an outside view, and it was hot and humid in the cargo bay within min-utes.

At the sound of the Gull's triangular wings deploying for at-mospheric entry, Michael unstrapped himself and went forward to climb the ladder leading to the cockpit. He knocked on the closed door there. "Queal," he said, and the door opened. There were three more unfamiliar faces: pilot, co-pilot and gunnery officer. Above the control panels a meter-high observing screen enveloped the cockpit. To the right, on the black velvet of space, *Belsus* was a flickering star, while straight ahead black turned to violet and then deep blue. As he watched, the curving horizon of an emerald green globe came into view, and the gunnery officer gestured to an empty chair beside him. "Better strap yourself in, Major. It'll be a little bumpy for a while."

Michael strapped himself in and watched the forward screen. There were wispy, white clouds over shades of green and blue. It was a watery world. His stomach sank as the Gull's wings bit into the thickening atmosphere. The craft shuddered for several minutes before steadying, and they were sailing in lazy, descending loops towards a dead-stick landing on the surface. Gull One was far ahead of them by now, going in under power and deploying wings at ten kilometers above the approximate landing site. He thought of Krisha standing before her observing screen, waiting for a flash of light, a puff of smoke that might indicate hostile fire. Her orders were clear. A hostile response would be instantly met with all the firepower her Gull could bring to bear. One way or another, they were going in, and although he was not a practicing New Christian, Michael prayed silently to whatever power had brought the human race this far that the landing would be a peaceful, uneventful happening. The image on the screen showed a pristine planet, unspoiled. This was no place for war.

"Landing area coming into view, sir," said the pilot. "Lansen, gunnery system to power, and clear the Gatlings."

The fingers of the young man next to Michael played the keys of a control board, and there was a brief shudder as the Gatlings fired a short burst of armor-piercing rounds into space. "Green board, sir," he said.

Michael unstrapped himself, and stepped up behind the pilot.

"There it is, sir, just coming up on the lower left. Security is over the drop zone, now. You'll need these, sir." The pilot handed a headset to Michael as the Gull made another, descending turn.

Michael put the headset on in time to hear Krisha say, "—boats spread out all over the bay. Looks like a fishing fleet. There's a village on the shore ahead. Copy coordinates 39-30-3-40-21-2."

"I copy," said Michael's pilot.

"We're being scanned, but nothing hostile yet. I've called twice on three-oh-seven, but nobody's answering. I don't think we're gonna get any help from these guys. Over."

"See any clearings, Captain?" said Michael.

"No, sir. The village is in a bowl at shore edge, and there's heavy growth down to the beach. Scattered houses, look like stone, a white tower on a hillock just east, and it's—yes, that's it. We just passed the tower, and the scanning power peaked. Maybe a homing signal, sir, for all those boats we saw. Heading inland, now, then back to shore. Didn't see a single person in the village. Very quiet."

"Try to find a clearing near the village, and close to shore. I want our backs to the water.

"Yes, sir. Turning, now. Scattered houses—dense forest and steep hills down there—one clearing—too small, though—water ahead, and—we're coming over a plateau, sir. Pretty high—steep drop to the beach, a couple of klicks west of the village. Looks good, sir. Request permission to land."

"Granted, Captain, but wait until we're in view to set up a perimeter, and keep your power up."

"Done, sir. Going in, now. Over."

29

A hiss replaced Krisha's voice in the headset. They waited expectantly as the pilot sailed towards coordinates 39-30-3-40-21-2, the sea below them smooth at first, and then rippling, dark splotches appearing beneath the waters. Clear water became shallower, and then ahead of them boats appeared, spread out in two long arcs, colorful sails taut. Michael flinched as a warbling tone suddenly came from the headset.

"Beacon, sir. They're down and deploying."

"Here we go, then," said Michael. He stepped back to the cockpit door and opened it. "Everyone buckle up! We're coming in. Everything is looking good so far."

The pilot turned left and trimmed so that the wings were in a para-sail configuration, and they were floating slowly west along the shoreline. A white tower jutted from the forest to their right, and then they saw the plateau dead ahead, a formidable-looking cliff dropping to a sandy beach. Gull One was fifty meters back from the drop-off, stirring up dust, maws opening fore and aft, and tiny figures were running down the forward ramp and fanning out in all directions. A cargo pod rolled down the aft ramp and instantly the maws were closing, the Gull rising in a yellow cloud and veering towards them, passing to their left at high speed and wiggling wings in greeting.

They came in to float ten meters above the precipice and landed with a gentle thump. Michael descended the ladder to the cargo bay. "Up and on! Everyone out in ten seconds and spread out in a line fifty meters from the flyer. Move!"

Light flooded the bay, there was fresh air, and they were running down the ramp. Michael led them. His feet felt thick grass and solid ground for the first time in eighteen years, and a gentle breeze brushed his face. He was startled by sudden exhilaration. He ran hard, heard the thump of the cargo pod being discharged, the whine of turbines. "Flank left!" he shouted over a shoulder, and pointed. When he turned around, Gull Two was already hovering meters above them, maws snapping shut. Hot wind hit his face as the craft drifted out over the beach and began to rise, engines screaming. In seconds it was a speck disappearing into a light blue, morning sky.

Michael could hear his heart beating in the silence that followed. They were on Emerson—and they were not alone.

His eyes found Krisha, and he walked towards her while the scientists scrambled to help Nik unload the cargo pod. Once emptied, both pods would serve as a command post and communications center, buried under two meters of earth. They were taking no chances on this drop, but Nik had orders to leave no trace of their presence when it was time to go. It was part of the drill for him.

"No movement of any kind, sir," said Krisha. "You suppose the whole village is out in those boats?"

"I doubt it. Our counselor friend has probably shooed everyone inside. I can't see the village from here."

"Just over that knoll, maybe a twenty-minute walk. A few meters from here there's a clear trail of bent grass, so people get over here often enough. Did you see anything besides the boats and the village when you were coming in?"

"No."

"Doesn't that seem strange to you, sir? I mean, after all these years could the colony still be so small? I'd have expected cities and highways all over the place by now, and all I see are trees."

"That's one of the things we're here to check out. By the way, I watched your deployment. Looked good."

"Thank you, sir. Excuse me, but we have a visitor." Krisha was looking past his shoulder.

Michael turned to see Osen standing only a meter away, his assault rifle cradled in one arm. "Osen, what the hell are you doing here? You should be pulling cargo with the others."

"Sorry, sir. I thought—"

"Don't think! All non-security personnel pull cargo. Do it!"

Osen showed no expression. "Sir," he said, then turned and marched back towards the cargo pod.

"The commander seems to feel I need an orderly on this drop."

"Maybe a watchdog, sir. With the size of this perimeter I can use another sentry if you think so."

"No, it's Mootry's orders, so I'll stick with it. I think we're exposed out here, so make sure all of your people have night glasses. A battalion could hide in all those trees. If you see something, call it in. If you're fired on, you have my permission for lethal response."

"I'll get on it, sir."

By mid-day two concentric circles of huts had gone up, and Nik had dug the trenches for the pods with his front-loader. By dusk the pods were buried, and Michael had set up housekeeping in one of them. He shared the space with Osen and a wall of communication gear. When he briefed Mootry on planet fall, on what he'd seen and not seen, he asked about the necessity for an orderly. All he got back was a terse, "Trust me on this, Mike." They agreed that without voluntary contact on the part of the colonials, they would march to the village the following morning.

31

Emerson's star looked like an ellipsoidal ruby when it touched the western horizon that evening, and darkness came quickly. Food odors came from the huts, where each marine was his or her only cook. Earlier in the evening they had all stood outside to watch the sails come in from the sea and disappear behind the knoll separating them from the village. The silence on the plateau was oppressive: no bird song, no animal cries, not even the buzzing of an insect.

By twenty-two hundred, Osen was asleep on his cot and Michael quietly left the pod to walk the perimeter of camp from west to east. He nodded a greeting to each sentry he passed. When he reached the east side a sentry had his glasses up, looking towards the knoll separating them from the village. Michael stopped, brought up his own glasses and saw two figures on the side of the knoll, burning like candle flames in IR. As he watched, they turned and marched away to disappear around the knoll. When he brought his glasses down, the young sentry was looking at him. "There were four of them a minute ago, Major. The first two had greenish lights with them; you could see the lights by eye. They've been over there for nearly an hour. Must have seen us looking at them just now."

"Good eyes, private. Keep it up, and be sure to call this in."

"The Captain saw them too, sir. She was out here half an hour ago."

So why hadn't he been informed? Michael started back towards the pods, his heart racing when a dark figure seemed to rise out of the ground in front of him, assault rifle slung casually.

It was Osen.

"You following me, mister? I left you asleep back there."

Osen grinned. "I go where the Major goes, sir. I believe you discussed all this with Commander Mootry. I have his trust, and I hope to earn yours, if you'll let me."

"Well, you stay out of the head when I'm in there. I don't need any help with that."

Osen grinned again, but Michael was noticing things about him as they walked: the easy, fluid stride, hand high on the rifle sling for fast deployment, eyes constantly moving, scanning the area.

"Your first drop, right?"

"Yes, sir."

"No combat experience?"

"Not in the traditional sense, sir. I saw some service during the Elsen overthrow on Brown's planet."

"Doing what?"

"Afraid I can't tell you that, sir. It's still classified."

By the time they reached the pods, Michael was damn curious about that.

* * * * * * *

The contact party left at sunrise, after Michael had argued Krisha out of her insistence that security personnel be included. He compromised by allowing her to place two marines on top of the knoll and in constant radio contact with them. They would enter the village without weapons. Michael chose four scientists and a linguist to accompany him, along with Osen, who again reminded him of Mootry's orders. Kari was with them, and Vilos Compagno, anthropologist and cultural historian. Takey Xu spoke seventeen languages and four Arkon dialects, although the initial radio contact made his usefulness seem unlikely. Biologist Utaka Fujioka and plant geneticist Cletus Euell rounded out the group and brought up the rear as they followed the faint, grassy trail away from camp. Kari walked beside Michael, and he wondered if Krisha was watching them as they reached the edge of the plateau. A well-worn trail curved out of sight around the knoll. Thick stands of Ellis pine covered the knoll; trees he knew were unlikely to be native to Emerson, since they had traveled with colonists as seedlings since the beginning of the expansion.

Beneath the trees the ground was carpeted in bizarre plants with leaves colored green, deep red and purple. Flowers were there in profusion. He saw one that looked like an orchid the size of a dinner plate, and a bush with crimson buds and what looked like walnut-sized raspberries.

When they rounded the knoll, even Michael had to stop, for the view was breathtaking. The trail suddenly turned to skree, and they were at the edge of a cliff dropping a hundred meters to a beach of white sand below them. Dozens of boats, sails furled, were anchored in a small bay of turquoise waters gently rolling in towards shore. The globe of Emerson's sun was just appearing above the eastern horizon.

"My God," said Kari softly, and then there was a chirp from the radio carried by Osen. He answered it, mumbled something and looked at Michael. "Security, sir. Just checking in."

To their left and below them the forest of great firs came right down to the beach, and rising from the base of a hill was a monstrous obelisk of white stone, towering above the trees. Even at this distance they could see the obelisk was topped by the inverted cross of The New Christians. "What do you know, it's a church," said Michael, and somehow the sight of that cross made him feel more at ease in this place. Small, white houses were scattered along the hillside to their left and below them near the beach, but they saw no people, heard no voices. It was plain these were fisher-folk, yet it was early morning and all the boats were in. Where were they?

They stepped gingerly across the skree at cliff's edge until they reached the trees again and the path turned to dirt, switching back and forth below them. They descended it and came out near the beach, hearing for the first time the sounds of surf, and all the time Michael was thinking to himself, *This is a paradise. I could live here.*

But nobody was there to greet them.

"May be everyone's in church," said Kari. "This could be a Holy Day."

"You might be right," said Michael. "Let's see if we can join them. Anyone wearing a cross?"

Kari, Osen and Vilas Compagno raised their hands. "Good," said Michael. "Keep them out and visible."

They skirted the edge of the beach and walked directly to the obelisk, crossed a large clearing surrounded by stone houses with uncovered windows and little yards packed with flowering plants. In the center of the clearing was a circular amphitheatre, concentric layers of benches dug from the ground and covered with short, carefully clipped grass. It was a meeting place, a stone podium in its center. They walked around it and came to the base of the obelisk. A long flight of polished granite steps led up to giant double-doors of pine, into which was carved the symbol of the New Christians. Michael climbed the steps and found the doors were locked from the inside. The obelisk towered above him, a needle pyramid with smooth walls and no openings except for those doors. Michael shrugged at the others. "Well, I guess we wait until someone shows up." He descended the stairs as Vilas came around from the side of the obelisk, pointing.

"There's a stone construction leading from the tower back here. The main sanctuary must be inside the hill."

"Let's all stay together, lieutenant. I don't want anyone wandering around here. If people are in there they'll be coming out, and we'll be waiting for them in the amphitheatre. Let's move." Michael followed them to the amphitheatre, and they sat down on the top edge facing the obelisk. Sunlight filtered through the canopy of trees surrounding them, and there was a gentle, salty breeze coming in from the sea. Michael closed his eyes and leaned back on his elbows in the soft grass. Something was missing, his senses were telling him, and yet he felt completely at home here. The peacefulness, a quiet feeling of solitude was there, even with the others around him. There was no scalding sun or clouds of dust—no sound, except for gently rolling surf—that was it. There were no forest sounds here: birds chirping, animal shrieks of territorial claim, the buzzing of insects. "Where are the birds?" he said.

"I noticed that, too," said Kari, sitting beside him. "I haven't seen a single bird, animal or other living creature since we landed. Doesn't make sense with such a lush ecology to support them. All those plants under the pine are nothing I've ever seen before, Mike. There must have been a profusion of life here at first planet fall, and it's been less than three hundred years since then. The sea must be loaded with life, unless all those boats were out there for pleasure cruises. How could a sea full of life fail to produce a single evolutionary line to mammals of some kind? Wasn't there anything in the ship's record about this place?"

"I read what was there," said Michael. "It says Class I, Earthlike, no sentient life forms observed. No data on flora and fauna not even a list of the colonists, just that they were farmers and fisherman, and the usual assortment of scientists and engineers. It was a small group, around a hundred. This might be the youngest colony in the federation. No strategic value, right at the edge of our expansion, so nobody cares. It's no wonder these people these people feel no connection to the federation; it has taken us over two hundred years just to say hello."

"It's so beautiful," said Kari.

"Yeah."

"Romantic. Let's go down on the beach tonight, Mike, and watch the sunset."

Michael opened his eyes, found her leaning close to him. "I'm sure Krisha would love that, lieutenant. Behave yourself."

Kari laughed deep in her throat. "I can remember a time when you would have taken my hand and led down to the beach without asking. We'd make a hollow in the sand so we couldn't be seen, and then we'd—"

"That was then, not now. Then was a long time ago."

"Only if you count deep sleep. I still love you, Mike."

"Right. And Krisha loves you. She all but said it to me face-to-face before we left the ship."

"I know. She told me about that conversation. Maybe it's an ego thing with you, Mike. You can't share someone. You can't see how a woman can love two people at the same time."

"One of them a woman, no."

"How can I make you understand?"

"Don't bother. And if you bring this up again, samples or no samples, I'm sending you up, so drop it."

Kari looked at him sadly, but Michael's eyes caught movement behind her. The others were dozing, but Osen was sitting up and alert. He pointed to the radio in his ear, then up towards the knoll and gave him a thumb up as if to say, *I'm right here, and everything is under control.*

He'd been watching them.

Michael leaned back again, closed his eyes for just a moment—and awoke to a loud sound of heavy wood scraping wood in front of him. Osen yelled, "Major, they're coming out!"

The others were standing when he got up, looking at the obelisk as the great doors opened out. A face peered briefly around a door, then disappeared. Beyond the door was blackness, then movement, and a white apparition floating towards them out of the darkness. The apparition took form; it was a man, very tall, in a white silken robe. His hands were folded together reverently on his chest as he came out into sunlight to stand in the center of the doorway. He was over two meters in height, huge hands, large features in a long face, and deep-set eyes glowered beneath a hairless brow. His head was shaven smooth, and hanging from his neck was a pendent of the symbol of the New Christians. "We have been with Toth," he said in a deep, resonant voice. "He has told us of your presence and of his will for us. Please be seated where you are, and we will talk."

The man turned, gestured to the darkness beyond the doors. "Come, please, there is no harm here. It's time for us to meet our neighbors from the stars. Come, now. Toth is with us in all we say and do here today."

He came sedately down the steps, and behind him people began to emerge from the obelisk. All were dressed in white robes. The people frowned, men, women, and children alike. All wore crosses, and the women had braided garlands of tiny flowers into their hair. Tall people, all of them, with Aryan faces, those of the men burned red and leathered from the sun. They followed their leader down the steps and across the clearing to the amphitheatre, fanning out behind him at the edge of it and standing there. Michael's quick count placed the number of them at only about one hundred and seventy, and no more were coming from the obelisk.

Michael said, "I am Michael Queal of Her Majesty's Survey Ship *Belsus*. I bring you greetings from the Rubion Federation of worlds and her people." With a wave of his hand he introduced the members of his party, giving their names and professions and carefully leaving out all military ranks. "We have a simple mission to survey the progress you have made, and we will only be here for a short while. If you will allow it, we would also like to take some samples of plants native to this planet. Your world is truly lovely."

"Thank you, leader Queal. I am Diego Segur, Counselor to The People, and a servant of Toth. I fear out first communication was cautious, but you did surprise us and we had concern for our safety. Please be seated—all of us. Let us get to know each other, if only for a brief time." He turned to the people standing behind him, gesturing them forward. "Come, come. Have you not heard the words of Toth this morning?"

The people, still looking suspicious of their guests, filed dutifully down into the amphitheatre. They sat down tightly together and as far from Michael's group as they could get while Diego walked regally to the podium and smiled back at them.

Michael was uneasy again. The man's words didn't ring true. Diego had spoken without expression, his face a mask, and his eyes never met Michael's.

For the moment, however, Michael was distracted by something else; it was the sight of a woman, tall, fine featured with a generous mouth, a mass of jet-black hair framing her face. She was holding the hand of a boy perhaps four years old, a beautiful child, and she kept his hand tightly in hers when they sat down. Her eyes met Michael's and quickly averted his gaze.

It was the most beautiful face he had ever seen.

CHAPTER FIVE

Diego's voice boomed in the hollow of the amphitheatre. "Leader Queal, these are the First Families of Tothwelt. Our Lord has assigned them as guides for your group. They will take you to examine our agricultural methods and yields, and the quantity of fish we take from the sea each year. There is nothing more to show you. We are a simple people. We lead quiet lives of devotion to Toth, and the world he has provided for us. You will find no technology or other monuments to human ego here. We are content to be caretakers of this planet, and to live peacefully, according to the laws of Our Lord. The information you wish to have should be complete within three days, Leader Queal. As a gesture of our hospitality, several families have volunteered to serve as hosts to you in their own homes. You should learn our customs, and appreciate the simple pleasures of our lives."

"Your offer is generous, Counselor. We appreciate your hospitality," said Michael. "We've established a camp on the high plateau just west of here, and can take care of all our needs rather than cause unnecessary inconvenience for you."

"Ah, but that would be most disappointing to the families willing to open their homes to you. It would deprive them of an opportunity to acquaint themselves with star-faring neighbors from other worlds. Please consider our offer carefully before you respond."

"I'll consult my superior about this, Counselor. I can bring you my answer tomorrow morning. I hope that is acceptable to you."

"Of course. I spoke with your superior when your ship first arrived. He is a military man, I believe, and there seem to be other military people in your group. Two of them are now trying very hard to watch us from the top of a hill while we speak. They have weapons, Leader Queal. Do you feel danger here?" Diego smiled, while behind him the favored people of the village sat stony-faced and silent.

"A routine precaution, Counselor. There are often many dangers when landing on an unknown planet, and we must be prepared for everything. Our armed personnel are present only for defensive purposes, and it is our faith in your hospitality that has prevented them from accompanying us today. Please notice that those of us here are unarmed."

"That is good, Leader Queal. Allow me, please, to anticipate a positive reply from your superior. Before you leave, let me introduce you to the families whose homes are open to you. As I call your names, please come down before me to greet each other. For you, Leader Queal, we have the family Grigaytes."

Michael stood up and stepped down the shelves of the amphitheatre to its center, was intercepted there by a man his height, perhaps fifty, bulky, face burned from a life at sea. "I am Davos Grigaytes, Leader Queal, and you are welcome in my home." He reached out a gnarled hand, sliding it up to grasp Michael's wrist when they shook hands. "My family also welcomes you," he said, and stepped aside at the approach of three women in single file, their heads bowed. "My wife, Leah, and the mother of my children," he said formally, and with pride. A tall, slender woman with pleasant features managed a faint smile, and bowed to him.

Michael bowed back. "My pleasure," he said, smiling.

"My youngest child, Deena," said Davos, and a lovely young woman with huge, brown eyes bowed without looking at him.

"Deena," said Michael, and then he held his breath, for behind her was the woman whose eyes had locked with his across the amphitheatre. Even now she looked directly at him, squeezing the hand of the little boy clinging to her robe.

"This is Gini, our first child, and our grandson Uhel. This family welcomes you to our home, Leader Queal, and will tend to your needs."

When Gini and Michael bowed to each other, their eyes never lost contact. For an instant he was speechless, but then managed to say "Hello, Uhel," and the little boy turned fearfully away from him. His mother said nothing.

"Thank you so much for your offer, Davos. It's my hope that my superior will allow us to visit together."

"Our home is there, near the shore," said Davos, pointing. "I'm a fisherman, and we live close to the boats. It is fishermen who live in these dwellings by the House of Toth. If you wish, I will take you on my boat and show you our ways at sea."

"I would like that very much. It is many years since I've been on a boat." Michael forced himself to look at Davos, with Gini just

39

out of his field of view. Names had been called out while they were talking, and now people were milling around them, even those who had not been called as host families, coming down for a closer look at the strangers from the stars.

Diego came down from his podium to join them, nodding sagely, and smiling as if he were directing the entire affair. He towered above all of them, dark eyes constantly moving, but when he neared Michael his gaze fixed on someone. He walked to her, and stopped.

It was Kari. She looked up, startled, but recovered quickly and bowed. "Sir," she said. Diego reached out to the pendant hanging from her neck and took it between thumb and fingers, turning it over in his hand. "How do you come to have this?" he asked pleasantly.

"I've had it since childhood, sir," said Kari, turning on her charm with a smile, "from when I was confirmed in the New Christian Church. I see the same symbol on your robe, sir, from when the first colonists came—"

"Toth has spoken to us about this," said Diego, so loudly that all conversations stopped to hear his words. "He has told us of his travels to other worlds, bringing harmony and goodness to others before choosing a few to be his people. Now you see the truth of this; his symbol, hanging from the neck of a visitor from the stars." As he said this, his other hand reached out, long fingers sliding across the back of Kari's neck and pulling her forward so that she was looking straight up at him. "Yet only a few have been chosen, and only those baptized may enter the House of Toth."

"I'm baptized a New Christian, sir," said Kari.

Diego shook his head sadly. "It is not the same. There are differences between us, but Toth has visited your people in the past and bids us to welcome you as brethren." He released Kari's neck, but she remained where she was, looking up at him with an expression crafted to melt the most stolid of male countenances. Diego showed no reaction, though he was slow to move away from her.

"Hurry, now. Our visitors must return to their camp, and all the Children of Toth to their homes for a day of rest. There will be more time for talk." He clapped his hands, and the villagers began to drift away. Davos shook Michael's hand once more, and his family followed him away towards a house near the shore without looking back.

Diego turned to Michael. "Tomorrow, then. I will meet you here at sunrise. In the meantime, I ask that you and your party remain close to your camp, and that you remove the armed observers from the top of the hill. We should trust each other, Leader Queal. There is nothing for either of us to fear here."

"I'll carry your message to my superior," said Michael.

Diego bowed, turned, and climbed out of the amphitheatre and up the steps into the darkness of the obelisk's interior. As he disappeared, the doors closed slowly behind him.

Michael spoke softly, his back to the obelisk. "Okay, let's march out of here. I don't think our host is alone in there."

They climbed the switchback trail and across the skree by the cliff, breathing heavy by the time they'd reached the trees again. Vilas Compagno strode up beside Michael and Kari at the head of the line, huffing and puffing. "So, what do you think? Is Diego for real, or is he putting on a show for us?"

"Some things don't fit, that's for sure. He says there's no technology, but has radio and scanning capability. The village seems too small, maybe a hundred or so people there and—"

"About two hundred in the amphitheatre area," said Vilas, "but a lot of people were watching us from the edge of the trees up the hill. Could be several hundred people here, Major, and we only met selected families."

"I think there were others inside the church, and did you notice how few children or young men were there? The age mixture isn't normal. And he made a big show about Kari's pendant, as if he had to explain how a visitor from the stars could be wearing the symbol of his church."

"He cut me off about that," said Kari.

"I think he liked you," said Vilas.

Kari rubbed the back of her neck. "When he touched me, I was a little scared, Mike. It wasn't just a friendly touch, his fingers were moving around back there, feeling and probing around, and all I could do was stand there."

"You did well," said Michael.

"He is one *big* man," she said. "His presence is intimidating. It's no wonder the villagers are so sober around him. They seemed to warm up when I was talking to them, but when Diego came up to me, they—well, they looked frightened."

"You sound awed, Kari," said Michael.

"Oh, get off it, Mike. He scared me."

"Sorry. He bothers me, too."

"So, are we going back?"

"Probably. I'll brief the Commander when we get to camp, but I don't like the idea of us being separated."

Emerson's sun was near its zenith when they saw the camp and its perimeter of scattered sentries. An earthmover was pushing sod up against the sides of the cargo pod, which now sported a spider-like antenna on its roof, and there was a small gathering of people at the edge of the cliff beyond it. Krisha came out to meet them beyond the perimeter. Her helmet was on, but she'd stripped down to under-shirt and khaki pants, her assault rifle cradled in one arm. "We didn't expect you back so soon, sir. How'd it go?"

Michael briefed her as they walked, Kari a step behind them. "Do you want me to pull my people from the knoll, sir? I think we need to keep up the surveillance."

"Let me talk to Mootry first, but if Diego makes a big issue of it we'll have to pull back."

"How could they have spotted them, sir? They're dug in under trees up there."

"IR sensors, probably. There's technology here, despite what Diego says. Anything happen while we were gone?"

"Haven't seen anyone, but we found something on the beach that you need to take a look at. Some of the scientists have gone down to inspect the thing, some kind of animal that washed up over-night. They seem pretty excited about it."

"I'll take a look," said Michael. "Carry on, Captain." He changed direction and left Krisha to commiserate with Kari about her experience with Diego, walked to cliff edge where a small group of marines was looking down at the beach. When he got there, Osen was right behind him.

There were four people on the beach, standing and kneeling around what looked like a shark or small whale glistening gray and white in the sunlight. "How do I get down there?" he said to a pri-vate who stood next to him.

"We've rigged a drop line, sir, over here. One at a time, sir."

Michael walked a few steps to a taut, motor driven double-cable angling down steeply to the beach from a tee-bar placed at cliff edge. A seat harness dangled from the cable. He strapped himself in tightly and said, "Going down, please." Behind him a motor whined, and he was dangling in air, the beach far below him but coming up fast, as he was swept down to land hard on the sand. Ending up on his knees, he struggled to get out of the harness.

Chelli Ganeff, a botanist, came over to help him up. "We've got something Utaki needs to look at, Major. I know a little zoology, but this is something I've never seen or read about."

They went over for a look and the first thing Michael saw were rows and rows of sharp, serrated teeth in the open mouth of a dead creature laying on its side. "A shark," he said.

"Definitely not, Major," said Chelli. "It's a mammal of some kind. See the blowhole over here? And the skin is smooth all over, the tail horizontal, and a tiny dorsal, swept back. This thing is built for speed. If I didn't see the head I'd say it was a small whale or a large porpoise. But the head's all-wrong: blunt-nosed, eyes right in front, and all those teeth. It's a predator, a very fast predator big enough to tear up a small boat."

Michael examined the creature from head to tail. There was indeed life, and sudden death in Emerson's seas. A mammal that looked like a shark grafted onto a whale. "I wonder if it's native?" he said.

"Probably," said Chelli. "It'd take a lot of imaginative bioengineering to come up with something like this." Chelli looked out to sea. "Uh-oh, Major, better inspect it quick. We have visitors coming in."

Michael looked up and saw a sailboat coming towards them, now moving parallel to shore just beyond the surf. Even at a distance he could see two, white-robed men standing at the bow of the craft. "Get any photographs?" he asked Chelli.

"Several, sir."

"Then hide your camera and quick dig a couple of samples out of the hide of this thing for Utaki to look at. The rest of you sling your rifles, and keep 'em slung."

The little boat tacked in the wind and swung towards shore, catching a small wave and riding it in smoothly to shallow. There were four men on the boat, all robed, two of them staying behind to deploy anchors fore and aft while their companions in the bow jumped into the water and slogged to shore.

They came close, and Michael studied their faces. He'd not seen either of them at his meeting in the village.

"Hello," he called out. "We've found a dead animal here. Can you tell us what it is?"

The two men came up on the sand, faces grim, and their eyes on the armed marines at Michael's side. "It is a Charni, and we have come to take it away before it begins to stink," said the taller of the two. They stopped a few paces from Michael, looking nervous. Both kept looking up towards the top of the cliff, and Michael suppressed an urge to turn around and see what was bothering them.

"Do you know if this animal is native to your seas?" said Michael.

The two men looked at each other, and the taller one said, "The Charni have always been with us. They attack our boats if we go out too far, and lately it seems they grow in numbers and come closer to shore. There have been two deaths from these things, and the fish are migrating further out each year. We must dare the Charni, according to the will of Toth. He has told us this."

"You've talked to Toth? You've seen him?"

"He appears to us from time to time. Please, we have been instructed to remove the Charni. Let us do so." The man looked up at the cliff again.

"Our scientists would like to study this animal. Maybe we can find a way to help you get rid of them," said Michael. "Could you let us keep this dead one for a while?"

"Please," said the man, and now there was fear in his eyes. "This is Toth's creature, and we must do as we're told. We want no trouble with you. We're only fishermen sent to get the Charni."

"Major, maybe if we—" Chelli started to say, but Michael waved him into silence.

"Well, then, you may take it from here. My people can help you."

"That isn't necessary," said the tall man. "There are two of us." They stepped forward timidly and Michael motioned for his people to move back from the carcass. "I didn't see you in the village this morning. Maybe we'll meet again tomorrow."

"You are mistaken," said the tall man, grabbing hold of the creature's great tail. "We were there, and heard your words. We hope you do not make difficulties for us."

The two men dragged the bloated carcass into the surf with great effort until it floated there, and then they pushed it gently to their boat where the others joined in with a mechanical winch and heaved the thing aboard. In a minute they had turned-to and broken through the small waves, setting sail again and moving straight out to sea without looking back.

"We just lost a good specimen, Major," said Chelli.

"Get something for Utaki?"

"Enough for a DNA sequence, if that's what you're thinking about."

"That's what I'm thinking, mister. But for now, at least, we keep the peace."

Michael was the first one up the cable, and he saw Osen kneeling at the edge of the cliff, handing a rifle to a marine. Another marine helped Michael out of the harness, and sent it down again. "A little tense down there, sir?"

"No. They weren't armed, and just wanted to take the body away."

"No problem, sir. Osen had a good bead on 'em the whole time."

Michael looked at Osen. "Come with me, private. We need to have a talk."

"Sir!" said Osen, and followed him back to the sod-covered pods. They pushed past radio and video panels to get to their cots, Osen dropping his helmet there. Michael took off his jacket and threw it hard on the cot. "Did you or did you not aim a weapon at those villagers down there?"

"I did, sir, but only for a minute until I could see they weren't carrying any weapons and didn't try to come close to you."

Michael scowled. "I was surrounded by marines with rifles slung, men with far more experience than yours, I would guess, but you had to take it on yourself to make a threatening gesture to people. For God's sake, son, we are trying to earn their trust, not *scare* them. What were you thinking of?"

"I was just following—"

"And don't give me that following orders crap! Get Commander Mootry on the horn. Now!"

Osen seemed stunned, but moved with lightning speed. His hands flew over the keyboard; he waited, saw nothing on the screen, and checked a small notebook. "They'll be coming over the horizon in ten minutes, sir."

"Sit there 'til you get him." Michael lay down on the cot, rubbed his eyes and thought about sharp, serrated teeth in an animal that breathed air and lived in the sea. Utaki would be thrilled, but frustrated. They hadn't brought a base sequencer with them, and the samples would have to go back up to *Belsus*. The fishermen had seemed most anxious to take the thing away. Why? At a sudden thought he got up and went to the door. "I'll be out at the cliff. Call me."

He walked quickly to the cliff and looked out to sea. It was still there, sails still visible, a tiny boat with four men and a monster; only it was not heading back to the village. It was going straight out to sea. He watched it as it became a bobbing speck, far out, and then Osen called.

"Got him, sir. You'll only have a few minutes."

Michael ran. He briefed Mootry rapid-fire on the morning's events and the creature they'd found. The Commander agreed to

45

their return to the village, ordered the surveillance team to leave a fixed video camera and move their position to just below the knoll summit. Full alert in camp. He listened to Michael's thirty-second tirade about Osen following him around, and the incident at the beach.

"Calm down, Mike. He's just watching your backside. Remember what happened to Duncan and Takahashi on their last drop?"

"That was war, sir."

"Well, we don't know *what* this one is, yet."

"But he's just a kid."

"There's more to him than you think. Anything else?"

Michael sighed. "Not for now."

"I'll have a flyer there in three hours. Type up a briefing for me, Mike. I gotta go." And he was gone.

Osen looked at him glumly. "You've got a friend there," said Michael. "There's more to you than I think, he says. So what is it?"

"You'll have to ask the Colonel, sir. I'm sorry about the thing at the beach. Maybe I over-reacted."

"Shit," said Michael. He sat down and wrote a four page report on the day's events, then went to his cot, lay down to close his eyes for just a little while—

And awoke to find Colonel Floyd Mootry standing over him. "When did you—?"

"Hi, Mike. You've been sleeping real sound," said Mootry, grinning.

"Your report is—"

"I've already read it, *and* talked to Osen *and* taken a tour of the camp. You okay?"

"Why do you ask, sir? Sure, I'm okay."

"I've just never known you to go to sleep in the middle of the day like that. Feeling the stress? Middle age creeping up on you?" Mootry smiled.

"Guess so. I closed my eyes, and boom I was gone. Didn't mean to sound defensive about it."

Mootry clapped him on the shoulder. "Didn't take it that way. Feel tuckered myself. This is the last time for me. God, I saw some beautiful country coming in. What do you think of it?"

"What I've seen looks like pictures of the tropical islands on old Earth."

"Pretty women?"

"You still thinking about settling here? We don't know *what* we're up against.

"We will. You're the best diplomat on the ship, Mike, and the smartest combat marine I've ever led, once upon a time. Leave the military stuff to Krisha and do your thing. I've decided. This is going to be the place for me, with or without you. When I come down here again, I'm here to stay. There's nothing for me anyplace else."

Michael bowed his head, speechless.

"It's the same for you, isn't it? You have a kid who's grown up barely remembering you, an ex-wife old enough to be your mother, and a long deep-sleep to anywhere else worth living on."

"I don't know, Floyd. I don't know what I'm going to do."

"There's time. I could do this much for you, Mike. I could make you Commander of *Belsus* for the trip back to Brown's Planet, and you could retire an old man. If you stay here, I've been thinking about naming Krisha for the job."

"Krisha?"

"Yep. Good experience, a military mind, and total dedication to The Corps. You disagree?"

"Well, no. I just never thought of her as a Commander."

"Think about it, then, but don't mention it to her, because I haven't. Oh, I think you'll find Osen a little more relaxed in the future. We had a chat."

"You sent him here as my bodyguard, didn't you, to keep the old Major from getting his ass shot off? He's a fuzzy-faced kid, Floyd."

"I want you around, Mike, and he's qualified, believe me. We get things settled here I'll tell you all about it, how I found him, why I trust him. Let's leave it that way."

"Yes, sir."

"Damn it, the name is Floyd. No more ranks, just two old farts getting ready to hang it up. I hope it'll be here, Mike. I really want it that way. What do you say we take a look around? I have lift-off in about an hour."

When they stepped outside, Osen was standing there, rifle slung. He fell into step behind them, and as Michael saw it, Floyd smiled. "Doing his job," he said quietly.

Cooking odors were thick in the air as they toured camp. They passed Krisha and Kari eating under the awning of their hut and talking in low tones. Dark clouds were moving in from the southwest, a swirling, foggy mantle below them announcing the coming of rain. They climbed to a ridge north of the knoll overlooking the village and saw unblemished, tree-covered hills north, east and west. The sea sparkled to the south of them. They stood in utter silence for a few moments, taking it all in, each man lost in his own thoughts.

47

As they left the ridge, Floyd muttered, "This is the place," and Michael knew that his old friend's decision was now irrevocable, and that what happened in the next few days would determine the future courses of both of their lives.

He was still thinking about this when they shook hands at the flyer. "Get it over with," said Floyd, smiling. "I'll be back when it happens." He climbed aboard as the turbines whined, and then the flyer lifted off and headed out to sea before soaring in a great arc towards the orbit of *Belsus*. Michael stood there with Osen, wondering why the boy's face was suddenly looking so grim.

That night it rained on them briefly, and when Michael went outside to walk the perimeter he saw the hills lit up in a green glow that took his breath away. Bright emerald streaks of light shimmered throughout the trees, as if some cosmic painter had been at work. He wished that Floyd had been there to see it, the sudden vista of shimmering color that came with the rain.

He was still thinking about it when they saw the warning sign on the trail to the village the following morning.

* * * * * * *

Kari and Krisha had also seen the flickering lights in the trees that night, but then they argued and Kari retired angrily to the hut, and flounced down on the cot to pout. With a little reflection she decided she was really angrier with herself, knowing Krisha's protective instincts where she was concerned. She should never have shared her fears of Diego, the way he'd touched her, his fathomless eyes boring into her face and body from so close up. And now Krish was insisting she withdraw from the visiting team, feign some illness, anything. She was always watching, jealous of a look or a touch, smothering her like a mother hovering over a small child. Sometimes, it was just too much.

She knew that Krisha loved her, loved her more than life, and would gladly die for her if the situation arose to require it. Her own feelings were deep, too, in ways Michael could never understand. Did she still love Mike? Probably. Hadn't she told him so? Or was she just being kind, saying things to ease the hurt and loneliness she knew was there inside him.

In some ways they were alike, Krisha and Mike: the hard, outer shell, a sense of total responsibility, but inside, something soft, sensitive, vulnerable. It was that extra softness that had drawn Kari to Krisha, that special understanding and knowledge that only a woman could have, a woman who knew her own body, the special places to touch, the—

Kari removed her clothes, and lay back on the cot in the bright light of the lantern. "Krish," she called. "Come in, now. It's getting cold out there. Please?"

The woman understood the tone of her lover's voice. The flap of the hut moved aside, and Krisha was standing there, looking down at her. "Let's not fight, Krish, I won't see you for three days."

Krisha's eyes were moist. She stripped off her clothes and turned the lamp down low, then crawled onto the cot and put her arms around Kari, snuggling her. "I'm sorry, baby; sometimes I don't know when to quit pushing people around."

"Mmmm," said Kari, massaging a hard bicep with one hand and a breast with the other. "I'm cold, Krish."

Their mouths met gently, and Kari sighed. "Oh, Krish, I do love you. Don't you ever doubt it. Don't you ever, ever doubt it."

They lay there cheek to cheek, Krisha breathing in her ear. "Baby, I promise I will always be there for you when you need me. Oh God, I love you, Kari. I worry too much about you."

Kari felt hot tears on the side of her face. She wrapped her arms around Krisha and rocked her like a baby. "Hush, now, my darlin' and hold me tight. Tomorrow is tomorrow, and tonight is real."

After a while, when they were both satisfied, they fell asleep in each other's arms.

CHAPTER SIX

They left camp near sunrise. The morning was shrouded in fog rolling in from the sea, and up into the hills in a network of misty tendrils. Krisha walked them to the edge of the plateau and Michael stopped with her briefly while the others went on. "I've placed two cameras and a receiver, sir," she said. "The knoll summit and north on the ridge. We can see most of the village, especially the area around the obelisk, and Osen has the radio. My people are just below the knoll, with a monitor linked to me. If there's trouble, they can give you cover fire and we can be there in fifteen minutes.

"Only on my orders," said Michael.

"Unless you're incapacitated, sir. In that case, do I have permission to take whatever action I think is necessary?"

"Yes, if you see we're threatened."

"I'd appreciate regular contact and a set rendezvous point. Kari tells me the trail goes along a cliff up there, just before the village comes into view. I'll have someone in the trees at all times, on the radio link. They'll also monitor any activity on the trail, and give you more cover if you have to pull out fast."

"Good," said Michael. "If all goes well, we should be back in three days. If we're not, get in there and find out why."

"Done, sir, and good luck."

Michael walked away in a hurry to catch up with the others, but he had only begun to traverse the seaward slope of the knoll when he saw them ahead, standing in a group, waiting for him. Kari gave him a worried look when he came up to them. "We have a message," she said. The group parted, and there in the middle of the trail was a flattened piece of bark protruding from a cairn of small rocks. Someone had written on the bark, neat block letters in charcoal:

DANGER FOR YOU
GO BACK

"Well, that sure gets our day off to a good start," said Utaki.

"A friend—or an enemy," said Michael. "We won't know until we get there." He pulled up the bark, threw it and the stones off the trail and down towards the sea. "Come on, we're late."

He marched them hard along the trail until they reached the cliff in roiling mist. The obelisk and the village were not visible at this height, and came into view only when they had descended the winding trail far into the trees. In the gloom on either side of them they saw the strange, green lights of the night before flickering dully. Looking closely, Michael could now see that the light was coming from long tendrils of moss hanging from the lower branches of the trees, and draped over the undergrowth like glowing beards.

They came around the last bend in the trail, and Michael saw Diego waiting for them in the amphitheatre. Several villagers were with him. He turned to the others and said, "Okay, here we go. Look sharp."

They walked casually into the village, and around them people appeared in the doorways of their white houses to watch. The fleet of fishing boats was anchored just beyond the surf, and several men were sitting on overturned rowboats on the beach to mend their nets. Michael smiled and said, "My Commander has allowed us to accept your hospitality for three nights. After that we must report back to our camp and the others will be expecting us then."

"Three nights are quite enough," said Diego, "and your host families await you. There will be no fishing today. It is a sacrifice for the welcome rain He has sent. You might first want to see our inland harvest areas, and get to know your hosts."

"Whatever your wish, Counselor. We're here because of your courtesy."

Members of the host families came forward to greet their guests. Davos Grigaytes shook Michael's hand firmly, held on for an extra heartbeat and muttered, "So, you have returned. We thought perhaps you would not, but the women have prepared a welcome. This way."

They walked together to a white stone house at the edge of the beach. Packed flowers and herbs fronted the house, and the weathered hull of a sailboat leaned up against the north wall in gloom. The little boy Uhel watched them from a window, his face somber. *He seems like such a sad little boy*, thought Michael, and then Leah Grigaytes was in the front doorway, smiling warmly and beckoning them inside. "This is our home," she said shyly as he stepped inside behind Davos.

51

The interior of the house was finished in wood, the furniture rough-hewn and sturdy. The wall of the entryway had a line of wooden hooks; a heavy jacket hanging from one of them, and above this was the carved symbol of The New Christians. The symbol of Toth, Michael reminded himself.

To his left was the kitchen with an open hearth, a kettle and spit hanging low over glowing coals, and the girl Deena stood at a massive chopping block, hacking away furiously at colorful fruits and vegetables. He smelled fish, and something sweet, both mixed with wood smoke.

Leah said, "We will eat soon. I'll show you where you sleep." They turned into a kind of sitting room with two large chairs and a rough cot woven from broad, flat plant fibers. A mat made from finer fibers lay folded at one end of the cot. The walls were bare except for one shelf over the cot, which displayed a colorful collection of seashells and pieces of driftwood twisted into bizarre shapes. A harpoon stood in one corner, tipped with a crude steel blade, the first piece of metal Michael had seen on Emerson. "This room is for you," said Leah.

"It's more than enough," said Michael. "Thank you."

A doorway led to a hall beyond the room. Gina emerged from it, bowed, and immediately Michael felt his heartbeat quicken. "Welcome, Leader Queal," she said. She was dressed like the other women: white blouse and long skirt patched together out of many pieces of multicolored cloth. Her hair was pulled back from her face, and held there by a wooden comb. "I'm pleased to be here," he managed to say, his eyes again drawn to hers, but then there was a knocking sound behind him and he turned to see a tall man robed in white standing in the entryway.

"The blessings of Toth for those in this house." He bowed to Toth's symbol, folded his hands across his chest and came into the room, looking only at Michael. "I am called Cainen Nimri, Leader Queal. I will serve as your guide while you're with us."

"Master Nimri will also be staying with us," said Leah, her face suddenly expressionless. "Let us now eat so you can get about your business."

The room seemed instantly cold with the appearance of Nimri, a man Michael had not seen previously, and another priest of some kind. Michael again wondered how many people had remained in the obelisk the previous day. The warmth of the Grigaytes family had abruptly evaporated, replaced with blank expressions and guarded talk. *Diego has sent him to watch us, to make sure the wrong thing won't be said.*

They went back to the kitchen and a long table with benches, on which was piled wooden bowls filled with fruits and vegetables. A plate was heaped with slabs of fish. Wooden plates and cups, knives, and forks with two tines were arranged neatly around the table. Nimri went to a place at the end without instruction, Davos sitting down opposite him. The three women sat down on one side of the table, Leah gesturing for Michael to sit alone opposite her in the middle, and when they were settled the Grigaytes family joined hands with Nimri and bowed their heads.

Nimri said, "Great Toth, our guest and provider, we give thanks for this food and the presence of your children from the stars. In this brief time together, grant us the understanding of each other and give us the courage we need to follow our separate paths as you have assigned them to us. According to your will."

"According to your will," said the others, answering his benediction.

Bowls were passed family style, and Davos named each dish as Michael served himself: a slab of Yellowfin, raw Garbas, and Trukyams seasoned with herbs, and a delicious, yellow pulp fruit called Arcot. Only water was served for drinking. A simple meal, but satisfying, and they ate quickly, in silence. Michael felt their eyes on him as he tried each new thing. When he finally could eat no more, he put down his fork and said, "That was excellent, and I enjoyed every bite of it." He looked around the room. "We're missing someone, the boy Uhli."

"He has already eaten," said Davos.

"You all live together in this house?"

"Yes, all of us. There is one house for each family and all its living generations," said Davos.

"And Uhli's father? I haven't met him yet."

The question seemed natural, but when Michael saw their shocked faces he knew he'd somehow blundered.

"His father is dead," said Davos softly. "Killed at sea—an accident—on my boat."

"I'm sorry. I didn't mean to bring up a bad memory."

"Don't feel badly," said Gini, looking straight down the table at Nimri. "It was two years ago, and I have my son. I still have my son."

"Gini," said Davos. "We have a guest."

But Nimri had shown no visible reaction to her outburst. "Toth provides pain to give us strength and correct our errors. Gini has done well, and her son brings new honor to this family," he said.

"This family has more than its share of honor," said Davos, looking down at his bowl. Michael didn't miss the sarcastic tone of the man's voice, or the heat of Gini's outburst. There was a terrible tension in the room, and people were making little effort to hide it from their guest.

"Would you like to visit one of our harvest areas, Leader Queal?" asked Nimri.

"Yes, I would."

"Fine. These women will accompany us, and you can see how food is taken from the land of Tothwelt. I can provide you with figures for our consumption, but they are far below the bounty Toth provides for us."

"And I have my nets to attend to," said Davos, rising from his chair. "Please excuse me, Leader Queal." He left the kitchen, and walked out of the house. Leah looked at Nimri grimly. "Do we have permission to clean up here before we leave, *Master* Nimri?" Gini gave Michael a look, eyes blazing, while Deena stared down at her empty bowl. The women were furious.

"Of course," said Nimri, unruffled, "but we should leave soon."

Michael waited with Nimri in his sleeping while the women cleaned the kitchen, mumbling and banging bowls and plates together. "Excuse me, Counselor, but they seem quite angry about something. What's the problem?"

"They're unhappy about my assignment to you as guide, Leader Queal. They would have preferred another."

"Might I ask why?"

"I know this family more closely than others, and have guided them through difficult times. As a servant of Toth, I've often had to be firm with them when their wishes were not those of Our Lord. There are some resentments. These are simple people, Leader Queal. They must be guided by those of us who are called for a life of service to Toth."

"You enforce the laws of Toth?"

"Yes, when it is necessary."

"And is there punishment for breaking these laws?"

"There are consequences, yes, but only after repeated warnings."

"What kind of consequences?"

Nimri looked away from Michael. "It is not my place to tell you. You must ask this question for Counselor Segur to answer."

"He's your leader?"

"No, he's a teacher and mentor. I've served with him since I was a boy. He is father to my spirit. You ask many questions, Leader Queal."

"That's my purpose in being here. You've been on this planet for over two hundred years, and we've had no contact with you. We want to see how you're doing, and offer any assistance you desire."

"We?" said Nimri, eyes narrowing.

"The Rubion Federation. Your world is a part of it, settled by people from Riga, all searching for a new life. Surely you have records of this? They were also simple people, Counselor, people devoted to the land and the sea, but they did bring technology with them, and so far I've seen none of it. I find that curious."

Nimri looked genuinely confused, made a teepee with his hands and touched his chin. "Toth has told us about our beginnings, about His bringing us here from a distant star as His chosen people. In the early days His creative work provided for our needs. There are no written records, Leader Queal. The transfigured presence of Our Lord reminds us of our past and our purpose in life. He has created all you will see here, and we are His caretakers. We are the chosen of Toth. There are no other allegiances here."

Michael sighed. "I can understand your loss of touch with the Federation after no contact from us in over two hundred years. We've experienced similar problems with other planets, and you're at the edge of colonized space. That symbol on your robe, it's the symbol of The New Christians, the major religion of the people who colonized all the planets of the Federation. It was the first religion on this planet, but it seems to have become something else. Who or what is Toth, Counselor? Your God? A supreme being with special powers?"

"His powers are indeed beyond understanding," said Nimri reverently.

"Is it possible for me to talk to him? He should have the answers to all my questions."

"Only the baptized may stand in the presence of Toth. He will speak to no others, though he is aware of your presence and watches over you during your stay here. It is His will that you be gone when your business with us is finished. As His servant, I will do all I can to satisfy your requirements, and enable you to leave quickly."

Wait until Mootry hears this, thought Michael, and the idea of retiring to the dusty deserts of Brown's Planet was suddenly real to him.

* * * * * *

The women each carried two baskets, and followed the men north out of the village. They climbed a winding trail through the trees on a steep slope leveling out into a broad valley heading east.

Wooden shacks on tree trunk pillars were scattered among the trees up the slopes and along the valley. People watched them sullenly from doorways before disappearing inside. The air was moist, and beneath each shack were lines sagging with the weight of drying clothes.

"These people are planters and caretakers of the fields," explained Nimri. "They live separate from us by choice, and do not enter the House of Toth. We provide them with fish for their labors, and all families do their own harvesting of fresh food. These are private people, Leader Queal. They will not talk to you. They are not The Chosen of Toth."

They came to a stream, and followed it in silence. The air smelled of pine and sweet flowers. Mushrooms with flat, red crowns were thick along the stream, and the women stopped to pick a few, hurrying to catch up with the men.

Far up in the valley was a roaring sound, and the stream was growing swifter. It tumbled over polished stones, and an occasional drowned log appeared. The trees began to thin, and suddenly were gone, and they were walking into a vast meadow filled with regularly spaced lines of small bushes with yellow flowers. The women rushed by Michael and walked out among the bushes to kneel and begin working with wooden trowels they had carried with them. Michael stepped up behind Gini, watched her carefully dig a circular trench around a bush. Buried Trunkyams appeared there, attached to large roots of the bush. She twisted them free, left one, covered the trench, put the yams in her basket and went to the next bush.

It's a farm, thought Michael. The rows of plants were so regular in spacing, and there was a criss-cross of shallow trenches leading to the stream for irrigation during the early season. "Each plant yields four or five fruits," said Nimri. "You may count the plants if you wish."

Michael did that, and estimated at least a thousand plants providing the vegetable staple for the village.

In minutes the women had half-filled baskets and were moving left to a row of short, broad-leafed trees lining the meadow. All hung heavily with the fruit called Arcot. Michael picked a few himself, and ate them on the spot, relishing the sweet, pulpy flesh. Juice ran down his chin. The women watched him, and giggled when he spat the large seeds of the fruit in high arcs to land meters from where he stood. Their baskets were soon filled, and still they moved eastward up the valley. Michael counted, made more estimates, and Nimri stayed right at his side.

The valley steepened to a crest, beyond which was the roar of falling water. The stream was now a trickle down the slope. All over the slope were vines laden with the small squashes called Garbas. Berries grew in profusion along the trickling waters, from plants flat against the ground and feelers creeping out in all directions. Michael picked and ate, growing exuberant with each new taste. His delight was an infectious thing, and now the women were also eating as they picked, until their faces were painted comically with the dark juices of the berries.

They were filling the last of their baskets when Michael climbed the final few meters to the crest and beheld the magnificent view there, the valley ending in a ten meter cliff of shear rock covered with tenacious brush and great beards of yellow moss. A waterfall crashed down into a circular, emerald-green pool surrounded by a beach of small pebbles. Mist blew in his face as Nimri came up beside him. "The waters come from underground just beyond our view, and the valley beyond seems to be a collecting place for the mountain rains we experience in the cool season. It is the source of our drinking water, but no harvesting is done there. The pool is deep, and our people come here often to bathe in it."

"It's beautiful," said Michael. From where he stood he could see all the way down to the ocean, and the obelisk thrusting up from the trees. To his left a sharp ridge led from the waterfall to the summit east of the village. To reach it one would have to climb the cliff by the pool, a formidable, slippery-looking ascent. The village church went into the hill. He wondered now if there was another entrance on the other side of what appeared to be a narrow ridge instead of a thick hill.

The women were finished, baskets heaped. They climbed to the crest, their faces glistening with sweat. "Our work is done, and we wish to bathe," said Leah, putting down her baskets heavily.

"We should return now," said Nimri. "There is more to show our guest."

Michael smiled. "There's time for that. I'd like to swim in the pool myself, but I brought no clothing for it."

"You wear clothing when you bathe?" said Leah, and stepped out of her wooden sandals. "Our custom is simpler. Please wait for us below while we wash ourselves. You can bathe another time with the men."

Gini and Deena had walked past them to the pebble beach, and Gini looked right at him as she began unbuttoning her blouse. Nimri's face was suddenly flushed red. "I must insist," he said firmly. "We do not have the time for this."

"Please allow it, Counselor," said Michael. "They've worked hard, and I still have to make some estimates for the plants on these slopes."

Nimri hesitated, obviously angry at the challenge to his authority, but thinking fast. "If you insist, Leader Queal, but only for a short while. We have just three days with you." He glared at Leah, who returned it with a defiant glare of her own. Michael turned away, but took one quick look back in time to see Gini's blouse dropping down across a long, lovely back before Nimri blocked his view.

They went slowly down the slope. Michael went through the motions of making yield estimates, totally distracted by the laughter and splashing sounds beyond the crest. His mind conjured up visions of what he might see there. Nimri watched him sullenly without a word, but in minutes the women appeared at the crest again, wet hair tangled about their smiling faces, blouses sticking to wet bodies so that every curve was visible there. Their arms hung straight with the weight of the baskets, and Michael stepped up to Leah, held out a hand. "Let me carry that down for you."

Her eyes sparkled, but Nimri said, "Our women are strong, Leader Queal. They are used to such labor."

Michael took both baskets from Leah. "I'm also strong, Counselor. It's a small thing to repay the courtesy of this family."

The women walked behind them, talked in whispers among themselves, and all the way down the hillsides Michael wondered if he had made a new enemy that day or had simply offended an existing one.

* * * * * *

The team was waiting for him in the amphitheatre when he returned to the village.

Kari rushed up to him. "We have to talk, Mike. Things aren't going right at all."

"I'll be out in a few minutes," he said, then went to the Grigaytes' house and deposited his baskets in the kitchen. Nimri was right behind him as he reached the doorway and stopped. "This is private, Counselor. I'm reviewing the day's events with my people."

Nimri nodded silently, but watched them from the doorway as they gathered in the center of the amphitheatre. In three other doorways Michael could see, white-robed figures also stood there.

"So, how was your day?" he said.

"Nothing," said Kari. "I've spent the whole time in the kitchen, learning how to cook Garbas twelve different ways. My so-called guide won't even talk to me, says I'm to learn about the work-life of the women, and he told me rudely I have no right to wear this pendant."

"Keep it out of sight, then," said Michael.

"Mike, I'm not even supposed to leave the house!" said Kari. "My guide won't take me anywhere."

"My hosts haven't said more than ten words to me all day," said Vilas. "My guide does all the talking, and he spent the entire morning listing the magnificent virtues of Toth. I did get out of the house, but only to watch the men work on their nets."

"Same here," said Utaka. "Same routine, but a little more action. Open resentment against my guide, a guy called Jezrul: tough looking guy, beady eyes, and sullen. Halfway through our meal the head of the house, Zeb Jiskra, suddenly glares at me and says, "Why did you come back here? You're making danger for all of us." Jezrul grabs the guy, hustles him out of the house while the rest of the family sits there looking terrified."

"Could be we've found the person who put that sign in the trail," said Michael.

"I thought of that too," said Utaka. "Anyway, Jezrul returns alone after twenty minutes or so, and the family has refused to speak to me the whole time he's gone, won't even look at me. When Jezrul returns he has this wooden staff with him, two meters of polished wood with a black cap on the end. The sight of that staff scared the hell out of people; they started to get up, and Jezrul ordered them to sit again. The rest of the meal he seemed calm and polite enough, talked about the different plants I'd want to take samples of and promised me a boat trip when the weather clears. After that I got the beach tour like the others, watched net mending, but everywhere we went the men seemed watchful and nervous at the sight of Jezrul and that staff. At one point we passed Osen, and—well, you tell it, Osen."

"I was plugged into the radio, sir, the open channel at one megahertz, and it was quiet. Then Utaka and this guy walk by and I get a sudden burst of static that made me jump. Real strong, sir, picking up a big power source, but just for an instant. Thought I'd picked up a scan. The static became faint, but every time I happened to get close to Utaka and his guide, it picked up again."

"It's the staff, Major," said Utaka. "There's a high frequency power source in it, and I think it's a weapon. Why else would the people be so scared at the sight of it?"

"Are you getting all this, Osen?"

"Recording, sir, the whole conversation."

"Send it as soon as we're finished here. See any other guides with those staffs?"

No others had been seen.

"I haven't seen any of our 'guides' before. For all I know Diego has an army of them buried in that hillside. When you hear this recording, Krisha, get everyone on full alert. There are weapons here, but we don't know what kind yet. I'll get an audience with Diego to ask for more freedom in looking around, and see if he'll put a leash on his watchdogs. I won't ask about Jezrul's staff. Not yet. Anything else for now?"

Everyone shook his or her head no.

"Send it, Osen."

Osen punched out a code on his hand-sized radio, and waited for the return beep only he could hear. "Prepare for level four transmission," he said softly, and then waited again. He punched a button, and the digitized recording of their entire conversation was sent to the receiver on the ridge above them. "Received, sir."

"Okay, let's get back to our hosts. Watch yourselves. The weather is clearing, and at least some of us will be out on boats tomorrow. I want to see everyone here at this time tomorrow. Everyone."

Cainen Nimri was waiting for him in the doorway when he returned to the house. "There are problems?" he asked.

"Complaints, Counselor. The team feels we're not being given the freedom to look around. Our activities are being restricted too much, and I need to talk to Counselor Segur about this. Can you arrange a meeting for me? This evening? I'll wait for you in the amphitheatre, alone, so no one will think you're neglecting your duties."

"I will inquire right away, Leader Queal. Please follow me."

Michael was aware of other faces at doorways as they walked away from the house.

Nimri went to the obelisk, and the doors opened as he reached them. In minutes he reappeared, and looked solemn. "Counselor Segur will meet you here after the evening meal," he said.

And that evening, after a meal eaten in silence and again without the presence of the little boy Uhli, Michael met the tall man in the amphitheatre to explain his problems.

"Your guides have been assigned to facilitate your work, and see to your personal safety, Leader Queal. Nothing more, yet I sense a suspicion about their presence on your part."

"The people say little in their presence, Counselor, and seem frightened. I'm the only one who has seen anything of value today. It makes us think you're hiding things from us, and I don't think either of us wants that. Give us the freedom to look around on our own, have our meals without your guides present, and our suspicions should go away. We meant to trust each other, Counselor, remember?"

"Lord Toth has assigned the guides. I will speak with him, but the guides must be present on the boats tomorrow. They are necessary to the success of our fishing."

"Fair enough," said Michael, "but on land we need the freedom to explore and talk naturally to people. We don't have that now, and if you want us out of here in three days you'll have to give it to us."

"I will consult with Our Lord," said Diego, "and give you his answer in the morning."

* * * * * * *

As night fell, the sky cleared, and Michael sat with Davos on the front stoop. They talked about the fishing fleet and the trip out to sea on the coming day. Michael, of course, would be on Davos' boat, as would Nimri. Davos explained the necessity of having the Counselor on-board, the way he evoked the powers of Toth to bring the Yellowfin to their nets when they seemed to have disappeared in the sea. Leah brought them a lantern, an open, wooden framework stuffed with the glowing moss that hung from the trees. The light would continue as long as the moss was kept moist, she explained. Another wonder provided by Toth. A God? No, thought Michael, not a God, but a man. A man with access to technology. Where was he? In the obelisk? That was where Segur had gone to consult with him. The people had seen him, heard his words, acknowledged his powers, his control, and yet there was no worship here, no worship of a spiritual being with infinite powers. They had brought that religion to Emerson. How had the religion changed so much in only two hundred years?

There was a quiet dignity and pride in Davos, a man who worked the sea and provided for his family. Michael liked the man, and sensed he was liked in return. He shared with Davos the loneliness of space life, the long sleeps, and the family that had aged beyond him, far, far away. Without thinking, he talked about the beauty he's seen that day, the quiet peacefulness he felt as they talked. *Belsus* moved across the sky, and Michael pointed to it. "That will be my home for only a little while, and then my life's work is done."

"You are still a young man, Leader Queal."

Michael laughed. "Older than you think, Davos, but there's a lot of energy left in me. I've thought of farming, raising crops like yours up by the waterfall."

Davos stood up and put a warm hand on his shoulder. "I think you will like the sea also. We rise early. I will show you *my* life's work. Good sleep to you." He went back into the house, which was already dark and quiet.

Michael sat in the green glow of the lamp for several minutes, then walked down to the beach, sat down on an overturned boat and stared out at the sea. There was a cool, salty breeze, soft lapping sounds of the gentle surf, and the smell of fish. He sat there, feeling old, lonely, and miserable, a feeling that had come suddenly, out of nowhere.

There was a snapping sound behind him. He turned, and saw Gini striding towards him across the sand. She wore a long, white sleeping gown, and her dark hair spilled down around her shoulders. She sat down close to him, so close he could feel her warmth, smell the herbs she'd used to wash her hair. "I heard you talking to father," she said, "but his place is not as you think it is. There are bad things here for you, for all of us if you don't leave soon. They will not tolerate interference from outsiders."

"They? You mean people like Segur or Nimri? The Counselors?"

"Cainen Nimri is my brother. His real name is Rico."

"What?"

"The first born son of each family generation is taken as a servant of Toth. Rico left us when he was five, and now he's one of them. They will take my son from me in less than a year. My husband objected, called for a change in the old ways, and—and they killed him. I know they killed him; it was no accident. Talk to my father about it. He likes you. They made it look like an accident, but Counselor Jezru was there, and he—he—ohhh!"

Gini shuddered, and clapped both hands to her neck, breathing hard. "They've seen us," she gasped. "I must leave." She jumped up and ran across the sand towards her house, whimpering.

Michael sat stunned on the boat and watched her disappear in the trees. He got up and followed where she'd gone towards the green glow of the lantern outside her house. His eyes caught movement off to the right; a tall man robed in white, walking away from him, an ethereal figure in the dim light.

The man was carrying a long staff with him.

CHAPTER SEVEN

Diego silently observed Zeb Jiskra's interrogation, and then fled from the room when the man's disciplining began. He paced the hallway, sweating, his big hands clutching at his robe as the screams went on and on. The sound sickened him, and a deep breath relieved a wave of nausea. He was fond of the old fisherman, had served on his boat when they were both younger men. And now this, a direct betrayal to newcomers who had only just arrived. What could bring the man to such an act? His needs were met, good fishing assured by the Counselors Diego selected carefully for his boats. All were children of fisherman like himself, who understood the Yellowfin and their habitat. He had a fine house by the amphitheatre, a place of honor in the village. What more could he want?

The screams subsided, replaced by moans, and Diego breathed a sigh of relief at knowing Zeb had survived the punishment. He must talk to the man; find out what was bothering him so much he could subject their world to a scrutiny Toth could not possibly tolerate.

Diego returned to his sleeping quarters, lay back on his bed and sighed again. Perhaps he was losing touch with the people, neglecting his communication with them. Each week he gathered them together to renew the promises of their Lord and give them The Pleasures that showed His affection for them. It was His thanks for the caretaking of all He'd created for their benefit. And Diego knew first-hand how one moment of Pleasures could dull the memory of past agonies of discipline.

Still, he sensed a growing discontent among the people, and it worried him. More specifically, the acts of the younger counselors worried him, for it seemed that in recent years more and more of them were taking on the responsibilities of exacting discipline on the people without first consulting him. Servants of Toth, yes, but had they forgotten they were first of all Counselors to the families that had nurtured their early years? How long had it been since they'd felt the wrath of their Lord, the pain that set the body afire through every nerve? Had they forgotten the mark of their baptism?

A sinister thought crept into Diego's mind. Perhaps these young counselors, and especially Jezrul, who had been a difficult boy, remembered the pain all too well, and sought to repay it in their positions of influence and delegated power over the people.

This thought disturbed him deeply. He arose and paced his room. He heard a scuffling sound outside, and went to the door, opened it. Two Counselors were holding Zeb up, his feet dragging along the floor as they moved him to another room to rest and consider the cause of his pain. They passed Diego, and as they did so the fisherman raised his head and looked right at him with tear-filled eyes.

"Why did you let them do that to me?" said Zeb.

Diego opened his mouth, but no words would come. He stepped back, closed the door and leaned against it. For the first time in years he felt the constriction in his throat, the sting of salt in his eyes. For the first time in years, Diego Segur wept—for a friend's pain.

In moments his grief had changed to a quiet anger. Jezrul's action had undoubtedly been witnessed by the visitors, could arouse even more suspicion than did Zeb's foolish remarks. It was time to have an understanding with Jezrul and the others. It was time for a reminder that Diego Segur was Counselor to them all, and the right hand of Toth.

His reverie was broken by a soft knock at his door. He went to it, wiped his eyes dry, and found Cainen Nimri there. His heart jumped, for he'd assigned Cainen as guide to Leader Queal and the most respected family in the village. "Is there a problem?" he asked.

"I bring a request from Leader Queal, First Counselor. There is some concern among the visitors."

Diego ushered the young man inside and listened quietly. Cainen reviewed Queal's request for more freedom to look around, and the absence of the Counselors at meal times. The request frightened him a little, for it went against Lord Toth's orders, and could only be granted by Him. "Tell Leader Queal I will consult with Our Lord, and give him the decision in the morning. This request displeases me, I must say. Surely you and the others are doing things that seem to intimidate both our visitors and the people, or we would not hear such a request. What have you personally done to incite this, Counselor?"

"Nothing, my Counselor. Nothing! I follow the will of Toth in every way." Nimri's eyes moved left to where Diego's staff leaned

65

against a wall. Diego saw it, and thought, *I should carry my staff when counseling these young people.*

"Perhaps," said Diego, "but I hear things that make me think otherwise. Your instructions come from me as I carry them forward from Your Lord, and one of them, you should recall, forbids the possession of your staff of office except at times you're on a boat, or during the ceremony on Toth's Day. Have you been carrying your staff with you, Cainen?"

"No, only as you've instructed, First Counselor."

"Has anyone else violated this in recent times?"

Nimri shifted his feet uneasily. "I'm not in a position to say about what the others—"

"I'm asking you a direct question, and you will answer it! Have you recently seen another Counselor carrying his staff in the village?"

"Yes—yes, I have. Jezrul, First Counselor. He was carrying it this afternoon, and there have been other occasions."

Nimri looked frightened, eyes huge. Diego said quickly, "Thank you, Cainen, and Jezrul will not be told I heard this from you. I think you fear him. Do you?"

"Yes, First Counselor, we all do."

"I see," said Diego. "Well, that will have to be corrected. You may go now, and give my message to Leader Queal. I have other matters to attend to." He waved a hand in dismissal, and the young man bowed, turned around, and fled from the room.

Jezrul had been a difficult boy, and now he'd become an even more difficult man. First Queal's demands, and now this. Lord Toth would have to be told, and Diego could only hope the man would be in a pleasant mood. He wondered if his own aging body could still hold up under the pain of discipline.

Diego left his room, descended a winding, stone staircase to the narthex, and followed the short corridor to the vast dome of the sanctuary deep in the hillside. Concentric, semi-circular rows of pews faced a great stone altar, above which hung the symbol of Toth in heavy wood. In front of the altar was a throne of polished stone, on which the transfigured image of their Lord appeared to them. Behind the altar, massive mats hung over the entire wall, hiding the back entrance to the sanctuary and the sacred, closed rooms used by Toth during His early days when He'd walked among the people as a normal man. They were the places of Toth's creative works, empty now. All equipment had been removed after His transfiguration, and taken by boat to the new temple at sea.

Diego went behind the altar, pulled out a drawer containing the controls that summoned Toth to the people, and other controls that brought The Pleasures and occasional pain according to His will. He typed in a sequence of commands, then hurried to sit down in a pew nearest the throne, and folded his hands in his lap.

Alone in the darkened sanctuary, senses acute, he heard a hum as lights in the domed ceiling came on, and formed a shimmering, pulsating veil around the throne. Suddenly, a man was sitting there, broodingly resting His chin on one fist, and looking away towards His left.

"Your call is early, Diego. It comes at an inconvenient time. What is it?"

"An emergency, My Lord, which requires your immediate advice before evening falls. I believe it has become necessary to discipline one of Your Counselors."

"Oh?" said Toth, looking suddenly interested. "Who is it, and for what reason?"

"Jezrul, My Lord. I fear he has been corrupted by his position, and exceeds his authority." Diego paused as Toth turned. He was now staring into the blazing eyes of His Lord.

"And what has he done?"

Diego told him, and as he did so it seemed as if Toth's eyes narrowed, His chin resting heavier on His fist.

"I'm aware of Zeb Jiskra's foolish and dangerous remarks, Diego. Jezrul was correct in bringing him to punishment; would you have done otherwise?"

"Yes, Lord Toth. I would have talked to him, found out his reasons for such an outburst. I would not have taken him away in a rough manner and aroused the suspicions of our visitors. I'm surprised, Lord, that you know about Zsalt's indiscretion."

Toth's smile was cadaverous. "Diego, all these years of service, and you forget that nothing escapes my observation. Nothing. I presume, of course, you would have told me about it this evening."

"Yes, Lord. I'm sorry." *Someone has told him. How?*

"The Jiskra family has become a problem," said Toth. "They complain openly about giving up first-born sons to my service, and others are siding with them. This cannot continue, Diego. It is your responsibility to stop it."

"Perhaps it's because they see what power has done to their son, My Lord. Jezrul has today brought his own father to us in terror and without authorization from me."

"Jezrul is no longer Zeb Jiskra's son, Diego. He is my servant, as are you. All that you say or do comes from Me. Your authority comes from Me and your judgments are Mine. Your will is My Will in all things. Has this become a problem for you?"

Diego felt a tingling inside the baptismal lump at the base of his neck. Warmth crawled down his spine, clutched at him. He stiffened, preparing for what might come. "You are My Lord and the Creator of my world. I have served You faithfully and enforced Your Laws for twenty-five years, and have heard You say that no other has served You as well as I. Lord Toth, have I done something to change your opinion of me?" The warmth in his back had changed to an ache spreading to his shoulders and legs.

Toth smiled. "I detect softness in your leadership, Diego, a reluctance to forcefully administer The Laws when necessary. Perhaps it's the burden of twenty-five years, the accumulated weight of difficult decisions. I remember a time when the celebration of My Day included admonishment of those who questioned The Law, another time when you banished half the village to the sea, all according to My Will. The people feared you then, dared not speak in whispers among themselves about perceived injustices that were only their own opinions. They obeyed The Law, and went about their lives in contentment. Now they question My Word, and I will not have it. And I will not have them arousing the suspicions of our visitors!"

Diego bit his lip as the ache changed to sharp fingers of pain stroking his spine and the long muscles in his legs. "I feel your anger, Lord Toth, but suspicions *have* been aroused, and I must deal with them. Leader Queal has noted what he calls intimidation by the Counselors. He requests their absence during meal times so he can talk freely with the people, and he wants permission to look around the village without their constant presence. The more we control his activities here the more he will feel we're hiding things from him. The zeal of certain Counselors has brought this about, My Lord, not any action on my part. Jezrul's action has contributed greatly, for the visitors saw it, and I must deal with that also. I'm your devoted servant, My Lord Toth. Please trust me." His words had become a gasp as pain enveloped him. He closed his eyes, and prepared for something much worse.

And the pain disappeared in an instant.

"Trust me, Lord," he said, his eyes still closed.

Toth was silent for a long moment, and then said, "Look at me, Diego."

Diego opened his eyes. His body was shocked numb, as if washed by fire.

"Perhaps I've been too harsh with you. You are indeed my right hand, my extension to the people. I too have times of uncertainty in making judgments. I would like to walk among them, touch them, and assure them of My devotion. I wish that My transfigured state would allow me to feel their touch in return. I know the feelings of age and fatigue, Diego. I am not immortal. I want to trust you. I must trust you, but I feel the day is coming when I will want you here with Me in the new temple."

"Your will is mine, Lord Toth," said Diego, his body tingling from toes to fingertips.

"You will grant Leader Queal's request, but the visitors must be gone in three days. If they aren't, I'll have to consider defensive action to protect our society. Both my ancestors and yours came to this world to escape from such people."

"A war, Lord? Can we fight them?"

"I have powers you have not dreamed of, Diego, powers that existed long before your birth, but never used."

"But others will be sure to come, Lord."

"In hundreds of years, perhaps. We are far from their worlds, and of little value to them. That has always been so. But you will help me avert a war by seeing to Queal's satisfaction, and sending him on his way. As to Jezrul, you may admonish the boy, but do not break his spirit. He has qualities which are desirable in a leader if properly tempered."

Diego could barely restrain his horror. "Yes, My Lord."

Toth leaned forward, and waved one hand limply in benediction. "Diego, My dear servant, you have done well for me in the past. I wish you to do well for Me now, and in the future. My blessings on you."

And as the image of Toth flickered and faded, Diego received the gift of Pleasures, beginning at the base of his skull and moving down over his body like a tender mistress with knowledge of every nerve ending. He tilted his head back and gasped as The Pleasures swam through him several times and then were gone, leaving him limp and sweating, and feeling wonderful. In one instant his pain was forgotten, and he was thinking, *how fleeting the wrath of My Lord is.*

After an hour, when he'd returned to his room, a terrible doubt crept into Diego's mind, a doubt that he knew could cost him his life. The inference of Toth had been clear; somehow, He saw Jezrul as a potential First Counselor, a cruel zealot to take the position Diego had held for twenty-five years. How could he consider this? He thought also about the increasingly fluctuating moods of His Lord, hard and punishing one instant, understanding and benevolent the next. Could this mean mental deterioration in a man one step removed from having all attributes of a supreme being? The thought seemed treasonous, blasphemous, but it was there, and it frightened him.

The fact remained that at least for the present he was in charge. The dissent of the villagers, for whatever reason, would have to be resolved, and the Counselors brought into line. He would begin with Jezrul.

A young man barely out of his apprenticeship served his evening meal. Diego sent him to fetch Jezrul for a meeting in the sanctuary, and then took his staff and walked down the hall to the room where Zeb was recovering from his discipline. The room was bare except for a cot where the fisherman lay on his back, one arm draped across his face. The man appeared to be sleeping, but his body tensed as Diego came to his side. He moved his arm, looked up at Diego, and his staff.

"So, you've come personally to finish the job. Why don't you just kill me, and be done with it?"

"Please, old friend, I came to see how you're doing. You're free to leave whenever you wish."

"How can you call me friend? You ordered my punishment, and then left me to them, and only the thought of my family kept me alive."

"You've said foolish things to our visitors, and questioned The Law in public. Toth is displeased, and considers you a problem. You could have been killed, Zeb, your family left with nobody to provide for them. I could have banished you to sea with the others, and certain death from the Charni that guard the routes to the outer islands. Would you rather such a sentence be passed on your entire family? No, Zeb, your pain was the least of what could have happened to appease Our Lord."

"Our Lord," said Zeb bitterly. He sat up and glared at Diego. "He's only an old man who hides himself from us, and rules our lives according to laws that haven't changed in centuries. They are laws we have nothing to say about. We are his work beasts with our own children as masters over us, and we are to say nothing."

"Zeb! It's this kind of talk that has brought you pain."

"So stop it, then. Use your staff of power!"

"I came here to use it, yes, but not in that way. I came to relieve your pain, to try and reason with you. I regret the severity of your punishment; it was more that I expected."

Zeb shook his head sadly. "More and more you've cloistered yourself in the temple, and given your responsibilities over to the young. I don't think you even know what's going on out there: the constant orders, the disciplining, even a murder, all unpunished. We are ruled by our own children."

"A murder?"

"Davos' boat and his own son-in-law who had openly opposed the taking of first-born sons for your army of masters."

"That was an accident, a chance encounter with a Charni."

"It was no chance encounter. Do you think we're so stupid that we don't know the power of your staff to call the Yellowfin to our nets, or to bring a Charni when you desire? Do you think we don't see that somehow the power that gives pain and pleasures is connected to something within each of us, a something that is put there at the time of our baptism?" Zeb grabbed the back of his neck, and squeezed hard. "Do the Yellowfin and Charni have baptismal marks, First Counselor? Are they also the baptized of Toth?"

"They are put here for the benefit of His Chosen People, Zeb. Our Lord does not condone murder. How can you say—?"

"Talk to Davos, then, and get his story. Jezrul has told you lies to protect his own skin, and you've believed him. You talk to Toth and the Counselors, and ignore the rest of us." Zeb leaned forward and put his head in his hands. "I've said enough. Do what you want with me. It will change nothing."

"No," said Diego softly, "but for the moment it will ease your pain."

He held out his staff so that the black cap on its end was near Zeb's head, twisted the thick shaft between his hands until he heard a single click. The fisherman moaned, and then looked up at him in surprise as The Pleasures swam through his body. He arched his neck and closed his eyes as something within him responded to the power of the staff. It washed away his pain and bitterness for what Diego knew would be only the moment at hand. And when it was over, Diego put a hand on Zeb's shoulder. "For now, it is all I can do, old friend, but we will talk about this later. Go home to your family, and try to trust me. Be careful about what you say. I will be watching."

Diego turned, left the room and marched directly to the sanctuary, the staff gripped tightly in his hand. Jezrul was waiting for him, pacing back and forth in front of the altar. Diego went directly to the throne in front of the altar, sat down, and gestured to the nearest pew with his staff. The young man sat down slowly, looking suspiciously

71

at him. "You summoned me, First Counselor, and I've been waiting."

Diego conjured up his sternest look and laid the staff across his knees. "I've had other things to attend to, Counselor. There are many problems in the village, and you have become one of them. This meeting is overdue."

Jezrul's eyes narrowed. "I'm a problem, My Counselor? I've only today solved one for you."

"And raised the suspicions of our visitors by forcefully bringing Zeb here as you did. It could have been done more discreetly after darkness had fallen."

Jezrul said sullenly, "There was no time for discretion. The man was making remarks to frighten our visitors, to make them feel there is danger here for them."

"As indeed there is. You know it, and I know it. How you know is not clear to me; perhaps you're favored with direct communication with Our Lord, and no longer have need of my counsel."

Jezrul stiffened, eyes darting. "Toth speaks to you, First Counselor, and I receive His commands in your words."

"Does he command you to use your staff to discipline the people? I can't recall saying that to you."

"No, but part of my function is to enforce The Laws of Our Lord, and preserve our society as He wills it. You have said this."

"I have said that all punishment, large or small, is a function of me and the temple staff personnel. Those of you who counsel the people on a day-to-day basis have been forbidden to carry a staff in the village. You have repeatedly violated this."

Jezrul growled, "Who has said this to you?"

"I've seen it myself," said Diego, and was thrilled by his own lie. "Do you dare to deny it?"

Jezrul paused, nervous but defiant. "No, I do not. I work for the protection of our society, and there are those who work against it, those who would change The Laws of Our Lord. I have sworn to uphold them, and soft words of admonishment are not enough for simple people. Just this evening I overheard a villager, Gina Veium, speaking in secret to Leader Queal about dangers here, warning him to leave. She seeks the help of our visitors in destroying what Toth has given to us."

"And for this you would punish her?"

"I—I gave her a warning, and her conversation ceased."

"A tingling, perhaps a bit of pain, Jezrul? A show of your power, a power that has not been given over to you, a power that has been given only to ME!"

"I am sworn, First Counselor."

"Where is your staff?" asked Diego softly.

"It is in the Jiskra house."

"You'll bring it to me by morning, and I'll keep it here. When you go out to sea you'll come here to receive it, and return it when the day's work is done, and for the next six weeks, on Toth's Day, you alone among the Counselors shall stand without your staff of office. It is my message to the people that you have violated my confidence, and usurped power."

"Has Toth decided this?" said Jezrul, a dangerous look on his face.

"I am His Right Hand. There is no other. Kneel before me. NOW!"

The young man knew what was coming, but seemed strangely unconcerned. He even smiled as he knelt before Diego, and looked directly into his eyes.

"Those who lust after power shall feel it," said Diego, and he stretched out his staff, twisting it between his hands until he heard the third click and Jezrul had gone rigid, head thrown back, mouth open "Ah—ah—ah—ah," he gasped, shivering.

Diego felt no pity, no compassion, only anger. He twisted the shaft again, and there was a fourth click. Jezrul remained on his knees, still upright, his body convulsing with great heaves, and still Diego stretched forth his staff. Finally, his arms grew tired, and the staff tip wavered towards the floor. He shut it off as Jezrul cried out, "Ahhhhhh!"

"Now get out of here, and bring your staff back to me before the sun rises again."

He'd expected Jezrul to collapse, but he did not. Instead, he saw a horrible grin and wild eyes as the young man lurched to his feet and said, "Yes, My Counselor."

Jezrul stumbled away from him and into the near darkness of the sanctuary. Diego sat shivering with fear and anger on the throne of Toth, thinking, *I've heard of such things. Even Toth has warned me of such people in the past, Counselors who used their own staffs of power to give themselves The Pleasures—or pain.*

This was no punishment for Jezrul. He enjoyed it.

CHAPTER EIGHT

A throbbing pain at the base of his skull awakened Rudy Hoffman. He sat up in bed; saw flashing red light below the video screen in his cramped quarters, and leapt to it. "Yes, My Lord?"

"I've been calling you for several minutes. Get down here, something is wrong with the system again!" Toth's voice shook.

"Right away, Lord," said Rudy. Fear clutched at him. The day had been long, with tedious observations of the ship orbiting above them. Their calculating and recalculating had been continuous as the thing kept changing orbit. Each time he reported a change to the four crews manning the laser and microwave cannons it seemed the men grew surlier, and reacted with increasing hesitation. Their expressions and unspoken words seemed an accusation of stupidity on his part. The orbital changes had begun only that morning, as if the captain of their target had suddenly sensed the presence of the awful weapons tracking his course. There was no way he could know this, of course, no signature of any kind to be seen beyond the tightly closed panels of the great palace dome. The huge fusion reactor itself was buried hundreds of meters below the island.

Rudy hurried down the hallway, past stairs to an elevator that took him quickly down to Toth's chamber. He was still rubbing the back of his neck when the doors opened to a sight that horrified him, the holographic image of his Master writhing on His Throne as if in terrible pain. His head was thrown back, hands clutching at the arm rests.

"My Lord! What's wrong?" Rudy rushed across the room, stopped just short of the image as a searing pain surged through him. He staggered back a step, legs wobbling. "Please, My Lord, I'm here to help. What is happening?"

"My chest," gasped Toth. "I—I can't breathe. What have you done to Me? WHAT HAVE YOU DONE?"

Rudy screamed, and sank to his knees. Flickers of light danced before his eyes. He rolled over on his side and cried out, "Release me, Lord. I'm your hands, and now I can do nothing for you. Please, Dear Lord, I've come to help. Release me!"

Toth groaned, and the pain was gone, replaced with numbness in Rudy's legs and chest. He lurched to his knees and crawled three meters to a computer terminal mounted before six screen filled with the output of Toth's life support system. He pulled himself up into a chair, and called up a routine that immediately displayed the status of the seven critical points of the system. All were normal: saline, oxygen flow, mineral levels, pace-rate, and the myriad of circuits for nerve stimulation. "You're having another attack, Lord Toth! The system is fine. Going to Beta-Choline. Hold on." Rudy's fingers flew over the keyboard, and there was a whine ascending in pitch behind the panel in front of him, then a thud. And Toth gave out a loud grunt.

"Beta-Choline flowing now, Lord. You should feel it any second."

"Ahhh," said Toth. "Yes—there it is. Oh, that's much better."

Rudy jumped from his chair, staggered a few steps to stand before the image of his Lord and Master. Tears streamed down his face. He held out his hands until they were bathed with green light. "It's all I can do, Dear Lord. It's all I can do."

Toth let out a long sigh, and closed his eyes. He breathed deeply, and in a moment seemed to relax, one hand moving to touch his forehead, then his eyelids. "Calm yourself, Rudy. It's better for both of us that way. Whatever it was has passed as before, but never with such severity. It reminds me I'm mortal, Rudy. It's another warning. I'm old beyond old at a time when I'm most needed by My People. You've saved my life again, and I've rewarded you with pain. In my agony I've lashed out at the one closest and dearest to Me. I'm sorry."

Rudy's eyes gushed tears and he fell to his knees. "You are immortal as long as I'm allowed to care for you, My Lord. Your pain is mine."

Toth opened his eyes and smiled, reached out towards Rudy with a slender, bony hand. "In my transfigured state there cannot be touch between us, but I wish it were not so. Arise and touch me, Rudy, and feel my gratitude for what you have done."

Rudy rose to one knee and reached out to touch the image of his Master's Hand, and as his own fingers glowed green, the waves of Pleasure flowed through him gently at first, and then rose to a crescendo that left him gasping. A warm tingling washed up and down his spine even after he'd slowly withdrawn his hand. "My life is for your use, Lord Toth. It will always be so."

Toth sighed again, and rested his chin in the palm of one hand. "Loyalty is admirable, Rudy, but it's not shared by your brethren. Over the years of my absence they've begun to bicker among themselves with ambitions for personal power. They've lost touch with the people, and there's growing unrest. Our visitors have arrived at a very bad time, a dangerous time in our history. Their presence here can only make things worse."

"We're tracking the ship, Lord, but since this morning it has been changing orbits in an erratic way. Even so, all weapons can be locked in well before they reach the horizon."

"You have data on the target?" asked Toth.

"Little, My Lord. There were two drop vessels, and a small force was deployed on the mainland. If it's indeed a survey, it's likely similar to the escorts used when you first made planet-fall, with engine pod aft and bridge pod forward. Our telescopes have not been able to clearly resolve the image, but it appears to be oblong. We've programmed for a three-beam spread within the image, and have the power to cut them to pieces if we're on track for a minute or so."

"Such a long burst might be dangerous for us, Rudy. I suspect their power to retaliate is equal to ours, and our laser beams give them a highly resolved target."

"There is risk, Lord Toth, but I'm confident one sustained exposure to our fire will reduce them to fragments incapable of retaliation."

Toth rubbed his chin reflectively. "It appears to me the issue is when we attack, not if. It's time for the people to see my power, and reconsider their ways."

"Even the islanders, Lord?"

"Especially them. You've seen the infrared halo there often enough to know there's growing technology on the island. They're planning something. I know it. Their boat crews grow bolder each year, circling the palace to observe us. I've hoped the islanders would remain where they are, and no longer contaminate those who expelled them. But contamination continues from within on the mainland. I tell you, Rudy, the day rapidly comes when I will excise all dissenters, and destroy those who will not follow The Law."

"Yes, Lord Toth," said Rudy, frightened by the words and the rising pitch of his Master's tone. Toth glowered at him, lost in the sound of His own voice.

"I will begin with visitors from the worlds we fled from to find this sanctuary of purity and simplicity."

Rudy's heart pounded. "I await your command, Lord."

"We will bring the people together again under The Law, and there will be peace and tranquility as before, without troublemakers, or interference from outsiders who seek to destroy what we have here. You will go to the weapons crews and tell them my words. My orders to them will come soon. Very soon. The future of our society depends on their vigilance and quick action, Rudy. Tell them that."

"I will, Lord Toth. We'll be ready to release the fullness of Your Power at a moment's notice. The ashes of those who oppose Your Word will be scattered in space and on the sea."

Toth smiled, and waved one hand in benediction. "Go then. I'll be with you in all that you say and do."

The image of Toth flickered and disappeared as Rudy bowed. He rushed from the sanctuary and went directly to the gun crews. All the men cheered in unison when he gave them the news. They were instantly alert and enthusiastic, their frustration with inaction answered at last. Rudy wondered how long they had indeed been mentally prepared for war. And when he was finished there, he called together his four ground-force lieutenants for a meeting in his room. They were astonished by his words, since six generations of the hundred-man force they commanded had served only as palace guards and observers of the sea. None had seen a single day of combat, had ever fired at another human being. Grim-faced, they voiced concern about the readiness of the men for hostile action, and their willingness to fire on people who even now could be relatives of their own families. Shrill voices expressed fear of the retaliatory power of the visitors, and demanded that threat be eliminated first and foremost, at any cost.

Questions were shouted out. The islanders were an unknown to them. What technology had they developed in the forty years since their expulsion from the mainland? What weapons did they possess to match the laser and projectile arms of their own force? They left Rudy's room quietly, faces etched with lines of deep concern, despite his assurance that once the visitors were eliminated, nothing could stand up to their firepower.

Sobered by the questions of his lieutenants, and sitting in the quiet of his room, Rudy felt a deeper concern stir within him, a concern for the very fate of His Lord. Somewhere behind the instrument panels of the sanctuary there was a chamber where the transformed being of Toth lived by himself, a man connected to his people only by electronic images and sounds for hundreds of years. He was growing older and older, alone, and mortal by his own words. At times during Rudy's youth, especially during the moments of Pleasures, he'd thought of Toth as a God, yet knew he was a man who had walked among the people in the distant past and brought forth the plants and the creatures of the sea by his own hand. He'd given the people a place that provided for their needs, and simple laws for living, a society for all the people without hunger or poverty or unequal justice.

Rudy stood up and paced his room. Something had gone wrong on Tothwelt: original disagreements with The Laws, the separation of the farmers, the expulsion of the islanders, open dissent among the mainlanders, and now the visitors, much of this in the last forty years. Why? He frowned in thought, and then a new revelation surfaced in his mind. He had been with Toth for twenty years, now, had witnessed His first attack while still an apprentice. These attacks, whatever their cause, had steadily become stronger and more frequent over the years, and could now only be controlled by Beta-Choline, a nerve stimulant which was at present a constant trickle in His Lord's life support system. Beta-Choline acted on nerve synapses to stimulate muscle response and brain function, was used primarily with the elderly. And Toth, transfigured, was indeed elderly beyond imagination. His mood swings over the years had become greater, more erratic, and now he talked of killing, an act totally forbidden by His Own Laws.

Rudy worried about the physical condition of Lord Toth and, quite suddenly, he worried even more about his mental state.

There was no sleep for Rudy Hoffman that night, and in the morning his worries were still with him.

CHAPTER NINE

The beach was illuminated by clumps of glowing moss that hung from poles, and the salty breeze was cool on their faces as they plodded across soft sand to the skiffs lying upside down near water's edge. Michael and Osen would go out with Davos Grigaytes and his crew. Vilos, Cletus, and Utaka had been assigned to other boats. Takey and Kari stayed on shore after Diego offered them an invitation to visit the sanctuary within the obelisk. He had offered the invitation in person, and now stood on the beach to see them off, a long staff in one hand. Kari and Takey were nearby. Kari still pouted. She had wanted to join the rest of them in the boats, and was feeling left out even though she understood the importance of getting a look inside the obelisk.

Michael and Osen went out in separate skiffs with Davos' crew, riding easily over light surf to where the boats were anchored in deeper water. There were ten boats, riding high, nets folded neatly over the railings. No engines were visible. When they neared the boats Michael smelled fish oil and oiled wood. He sniffed the air, and Davos, pulling on an oar, smiled at him. "A good way to wake up in the morning," said Michael.

"Yes, and a good way to live," said Davos. "I think you will like this day."

Again Michael felt respect and growing affection for this man: quiet dignity and strength, responsibility for family, molded by a simple life of physical labor at sea. There was a serenity that he envied; a serenity he suddenly realized was missing in his own life, a sense of meaning, of place.

They clambered aboard a boat painted white, bow pointed seaward, and the crew of eight scattered to their stations. Long lines to the stern tied the skiffs. Michael and Osen stood in the bow as sails were unfurled to catch the morning breeze, and two men cranked up a great stone anchor at their side. There was a gentle shudder as the sails filled, and they were moving out to sea, Davos pulling at the rudder astern. On both sides of them the other boats were on a parallel course, bows rising and dipping under white sails.

Osen turned to Michael and said, "Ever been on a boat, sir?"

"Not like this. Not with sails, and on a real sea. There were some small rivers to cross on Rigal Six, and we did it in little rubber boats at a time when we were running for our lives. No, it wasn't like this at all."

"I've never been on water, sir. It's—peaceful."

"Not much water on Brown's Planet, at least not on the surface. The vineyards I saw there had wells going down at least forty meters, maybe more. Did you grow up there?"

"Yes, sir?"

"Go to the academy?"

"Just basic, sir."

"No further? No officer training?"

"Couldn't, sir. The revolution started, and I felt I should be with my mother. A lot of the farms were being raided, and she was alone." The boy looked away from him, and out to sea.

"And your dad was in deep space."

"Yes, sir."

"So how did you hook up with Mootry? He's particular about his crew."

Osen still wasn't looking at him. "Volunteered, sir. After the revolution, a lot of lands were confiscated and parceled out to whoever would work them. A good part of Colonel Mootry's crew mustered out there, and took up farming. Mom was sick, and we couldn't sell the farm with all that free land available. She died a week before I shipped out."

"I'm sorry," said Michael.

"Yeah, well, I'm where I want to be, and the farm's still there." Now Osen looked at him again. "You going back to Brown's, Major? This is your last drop, isn't it?"

"Probably, but I haven't decided yet. Mootry wants to muster out here, but I don't know if that's wise."

"Kind of a hostile place here, sir. Some funny things going on."

"Seems that way," said Michael, but then Cainen Nimri, who came up beside them and pointed his staff out to sea, interrupted them.

"We're nearing the fishing area, Leader Queal. The men will soon deploy their nets if you would like to watch. Today we fish deep for the Yellowfin."

"Lead the way," said Michael, and without thinking he put a hand on Osen's shoulder, startling him. "Let's do some fishing, private."

Behind them the crew had begun unfastening nets rolled up on thick poles along the railings. There were two each on starboard and port sides, hinged and connected by thick ropes to two hand-winches amidships. Davos was standing, the tiller between his legs, and guided the boat by leaning from side to side as he looked ahead. Nimri stood at the bow, staff in hand, and watched the sea. Land was still visible, the hills above the village, the dark speck that marked the encampment on the plateau. It occurred to Michael they were not nearly as far out as the time he'd first seen the boats during the drop.

Nimri held up his hand, and the men watched him, and when he suddenly lowered it they swung the poles out from both sides of the boat. Cranks on the winches whirred as the weighted nets sank into the sea. Only when the nets were fully extended did the crew shorten sail. Michael noted the high angle of the poles aft, the forward poles parallel with the water. He surmised the nets formed giant scoops traveling along with the boat. *The Yellowfin must be school fish*, he thought. He walked the length of the boat to stand by Davos, who scowled at him.

"We're not out far enough," said Davos. "There will be no fish here. I think Nimri prefers we not see a Charni today, with visitors on board, but the Yellowfin have moved out to the barrier, and that is where we must go to find them."

"What is the barrier?" asked Michael.

"Far out, maybe an hour, it is the place where the Charni live. Toth has put them there to make a barrier we are not supposed to cross. The waters beyond are dangerous."

"There's a large island out there," said Michael. "I saw it from our ship. Hasn't anyone ever gone there?"

Davos looked at him nervously. "One time—years ago, some people left the village and tried to go there. They never came back. We all knew the Charni would get them.

"So you know about the island. Why did you let the people go?"

Davos looked away from him. "They—they wished to leave the village. They'd made trouble, and rejected The Law. We could not stop them from leaving. Perhaps some of them reached the island, but I doubt it. Their boats were very small."

"They were expelled from the village for questioning the Law," said Michael.

81

Davos gave him a quick glance. "Yes."

"Sounds like a death penalty to me. Is that part of The Law?"

"It's not meant to be," said Davos.

Michael looked around him. The crew was at the railings. Osen talked to Nimri at the bow. Michael leaned close to Davos. "People still question The Law, Davos. I've even heard you say things about it. I know Nimri is your first-born son, that all first sons are taken from their families to be servants of Toth, and that your son-in-law opposed The Law before he was killed on your boat."

Davos looked at him, horrified. "Who—?"

"Who is not important. I know. Right or wrong, there are people who think Gini's husband was murdered because he opposed The Law. What happened? How did he die?"

Davos' face was grim. "It's not a thing I want to talk about. He was a good man, a good father and husband. My daughter still grieves for him, and your arrival has brought her new pain. I think you remind her of Lebyn, her husband. There are similarities between you."

Michael touched the man's shoulder. "If there are wrong things happening in the village, I can't leave until I know about them. It's part of my job. Tell me."

Davos glanced towards the bow, swallowed hard and said, "Jezrul was our guide that day. We were in close, and suddenly the Yellowfin filled our nets to bursting. One net tore at the surface, and Lebyn, my son-in-law, leapt into the water with rope to repair the break. Jezrul went to the railing, and stretched out his staff, and—and suddenly a Charni was there. A Charni, so close to shore!"

Nimri was now watching them standing close together. He interrupted Osen's conversation with a wave of his hand, and started walking towards them. Both men saw him coming at the same time.

"It cut Lebyn is half at the waist with one bite, and was gone in an instant. It didn't attack the net, didn't stay to feed on the Yellowfin boiling around us. It killed Lebyn, and swam away."

"Do you have questions I can answer, Leader Queal?" asked Nimri, stepping up in front of them.

Michael smiled. "I was learning about the nets, and Davos thinks we'll have to go further out to catch fish today. He says we might even see a Charni."

"The Charni are further out, and the Yellowfin are near. You will see. Toth will bring them to us, and I am his instrument. Watch me, and you'll believe." Nimri wasn't looking at Michael; his blue eyes were focused directly on his father. "This boat will be low in the water when we return." He turned, and walked back to the bow where Osen awaited him.

Michael patted Davos on the shoulder. "Another time," he said. "I want to talk some more about this." Then he joined Nimri and Osen at the bow.

They sailed for over half an hour before the Yellowfin came. Nimri stood silently at the bow, studying the water ahead, and for the first time Michael noticed the plug in Osen's left ear. He had his radio, alert for an emergency message from Krisha or Mootry. Again, Michael was impressed by the boy's professionalism, his watchfulness. They watched with Nimri, and suddenly the water ahead of them turned a deeper blue, and there were choppy waves swaying the boat from side to side. Nimri held out his staff over the water, and closed his eyes. A hum came from deep in his throat.

Osen's hand slipped inside his jacket. He looked at Michael, and wiggled an eyebrow at him.

Nimri hummed a kind of mantra, and behind them the crew stood silently at the railings, watching him respectfully. The hum, the gentle rocking of the boat seemed to penetrate Michael's mind, blanking it out, lulling it into a relaxed state approaching twilight sleep. He closed his eyes …

"YELLOWFIN!" screamed a crewmember.

Michael's eyes snapped open, and ahead of him the surface of the water boiled with thrashing bodies on a collision course with the boat. The characteristic yellow-tipped dorsal fins waved like sails. In an instant they had passed under the bow, and the boat lurched, groaning, slowing so rapidly that Osen's arms came around Michael to prevent his being thrown into the sea. Nimri stood firm like a statue; staff outstretched, and behind them the poles holding the nets sagged with the sudden weight of countless fish swarming below. "Bring them in!" yelled Davos, and two men rushed to each of the great winches and began cranking furiously. Others pulled up on the nets, the thick poles holding them now bending close to the water.

Men yelled as a frothing, struggling mass of fish appeared beneath the water on both sides of the boat, then above it. One pole creaked, and made a popping sound. The crew leaned over the side, and began pulling Yellowfin one-by-one from the nets, throwing them flopping and gasping on the deck before the nets were even clear of the water. There were smiles, and glances towards the bow where Nimri still stood, humming his deep-throated mantra. Somehow he had brought the Yellowfin to them, and they were grateful. Michael and Osen watched in awe as the collection of struggling fish became a pile, a mound, a small mountain writing on the deck from rail to rail, until finally the nets were empty and one crew-member was wrapping a small break in one pole with a short length of rope.

Nimri turned to them. "It is enough," he said. "Give thanks in your hearts that Toth has again provided for our needs." He walked to where the men were already reaching to swing the poles back along the railings and roll up the ends of the nets. He stood tall as they gathered around him, and hands reached out to pat his back and shoulders.

"Incredible," said Michael softly. "How could he see a school of fish under the water like that?"

Osen touched his shoulder, pointed to the plug in his own ear. "He called them," he said in a whisper. "There's a transmitter in that staff, and I heard the signal, just like I heard it on the beach. He sent a signal that brought the fish here, a rising squeal that repeated over and over. I had the radio on scan, and this time it locked right on the frequency. Clear as a bell."

"But under the water, how could it?"

"CHARNI!" screamed someone, and everyone jumped back from the railings. Michael followed their faces to port; saw a great dorsal fin slicing through the water fifty meters away, heading right for them, a long, shadowy shape just below the surface. Men cried out, and fell back into the mountain of fish. Other boats were visible, but closer to shore, and they were alone with a killer, a missile armed with razor teeth, coming straight at them like a torpedo half the length of the boat. But Nimri remained calm, stepped up to the railing and twisted his staff sharply between his two hands. He thrust it out towards the attacking Charni. Osen grunted beside Michael, and ripped the plug from his ear.

"By the power given to me through Our Lord Toth I command you to be gone!" shouted Nimri, and he closed his eyes as if in prayer. Michael and the others watched in astonishment as the giant fish leaped from the sea only meters away from them, snapped its jaws in fury, and crashed into the water to throw a wave of spray over the men and the boat. It turned sharply, and Nimri followed it with the tip of his staff. "Be gone!" cried Nimri, eyes now open.

Michael stepped back to the bow and watched the huge dorsal fin streaking away from them, heading towards the southern horizon from which the Yellowfin had come, the horizon on which floated the hazy shadow of a distant island. In seconds it was gone, and the men were cheering Nimri, crowding around him. Even Davos was smiling with pride for the servant of Toth who was his son.

Osen had a finger in his ear, rubbing softly. "Maybe putting the radio on scan isn't such a good idea. I think I've hurt my eardrum."

"The staff again?" asked Michael, and Osen nodded.

"If you're right, it can call the Yellowfin and chase the Charni away. If it can do that, I think it can also call the Charni. I wonder what else it can do. And how?"

They walked from the bow to join the happy throng of men surrounding Nimri, and offered him their congratulations.

Nimri was pleased.

CHAPTER TEN

Kari watched the sails of the boats get smaller and smaller, and thought about marching right out of the village and up the hill to the plateau. Suddenly she was lonely again, and missed Krisha. Michael was hardly speaking to her, and when he did it was strictly business, talk between officer and subordinate. She felt the hurt in him, the sense of abandonment, but what could he expect with the long deep sleeps out of synch with her own time in the cocoon. And Krisha was always there when she awoke. Age had changed Michael, made him softer, diplomatic, and careful with words. He was certainly not the randy young captain she'd first met and bedded. Krisha was now a constant in her life, strong and protective, but still a woman, understanding her deepest needs, and always satisfying them.

Diego Segur stepped up beside her, staff in hand. "Are you still angry?" he said softly.

"Of course. The others are allowed to go out to sea, and I'm left behind. I suppose it's because I'm a woman."

"This is only partly true," said Diego, looking down at her, "but it's a tradition, and not part of The Law. Our women accept it and go about their tasks at home. Besides, I thought you'd prefer to visit Toth's home among us and witness the baptism of a child. That is another tradition, and a ceremony attended only by our women. It acknowledges their special gifts in giving birth to our children."

His words softened her anger. "I appreciate your invitation, Counselor, really, and I do look forward to it. But I've never been in a boat before and I'm a little disappointed. When is the baptism?"

"Soon. We have enough time to see the sanctuary before the ceremony begins. Shall we go?"

Diego took her by the elbow, his huge hand enveloping it, and standing next to him she was again awed by his size and piercing gaze. How old a man was he? Did he have a woman, or was celibacy a part of his life as a servant of Toth? His grasp moved to her arm and she felt his warmth. Was he attracted to her? She remembered his fingers rubbing across the back of her neck, rough fingers that had sent a chill through her. Was she, in fact, attracted to this big man in a subliminal way he could sense? His hand closed warmly on her arm and she made no effort to break the contact. "Baptism is our most important ceremony," he said. "We dedicate our children to lives of husbanding all that Toth has provided for us, living free under His simple rules."

They were walking slowly towards the obelisk, and the doors opened to receive them. "Is the child a first-born son?"

"No, it is a girl, second-born to the Kaziel family. Their first-born was also a girl, but there is still hope."

"You place great importance on sons," said Kari.

Diego's thumb stroked her arm. "Only the first-born are ordained as servants of Toth. It is necessary for each family to be represented so each of us who serve Him will remain close to the people in guiding their ways under The Law. You must understand, Kari, that we are the eyes and hands of Our Lord. In His transfigured state he can no longer be among us, and can only give us His Word. Oh, may I call you Kari?"

"Yes."

"Good," said Diego. He squeezed her arm, and then released it. "Let us now go inside."

They had reached the great doors beyond which were darkness. Takey had gone back to the home of his host to await his tour of the obelisk. He intended to study some of the early writings of counselors from the days when Toth had walked among the people. The rest of the team was out to sea, and it was Kari who entered a dark place with a near stranger towering over her. As they stepped into the darkness another counselor suddenly appeared and closed the doors behind them. Kari breathed deep to control her fear, but it was short-lived. Rope globes of the strangely fluorescent moss glowed along the hall before them, and her eyes quickly adjusted to the gloom.

The other counselor, barely out of his teens, scurried ahead of them and pushed open two heavy, carved wooden doors. Diego's hand rested lightly on her waist. "This is our meeting place, and Toth's sanctuary among us."

They entered a huge room with a domed ceiling glowing green from drapes of moss hanging from trestles five meters above their heads. Kari saw concentric semi-circles of pews, the throne, the great stone altar behind it, a back wall covered with a great, plane tapestry made from plant fibers. A heavy, wooden symbol of the New Christians hung in front of it. "Very impressive," she said. "Toth meets with you here?"

"His image appears to us, sitting in the throne you see. He dwells in another place, but is always with His People."

"He talks to you?" Kari reached inside her shirt, withdrew the pendent she wore and held it in her hand.

"Yes, he talks to all the people on His Day. He reminds them of His Law, the tasks they must do to maintain all He has provided for us. He has great affection for the people and wishes He could still be with them."

"Why? Why can't he be with them?" Kari fingered her pendent and Diego's eyes were drawn to it.

"He is a man, Kari, not one of your gods. Long ago he was old, near death, but His wisdom was needed and could be found in no other man. Long before I was born, Lord Toth created for himself a transfigured body that would age no more, a state beyond human understanding. It was necessary for him to physically dwell in a place far from His People whom he loved and continues to love. What He shows us is His image before the transfiguration, a familiar image the people can understand. In this way His counsel has been with us for hundreds of years, holding us together and maintaining the world he created for us.

"Was he one of the original colonists here?"

"Yes."

"But that was nearly three hundred years ago!"

"Yes. I can tell you no more about him except that he was a scientist. He created the plants and the creatures of the sea to provide for all our needs. We have dwelled happily here, and want nothing to change that. If we have appeared unfriendly at times it is because we want things to remain as they are. You and your companions are our first visitors from the stars. You are an unknown, and there is some fear among the people. We have no desire for contact with other worlds. Toth has instructed us to answer your questions so that you will then leave. I follow the words of My Lord."

"We have no intentions of disrupting your life here, Counselor. We've come only to offer our services if they're needed and asked for. I do have another question, though. This pendant I wear is the symbol of The New Christians, a symbol of the God we believe in, and I see you wearing the same thing. How can this be, unless the first colonists were New Christians?"

Diego reached out and touched her pendant, fingers lightly brushing her chest. "We worship no gods here, but give thanks to Toth for his gifts. He came from your world and I can only speculate that He adopted this symbol for His own use. The circle on the cross represents the unity of the people, and the three spokes speak of a simple, harmonious life on His world."

Diego looked into her eyes and smiled. "So many questions from such a lovely woman. You are very perceptive, Kari, and intelligent."

"Thank you," said Kari, feeling his fingers brush her throat as he placed her pendant back inside her shirt. "Will the baptism be in this room?" she said quickly.

"Yes. There is a place behind the wall covering where you may listen, and see a little. The people must not see you here. Come, I'll show you."

Kari followed Diego to the wall behind the altar, where he pulled aside a flap of the great fiber-hanging to reveal a small alcove. "You'll be here during the ceremony and I'll come for you afterwards. Now I must quickly show you the rest of the sanctuary."

He took her arm again and ushered her from the room to a long hallway lined with closed doors, the sleeping quarters of his aids, he explained. As they walked, his hand left her arm and went to her waist, pulling her lightly to his side. There was no doubt in her mind, now. He was attracted to her, and allowing her to witness the baptism was an illegal thing, something he had to hide from the people and from Toth. How far could she play this, and what would be the price? For a brief instant she entertained a fantasy of what it would be like, beneath him, his huge hands moving over her body. As she thought this, she leaned against him ever so lightly, and he smiled down at her. "The stairs are quite steep and dangerous. There is an elevator to take us to the next floor."

So there's electrical power here, she thought. They rode in silence to the next floor, a curving hallway with more closed doors, a spiral staircase leading upwards to darkness, rope globes filled with glowing moss at regular intervals along the walls. Diego went before her to a door, opened it, ushered her solemnly inside. "As an example to the people, we who serve Toth give up the pleasures of the world and live only for His service. This is my room."

The room was Spartan, the wooden symbol of Toth over a crude bed that was only a fiber mat on thick boards. Robes hung on two wall hooks. There was a chair, and a table on which a globe of moss glowed dimly. There were no windows, and the air in the room smelled stale. "It's—it's simple," said Kari. "I'm surprised, Counselor."

"There is no luxury for me, you see. My life is devoted to Toth and to His People. It has been so since I came here as an apprentice forty years ago."

"It's so quiet." Kari walked over to the bed, pressed down on the thin mattress with one hand. It was hard. "Isn't it lonely here?"

Diego walked up behind her. "There are times, in the late evening, when there are problems to consider and only the walls to share my thoughts with. There are times when I think of the dead family that gave me up when I was a boy, my father who was a fisherman, my sisters, the long conversations over eating, hauling on nets with sea spray in my face. They were good times, but they're in the past. As a first-born son my life is here. It is The Law, and I have no regrets. Each of us does what is commanded by Our Lord."

Kari turned around, looked up at him. "I've never met a man who lived his life only for others. Even the priests of The New Christians have families and live normal, social lives. I think you've made a great sacrifice. I admire that. Counselor, but something is bothering me. This visit, my being here, it isn't something that will cause you trouble, is it? Should I be here?"

Diego put a hand on her shoulder. "I've made a choice, but we must be discrete. Only Danen my apprentice knows you are here and he has my trust. You must not be seen or heard when the others arrive."

"Why me?" said Kari. "Why did you invite *me* here?" His hand was warm on her shoulder and she felt her vulnerability strangely without fear in the near presence of this huge man.

"Ah Kari," he said, his hand moving to her face, a long thumb stroking her cheek once. "I think you are the loveliest woman I've ever seen. Please forgive the desire of an old man to spend a few moments alone with you."

Kari looked up at him, touched his hand with own, a rush of heat surging through her as her earlier fantasy about him returned. "You don't seem old," she said softly.

"Thank you," said Diego. He leaned down towards her, cupping her chin in his hand. She closed her eyes, lips parting; heart pounding in anticipation, but what she felt was the gentle touch of his lips first on her forehead, then on the cheek. "Thank you for saying that," he murmured, "but now we must go."

He took her hand and led her from the room; Kari felt disappointment and relief at the same time. They took the elevator down to the sanctuary and there he hid her in the tiny alcove behind the altar. "Be very quiet," he said. "I'll return for you as soon as I can after the ceremony." He dropped the flap of the great curtain, and she was plunged into darkness.

In moments her eyes had adjusted to the gloom. Slivers of light leaked through breaks in the weave of the curtain. She could see the altar, the back of the throne to its right, the end of a pew, a portion of the glowing ceiling above her. She waited for what seemed an eternity and then there was the creaking sound of doors opening and voices beyond the sanctuary. Women's voices. Footsteps in the room, the rustle of long skirts, and the creak of wood as people settled themselves in pews beyond her view. Diego's voice was soft; "Our Lord is with us for this moment," he said, and bright points of green light suddenly burst from several places in the ceiling, beams falling towards the throne in paths made visible by sparkling dust motes. The top of a cloaked head appeared above the throne, an image through which Kari could still see the edge of a pew. A hologram, she thought. Diego was projecting an image of someone sitting on the throne. The image of Toth, which she could not see from her hiding place. The head moved.

"I come to rejoice with you," said the image on the throne, a deep, resonant voice. Kari stifled a gasp.

"Our Lord, we present to you Andrea Kaziel, a new addition to Your Chosen People, a daughter born of Tal and Ona." Diego stepped before the throne, robe glowing green, and in his arms he cuddled a tiny child. The baby was awake, wide eyes blinking at first then closing against the bright light. It whimpered in displeasure, and Diego cuddled it closer to him.

"She is a wonderful child," said the voice from the throne. "I welcome her to My People, and send my blessings to all who join in this celebration. May all who are here nurture this child and bring her to womanhood according to The Laws I have set forth."

"We so promise, Lord Toth," came a soft chorus of female voices from the pews.

"May she grow in strength and happiness in a life of simple tasks, enjoying and caring for the fruits of My World. May she forever be free from harm, for she is one of those blessed and chosen by Me, and is under my protection for as long as she lives. Now do we instill in her the connection that binds us together."

Diego bowed and walked past the throne to the altar, his back to Kari. He laid the baby face down on the altar, opened a drawer in it and took out a small tray. Kari stifled another gasp as he took from the tray a small knife and what she recognized as a pressurized epidermal syringe. She heard the hiss of it as Diego leaned over the child, but the little girl did not cry out. He was going to cut the baby! She remembered Diego's fingers on her neck that day, searching for something. A baptismal mark, a scar? She held her breath as Diego spoke, his hand grasping the knife.

"Andrea, we give the tie that binds you to your Lord Toth, the gift of Pleasures given only to His Chosen, The Laws you will follow all the days of your life."

And then, to Kari's astonishment, Diego stretched out his arms to his sides and began to sing in a deep, basso voice, and a mesmerizing chant that so filled her head with sound she realized when the song had ended that she hadn't registered a single word of it. He leaned over the baby again, the knife flashing in his hand, moving quickly to the tray to remove something tiny, a gray thing held loosely with wooden tweezers, and leaning over again as the baby cried out for the first time. He picked up the squirming infant, held her out over the altar to face the spectators and Kari saw what looked like a small bandage at the base of her neck. "Andrea, go in peace with those who have accepted responsibility for you," he said.

"And with My blessings," said Toth from the throne.

The baby instantly ceased crying and Kari heard a collective sigh coming from the pews as Diego carried Andrea away from the altar. "Peace be with you always," he said, and then there was the scuffling of feet as people began leaving the sanctuary.

"Diego," said Toth. "I wish to have a moment of your time."

"Yes, My Lord." Diego came into Kari's view again and stood before the throne. The women's voices faded, and then were gone as the outer doors closed with a thump. "We are alone now."

"We discussed the matter of Jezrul, and I've been thinking about it. I feel he should be admonished for his behavior."

"I have already done that, Lord."

"It is not enough, Diego. It is time for an admonishment directly from Me. Bring Jezrul to me at once."

"He is at sea, Lord. Our visitors were taken out on the boats today."

"They return as we speak, Diego, and with a great catch. Go and send Jezrul to me, then spend some time with the people and convey my blessings on them for a job well done. They need to see more of you outside the sanctuary. I will send a more humble Jezrul to fetch you when we are finished here."

Diego hesitated; his eyes darting briefly towards Kari's hiding place then back again. Kari held her breath. "If you wish to break contact, Lord, Jezrul can call you when he arrives here," said Diego.

"That won't be necessary. Go, now."

"Yes, My Lord," and Diego hurried away.

92

The outer doors opened and closed, the silence of a tomb descending on the room. Kari stepped away from the curtain, pressed her back to a cold wall, her breathing shallow. Could he feel her presence? How far did his powers extend? And if he found her here, what then? She was suddenly frightened in her dark hiding place. Any possible exit was in view of the throne. Could he actually see what was in the room? Likely there were video cameras everywhere, so she must stay where she was until Diego arrived to get her.

The wait seemed endless and her legs were tired, the cramped space too small for sitting. Her nose felt stuffy from the cold air. She breathed through her mouth, heard a tiny wheeze that wouldn't go away no matter how shallow she breathed. Finally the outer doors creaked and there were footsteps in the room once more.

"I am here, Lord Toth." It was Jezrul.

"Must I call you to me? Where were you last night?"

"Diego sleeps poorly these days. He was walking the halls until morning, and I dared not chance it. Forgive me, Lord."

"No matter. You are here now, and it's soon enough. Hear my words, and act upon them. Sometime during the early morning hours I will attack the ship of our visitors from the stars and destroy it. I cannot give you the exact time and you must be watching for the ship each time it passes over us. There will be a light mist at sea level and our beams should be visible from the beach. Assemble the men, and keep them alert in their rooms until the time comes. Are you absolutely certain of their loyalty, Jezrul?"

"They are loyal only to You, Lord, and I am Your spokesman to them."

"I hold you responsible, Jezrul. Look for the flash in the sky when the ship is destroyed, then go to the men and disperse them to the village to take the visitors as prisoners. If they resist you, kill them. Kill them all, if necessary. Is this a problem for you, Jezrul?"

"Your Words are The Law at all times, My Lord. I obey The Law. But what about Diego?"

"Do not kill him. He's a weak fool, but I will repay his days of faithful service by sparing him. He will soon take his evening meal and you will arrange to have it drugged so he will not awake until all has been accomplished. You will bring him to me in the airboat, the rest of the prisoners in fishing craft. My beacon will give you all safe passage through the barrier. The Charni will swim deep to escape it."

"We must move quickly, Lord. There are still observers on the ridge and their soldiers can be in the village within minutes."

"So it is, but you will move quietly as well as quickly. By the time they sense something is wrong and move to stop it you will be well out to sea and they have no watercraft. If they take boats and follow you I will destroy them all."

"Yes, Lord Toth."

"Go, then, and gather your brethren together. When the morning comes, My Laws will no longer be questioned. Our world will be safe from foreign contamination."

"It will be done, Lord."

"Jezrul, my most trusted servant, your hour has come. Bring to me those who would change that which must not be changed, and you will lead the people according to My Law. Our future is in your hands. Leave me now, for I must see to my gun crews. Tomorrow, Diego's office will be yours if you don't fail me."

"I go, Lord Toth! I will not fail you!"

"Until tomorrow and now ask Diego to return. I have chastised you, and you will show humility to him," said Toth, and in her hiding place, listening with increasing horror, Kari was suddenly plunged into darkness as the green lights in the ceiling went out.

She heard Jezrul striding away, low voices, the great doors creaking once more, and then silence. She had to get out, must get to Michael and warn him. The doors were only meters away, a path visible in the gloom. She pushed the flap of the curtain aside, stepped out cautiously, looked around, took two steps towards the altar and froze.

The doors were opening again, outside light leaking into the sanctuary. Kari darted back to her hiding place, cursing. She distinctly heard Diego's voice, and others, all growing fainter as they moved away from the sanctuary. Diego had returned. He would come for her soon. She waited—and waited—the door opened and closed twice more—finally she heard deliberate footsteps coming towards her in the gloom. She would tell him of Jezrul's treachery, his own danger, surely he would allow her to warn Michael before it was too late. If he really were attracted to her he would allow this. Wouldn't he?

The footsteps came towards her on a line. She leaned back against the wall, hands behind her, and conjured up a welcoming smile for him. A hand seized the curtain flap in front of her and pulled it aside. Kari squinted to see his face in the gloom.

It was Jezrul, and beside him stood the young man who'd closed the door behind Kari and Diego earlier in the morning.

"Well, well," said Jezrul, "just how long have *you* been in there?"

Kari ducked down, sprinted towards Jezrul's right, but he caught her by the hair, a hand chopping hard alongside her head. She grunted as he pulled her upright and clamped a hand over her mouth and nose. There was a roaring sound in her ears, colorful stars dancing before her eyes, and then there was nothing at all.

CHAPTER ELEVEN

Michael was caught up in the merriment of the men and joined in with their work after a moment of instruction from Davos. Each fish was sliced open from gills to tail fin, organs removed and thrown into a tank below deck that smelled of alkali and fresh dirt. The meat went into an adjoining tank into which salty water now issued in a fine spray from port to starboard. Finely honed steel knives had appeared from some hidden place on the boat, issued one to a man by Davos and to be returned to him for safekeeping. So metal *was* used by the villagers, but in a tightly controlled way. The implements themselves, Michael concluded, dated back to the founding of the colony, and had been used for centuries without re-placement.

He caught on to the work quickly, flinging fishy carcasses and organs right and left, his hands bloody. Osen was curiously absent from the work, standing at the bow, the radio again in his ear, but the men took no notice of him. Even Nimri had joined in cleaning the fish, sitting on the deck, staff across his knees. By the time they felt the surf building beneath them they had worked their way through most of the Yellowfin and the other boats had drawn close. Men shouted back and forth to each other. All had taken fish, and according to the shouts, each boat had exceeded the catch of all the others.

They dropped anchor at surf' edge, and a small crowd was on the beach to greet them. Diego Segur was conspicuous by his great height. Michael went ashore in a skiff with Osen and Nimri, the rest remaining behind to finish the work and begin the task of hauling the catch to shore. Diego went straight to Jezrul as he was wading the last few meters to shore, spoke to him, and the younger man walked off towards the obelisk. Women were turning over rowboats and pushing them to water's edge when Michael felt sand under his feet. A swaying feeling remained in his legs and body. As Diego approached him, staff in hand, Michael smiled. "Your people have had a good day at sea."

"And you've had an opportunity to see just one of the many blessings Toth has bestowed upon us. Did you enjoy it?" said Diego.

"It's been a long time since I've felt so alive," said Michael. The work, the camaraderie of the men, the excitement of the catch, even the appearance of the Charni had filled him with vigor and exhilaration he hadn't experienced in many years. He felt as if he were a young man again, experiencing things for the first time. Michael looked around him. "Where are Kari and Takey? I thought they'd be here to meet us."

"They are still in the sanctuary and I must return to them. The young woman has witnessed a baptismal ceremony I'm sure you'll find interesting. The man has read what few books and written records we could provide for him. They will return soon."

"I'll be waiting," said Michael. He turned to find Osen standing right behind him, looking grim. The boy tapped the plug in his ear. "Message for you from Colonel Mootry, sir. I intercepted it while we were coming in and you need to hear the tape right away. He's put our backup on full alert and Krisha, uh, Captain Elg is moving people up towards the village."

"Back to Davos' house," said Michael, and Osen followed him away from the beach. Behind them Diego was shouting to the men, bringing them the blessings of Lord Toth and on the boats the men working there broke into a song of praise for the creator of their harvest.

Gini and her mother were in the kitchen when they arrived. She gave him a lovely smile that made his chest tight, then a perplexed look when he grinned and darted away from her to his sleeping quarters to plug into Osen's tape.

The message from Mootry to Krisha was short and to the point. The ship was being scanned regularly and they were taking evasive action. The scanning signal was coming from a small island fifty klicks east of the big island some forty kilometers offshore from the village. The big island itself was showing them a variety of signatures, mostly in the infrared, and concentrated inland within a ring of mountains. Mootry was now certain the island was inhabited. The IR spectra indicated something geothermal or the waste heat of engines; he couldn't be sure which. The small island east could be a military installation or simply a lookout, but the sudden, intense scanning worried him and his crew was at battle stations, under orders to make random orbit changes for each pass over the islands. He ordered Krisha to move a party of marines to the ridge and the summit of the trail leading to the village, and be prepared to return at a moment's notice for pickup by a flyer. He saw no need to bother Michael with the news just yet. Let him do his job and get out, but if there were any signs of trouble in the village Krisha should move in without further orders. Krisha had no questions. Her people were already on the move. Mootry clicked off and then Krisha said; "If you hear this, Major, don't worry about it. If anything happens, we'll be there."

Michael took the plug from his ear. "Erase all that, Osen."

"Yes, sir," said Osen, and he erased the tape clean.

"So now it seems the village isn't alone. There are people out on those islands and the villagers say they won't go there because of the barrier, the place where the Charni live. I think this fellow Toth doesn't want the people back together again. Nimri controlled the Charni we saw today with a signal from his staff. My bet is the big island out there is sending out a beacon that keeps the Charni in one general area the villagers dare not cross. Why? Because Toth is there. Technology is there. The real civilization for this planet is on that island, and we've got to get out there. It's not that far; I could see it from the boat today when we were still in sight of shore. Get your night glasses and meet me at the amphitheatre. We're going to take a little hike."

Osen left without a word. Michael started for the door, and Gini was suddenly there. "Are you leaving again?"

"Just taking a little walk. I'll be back by dark."

Gini smiled. "I could come with you. We could swim in the pool by the waterfall." She came up to him, stood close.

"Sounds good, and I'd like to do it, but not now. I want to see more of the area from a high point and Osen and I will be doing a lot of fast climbing. Can we do it tomorrow?"

Gini nodded. "Of course, if you wish."

"It's a date, then. Tomorrow we go swimming." He touched her arm, felt firm muscle there, then turned and rushed from the house.

He met Osen at the amphitheatre and they started up the trail to the gathering fields, pausing once in the trees and looking back in time to see Diego cross the village square and enter the obelisk with two other counselors. They hiked hard, Michael taking the lead through the trees, and skirting the edge of the gathering fields to a point just below the pool. They angled right, and bushwhacked down a slope into a deep gully and up again at a steep angle towards a ridge. By the time they reached the ridge Michael was exhausted, chest tight, and legs burning. Osen wasn't even breathing hard. They paused, Michael gasping for breath.

"Where are we headed, sir?"

"The summit above the obelisk. It's—it's the highest thing around here. Good for me it looks pretty flat between here and there. Whew!"

"You're doing fine, sir."

"For a man of advanced years, you mean. Come on, let's get it over with."

It took one hour to walk the length of the undulating ridge to a broad summit overlooking the obelisk. Wind from the sea whipped at their faces and Michael was still breathing hard when he peered cautiously down at the tip of the obelisk a hundred meters below them in shadow. Tothwelt's sun glared at them, just touching the ridge beyond which lay their encampment. He searched that ridge with Osen's night glasses; looked for signs of movement, saw nothing. "I hope they're watching," he said, then turned the glasses seaward. The big island was there on the horizon, a long, gray shadow of land sloping to the sea at both ends. Mountains thrust upwards from the center. "Big thing," he said. "Must be a hundred kilometers long." He handed the glasses to Osen for a look and walked to the east edge of the summit. Rolling hills as far as he could see, and below him a deep canyon ran from the escarpment by the waterfall down to a small beach. Something there glinted in sunlight at water's edge.

"I need the glasses again. Something down there."

Osen handed them to him. "It's going to be twilight pretty quick. We'd better get going," he said.

Michael peered through the glasses, zoomed in on the beach and saw two ribbons of polished metal running from the water and across the sand. They curved towards him, and disappeared into shadow below where he stood. "Rails," he said. "Some kind of tracks running from the hill to the water. Shiny, too; they've been used. Take a look."

Osen took his turn at the glasses. "Look like train tracks, but there's no bed. Could be for a cart to move supplies from the beach."

"So there's a rear entrance to the obelisk. I'm not surprised. I'll talk to Takey and Kari, and hear what they saw inside. Before we leave I want a look at the island under IR." He took back the glasses, dialed in image enhancement in the IR range and focused on the sea to set the polarizers, and filter out all highly polarized, reflected light. The view was dim until he raised the glasses to the horizon

99

and the island was suddenly there, bathed in an aura of green light concentrated mainly near the mountains, a long plume stretching east. Pinpoints of brighter light flickered near the base of the mountains, some so low they had to be on the water, and as he watched, one of the points moved slowly from east to west. "That's enough for me," he said, handing the glasses to Osen for a look. "There are people out there, and technology. We've landed in the wrong place and for all I know these people in the village might be a splinter group from the main colony. I wonder why *they* contacted us and not the others. When we get back I'm calling Colonel Mootry to get a flyer down here so we can pay those islanders a visit."

"There's movement out there," said Osen. "Could be power boats. Mountains don't look like any volcanoes I've ever seen on Brown's, but that central glow is sure uniform."

"We won't know until we get there. It's getting dark below. We'd better move."

Osen put the glasses away and they walked quickly down the ridge, descended into shadow near the waterfall and pool. Michael again thought of his date to swim there with Gini. No swimming suit necessary, she'd said. He'd never been swimming that way before, with or without the presence of a beautiful woman. Years ago he wouldn't have hesitated, but now—well, now it seemed different. You're not a kid anymore, he reminded himself. Now everything is different. His knees responded in the affirmative as they plowed down the steep slope in shadow.

They followed the lines of harvesting plants, and wandered awhile to find the trailhead at the edge of the trees. By the time they made the final descent to the village it was dark enough to see the brightest stars above them. Michael's eye caught movement, and they stopped. A long line of robed figures was nearing the obelisk, the doors opening to receive them. Counselors, and as they entered the obelisk one figure stood in dim light by the door to touch each man, and look at him closely. It was Jezrul. When the last man was inside he entered quickly, and pushed the doors closed behind him.

"Every counselor in the village," said Michael. "I wonder what *that's* all about. When's the next flyover for the ship?"

Osen looked at his watch. "Twenty-four minutes, Major."

"I'm expected back for the evening meal. When's the best time to make contact after that?"

"A little past nine, sir. Nine-twelve, to be exact."

"Meet me on the beach at nine. I want a flyer down here tomorrow. Let's split up, now. I'll go first."

Osen nodded and Michael walked quickly across the square to Davos' house. Takey intercepted him, coming out of deep shadow from a neighboring building. "I've been looking for you, sir. Have you seen Kari?"

"No, I just got back. I thought she was with you."

"We had separate tours, sir. I haven't seen her since she went inside this morning. She must still be in there."

"When did you get back?"

"About an hour ago. I've looked all over and can't find her. She should have been back before me."

Michael had a crawling feeling in the pit of his stomach. "Look again, and get back to me at Davos' house. Did you see all the counselors going into the obelisk just now?"

"Yes, sir. I wanted to talk about that too. There were some faces I didn't recognize. It must be all of them. They came up from the beach and there's one of them down there now. Looks like he's watching over the boats, and Major, I got close enough to see he's carrying a laser rifle. A *laser* rifle, sir! What's going on?"

"I don't know. Look for Kari and get back to me quick!"

Michael hurried to Davos' house where he found the entire family patiently waiting for him at the dinner table. "Sorry I'm so late," he said. "I took a walk above the waterfall and forgot about the time."

Gini smiled at him warmly and they served themselves from the bowls and platter on the table. After a few bites Michael said; "Has anyone seen Kari, the young woman who's with my group?"

"Not since this morning," said Gini, who'd moved herself to sit opposite him. "I saw her enter the sanctuary with Counselor Segur."

Davos gave her a horrified look. "The House of Toth? That is forbidden to all except the baptized."

"I thought it strange at the time, father, but First Counselor was with her."

"He invited her to witness a baptism," said Michael. "I was there when Diego himself offered her the invitation."

"Yes, Andrea Kaziel was baptized this afternoon," said Leah. "I was there for the ceremony, but if the young woman was present I did not see her. That was hours ago."

"Diego enforces The Law for his own convenience," growled Davos. "It does not apply to him."

"Father!" said Gini.

Michael said, "Diego gave the invitation himself. I didn't realize—"

101

"There are dangers for you here, Leader Queal," said Davos. "They are not of your making. You have come at a bad time when there are again questions being raised about The Law, and distrust of those who enforce it. I will be direct with you, Leader Queal, because I think you are an honest man. There are those of us who believe that Toth is long dead, his so-called transfiguration a trick made up by the counselors to control the people and maintain their power over us. Our planters and growers were the first to assert this, and now they will not enter The House of Toth. The counselors have tolerated them because they are necessary to our survival. Years ago there was revolt, and many were banished to the sea. It was said to be by Toth's words, words we heard directly from the image of an old man sitting on a throne in the sanctuary, and an image you could see right through, not a real person!"

"Davos, please!" said Leah, but he waved her into silence.

"I was a little boy and I heard those words ordering nearly two hundred people to certain death with the Charni even though The Law forbids killing. Our best thinkers, all those whose forefathers were technologists and desired to make our lives easier were forced to leave at gunpoint. At the beach there was much upset, people crying and shouting as the condemned were forced into boats with provisions for one day. The counselors were everywhere, giving pain with their staffs. Pain to the once Chosen of Toth, those to be blessed with The Pleasures! Pleasures if you say yes, pain if you say no. It is the counselors who rule, not Toth. The man who created all that we have has been dead for hundreds of years. And it was Jezrul who killed Lebyn. He is the worst of them."

Gini's eyes were suddenly flooded with tears; she jumped up from the table and fled from the room. Leah was crying softly. "Oh Davos, you'll destroy us with your talk. Deena, please leave the table."

Deena Grigaytes sullenly looked at her mother. "I'm old enough to hear this, and someone has to say it. We are slaves to The Law. Our lives are defined for us and there are no choices. I will spend my life gathering, cooking, cleaning after men and bearing their children. There is nothing more for me. No choices!"

Michael expected an outburst from Davos, but the man just looked at him and shrugged. "I have the sea," he said. "That and my family is my life. It is fortunate for me that what Toth has defined as my tasks in life would also have been my own personal choice. But this is not true for many others. We cannot explore the sea, we're forbidden to walk beyond the gathering places or build our homes where we wish, and missing a ceremony on His Day can mean terrible pain unless a person is seriously ill. The counselors watch us constantly through our own sons and we cannot speak freely as we do at this moment. They make our children rulers over us, even my own son!"

"I will not listen to any more of this," said Leah. She arose and went to the next room, pausing at the door to look outside. "Come in, Gini. You'll get cold out there." There was no reply.

"She is afraid," said Davos.

"So am I," said Michael. "A member of my team is missing, and more counselors than I've ever seen before have gathered in Toth's House. They've posted a guard on the beach and he's armed with a laser rifle. Do you know what that is?"

"Hot light that burns. On the day the condemned were put to sea such weapons were used to destroy their homes and belongings. I have not seen them since, but the counselors have the staffs proclaiming their office. Pain has been a sufficient weapon against us."

Michael thought of his first conversation with Gini on the beach that night, her gasps of agony, and the robed figure of a man carrying a staff and sneaking away from them. "A counselor can point his staff at you and give you pain?"

"Or pleasure," said Davos, "depending on what you've said or done, or the mood of the man. It is the same with the image of Toth on His Day. Some people live for the gift of Pleasures. They will do anything to receive it."

"The staff can bring the Yellowfin to your nets and chase a Charni away. Do you know that?"

"I think it is obvious," said Davos.

"Each staff is a transmitter that sends out electromagnetic waves. One frequency brings the Yellowfin, or a Charni; still others can chase them away. Pleasure, or pain, Davos. Something in the people and the sea animals here responds strongly to electromagnetic radiation, but I don't know what."

"I do not know of such things," said Davos.

"Where do you feel the pain?"

"It begins here, and then goes throughout the whole body, arms and legs, everywhere." Davos pointed to the back of his neck.

"Let me see," said Michael. He looked at Davos' neck; saw only a faded semi-circular scar there. He pressed it with a finger. "What is this?"

"It is the mark of my baptism, from when I was a baby."

"Hmmm. All the people have this?"

"All are baptized," said Davos, "even many of the older planters."

There were voices from outside, and Takey appeared in the doorway. "Kari is gone, sir, we can't find her anywhere, and Osen just got a message from Captain Elg. Colonel Mootry has ordered us to move back to the camp immediately. He's expecting an attack and Osen's telling everyone to get his or her things together.

Michael went to the door, heard Osen screaming orders from the next house. The boy sprinted towards him. "Grab your things, sir. The others are on their way to the trailhead in a minute. Ten minutes ago, Colonel Mootry detected a feeler beam on the ship. Someone has them locked in a laser sight! He wants us out of here *now*!"

"Not without Kari," shouted Michael. "Get the others moving. I'm going to the obelisk."

"I'm staying with *you*, sir! Mootry's orders."

"Shit," said Michael. "Come with me, then, and watch your rear. The people in the obelisk are probably armed."

Gini stood with both hands over her mouth, eyes wide. "Get inside. There might be trouble," said Michael, but she stood frozen there. He put an arm around her, pulled her towards the house. "Please?" Reluctantly she went inside where Davos grabbed her and hustled her towards the back of the house.

Osen was right behind him when he reached the amphitheatre. Behind him his crews had assembled their kits and were trotting in a line between two houses towards the trail leading back to camp. The doors to the obelisk opened slightly, someone peeking out before slamming them tightly shut again. Michael ran, but was too late. He pounded on the doors with the flat of his hand, then a fist. "You have one of our people in there and we've been ordered to leave at once! We're leaving the village; do you understand? Now send the woman out, and we'll be gone!"

No answer. Michael pounded again. "We're not leaving here until you send the woman out!" He threw a shoulder against the doors and they creaked, giving a little. "I'll force my way in if I have to!"

The smell of ozone wafted from the crack between the doors. "Down, Major!" screamed Osen, slamming into him. Burned wood exploded from six places in the doors, and Michael felt laser heat stroke the top of his head as he hit the ground. They crawled away. Four more searing columns of orange light burst through the doors, and then Michael and Osen were running zigzag across the square towards Davos' house. The doors banged open behind them, and beams exploded tree limbs and brush beyond which Michael's team had just reached the trailhead and were climbing fast. Someone cried out in pain.

They reached Davos' doorway and crouched there. Michael glanced at Osen pressed to his back, expecting to see fear there, but what he saw instead was a thin smile and narrowed, dark eyes, a look devoid of emotion or feeling. The doors of the obelisk were open, and counselors streamed outside in a line moving towards the trailhead. One man broke off, and headed straight for the house. He trotted towards them, a laser rifle in his hand.

A second swarm of counselors appeared in the obelisk doorway, fanning out in all directions, but not fast enough as the roar of assault rifle fire from the ridge suddenly beat against their ears. Men were hammered to the ground. One man's head exploded, and a door to the obelisk suddenly disappeared in splinters. Those few remaining stumbled back inside, and closed the remaining door that was shot to pieces in an instant. Tracer rounds screamed into the obelisk, shattering stone, lighting the interior with death for those near the doorway.

The counselor running towards Michael ducked, but came on. Michael looked for a weapon, a knife, a pot, anything. He jumped across the doorway to the kitchen, found only a pot to throw, turned back and saw Osen crouched like a cat at the door, his face a horror, and in his right hand was the biggest knife Michael had ever seen, a curving thing with serrated blade. "Where the hell did you get that?"

"Boot, sir," said Osen, and then Davos burst from the adjoining room to stand in the doorway, blocking it.

"You'll kill no person in this house without killing me first!" he shouted.

"I'm not here for that. Follow me to the beach, to the boat, *everyone*! You're cut off from the others. Quick!"

It was Nimri, Davos' only son.

"Father, *please*! We have no time!"

Michael stepped to the doorway, saw Nimri's rifle leveled at him. "I'm going with you; don't try to stop me. Everyone, father, not just these two. I'm getting *all* of you out of here! *Trust* me!"

Davos hurried to the back of the house as Michael and Osen stepped outside and Nimri saw the big knife. "There's a guard on the beach," said Michael.

"I have a rifle."

"We'll need that," said Osen. "I'm on it, Major." The boy
pushed Nimri's rifle aside with lightning speed and ran crouched
over into the trees and brush between the house and the beach.

Davos arrived with his family: Gini, Leah, Deena, the little boy
Uhel in his mother's arms. There was a horrible scream from the
hillside above them, someone hit by laser fire. It had to be a member
of the team. "Follow me," said Michael. There was no movement
near the obelisk as gunfire continued to tear at earth and stone. They
crept through bushes along a sandy path and despite their care the
dry grass crunched underfoot so that when they crouched at the edge
of the beach they saw the guard well out on it, rifle leveled towards
them. Brush suddenly crashed forward meters to the left of them,
and the guard fired twice into it, advanced, and fired again. He
probed the brush with his rifle. A dark figure emerged silently from
bushes to his right, and crept up on him from behind with the speed
of a great cat, the knife flashing as it severed his throat from ear to
ear. The guard fell gurgling to the ground. Gini moaned, and pressed
up against Michael's back.

Osen held up the guard's rifle. "Now we have two. There's a
staff over there by the boat."

They turned over a skiff and collectively shoved it into the surf;
Gini put Uhel in, crawled up over the stern ahead of the other wom-
en, and hunkered down. Weapons in the boat, the men swam holding on to railings, and Michael pushed. From shore it seemed as if a
boat had broken loose, drifting beyond the surf. But in minutes they
had reached Davos' fishing craft and clambered aboard, hauling anchors, Nimri helping his father set sail. Gunfire was scattered now,
occasional tracers still descending from the ridge.

"Hope the others made it," said Michael, but the instant he said
that there was a horrible explosion of gunfire atop the cliff between
the village and their encampment, a long barrage of sustained fire
interspersed with screams. *Krisha*, thought Michael. *She intercepted
the pursuing counselors. How many of our people are still alive?*

The boat moved straight out to sea, Davos at the tiller, Osen
checked the rifles. Michael went to him, clapped him on the shoulder. "Nice job, Osen. You're a real killer."

Osen gave him a dark, frightening look. "You're right, sir,
that's exactly what I am." He went back to checking power levels on
the rifles. Without the heavy power packs normally carried by combat infantry each rifle could only be fired twenty to thirty times. Michael went to Davos. "How far out do we go?"

"As far as you wish."

"Okay, stay on course half an hour, then turn west. I want to go back to the encampment."

Davos nodded, and for several minutes they sailed in silence. Stars sparkled above them, and the usual blanket of evening fog rose from the sea ahead.

The silence was broken by the sound of a powerful engine, faint at first, back towards shore, growing louder. Far off to their left something skimmed over the water, throwing up a fountain of spray in all directions. It passed them hundreds of meters away and sped out to sea, engine shrieking. Davos gasped; "What is that?"

"Airboat," said Osen. "A big one, heading for the island. Major, what do you want to bet Diego and Jezrul are on that thing?"

"Yeah, and I wonder if Kari is on it, too," said Michael. "So much for the village not having technology."

"I've never seen it before," said Davos. "Should we try and follow it?"

"No. Back to camp and regroup and I'm calling down a flyer. We're going to make an unfriendly visit to that island, and soon. Osen how's the radio?"

"Damp, but okay, sir. We need to be further west before I can get the camp. The cliffs are still in the way."

"We're far enough out, Davos, so let's head west. Osen, you work the radio and as soon as you can, patch a relay to Colonel Mootry. I'm going to call for a flyer right away."

They turned west, and sailed for several minutes, Osen tried unsuccessfully to reach the camp by radio. Michael watched the sky, and suddenly a bright star was moving up from the western horizon. "Here comes the ship. Any luck?"

"Nothing, sir. Captain Elg must have cleaned out the camp for now."

"We'll have to wait until next orbit, then," said Michael. He watched the star that was his home in space, the star he would reluctantly return to when the job was done. *I don't want to go back there*, he thought. *If the circumstances were right I would much rather be where I am right now*. The star reached its zenith, moved down towards the eastern horizon, flickering in light wisps of fog. At the horizon, three converging beams of orange light surged upwards to meet it, pulsing once, twice, then holding steady. The star brightened like a sudden nova, a trail of mini-stars in red and yellow scattering behind as it disappeared comet-like over the horizon.

Osen saw it, too. "Holy Mother," he said, "they're attacking the ship! What are we going to do now?"

Michael felt a chill in his stomach. "Head for the camp," he said.

CHAPTER TWELVE

Kari awoke in darkness and panicked when she tried to take a breath. The gag was tight, filling her mouth, and she inhaled sharply through her nose. Her hands were bound numbly behind her back, her legs and ankles tied together and bent upward towards her hands through a connecting bond. She squirmed, and the ropes bit hard. She was lying on her side on a cold floor in absolute blackness. Her jaw and neck hurt where Jezrul had struck. *Still alive*, she thought, *but for how long?*

She was in a room of some kind and there were voices outside, soft, then loud, then shouting and she distinctly heard gunfire from a distance. Footsteps pounded the floor outside and the door rattled, opened, and flooded her with green light. Jezrul came into the room and swept her up in his arms, face close to hers. "We certainly wouldn't want to leave you behind, would we?" He carried her down the hall. She struggled to look back around him, and saw two counselors drag Diego stumbling between them from his room. They took the elevator down. Diego groaned softly, a bloody gash on his forehead. "Ah, our Master Counselor awakes. If you'd accepted the evening drink I offered, you would be enjoying the trip," said Jezrul. "I will enjoy it for you, holding this little treasure in my arms."

Diego didn't respond, near unconsciousness, but Kari twisted and squirmed as Jezrul's long fingers found her right breast. The sounds of gunfire were getting louder as they descended, and when the doors opened the roar was deafening, men running, screaming, and the hallway filled with acrid smoke and pieces of burning wood. Tracer fire was coming through an open doorway, the bodies of dead men jumping with the impact of armor-piercing bullets that splattered blood and stone from the floor. Jezrul leapt past the doorway in one bound, but behind them one of the men holding Diego went down screaming, the other dragging his burden miraculously ahead without harm. They went to the sanctuary where several cloaked men and boys stood silently, eyes wide with fear. "Stay where you are," shouted Jezrul, "and if they attack the sanctuary throw down your arms. It is not Toth's will for you to die, and I will return with His own army to free you!"

He carried her beyond the altar and to the wall-hanging left of where she had hidden, another flap covering the entrance to a corridor lit by globes of moss. They passed several doorless, empty rooms smelling of dust and mold, into an area with a high ceiling, and ascending wooden stairs to a walkway ending in a few steps. Jezrul jumped lightly from the end of the walkway. A wooden floor rocked beneath them as they landed. He dumped Kari hard at his feet, and then helped the other man with Diego. She saw a control console, a wheel for steering, railings, and the smooth curve of wood facing one wall of the room. They were in a boat! She was lying on the foredeck, a low-slung cabin aft.

Jezrul flopped Diego against a railing opposite her and tied his hands to it with two pieces of rope. "Get the door," he shouted, then went to the controls of the boat and turned a key there. A whine began in the bowels of the craft, ascending in pitch as Kari wriggled on the deck, trying to get on her knees. Her legs had gone numb and she fell over facing the bow, staring at a huge door rolling upwards. Night air flowed coldly over her. The other man jumped into the boat as Jezrul pulled hard on a lever and they were suddenly moving, metal screeching. The whine of what had to be a turbine screamed beneath her. The boat moved slowly at first, past the door and she looked up to see stars twinkling, feeling a lurch, as they turned right, picking up speed. Hills loomed on both sides of them as they slid at an increasing angle of descent. Trees sped by, and wind whipped her face, and then a sudden deceleration rolled her completely over once. There was a spray of water on her face, and the sudden roar of an engine aft. The boat accelerated, surf jarring them, then smoothing as they came up to speed. Jezrul gestured for the other man to take the wheel, then came over to Kari, untied the rope binding her feet to her hands, the one around her thighs. He sat her up and removed the gag, running a wet finger over her lower lip. "That's better, No use covering such a pretty mouth now."

"Where are you taking me?" she said.

"To Lord Toth, of course. Perhaps he will be in a merciful mood. And if the others come after you, as I hope they will, we will kill all of them and leave their bodies for the Charni."

The boat roared on as they headed straight out to sea where the man-god called Toth awaited her arrival.

Later on, she did not see a moving star suddenly flare brightly above her.

* * * * * *

Krisha was filled with fear for Kari and the others, but remained her professional self throughout the afternoon and evening. After Mootry's first message, she had moved all her marines to the ridge and the place where the trail skirted the high cliff. One marine and Nik Balestrieri had remained behind with her; Nik was on the radio as they waited for the next flyover. She assembled her kit, with knife, sidearm, and radio and assault rifle, checked each piece and covered her face and hands with black greasepaint. Now she paced the perimeter of the camp, mumbling to herself; "Why did you have to go, baby, why?" At best she was missing, swallowed up by the obelisk. How could Mike have risked letting her go in there? *I thought he'd be with you all the time. I worried that you and he would—*

"Captain! Colonel Mootry wants you *now*!" Nik screamed, and waved his arms at the door to the earth-covered radio shack. Krisha sprinted to him, kit rattling, and rushed to the radio. "Just got on the line," said Nik.

"Patch this through to the ridge and cliff parties," she said breathlessly. "Colonel? What's up?"

"We just detected a feeler beam at four thousand angstroms, Krish. Someone has us in a laser sight and I'm going to a high orbit. Get our people out of the village right now and move everyone up to cover them!"

"They're already in place, sir, only three of us left here."

"Get up there yourself and do whatever's necessary to protect our people. I'm going to boosters in one minute as soon as we're past your horizon. That feeler is still on us."

"Good luck, sir. I'm on my way. Emerald Base out."

"*Belsus* out."

Krisha stood. "Get your rifle, Nik. You and Dala are holding the fort. Shoot anyone you don't recognize and make sure Dala watches the sea for any incoming boats. Pull the cable sling up and keep it up until I'm back."

"Got it," said Nik. "Watch yourself, Captain."

Krisha didn't hear him, already out the door and charging towards the camp perimeter. She slammed home the bolt of her assault rifle and flicked it to full automatic as she ran. She headed toward the trail at full gallop, stopping briefly at the base of the ridge to shout into her radio; "Tango, you there?"

"Here, Captain. Quiet, so far. We saw Queal and Osen come down from a ridge a while ago. We've patched the news through to Osen and they should be moving by now."

"You hear one shot, you open up immediately. Our people can only come up the trail, so cover them."

"Can't see the trail from here, Captain."

"Then spray the village. Let 'em know you're there. I'm going up the trail." She clicked off and trotted up the trail away from the lights around the camp perimeter, now suddenly in darkness. With rifle, grenades, and ten magazines her total kit weighed thirty pounds, but with the adrenalin rush her body was experiencing, her legs refused to acknowledge the weight. The night was eerily quiet, a light mist floating far out to sea in the last gleams of twilight. Her breathing was loud, boots snapping twigs, crunching stone and suddenly, ten meters ahead, a dark figure leapt from the brush and into the center of the trail. "Get off the trail!" she shouted. "It's Elg!"

Figures moved in the trees and brush as she stopped at cliff's edge, gasping; "Hear anything?"

"Shouting down there a few minutes ago," said a marine.

"Get down and listen." Krisha stepped off the trail and crouched shoulder to shoulder against a boy with wide eyes. *First combat*, she thought. "Load and lock," she said and bolts snapped. *I had to tell them. Oh boy!*

They waited, listening. She heard a shout, then another—closer. There was another sound, like a metal string plucked, then a shrill scream. "Follow my lead," she said. "Fire at my command, full auto." Two fire control levers clicked in the darkness.

Ahead of them a laser beam flashed on a tree at cliff's edge, smoking a branch and simultaneously they heard another shrill scream of pain and the roar of assault rifle fire echoing from the village. "Steady. Fingers off the trigger until I fire." She leveled her rifle at the bend in the trail ahead. Feet pounded the ground, people groaning, and stumbling around the bend, Utaka in the lead. The remaining members crashed by them, unaware of their presence, but others were coming, robed figures, three, four, now six of them, one snapping off a shot that blasted dirt over her. "Now!" she screamed and fired, emptying a thirty round magazine in a six second burst of death. As five other magazines emptied, Krisha snapped a new one into her rifle and sprayed the pursuers again. Men screamed, two of them disappearing over the cliff, the rest hammered to the ground in a pulpy mess. In fifteen seconds it was over, but still the roar of rifle fire came from the village. Krisha held up a hand and they waited for a moment, but nothing moved ahead of them.

She walked up the trail, probed a body, and motioned to the others to follow. Five bodies, five laser rifles, which they picked up. *Shit! Laser weapons, and here I thought we could intimidate them.* The rifle fire from the village was now scattered, and deliberate. Krisha made a hand signal and they moved around the bend of the trail.

They found Vilos Compagno there, lying on his face, dead, two laser burns in the middle of his back. Ahead of them another body sprawled in the trail. No robe. Krisha took a deep breath, heart pounding from fear of whom it might be. They moved ahead.

It was Takey Xu, wounds burned black in hip and lower back. He groaned. "He's alive," said Krisha. "Turn him over, carefully." An exit would through his stomach was huge, boiled intestines protruding from it. She shook her head at the others. "We'll come back for him. Move out."

"We can't leave him here!" said a young marine.

"I said move out, mister," and they followed her obediently while she thought; *What if it had been Kari? Would I have left her behind like that? Could I have done it?* But Kari was somewhere ahead, so were Mike and Osen. The others were safe for now if Nik didn't blow them away when they got to the camp.

The village came into view, doors of the obelisk obliterated and smoking, sporadic tracers still raking the interior. Krisha dug out her radio. "Tango, this is Elg. Cease fire, but cover us. We're moving in."

"Affirmative, Captain," said Tango. "There are still people in the obelisk, all with laser weapons, but we shot down a bunch of them."

"We'll dig 'em out," said Krisha. She snapped instructions and led her marines in a crouch to the village square where they fanned out, sprinted past the amphitheatre to the obelisk and knelt at both sides of the open doorway. "You in there!" she shouted. "I'll give you one minute to come out with your weapons over your heads, and then we're blowing this place to pieces! Let's hear you!"

The reply was immediate; "We're coming out! Don't shoot!" Eight men filed out of the obelisk, laser rifles held loosely above their heads.

"Move over here and drop the rifles. Hands on top of your heads. Anyone left in there?"

"Only our dead," said a young man.

113

"Yeah?" Krisha looked at the marine opposite her by the door. "Toss me a grenade." He tossed it underhand to her; she tapped its base on the wall. Seven seconds. "Anyone still in there? Kari, you in there?"

No answer. Four seconds—three—two—

She flipped the grenade backhand into the darkness beyond the doorway.

The explosion was deafening, a cloud of burned wood and rock belching forth. "Inside!" she screamed and they charged inside to find broken, bloody bodies in the entrance and along the hall. "You," she said, pointing to one marine, "stay with the prisoners. The rest of you scatter and search."

They searched the obelisk from top to bottom: living quarters, an elevator powered by huge batteries in a basement, a place like a church, hidden rooms empty behind it, a storage bay with tracks leading outside through a huge door and down to a beach, two musty rooms on a third floor where they found a few books and then returned to meet Krisha at the front entrance. "That's it? That's all you found?" she said.

The marines nodded, but then there was a shout from the church area, and they rushed inside again. A marine was at the altar, fumbling in a tray he'd placed there. "Medical stuff," he said, "just below the altar here. Some tools, a syringe. What's this?" He held up a vial filled with clear liquid. Two lumps of dark gray matter glistened there. The marine looked closely. "Ugh," he said, wrinkling his nose. "Looks decayed."

"Wrap it all up and put it in your bag. The books, too. What's the console for?"

"I tried it, but it has to be unlocked with a key, on the right, there."

"That's enough for now. I want to chat with the prisoners."

They went outside and found the prisoners sullenly sitting on the ground, hands on heads. She went to the oldest, meanest looking one in the group and stood before him, the muzzle of her rifle inches from his nose. "Get up," she ordered and he did it, smirking at her.

"Three of our people are missing. Where are they?"

"I don't know what you're talking about," said the man, his smirk fading as he looked into her eyes.

"That is the wrong answer, sir. Two men and a woman; where—are—they?"

114

The man shook his head, mouth closed tightly. "Take this," said Krisha. She handed her rifle to a marine, took out her handgun and released the safety.

"Captain, the prisoners are unarmed. You can't—"

"I'm not going to kill him, private."

Krisha aimed her pistol deliberately, and shot the prisoner in the left knee.

He screamed and dropped to the ground writhing as she bent over him. "Just to clarify your situation, I am *not* a nice person. I will ask you one more time; where are—?"

"I saw the woman!" screamed another prisoner, a young boy obviously terrified by what he'd just seen.

"Shut up," said another.

"No—no, they'll kill us! I saw the woman! Jezrul carried her out back; they took the airboat to the island, to Toth."

"Was she alive?"

"Yes," said the boy. "They took her to Toth. I saw no others, only the woman. This is the truth, I swear!"

"Maybe. I want a house-to-house search, two to a house. Do it now." She pointed at a marine, then another. "You get this guy's knee cauterized and wrapped. *You* watch the prisoners. I'm checking the beach."

The marines scattered to the homes, herding frightened people outside. One house was empty, a family missing. Krisha went to a neighbor of the house, a woman who clung fearfully to her husband. "Where are the people who live next door?"

"I don't know. Leader Queal was with them earlier. Please, we want to go to Toth's house. Our sons are there."

"Later, when we're ready to leave. Your sons attacked us without provocation. Some of them are dead, the rest are our prisoners. We're taking them to our camp until this whole mess is sorted out."

The woman burst into tears as Krisha walked away. *We've shot up their village and killed their sons. I'd cry too. But we didn't start this, lady.* She went down to the beach, saw the guard lying there, throat gaping. He had no weapon, and a depression in the sand showed one boat missing. She looked out to sea, several boats anchored close. There was a conspicuous gap between two of them. *Mike never sailed in his life, but he just might have done it.* There was mist out to sea, stars twinkling overhead. She looked at her watch in penlight, and it was ten-forty-two. The next flyover was at eleven-thirty, and she had narrowly missed an opportunity to contact Mootry. *What will he say when I tell him we had to kill people? Did we provoke them?* She thought about regulations, survey ships authorized to intervene in cases where a colony had gone in directions not defined by the Rubion Federation. They were, in effect, a police force. *Did Mike make that clear to the villagers? And did Mootry make it clear to the assholes on Brown's Planet when their retrofit was put off until after this landing?*

She turned from the sea and walked back to the village. The people had assembled in the amphitheatre there, surrounded by marines. She walked to the podium at the center, looked out at their faces, some angry, some weeping.

"A terrible thing has happened here tonight, but you need to understand that we were defending ourselves and the people who were your guests. At least one of our people is now dead, two are missing and one, a woman, has been taken by force to an island out to sea. We came here with good intentions, and have done nothing to provoke such hostility, but you have given it to us and we have responded in kind. I assume no guilt for that. You are a colony of the Rubion Federation, established by contract, and that contract does not include the right to kill federation representatives."

"We had nothing to do with that," said a woman.

"I intend to find out who did. Until then, some of my people will be kept here to watch you. They will not interfere in your normal, everyday lives, but further hostile actions will not be tolerated. Our prisoners go with us to our camp, and they'll be well cared for. When we leave depends on when we get our people back safely and how soon we can resolve the mess this colony has apparently become. Any questions?"

"May we bury our dead?" said a man.

"Yes. I will need a list of their names."

"We bury our dead at sea, it is our tradition."

"You'll have to bury them on land until everything is settled here, at least for the next couple of days. By normal, everyday life I mean life in the village. For the next two days I want no fishing, no gathering of food. You have more than enough food in your homes. For the next two days and hopefully no more, everyone remains in the village at all times. Any other questions?"

"You have no right to do what you've done. Toth will punish you for this," said a man.

"Then he'd better be a quicker shot than I am," growled Krisha, and she stomped out of the amphitheatre to bark more orders. Two marines were assigned to village duty; two others to retrieve Takey and speed him back to camp. She ordered the prisoners to carry their wounded comrade, and then marched them out of the village without looking back. The going was slow, penlights waving to keep the trail in sight and they stopped at the cliff. Krisha again checked her watch. It was only a few minutes to flyover. She opened a channel on her radio: "Nik, it's Krisha. Come in."

No answer and she cursed silently. They moved out, picked up Vilos' body, and walked hard until they saw the lights of the camp perimeter. Krisha stopped, the rest moving on. "Nik, come in. It's Krisha."

"Got you, Captain. Some tired, scared people here, but they're okay."

"We're coming in with prisoners, Nik, and patch me through to the ship. It should be coming over now."

"You've got it in ten seconds on one-zero-four."

She counted to fifteen. "*Belsus*, this is Captain Elg, reporting to the Colonel, please. Over."

No answer. She called again, looked up at the sky. The stars were still and quiet. Five times she called, and nothing came back. By now they'd be out of contact again. Where was the ship? WHERE WAS THE FUCKING SHIP? She pocketed the radio and hurried to join the others as they reached the camp perimeter.

A small crowd was waiting for them, tired-looking people eating a quick meal. They were cold and shivering, more likely from shock than the night air. They stared silently as Krisha sat her prisoners down in a cluster by the huts and posted a guard over them. Nik came up to her. "More guests, I see. Where do we put them?"

"Where the front-loader is, I guess. It won't hurt the machine to sit outside a couple of nights. I couldn't get Mootry just now. What's wrong?"

"I don't know. Not even a click or a buzz. He just wasn't there."

"I was watching the sky, and the ship didn't come over."

"He must have changed orbit, Captain. We were expecting that. I'll stay on the radio and get to you when he comes in."

"How's Takey?"

Nik shook his head. "Dead on arrival, Captain. He didn't have a chance; his insides were boiled out. Is that Vilas's body you brought back?"

"Yeah." Krisha wiped her forehead. Quite suddenly her legs were shaky. Two dead, three missing, one of them the Major, another who was central to her life.

"Want a burial detail?"

"No. Bag 'em overnight. Hopefully, a flyer will be down here pretty soon." Nik raised an eyebrow at her. *Something has happened to the ship. There might not be any flyer coming for us—ever.*

117

Krisha briefed Nik on the action in the village, Kari's predicament, and her suspicion that Mike and Osen had somehow escaped to sea. As she talked, it seemed as if all her energy was draining through her feet and into the ground. Her knees began shaking and she passed a hand across her face.

"Pardon me, Captain," said Nik, "but you don't look so good."

"Don't feel so good either. Get the others to bed, will you? Tell them I'll want a briefing tomorrow morning on what happened in the village. And stay on that radio. Right now, I've got to flop."

"I'll handle it," said Nik. "See you in the morning."

Krisha went to the hut she'd shared with Kari only nights before and crawled inside. Kari's perfume still lingered there and as she smelled it Krisha felt the sting of salty tears in her eyes. Sitting down on the cot, her legs weren't shaking anymore and she cleaned her rifle, the sharp odor of powder solvent masking Kari's scent. The faces of the villagers still haunted her: expressions of anger, sorrow, and resignation. She was an invader, a murderer of their sons, a destroyer. She had gone in to save the team and now at least two of them were dead. Three were missing, the ship missing, eight prisoners to guard, and a powerful enemy somewhere out to sea.

She stripped off her clothes, lay down naked on the cot and sighed. In the dim light of her lamp she saw a rumpled pile of underclothes tossed carelessly to the end of the hut. Kari's, from the night before she'd left for the village: bra, panties and tee shirt. She reached over and picked them up; put them under her hard pillow beneath her cheek. Her lover's scent was there again and she closed her eyes to squeeze out the tears, biting her lip and crying soundlessly into the pillow. And as the blessing of sleep began to descend on her she mumbled a promise to herself and to another:

"Oh, Kari, I'm coming for you. I'm coming for you, baby."

CHAPTER THIRTEEN

Michael stood at the bow of the boat and stared morosely at pinpoints of light scattered atop the black silhouette of land four kilometers north of him. He searched it with Osen's night glasses, but saw no signs of movement and didn't want to chance using the radio until certain it was safe to do so. Osen stood next to him and yawned. Neither of them had had any sleep that night. Davos was at the tiller; his women huddled at one railing, dozing, Gini held her son to her chest. Nimri sat with his father, staff ready in case they encountered a Charni, which they had not. It had been a quiet, slow trip after they'd seen the blaze of light when *Belsus* was hit. Michael dared to hope the ship had somehow survived, but at the time of each successive flyover in a clear sky no moving star had appeared above them. The ship was simply gone, but even that observation gave him reason for hope. If *Belsus* were destroyed or crippled it would surely remain in the orbit it had occupied when attacked. Had Mootry powered out, then? Was he in fact hidden in some geosynchronous orbit at this very moment? Whatever the situation, there was no radio contact to be had and without that no pilot crazy enough to fly in for a pickup. They would wait, but for how long? Kari was gone, perhaps on that airboat they'd seen, maybe dead in the obelisk. There had been screams during the firefight. His own people?

Too much speculation. Michael sighed and left Osen behind to walk the length of the boat to where Davos and Nimri had been quietly talking to each other. "How long before we reach shore?"

"An hour, maybe two," said Davos. "The morning wind will come soon."

"No hurry. I want to be sure my people are there before we go charging in. I've had enough surprises." He looked down at Nimri, whose eyes were averting his. "One surprise was your son, here, helping us. Why did you do that, Counselor, I thought you were a sworn servant of Toth?"

119

"I am," said Nimri, looking starboard to the sea.

Michael chuckled. "Perhaps you can explain that to me. You might be the only counselor left alive right now."

Nimri smiled. "Oh, I'm sure Jezrul has seen to his own safety, and it was he who ordered your capture."

"Not Diego?"

"He was confined to his room when I arrived. Jezrul said Lord Toth had ordered him to take control and seize our visitors, that Diego was too weak to do it. He said if we didn't, your military was about to attack the village with heavy firepower from your ship. All the others believed him. I did not."

"Why not?" said Michael.

"He ordered us to kill you if you resisted. Lord Toth would never give such an order. It's forbidden by The Law to kill another human being for any reason, even in defense of your own life."

Davos made a rude sound. "You still think Lebyn's death was an accident?"

"No, father, I do not. It was Jezrul, acting on his own. For two years he's been talking secretly against Diego, claiming himself favored by Toth with private audiences preparing him to seize power, and that Diego had grown weak and indecisive. A strong leader was needed in an hour of great danger, he said, and Toth has put him in charge. Jezrul is a brute. He always was, even as a boy. Toth would never trust him with such power."

"Yet the others believed him and you didn't?"

"He worked on all of us, and Diego *was* weak. Your arrival sent him into despair. He'd become reclusive. The only times the people saw him were on Toth's Day. The Chosen were missing services, and he did nothing. That was when Jezrul first took charge. He wielded his staff, and the sanctuary was full again for His Day. I respected that. We all respected that. We were trained to uphold The Law. But The Law does not include killing, and Toth must be warned."

Davos shook his head sadly and sighed. "They trained you well, and turned you into a fool."

"So where do we find Toth, if he needs to be warned?" said Michael quickly.

Nimri swept one arm out towards sea. "There is an island, a fortress far out to sea where Our Lord now dwells in his transfigured state. Two of my boyhood friends were assigned to go there when they were only apprentices. They were simple boys with no particular talents, and the rest of us were quite envious of their assignment."

"How did they get past the Charni?"

"There is a large boat, very fast I'm told, a boat without sails. Toth kept it when he was with the people. I never saw it, but I heard it the night the boys left. I think it was the same one we saw last night. Jezrul was on that boat. He will lie to Toth; blame you and your people for everything. The other counselors are like the Yellowfin, they will follow the wave of his staff, the excess of Pleasures he gives to his friends with it. He has perverted the symbol of his office. I think Diego would have the courage to speak the truth, but I'm sure you will find him dead. I think Jezrul has killed him, just as he killed Lebyn."

And now I know why you oppose Jezrul, thought Michael. "I'll promise you this, Counselor; if you continue to help us I will somehow get you out to that island, even if we have to fight our way through the Charni. I think one of our people is out there and we're not leaving this planet until we get her back safely. If your Lord Toth is in charge of things the way you say he is I will hold him responsible if Kari is hurt or killed. Do you understand?"

"If she has not violated The Law, Toth will not allow her to be harmed, and under no circumstances will he allow her to be killed. My fear is, if Jezrul has her he will arrange another 'accident'."

"If Toth is as wise as I'm told, he will see through this and Jezrul will be punished by him. That will be enough."

"And then you will leave?" said Nimri.

"When all is back to normal, we will leave." *But it will be normal when Toth is no more*, thought Michael.

"Then I agree," said Nimri. "I will help you if you take me to Toth." He stood up and walked sedately to the bow of the boat to watch the shore. Michael turned to see Davos smiling at him. "You are good with words, Leader Queal, and quick to make promises, but the barrier must be crossed and if your ship is destroyed there will only be boats like this one to do it with. A single Charni can sink this boat. Think about that. What you promise could mean many deaths, including yours and mine."

"I know that, Davos, but there are other reasons I have to get to that island, and Kari is only one of them. During my hike last night I saw lights out there, moving lights, and I think there's a lot more than a fortress on the island. We have to see it or our mission isn't completed."

Davos smiled again. "And so you will remain. I'm thinking you will remain for a long time."

121

It was said without sarcasm, simply a statement of fact. Michael smiled back at him. "After what we've been through, there's a favor you can do for me."

"And what is that, Leader Queal?"

"From now on I'd be pleased if you would call me Michael."

Davos nodded. "Very well—Michael," he said.

It was over an hour before the morning breeze came, and it quickly pushed them to shore. As they came close in Michael instructed Davos to tack back and forth while he scanned the cliff and in moments he saw a marine there, looking back at him through night glasses. The marine disappeared, came back with another. Michael waved to them, and there was no response. The first glow of Tothwelt's sun appeared on the horizon as they zigzagged closer to shore. More marines appeared on the cliff. Michael breathed a sigh of relief when he saw Nik Balestrieri lower a pair of glasses and rush away. A minute later he reappeared, accompanied by a tall, muscular marine who could only be Krisha. When she raised her glasses, Michael put his down and waved to her, smiling. Immediately the marines were moving, two of them coming down the sling cable to the beach. "Okay, we're recognized!" he shouted to Davos. "Take it in." Gini awoke at the sound of his voice, then Leah and Deena. They stood up and stretched, groggy. "We've reached the camp," he said to them. "You'll have to get wet going in."

The surf was gentle near the cliff, a continually rolling thing over a broad, sandy shelf that reached out a hundred meters from the beach. They dropped anchor fore and aft where the water was only five feet deep and one by one plunged into the cold water to wade to shore. In their rush to escape they had left the skiff behind. Gini handed Uhli down to Michael, and the little boy clung fearfully to him. He'd never before been in the water. Davos was the last to jump in, and they swam-walked the last forty meters to the beach, where two armed marines awaited them. "Good to see you, Major," called one marine. "Captain Elg figured you somehow got out to sea. That man your prisoner?" He was pointing to Nimri, who slogged his way in, staff in one hand, and laser rifle in the other. The marine looked nervous, the muzzle of his rifle coming up.

"No. Put down your rifle. He's helping us. This is all one family we're bringing in here." He put Uhli down on the sand, turned to watch the others. Gini was soaked to the neck, her blouse transparent and sticking to her and what he saw there made his heart take a few extra beats. They were all shivering the instant they came out of the water. Uhli ran to his mother and hugged her. "Elevator going up, two at a time, women first," said Michael. "Gini, I can take Uhli up with me if you like."

Uhli whimpered and clung to her. "He's frightened. I'd better take him," she said. The marines put her in the seat-sling and strapped Uhli to her and she was the first to ride the cable up to the top of the cliff. Her eyes were closed the entire trip. Leah and Deena went next, clinging to each other in terror, then Davos and Nimri and finally Osen with Michael. Krisha met him at the top, her face still smeared with grease paint, looking every inch like a combat marine. "Didn't know you were a sailor, sir. Welcome back."

"Thanks, Krisha. I didn't think we'd be back for a while there. Thanks to you and your team, here we are. What's the situation?"

She briefed him as they walked back to his quarters in the radio shack, and the others were hustled off to get into dry clothes. He took the good news with the bad, feeling grief for the loss of Vilos and Takey; was relieved the rest of the village team was safe. Nik greeted him with a slap of hands from where he sat at the radio. "Been trying to reach the Colonel, sir. We haven't heard from him since last night."

"I'm afraid there's a reason for that," said Michael. He stripped down, and put on dry clothes as Krisha watched him calmly, without embarrassment, and then he told them what he'd seen last night: the laser or particle beams reaching towards the ship, an apparent explosion, what looked like debris trailing the ship as it dropped below the horizon.

"We've looked for it all night, Major, and it's not there anymore," said Krisha.

"Even in pieces it should still be there. I find that encouraging."

"I was thinking the same thing, sir. I've never heard of a ship like *Belsus* vaporizing under any kind of fire. I'm thinking it's in geosynch out of our view."

"And out of communication," added Nik.

Michael looked solemnly at Krisha. "We didn't find Kari. I'm sorry. But we saw an airboat headed out to sea, and I think she was on it."

"That's what out prisoners said, sir. She was alive the last time they saw her. She's being taken to Toth. When do we head for the island, sir?"

"Soon, Krisha, as soon as we have a plan and you'll be a part of it. You'll be right there."

"Thank you sir." Jaw set, her expression was one of grim determination. At that moment she looked very dangerous for anyone who might harm her lover. *You really are in love with her*, he thought.

"Whatever we do, we can't wait long, not long enough for a flyer to get here. If one comes, fine, and things will be simpler, but I'm not going to count on it. Did you lose any people?"

"We're at full force, Major, but we need to keep at least two guards in the village. There are still some folks who blame us for what has happened."

"That's understandable."

"Yes, sir."

"Nik, stay on that radio. I've got to have something to eat, and then we'll meet here and talk about our next step. There's a fortress out there and a Charni barrier to cross. This is going to take some careful planning."

"I'll be here, Major," said Krisha.

Michael brushed past her on the way out the door, paused and put a hand on her shoulder. "We'll get her back, Krish," he said softly, and she smiled.

"That's a plan, sir."

He saw to the Grigaytes family, all of them now dressed in fatigues, and munching an originally freeze-dried concoction passing for bacon and eggs in the military. Uhli sat clown-like next to his mother, engulfed in a down vest and long underwear someone had found for him. The smile Gina gave Michael when he passed by did not escape the little boy, and Michael saw a critical frown pass over his face. He ate quickly, and then motioned for Davos to follow him back to the radio shack where Krisha and Nik were waiting. He tore a sheet of paper from Nik's log and scribbled on it, a rough map of the mainland and the island, drawing in mountains, the spots where he'd seen individual lights there, the area of IR glow.

"If I go by optical activity the fortress and any villages around it are right here in the center. Davos, do you have any idea how the Charni barrier runs along here?"

Davos took Michael's pen, drew a wavy ribbon parallel to the island about halfway to the mainland. "I don't know how wide, or how deep the water is there. It could go all the way to the island. The water suddenly gets deep on the edge nearest us, I know."

"Maybe a channel?"

Davos nodded. "The Charni appear suddenly, and in great numbers there. Yes, I think they swim deep."

"Kept there by something like a staff, only stronger. A signal they respond to, like thrashing sounds or the odor of blood is to most big sea predators. Can't be electromagnetic, like a staff. Too much absorption. Could be a pressure wave of some kind, but in a finite strip parallel to the island. I don't know of a transponder that can do that." Michael looked up, and saw puzzled faces. "Just thinking to myself. If the barrier has a width, it has a length, and if the signal source is at the center of the island, the intensity should go down as we get further east or west."

"There could be signal sources all over the island," said Krisha. "The barrier might surround the whole thing."

"Maybe, but if I were Toth I'd protect against a frontal assault first. All those mountains will make a flank attack a real chore for people on foot. If we landed on the west end we might get in, sailing far west and south, and then coming in from seaward south."

"Assuming no surrounding barrier and no observation posts," said Krisha, looking doubtful.

"We could wait for a flyer and just storm the place," said Nik.

"We don't have a flyer, Nik, and we might not have a ship. If a flyer comes, fine, but we're not going to sit around and wait for one. The island is only forty klicks out and we're making our move in the next forty-eight hours if we're serious about getting Kari back. We don't have time to wait. The only question is how we get there."

"I agree, Major," said Krisha. "Three boats close together, and all the firepower we have in camp."

Davos shook his head. "The Charni come in groups, many from beneath the boat. They smash the hull with their hard heads and chew their way inside. I've seen a boat sunk in minutes by only a few of them while two counselors used their staffs without effect. They're crazy in the barrier, and your weapons will not stop them. I have seen this, Michael, believe me."

It was a sobering thought for all of them. "We're not going to sit here and do nothing."

"No, I'm saying you don't know what the Charni can do. They are stupid animals with unending appetite, attracted only to food. You need a diversion, a scent of food to attract them away from a boat. We gave up half a catch of Yellowfin in minutes to escape the barrier when our neighboring boat was attacked. They fought over the fish while we escaped."

"And how do we do that?" asked Michael.

"You will need the support of my people. I will talk to them," said Davos.

"This is a bad time for us to be asking them for help."

"Not as bad as you might think. Jezrul was despised, and he is gone. Many will talk freely now, people who said nothing in the past. There will be opposition from those who lost sons last night and the few who are truly faithful to Toth. I think I can persuade many of them."

"When?"

"I can begin today. Our food stores are plenty, but we'll need several boats."

"We'll return to the village this afternoon, then, all of us."

"Your armed people also?"

"Yes. We're in charge, Davos. We also intend to repair the damage we've caused. They need to hear that, and other things."

They set a time, and Michael left the shack to talk with the survivors of the village team. He walked back to the huts to do it. As he approached, Cletus Euell, the biologist serving as Kari's backup as botanist, waved to him from a table at the entrance of his hut. "Major, you've got to see this."

Michael went to him. "What's up?" A microscope was on the table and Cletus was peering into it. "I've been looking at some material Krisha brought back from the obelisk. They found it along with surgical tools inside an altar; looked like lumps of decayed flesh until I got a closer look at it. Here, see for yourself."

Michael looked in the microscope. At first all he saw was a field of gray broken into small compartments separated by rippling walls, and connected by a myriad of filaments. "Move the slide, sir, so you can see the edges of the thing."

The edges were sharp and protruding from them were thick tendrils of matter waving in the liquid drop housing the sample. "Looks alive," said Michael. "Little legs along the sides."

"Not alive, sir, but it's organic. The 'legs' are connectors to an external system, with polar molecules specific for linking. I haven't seen these things since I was in graduate school; we've been using thin-film devices for a couple of hundred years now."

"So what is it?"

"A biochip, sir, big and crude by our standards, but healthy and active. Each compartment there has a specific function and there are lots of them, so it's not a simple device. Could be a microprocessor or complex stage amplifier. Maybe an oscillator."

"How about a receiver?" said Michael.

"Possibly. Can't tell by looking at it. But all those connectors mean it's part of something bigger."

An organic, electronic device found with surgical tools in an altar within the sanctuary of Toth. Part of an organic whole. Something fluttered up from Michael's sub-conscious mind, and then fled before he could grasp it. "Any way to test it, see what it does?"

"Not here, sir, but there's a circuit analyzer on the ship. It'll tell us what each compartment does and then we can run a simulation on the whole thing to see what the output is for various input."

"Save it, then. Nice job, Cletus. This might be important."

Michael talked to the rest of the village team, lending a sympathetic ear to their story of terrified flight. He explained the situation with Kari, and his vague plan to reach her, the danger of the barrier, and the need for cooperation by the villagers. As he did this his mind wandered, going back to the blob under the microscope. Surgical tools, in the altar, a baptism attended by Kari, the mark of baptism at the base of the skull for every villager. Davos had pointed to it as the initial point of pain, or pleasure, when a counselor wielded his staff with its hidden transmitter. An implant? Could it be an implant inserted at baptism, a receiver responsive to electromagnetic waves? Could the greater whole it was a part of be the human nervous system itself? And could a genetically engineered version of this same thing be a part of every fish in the sea? A test came to his mind, a test so simple it seemed absurd. He suddenly excused himself and searched for Nimri, found him with Davos and Leah in one of the huts. "Bring your staff, Counselor, and come with me. You too, Davos."

They followed him bewildered to the radio shack where Krisha was already waiting for him. He pointed to Davos. "You have a helmet and vest that will fit this man?"

Krisha looked Davos up and down. "Try mine. The vest might be too long." She went to her hut and was back in a minute with steel helmet and a vest capable of resisting all but direct impact at close range from small laser fire or a heavy assault rifle bullet. "Take the fabric off. I want to test the metal."

The fabric unbuttoned from the reflective metal shell, designed to cover body and throat and fitting snugly at the neck and throat. Michael turned to Nimri. "Pleasure or pain, can you control the intensity of what your staff does to people?"

"Yes."

"Okay, I want you to set it for what you call The Pleasures, but gently."

Nimri twisted the staff between his hands, looking suspiciously at Michael. "And now?"

"Point it at your father," said Michael.

"I can't do that, it's not right to arbitrarily—"

"Please do it, Counselor, it's important."

127

Reluctantly, Nimri raised the staff at close range and pointed it at his father. Davos shivered, hands clenching.

"Enough," said Michael. "Stop it, now. Davos, put this vest on, then the helmet."

Davos did as he was told, Nimri and Krisha both looking confused. Michael snapped the metal vest closed around the man, adjusted the helmet so its rim was in contact with the vest at the back of the neck and then pressed down on it. "Okay, counselor, do it again."

Nimri pointed the staff again, but Davos just stood there, without reaction. "Feeling anything?" asked Michael.

"No—nothing."

"Turn it up, counselor, all the way up to full power."

Nimri twisted the staff again, a faint hum now coming from it. "Hmmm," said Davos. "A little something, now, just a little in my neck."

"Turn it off, counselor. That's all I need."

"What is it?" said Krisha.

"I know the source of pleasure and pain in these people, Krish. It's sitting over there under Cletus's microscope, if you want to take a look. It's also lurking under the baptismal scar of every villager, and now I know how to control it with a simple electromagnetic shield. Not bad for an old marine, huh?"

Michael led them to see Cletus's biochip, feeling pleased with himself, but thinking; *I can't put a shield on every Charni in the sea, but Toth can forget about using pain against any villager who goes along with us.*

CHAPTER FOURTEEN

A skull-shaped island loomed ahead of them, and the boat slowed. Jezrul was at the wheel. Diego had awakened at last, but had said nothing. He looked sadly at Kari sitting opposite from him, still bound hand and foot. The other counselor was at the bow, waving a lamp slowly back and forth as they came closer in, passing to the south a few hundred meters from a steep, featureless slope. It was not a large island, more a monstrous boulder thrust up from the sea, dark and dangerous looking, devoid of life. Kari lost sight of it as it passed behind her position on the deck by the railings. They circled it, turned sharply, and headed in on a collision course from the east side. "There it is," said Jezrul. "Bring us in straight to the platform."

The other counselor nodded, put down his lamp as the engine of the boat came down to near idle speed. For the next minute he gestured for Jezrul to move the boat right or left, stars disappearing as a mountain of solid rock blocked out the western sky nearly to the zenith. They came to a stop with a gentle bump. Immediately there was a whirring beneath them and the boat was rising from the water. Two lines of yellow lights converged into the rock before them. They stopped suddenly, and then slid forward, passing into the mountain through an opening only meters high above their heads, and there was the rumble of a huge door closing behind them.

Light appeared with the brilliance of a sun. Kari squeezed her eyes shut, opened them slowly to see a cavern. Hand-railed walkways wound up vertical walls to closed, metal doors, and racks of blinding lamps hung from a ceiling tens of meters above them. Immediately it was warm in the cavern. Jezrul came over, pulled her to her feet and untied her ankles. "Welcome to the true House of Toth," he said. He took her arm and steered her towards the bow where five men in full battle dress were waiting. With visor helmets, shining vests, and laser rifles at the ready, the men stood silently as Jezrul lifted Kari out of the boat and placed her on her knees on a metal grate. "Take her downstairs," he said, and two of the men lifted her to her feet. A thousand needles reminded her feet were still there, but just now waking up again. They marched her along a walkway to a red door and down a gloomy, rock staircase to another door that opened to a cold hallway. There were closed doors with small windows covered by thick wire mesh. They opened one door, and pushed her rudely inside, hands still tied behind her. As the door slammed shut a light came on, a bare bulb hanging two meters above her head. There were bare walls, a toilet, and a torn cot in a corner. *Home sweet home*, she thought in disgust, and sat down on the cot, twisting her wrists against the rope. They were sore, but the bond had loosened enough that feeling had returned to her fingers. *When you have pain you know you're alive*, she assured herself, *but for how long?* She leaned against the wall and waited for a long time. Finally, Jezrul himself came for her.

The door rattled and opened, and he was standing there. "Lord Toth will see you now. Get up." He walked behind her; his breath heavy on her neck as he untied her hands, then took her arm in his hand. "I think you are fortunate, for He seems to be in good humor tonight. Your ship is destroyed, and your companions are scattered."

"It didn't seem that way when we left," muttered Kari, but Jezrul squeezed her arm so tightly it was immediately numb.

"Be careful what you say and it will go better for you."

He took her to the stairwell near her cell and they descended three flights to a door with fingerprint entry. Jezrul pressed his index finger against a lighted, opaque pad and the heavy door clicked open. Two men met them, one quite young, in a long robe. "Rudy," said Jezrul, "our guest has arrived."

The young man nodded and gestured to his left to a gloomy room lit only by the screens of many computer terminals lining the walls around a central, stone chair, now empty. He walked in front of them and stood before the chair. "Lord, the woman has arrived as you requested," he said reverently.

A ring of lights in the floor around it illuminated the chair, and suddenly a man was sitting there, head cloaked by the hood of his robe, a sharp chin and beak of a nose protruding from darkness. Slender, bony fingers gripped the armrests. "Ah, our visitor from the stars, and as lovely as you said, Jezrul. I have not seen your kind in hundreds of years. What is your home planet, Miss?"

"Ceti, sir. Why have you brought me here?"

"Ah, Ceti, a site of the Rubion wars. I served there as a young man aboard Her Majesty's Vessel *Turlock* to help undo the foolish destruction caused by political ambition. Do you remember trees on Ceti, miss?"

"Many of them," said Kari. "Lumber was a major industry when I was a child. Sir, why am I here?"

"After the war not a single tree was left standing. The reforestation project was my first of many. I love trees, don't you? They give beauty to the land and oxygen to the air we breathe. I miss the smell of them."

"Yes, sir," said Kari.

"It's one of the few things I remember fondly about your world. It has been a long time, of course, but I suppose the Church is as corrupt as ever."

"Sir?" Jezrul was still squeezing her arm, and Kari glared at him.

"The heavy tithing, the forced confiscation of property, required membership for political office, that sort of thing."

"You're talking about hundreds of years ago, sir. None of that exists now."

"Hmmm. Well, it was true when we came here to escape it. We have no church, worship no gods, and live simple, productive lives. Would you change that if you could?"

"We didn't come here to change anything, sir. We're a survey ship. Our job is to take a census and report on the progress of the colony, nothing more. We've come with no bad intentions, and now you've attacked our ship and kidnapped me. Why? We've done nothing to provoke you."

Toth leaned forward. "Your very presence here is a provocation. You've brought a military force with you, encouraged dissent by your questioning, and violated The Law. For example, you knew that only The Baptized were allowed in My Sanctuary, yet you accepted the invitation of Counselor Segur to join him there.

"We're told that First Counselor is your spokesman, and since the invitation came from him we naturally thought—"

"He hid you away for his own purposes and used you as a spy!" The old man had become suddenly angry, his voice rising in pitch.

"I deny that, sir! He hid me during a baptism I was invited to see. He didn't want the people there to be upset by my presence. I was supposed to leave right after the baptism, but you sent him away and I couldn't leave."

"You remained to hear my conversation with Jezrul. That's spying, and it is why you are here."

"I'm not concerned with the overthrow of Counselor Segur; that's your business. But you plotted to kill us and destroy our ship!

It makes no difference whether or not I was there to hear it! You were going to do it anyway! You have committed a hostile act against the Rubion Federation, sir, and the responsibility is entirely yours! And tell this servant of yours to let go of my arm. He's hurting me!"

Toth leaned back and smiled. "Release her, Jezrul. It's enough that she's here and we should be courteous. My only concern now is their land troops and they will surely come to us in search of the woman. Rudy, is there anything new about the ship?"

"Nothing, Lord, it has disappeared. The ship was under drive when we fired. It might have been vaporized."

"Perhaps," said Toth, rubbing his chin reflectively. "You will keep watch over the skies and the sea. Any approaching boat is to be incinerated without warning and if you *do* see another planet-fall vessel coming in, I want it shot out of the sky immediately."

"Yes, Lord Toth."

"As for you, young woman, I will not hold you entirely responsible for the people who have sent you here. For the moment we will be gracious hosts. Jezrul, I put her entirely in your care. See to her comfort in any way that seems fitting to you."

Jezrul smiled. "I will, My Lord, with your permission."

"You may leave, now, and bring Diego back with you."

Jezrul bowed, took Kari gently by the arm this time and guided her from the room. Five long flights of stairs ended at a brightly lit, curving hallway along which two counselors were coming towards them, nodding a silent greeting as they passed by. "These are our quarters, and I have a room for you here. I'm sure you'll find it comfortable."

The tone of his voice had changed, softer now, but there was still that slight smile, brightness in his eyes that disturbed her. They stopped at a door, and Jezrul unlocked it. "You will be locked in, of course, but I'll return in a short while to show you some of what we have here."

"What will happen with Counselor Segur?"

"Who can say?" said Jezrul, opening the door for her and following her inside. "He seems in fine humor tonight, but Our Lord's moods can change quite suddenly, a common thing among the elderly. I think he'll be merciful since Diego has served him well in times past. The man has accomplished what he can, and I will build on it. As of this night, I am First Counselor."

The furnishings were elegant compared to what she'd seen in the village: a large, wooden bed with thick mattress and blankets of finely woven polymer, a dresser with mirror, standing closet, plastic writing table with chair. On the walls, three liquid crystal mood panels backed by a myriad of programmable heating elements pulsed a display of color. "There are robes in the closet and you can see me through the aperture in the door. Let no other person in this room. The other counselors are forbidden to fraternize with you. Do you understand?"

"Yes."

"Good. I'm leaving now. Please refresh yourself."

He turned and left the room, closed and locked the door behind him. Kari rushed to the door to peek through the fish-eye aperture there and watched him walk down the hallway, curving out of sight. *Talk about mood swings. One minute he's bruising me and the next he's polite.* She pulled on the door handle, locked tight, a keyhole above it, and then went to the bed, sat on it, bounced on it. *Very nice.* She got up and opened the closet, finding three robes there, a kind of muslin, but soft. She picked one and tried it on over her clothes, looking at herself in the mirror. Suddenly she felt dirty, her face smeared with sweat, ash and wood smoke, her hair a rumpled mess. She stripped and went to the bathing cubicle, a familiar thing much like those on the ship. *Bathrooms haven't changed much in two hundred years*, she thought.

The hard spray of the shower stung the chafed places where the ropes had rubbed on her wrists and ankles. There was liquid soap, perfumed, which she rubbed over her body and into her hair twice with long, hot rinses in between. She caressed herself languidly, nipples suddenly hard and erect as she remembered the times on the ship when she and Krisha had showered together. Krisha was alive, of this she was certain, but what would she do now? Dear, protective, tempestuous Krisha. Would she try to come after her? *Could* she? If the ship were destroyed she would come by boat, and Toth was waiting for that, Toth and the Charni, waiting to destroy all who would dare to invade the stronghold. Diego's attraction to her had perhaps cost him his life, might result in her own death. Now there was Jezrul, cruel one moment, polite the next, but always that strange, frightening light in his eyes. In all her years with Krisha she had almost forgotten her power over men, her usually submissive nature interspersed with moments of defiance that seemed to draw them to her and into her bed. Mike had truly loved her, but the long sleeps—and she needed the closeness, the intimacy. She needed it constantly. Krisha was always there—until now.

She was alone on a hostile planet, and in the fortress of a powerful old man who appeared only as a holographic image to his faithful servants, a man whose single order could mean life or death for her at any moment. Krisha, Mike, the others, would they leave her if the ship had been saved? No, they couldn't, not with Krish and Mike there and besides that their mission wasn't complete until they'd solved the problem of Toth. They would come for her. She knew it, and so did Toth. And if they all died, what then? Death, or torture, or even worse a lifetime at the mercy of a man-god and his followers.

Her only power lay in her own sexuality, and she would use it fully, first of all to stay alive, and secondly to make the best of whatever life was ahead of her. She ran her hands over her breasts, down to her hips and touched the place between her legs that gave her the power.

Kari toweled down and dressed in the robe, feet bare. She lay down on the bed and stared at the mood panels for several minutes before she heard voices in the hallway outside her room. She tiptoed to the door, looked through the aperture there and saw two guards coming along the hall, holding Diego up under his arms. His feet dragged on the floor. His face was ashen, blood coming from his nose and one ear. The guards were laughing and when Diego groaned they shook him roughly. "Shut up," said a guard. "You're lucky to be alive. If it was up to me, I'd have torn your balls off and fed you to the Charni!"

They dragged Diego to a room three doors from Kari's and heaved him inside, closed and locked the door, then came back towards her. As they passed her door one guard jerked a thumb at it and said; "Nice piece in there. We keep our noses clean, Jezrul says we're gonna get some action with that one."

Their laughter followed them down the stairwell at the other end of the hall.

Kari went back to her bed, lay down on it, and wept.

* * * * * * *

A knock on her door awoke her and she rubbed her eyes. How long had she slept? Another three knocks, softly.

"Yes?"

"Are you dressed? It's Jezrul."

"Yes."

A key rattled in the lock, the door opened and Jezrul came in awkwardly balancing a plate of food and a bottle in one hand, his staff in the other. "Something to eat and drink," he said. "You were sleeping?"

"A little." She stretched, and yawned.

He put plate and bottle on the table. "You'll find eating here to be more varied than in the village, and the wine is quite sweet. It is an extra privilege for those who work closely with Our Lord. Please, try something."

"Thank you," she said sweetly. She went to the table and sat down while Jezrul rummaged in a drawer of the bureau. He returned with two plastic glasses, and filled them with wine. She wasn't really hungry yet, but the food looked delicious. There was the usual slab of fish, but also a thick piece of bread, and vegetables familiar to her from the ship: miniature green squash, lettuce covered with slices of real tomatoes and two small, skinless potatoes cut like an opening flower and covered with a white sauce. "Where does this come from?" she said in amazement.

"Toth provides for all. I will show you his gardens, and other wonders, when you've finished." He sipped his wine. "Try some."

It was delicious, sweet and very alcoholic, burning a path warmly to her stomach. She drank two glasses and quickly ate every bite of food on her plate while Jezrul sipped wine and stood watching her, amused. Finished, she looked up at him expectantly and he said; "Are you comfortable here?"

"It's all very nice, considering I'm a prisoner."

"Ah, well, that is true as long as your companions are running about, but that shouldn't be for long. When they're gone, life will go on as usual under Toth's guidance, and he bears no malice towards you. I've convinced him that the circumstance which brought you here was caused by Diego's weakness. Toth has dealt with him for his actions, and your part in the incident has been forgiven. But Diego's punishment was somewhat severe for a man his age."

"He looked half-dead when I saw the guards bringing him back to his room."

"But he will live. Our Lord is more merciful than I would be in such a case. He rewards those who have given him faithful service in the past, regardless of their stupidity, but Diego's days are finished. I am First Counselor now, and Toth has placed you under my care. You heard his command. I will carry it out all the days you're here. You are mine, Kari, from this day on. You will be one of The Baptized in Toth."

His soft voice helped Kari keep her composure. "Assuming I'm not rescued first, of course," she said. "In the meantime I will do what I'm required to do." *He'll like that.* She looked at him submis-

135

sively, saw the light come to his eyes again. *I will use my own, special powers to do that*, she thought.

"Shall we go now? There's much for you to see, and if there is to be the fighting I expect, you'll be confined to this room until it's finished."

He escorted her from the room. Kari expected to see a cloistered, dreary place like the interior of the obelisk, and at first it was like that. Hallways curved around the perimeter of the great rock mountain, room after room with closed doors, and the floor was cold on her bare feet. There were no elevators, only stairwells with spiral staircases of stone. As they toured the fortress, she counted twelve distinct levels above the throne room of Toth. Power came from a great fusion reactor far beneath the island, Jezrul explained, providing power and desalinized and heated water for their needs. A virtually unlimited source of power fed seven gun emplacements with laser cannon and electromagnetic rail weapons huge in size. *Two-hundred year old technology*, she thought, *but clean and functional and deadly*. Jezrul held her arm gently wherever they went; leaned close, spoke intimately to her. Gun crews and robed counselors noticed her with delighted surprise, but looked away as she came near. *I am his, now*, she thought. *I am his status symbol, like the staff he carries.*

There was something else going on, she decided, She saw it in the looks of the men when Jezrul was near, their deference to him, reporting to him as a leader, and drawing him aside for private words. These men, these military men, were loyal to *Jezrul*, now their First Counselor. How deep did that loyalty go? And just how deep was Jezrul's loyalty to Toth?

He showed her a bay where the Yellowfin collected, attracted there by an unexplained device designed by Toth himself. There was a submerged tunnel leading out to the sea, and then he took her to the center of the mountain below sea level and showed her a vast hydroponics farm, acres and acres of rock baths from which vegetables and flowers grew to monstrous size. Soft blue, red and yellow lights illuminated the area, and a dozen men worked there. Again, the men smiled when they saw Jezrul and his lady. They showed them examples of their produce, and beamed at Jezrul's generous compliments. *The soldiers, the workers, he has them all. Who is the real power here?*

He took her up three levels to a simple metal door deep inside the mountain where he paused dramatically to put an arm around her and speak close to her ear. "I have saved this for last. Prepare yourself for the first wonder Toth has bestowed upon us."

He opened the door, and she heard the roar of water falling. Her senses reeled from a deluge of fragrances as they pushed past a heavy polymer curtain and stood on a platform near the top of a mammoth room two hundred meters across and as many from floor to a ceiling, where racks of yellow lamps glowed fiercely through swirling mist.

The first thing she saw was the waterfall opposite them. A raging torrent tumbled fifty meters into a circular, green pool lined with boulders on which two robed men sat reading. The floor of the room was a tropical forest: gnarled, moss-covered trees, ferns and colorful flowers everywhere. Stone trails wound crazily among the foliage, and below them was a second pool with a bridge on which another robed man stood staring into the water to watch colorful fish swimming. "Shall we go down?" asked Jezrul.

Speechless, Kari only nodded her head. He took her hand and they descended four long flights of steep metal grating stairs past two other platforms. Something fluttered past her head, a butterfly with wings of yellow and red. As they descended there were more of them, a rainbow of colors, and then a bird flew past her, a tiny thing plumed in red. As they reached the floor the butterflies were everywhere, and birds were fluttering in the trees, chirping.

They walked the pathways, Jezrul still holding her hand and when he spoke there seemed to be true reverence in his voice, even a sense of sadness; "This was the second stage of Toth's plan, to turn our world into a garden of great beauty, but it was not to be. He grew old, and the work became slow, and then there was the transfiguration. All he was working on was moved here, and little by little it has become what you see. Someday, when the time is right, and all the people are again together under The Law, this will be Our Lord's gift to them. I will see to it."

"I've never seen such beauty," said Kari, "but some of the flowers seem familiar."

"Yes. We've been introducing new species slowly over the last centuries, and inland, far from the village there are now three forests similar to this one. The process has begun, but it is slow. Toth was a great scientist and teacher, and this is his legacy, but only for The Chosen who follow His Law. It is not for those who inhabit the corrupted worlds he fled from. It is not for your people."

"But I'm here," she said, looking up at him.

"You are one person, and Toth has made the exception, but only because you will become one of The Chosen. This is His word to

137

me. Resign yourself to this, Kari; when your people are gone you will still be here—with me. It is Toth's will. It is mine."

"I'm Toth's reward to you for overthrowing Diego," she said calmly.

"Yes."

Her mind whirled, and she dared to ask the question: "And a reward for the men who follow you?"

Jezrul's eyes narrowed. "I don't understand."

"Will I be a sexual plaything to be shared with your men? Is that why I'm still alive?"

"Certainly not!" he said.

"You'd better make that clear to your men. They might have other ideas."

His eyes clouded over darkly. The seed had been planted, and she could only hope it would take root. "I will talk to them, and there will be no misunderstanding, but you *are* mine, and how you live here depends on your relations with *me*. Let there be no misunderstanding about that, either."

"I will accept that—for the moment," she said, a hint of defiance in her voice that brought light to his eyes again. "The pool looks inviting. May I wade in it?"

"Of course." Jezrul smiled.

She waded in the big pool, cooling her sore feet and pulling the robe up to her hips while Jezrul watched silently, appraising her legs. The two counselors sitting on nearby boulders had watched them furtively, but were now deeply engrossed in their reading. And when she was finished they walked the length of the forest path and returned to her room.

Jezrul paused as he opened the door and she was squeezing past him in the doorway. He put his hands on her shoulders and looked at her fiercely. "More food and drink has been brought to your room. I will return this evening."

Her answer was a shrug of her shoulders against his hands, a shy roll of her eyes upwards towards his face. He stepped back quickly, eyes wild, and closed the door.

Kari went to the bed and lay down on it, thinking, *your battleground will be the sky and the sea. Mine will be right here on this bed.*

Late that evening, he came to her.

She had bathed again, eaten, and drunk nearly two bottles of the wine. When he knocked three times she was lying on the bed, a fresh robe pulled up to her hips, a glass of wine in her hand. "Come in," she said. He entered the room, staff in hand, and locked the door behind him. For a moment he looked at her silently, then came to the bed, sat down, and took the glass from her hand, his own hand shaking ever so slightly, but enough to create tiny wavelets in the liquid. "You're not afraid?" he asked softly.

"Should I be? What do you have in mind for me?" she whispered. The look on his face *did* frighten her, and her own heart was beating hard.

"Not what you're thinking," he said. "Not until you're baptized in Toth, but that will be soon, Kari, I promise you. Here, take this." He handed her his staff, and lay down beside her. "Now, sit up."

She obeyed, confused. He guided her with his hands until she was straddling him and the end of the staff was positioned at the side of his neck. His hands moved over her body and up beneath the robe until she gasped. "You see the marks on the staff? Put your hands there and twist as if you were wringing out a wet cloth. You will hear a click."

She did so, heard a click and Jezrul's fingers gripped her thighs hard. "Ahhh, that's it," he said, closing his eyes. His breathing was suddenly heavy, mouth open, and beneath her she felt him harden. "Again," he gasped, "two more clicks."

She obeyed, heard a hum, and instantly Jezrul was writhing beneath her, his hands moving everywhere, squeezing, probing painfully, the cloth of his robe hard against her, chafing and burning, and she cried out softly as his eyes opened, rolling wildly. "Ah—ah—ah—" he gasped as he rocked her roughly with his hands until blood ran down his chin from a self-inflicted bite on his lip and the robe was wet between her legs. His skin became ashen, and he fumbled at the staff. "Off," he said weakly. "Turn it off."

She did so, the hum ceasing as she sat there terrified, looking down at him. Breathing hard, he grasped her arms and pulled her down on him, burying his face against her throat, his cloth-shielded organ still hard against her. "Kari—Kari," he murmured, "there is power in pain, a power only I can stand up to. Not even Toth can hurt me! You see? *Not even Toth!* And when you are baptized, Kari, that power will also be yours, the power of pain—and pleasure. We will share it, Kari. We will share it forever!" He moaned and clutched her to him, and in a few moments was deep in sleep.

Kari lay beside him, his arm tightly around her in a protective way, yet she wept silently, and shivered uncontrollably with terror and despair.

She had fought the first skirmish on her battlefield, and already she knew that her war was lost.

CHAPTER FIFTEEN

The debate was heated, but Michael was optimistic from the start. Davos had gathered everyone at the amphitheatre and argued strongly against the unprovoked attack by the counselors and then Kari's kidnapping. Nimri joined in and the people listened quietly as he described Jezrul's long campaign against Diego, his desire for power and probable involvement in the death of Lebyn. It was clear Jezrul had long been despised for the frequent use of his staff against the people, and several of them gave accounts of his atrocities. Nimri's zealous support of Toth swayed others, for his mission was to warn His Lord of Jezrul's treachery and misdeeds among the people. But there were those who had lost sons in the fighting, mothers still on the edge of hysteria, and their tears won denouncements of their visitors from the stars, without whose presence the fighting would never have occurred. It was at that moment Michael chose to say something. He went to the podium, and the people were suddenly silent.

"You've lost sons and we've lost comrades, two of them. They died horribly, their insides boiled by laser fire from some of your sons. They had families, loved ones, and they are grieved. They were not soldiers. One was a man of letters who came only to study your history, the other a biologist who marveled at the beauty you have here. They carried no weapons, but were shot in the back, and they are dead, as dead as those who killed them. This is not justice, it is a tragedy, a tragedy that should end right here, right now. The physical damage can be repaired, and our people will work with you until it is finished, but we cannot bring back your sons, and you cannot bring back our comrades. Let us bury our dead together—at sea, and then get on with what we must do. I ask for your help in reaching Toth. If Jezrul can blame us for what has happened here he can also blame you, and I want no further harm to come to this village. Please help us—and help yourselves. We need your decision now."

140

He left the podium, eyes downcast and Davos shouted after him; "Let my pledge to help Michael Queal be the first. Now, who else?"

"I make my pledge also," said Nimri, "in support of Our Lord. Who will go with me?"

In minutes it was done, all but three families pledging support for the journey to Toth's stronghold. The deciding factor had been Jezrul, not Toth. In private discussions after the meeting broke up, Michael finally heard the stories of hard discipline forced by Jezrul on the people. They wanted to bring him down. There was little mention of Toth, and Michael wondered how many shared Davos' view that He was, in fact, long dead, and the counselors had become the true power on Tothwelt.

Another revelation awaited him when they returned to camp to begin gathering their gear for war. Cletus Euell came up to him, and held out a mold-stained book. "One of the books we found in the obelisk, sir. The author's name hit me right between the eyes. He was a plant geneticist, a bioengineer and devout atheist, from the sound of his writing. The book includes several tirades about controlled thinking by The Church."

Michael opened the book to the title page.

The title was *The Role of Bioengineering in Environmental Restoration.*

The author's name was Edward Tothman.

"My God," said Michael. "And the copyright is 3287. This book is nearly three hundred years old!"

"Yes, sir. I wish we had a list of the original colonists, but we don't. And back in those days there were some major purges by The Church, until Victoria took charge of them."

Edward Tothman. Toth. A bioengineer that had fled with farmers and fishermen to found a new world. A paradise. It had to be. The exotic plants, the Charni, the biochip, the atheism of the people, it all fit. "It's Toth," he said, and Cletus nodded. "By now he'd have to be nearly three hundred years old. How?"

"A bioengineer, sir. Who knows?"

"Only Toth," said Michael, and he hurried away to tell the others.

* * * * * * *

The boats were loaded in the darkness of early morning, globes of moss on the beach and the boats casting faint shadows as people moved to and fro between the skiffs. Michael sat and watched Osen load their rifles and other battle gear into a skiff. He sat alone, and thought about going into combat again, an old marine whose legs had nearly given out climbing a single slope only days before. He was done, finished as a marine, this he knew for certain. It was people like Krisha who would carry the action; her fresh-faced troops now had a taste of war. And then there was Osen: young, like a puppy at times, but on that one night a silent, efficient killer. You're a real killer, private, he'd said. *Yes, sir, that's exactly what I am.* Mootry's orderly, a trained killer? *There're things about him that Mootry hasn't told me. What are they?*

Gina came down to the beach, looked around, then started towards him, and he thought of the night before, sitting on a skiff to stare out at the sea, and the woman suddenly there beside him, sitting close, touching his hand, his arm going around her. They'd sat in silence for several minutes, and then Gina had put her head on his shoulder and said; "I've lost one man at sea. I don't want to lose another." And when he'd looked down at her in surprise she'd kissed him gently on the mouth, a kiss they held for an eternity, and then she'd jumped up and rushed away.

He still felt that kiss.

She sat down on the sand beside him. "The loading is nearly done," she said.

"Yes, it is. Gini, I want you to promise me something."

"What?" She leaned against him, looked out to sea.

His arm went around her waist. "I don't know how long we'll be gone, or what we'll find out there. I don't know if help is coming from the ship or if we even have a ship, but until it's over, one way or another, there's a chance that Toth may send some people here to occupy the village and hold you as hostages. I've given orders to fall back to our camp if that happens. Promise me that you and your family will go with my marines if that time comes. What few men we're leaving here will have plenty of firepower and I want you protected. I want you here when I get back."

"I want to be here," she said, snuggling against him. "We have a date."

Michael smiled. "Yes, we have a date."

Osen and Davos had pushed the skiff into the water and waved to him. "That's it, I have to go." He stood up, took her hand to pull her up, and backed away a step. Gini threw herself into his arms, face against his chest. "You will come back," she said. "You *will* come back."

He kissed her forehead, turned and walked to the skiff without looking back. *That's my intention*, he thought.

Only a few had come to the beach to see them off; goodbyes had been said in the privacy of homes. A new solidarity had been welded the afternoon before when three boats loaded with mourners had sailed south and west to a place ten kilometers from shore. There they had all bowed their heads while words were said over the shrouded bodies of twelve men who had died in battle. A servant of Toth, and a military Major had said the words, and when they were finished the weighted bodies had disappeared into the sea, two of them far from home.

When he was on the boat Gini waved to him and he waved back, Davos was beside him. "You will break her heart," said the fisherman.

"When I leave?"

"Yes."

"And what if I stay, Davos? This was supposed to be my last mission, with retirement at the finish of it. I can go to Brown's planet and retire as an old man, or go to Arkon in deep sleep and wake up to a world that isn't mine anymore. It would be easy for me to settle here for the rest of my life if—if it were allowed. Right now, I don't see that happening."

Davos looked surprised. "It could be possible."

"Not with Toth or Jezrul here."

Davos patted his arm. "We do what we can, for now. The future will have to wait for us, but know this, Michael Queal, I do not oppose you're settling here. I do not oppose it at all." He squeezed Michael's arm, and walked back to the tiller through the crowd of marines setting sail under Nimri's directions. In a moment, they were underway.

Seven boats sailed in v formation that early morning, an inverted phalanx with two marine-filled craft at the apex, the other five filled with village men who immediately set to work cutting up Yellowfin as a tasty distraction for the Charni. They sailed south until the water was deep, depth measured by stones on long ropes, for it was still dark and they could not see the color of the sea. They turned west, and ran for several hours in a strong breeze until the sun was well above the horizon, and then turned south again. The sea bottom was now visible, a sandy plane only meters beneath them, and in all this time they had not seen a single Charni. The big island was visible to the east, mountains looming clearly, and they were now further south than the barrier off shore from the village. Still no Charni, but they were ready, and Nimri was at the bow with his staff. Village men stood at other bows with captured staffs he had taught them how to use. Two laser rifles had been distributed to each of the Charni chumming boats of the outer phalanx, while the two inner boats bristled with laser weapons and assault rifles.

The tip of the island moved north of them. Still no Charni. They turned east and tacked in a zigzag pattern, progress now slower. Michael went to the bow with Nimri, watched for the deep blue of a trench, or a canyon, where the killer fish might be awaiting them.

The tip of the island drew nearer. White cliffs dropped to the sea. A kilometer away, perhaps closer, and Michael pointed, shouted to the other boats; "Straight in! Head for the cliffs!" Standing on the bow, he could see a strip of white, a small, narrow beach straight ahead. Looking outwards he did not see the water beneath him turn suddenly dark blue, did not see the trench there, or the silver sides of countless, living torpedoes rising from the deep.

The Charni hit all boats simultaneously, and men screamed.

"CHARNI!"

Nimri swept the water with his staff as the boat shuddered again and again with the impact of bone and tooth. Darting shapes in the deep, and then dorsal fins homed in. There was a sight of a horrible head, jaws snapping, and an eye exploded in gore at the roar of an assault rifle. The body was ripped to pieces in seconds in a boiling mass of attackers. The other boats were dropping masses of bloody fish into the sea, rocked by the swarm of attracted killers. Men shouted, and one boat was already listing dangerously and sinking rapidly. Men leapt from one boat to another in panic, only to fight a new battle. A thousand shapes rushed to the sinking boat, penetrating it to the tanks of butchered Yellowfin, and pulled the entire craft under the waves. Another boat sank on their port side, men in the water, shrieking, two pulled under with a single tug, another cut in half by one monstrous bite, and a barrage of rifle fire as a boat slowed and jerked the six survivors on board. One man was pulled right out of the mouth of a Charni, only to find his foot missing, a stump spurting blood.

The beach was two hundred meters away; the water boiled around them, but the phalanx was working, the Charni going for the Yellowfin chum.

A huge head rose from the sea only meters away, and Michael shot it seven times in head and eye, watched it roll over on its side, floating.

Floating. Nothing came to claim it.

The Charni were suddenly gone.

144

Five sailboats were coming around from the north side of the island and heading straight towards them.

"Prepare to fire!" screamed Krisha, and her men turned, aiming their weapons.

Davos screamed with her, pointing to the bow. "Shorten sail, shorten sail! He pulled hard on the tiller, the boat turning sharply.

Twenty meters ahead, something was raising from the depths, sparkling in sunlight, then popping to the surface like a cork, a thing ungainly yet beautiful, a thing of glass, two pontoons and a geodesic dome, inside of which was a man staring at them in amazement and fear, peddling furiously to move the little craft out of their way.

"Drop sail!" screamed Davos. "Drop anchor! We're nearly aground!"

Boats spun, running into each other, anchors splashing. Krisha yelled at villagers to drop down on deck and get out of the line of her fire.

A hatch popped open on the little glass boat, and its occupant stood up, shaking his fist at them. "Get out of here!" he screamed. "You're on the rocks and wreaking my beds! Get your anchors up! You, Counselor! Get your people out of here! We don't want any of your kind here, and I'm not afraid of your guns, either! Get out! Help! Helllp!" He was looking at the on-coming sailboats and waving his arms.

"Please!" shouted Michael. "We've escaped from the mainland. Toth has taken one of our people, and we've come to get her!"

"Go away! Toth isn't here; you're too far west, way too far. Now go! My Lonia will choke in all the sand you've stirred up!"

"Ready!" screamed Krisha. "At my command!" Twenty-one guns were aimed at the charging sailboats, close enough now to see they were filled with angry men brandishing knives and harpoons.

"Wait—wait," said the glass boat man, waving his arms over his head. "Heave to! Stop! They are not from Toth!"

The sailboats stopped with amazing quickness, sails coming down, anchors splashing.

"Oh, NO!" screamed the man, red-faced. "*More* anchors! My Lonia will crawl under the rocks and I'll *never* get them out! You're all ruining my livelihood! I have children to feed!"

"What do you want here?" shouted a tall, sunburned man on one of the newly arrived boats. He carried a long harpoon of black metal, and pointed it at Michael.

"There's been a battle on the mainland, several people killed and one taken to sea as a hostage. We've come after her, expecting to find Toth here, but this man says—"

"Toth's fortress is in a small island to the east of here. Who are you? You're not from the village, and I don't recognize your weapons."

"We come from the stars," said Michael, holding his breath, but the man was suddenly calm.

"We saw your ship come over days ago. Have you come to rid us of Toth?"

"That wasn't our intention, but his people have taken one of ours and we're not leaving until we have her back." Michael gave the man a quick summary of where they were from and why they'd come to Tothwelt. Behind him guns were still leveled at the newcomers and there were repeated shouts from the little man in the glass boat demanding that *everyone* get out of his *Lonia* beds so he could get on with his work.

"You have a counselor with you, and he has a staff. I see others as well."

"This man helped us to escape. He's a friend."

"Then put down your weapons and follow us. We will show you the way to Toth, but no more than that. He is our enemy, and his forces could easily destroy us if we helped you."

"Fair enough," said Michael. He motioned to Krisha, and she ordered her marines to port arms. Sails went up, and anchors hauled. "Follow us in a line," said the big man, "close to shore. The Charni are nearby, but run deep along here."

"We have a badly injured man here," said Michael. "A Charni took off his foot."

"We can care for him," said the man. "Follow us."

"And don't come back!" shouted the man in the glass boat. He climbed back inside, cranked furiously on a lever, and there was a sucking sound from the glass pontoons on either side of him. The little craft sank like a lead weight, and as they drifted away, Michael could see it crawling among the rocks on the bottom, pinching at them with accordion appendages, and withdrawing to drop what looked like shiny, flat stones into a basket attached forward.

"Isaac is back to his harvesting," shouted the big man, "and glad to be rid of us. But the shellfish he raises here are an important part of our diet, and we respect his wishes. Be glad he stopped you. The sharp rocks surrounding his beds could have torn the hulls out of your boats."

"Thanks, we understand!" shouted Michael.

They sailed single file along the northern shore of the island past knobby cliffs of brown and black rock streaked with yellow.

There was a rotten smell as they passed a steaming cascade of water issuing from cracks in the rock and ahead of them there was the beginning of a beach. Women and children dug in wet sand at water's edge. They waved, and then stared as the boats passed them. Ahead of them more people appeared on the beach, half-naked, even the women, and the clothes they wore were tattered. There were two sailboats a hundred meters offshore and people were jumping in the water there, staying under a long time, and coming up to place things in floating baskets before diving again. Realization struck Michael hard. *These are the ones who were expelled from the mainland. They've survived, and built their own world in the last forty years, and now here they are, maybe relatives, together again.* He waited for the villagers on his own boats to show signs of recognition, but there were none.

They dropped anchors in a line, bows pointing to sea where the water was nearly two meters deep, and then swam and waded ashore to the crowd of people gathered there. There were nervous looks at Krisha's marines and Krisha herself as she ordered her people to sling rifles held overheads on the way in. Many were young, only a few old faces and the first, shy smiles came only from the children. The big man with the harpoon came up to Michael, put out his hand. "I am Eves Ekren," he said.

"Major Michael Queal of Her Majesty's Survey Ship *Belsus*. This is Captain Elg, my second in command, and Davos Grigaytes, a fisherman from the mainland, and—" He looked around; saw Osen knee-deep in surf, talking on the radio. "Got something?" he shouted.

"Talking to Nik, sir. He knows we're here!"

"That's private Osen, my orderly."

Villagers carried the injured man ashore. The stump above his missing foot was wrapped in blood-soaked cloth. His face was ashen, but he was conscious, and moaned in pain. "We've got a badly injured man, Eves; can we get some help for him?"

"We have dealt with such things," said Eves. "Gareth! Hemmo! Help them take him to Timannie, and heat the metal for her!"

Two young men rushed to help carry the man from the beach and up a gully disappearing into a stand of trees.

"We will do what we can," said Eves, but then he looked left to where Nimri stood silently a few meters away. "You say this man helped you escape?"

"Yes. Davos here is his father. The man is a counselor."

"I recognize a counselor and his staff when I see one," said Eves, eyes narrowing. "I thought we'd seen the last of such people."

147

They walked up the gully, at the end of which were stone stairs cut out of a five-meter cliff. "You *remember* the counselors?"

"I was a little boy when they forced us into boats and made us come here. Have you heard the story?"

"Yes. It's still a bitter memory for the villagers on the mainland. That, and other things, including our arrival, has led to the fighting and killing."

"I don't think that's our problem, but it is not for me to decide. Derald Hudak is our Elder, and head of The Council of Eight. I'm taking you to him now to discuss your wishes."

They climbed the steps, walked a worn path through thick trees and came out at the foot of a wide, steep canyon rising to the mountains a thousand meters above them. The canyon was devoid of vegetation. Houses of stone lined it, and at its foot was a circle of buildings surrounding an amphitheatre. Sharp odors assailed Michael, odors of cooking, hot metal, sulfur, something rotten. The houses were similar to those on the mainland, but with one significant difference. The windows. They were covered with panes of glass in every imaginable color: reds, yellows, greens in single color sheets, some with swirls of multiple colors, others with a complex of many smaller panes fastened together to form geometric shapes of great beauty. Michael pointed to a window as they passed it. "That's lovely. I've never seen such wonderful work with glass."

"It has become a minor industry," said Eves. "The development of our technology has accelerated in the last ten years, but I expect you will find it crude. Toth has the weapons of our forefathers and even if he continues to leave us alone it will be a long time before we're capable of opposing him."

"He knows you're here?"

"Oh, yes. We see his boats out in the barrier and on the south side quite often, now. The increasing regularity of their appearances is bothersome. Now, have your people seat themselves in the amphitheatre, and we will bring food."

The group following them nearly filled the amphitheatre, and when they were settled, Eves said, "You and I will eat later. I want you to meet our Elder and explain the situation to him."

"Of course," said Michael, but as he turned, Osen was once again at his side. "Yes?"

"Permission to accompany you, sir? Nik will be reporting in, and it could be urgent."

"Do you mind?"

Eves shook his head. "If you wish. We're going to the larger building halfway up the right side of the canyon. Please follow me."

They followed a worn groove of a trail snaking around boulders, then straight up the canyon. Eves was several steps ahead of them when Osen came up to Michael's side, and spoke in a near-whisper. "All okay at camp, and Nik knows where we've come in, but the real news is he thinks he heard something from *Belsus*!"

"When?"

"Couple of hours ago, just a few words, but he heard your name and by the time he tried to answer the signal was gone."

"There's hope, then, more than hope. Keep yourself plugged in."

"Yes, sir."

Michael was puffing again, his legs burning when they reached a windowless stone building perched on a shelf high in the canyon. Eves went to the open door, and paused there. "Derald, we have visitors. The ones whose ship flew overhead have arrived, and there are villagers from the mainland with them. There has been fighting, and they are searching for Toth. Will you see them?"

He turned, and gestured for Michael and Osen to enter. The interior was dark, except for a single lamp on a table piled with debris, behind which sat an old man with long, white hair flowing down over his shoulders. He put out a hand and Michael shook it. "I am Derald Hudak," he said.

Michael formally introduced himself and Osen as representatives of the Rubion Federation, and his eyes moved around the room. Rods and sheets of dark metal leaned against walls, and the model of a ship with multiple balls of blown glass was mounted on a metal framework with pontoons, also of glass. Stacks of thin wooden sheets were covered with diagrams and writing. The man's table was heaped with such sheets, and a crayon he held between them blackened his hands.

"I should not be surprised by your visit," said Derald. "We saw your ship pass over days ago, and assumed it was a matter of time before you found us. But what is this about fighting on the mainland?"

Michael gave him the whole story: their mission, the hostile reception, the attack on *Belsus* and resulting firefight, during which Kari had been kidnapped and taken out to sea.

"As much as I regard Toth as an enemy I find it difficult to believe he would sanction overt killing," said Derald. "It violates his own law and he has always found other ways to eliminate his adversaries. Have you heard the story of how we came to be here?"

"Yes, I have. I think a counselor named Jezrul somehow initiated this whole thing. The first counselor has been overthrown, and since we haven't found his body I assume he was taken out to sea with Kari as prisoners of Toth."

Derald frowned. "Who is this First Counselor?"

"His name is Diego Segur. I think he'd been First Counselor for many years. Do you remember him?"

"I certainly do. It was he who ordered us into the boats, and sent us here. His own mother died here only five years ago. But it was also Diego who came to us secretly the night before we were thrown away, and he brought four, dismantled staffs, which he taught us how to use. He hid the pieces in the clothing we wore, and the few possessions we were allowed to take with us. Without these staffs all of us would have perished in crossing the barrier, not just the twenty of us who did anyway. He saved our lives."

"But why?" said Michael. "He is a servant of Toth."

"He is also my son," said Derald.

CHAPTER SIXTEEN

Rudy Hoffman stood before the throne of Toth, and he was deeply concerned about the health of His Lord. He'd been summoned once again in the previous night, had administered an ever-increasing dose of Beta-Choline into the life support system while the image of his Master gasped in pain, and struggled to breathe. And when the drug had taken effect, Toth had closed his eyes, leaned back wearily in the throne, and said, "Ah, Rudy, each time I grow wearier and the pain is slower to go away. I think the time draws near when even my transfiguration won't sustain me. Our present crisis must be resolved, and quickly—before I am gone. Bring Jezrul here in the morning. I must talk to both of you."

He had obeyed. Jezrul had just arrived, and was standing in the gloom just outside the scattered illumination from the throne. Rudy did not like the man, did not trust him. *He thinks me blind that I don't know about his politicking among the men, his promises, and his ambition. Given a chance he will set himself above Our Lord, even destroy him by manipulation as he has done with Diego. Dare I say something? Do I dare express my concern to Toth in his present condition? No, I will not. The strain would be too much; better to let Jezrul hang himself with his own rope.*

Toth appeared, slumped in his throne like a man asleep. "We are here, Lord, as you requested," said Rudy.

Toth raised his head, and for a long moment his eyes seemed unfocused. "Come closer, Rudy. Is Jezrul with you?"

"I'm here, Lord," said Jezrul, and both men stepped up to the apron of light before the throne.

"Ah, good, both of you here, the two who will be my hands in this hour. My blessings on you."

They received the Gift of Pleasures.

"There are matters to discuss," said Toth, now focused on them, and resuming his regal posture on the throne. "Can we now assume the starship has been destroyed?"

"There have been no sightings, Lord, either of the ship or any planet-fall vessels. This is not conclusive, of course, but it seems at worst case that the ship is heavily damaged and unable at this point to retrieve the people they sent here. If able, they would surely have done this by now, and might even be attacking us. But there are no signs of activity at sea, and even the usual boats from the island are absent this morning."

"I hear nothing from the village," said Toth.

"It has been taken, Lord," said Jezrul. "I ordered our men to lay down their weapons if the sanctuary was threatened with destruction, but I promised we would return to free them. I spoke as Your Servant, Lord; my instincts told me this would be Your Will."

"Indeed it is," said Toth, "and we will return in force when the time is right. But tell me, Jezrul, what would you now do if you were Michael Queal, your ship lost, one of your people taken away, but much of your force intact? How would you proceed?"

Jezrul rubbed his chin reflectively. "The man has not lived under the guidance of The Law, Lord. His moral values are different from ours so I can only guess at what he might do."

He gives himself time to think, thought Rudy.

"I understand," said Toth, "but give me your guess, and we will see if it matches my own."

"Forgive me, then, for some of the things I say may seem brutal to you. Having taken the village by force, and with much damage, I would need to control the outraged people there. I would force the surviving counselors to do this or be killed. With my ship gone, marooned on a hostile planet, but with a small, well-equipped military force intact my only possible survival would be to take total control of that planet, bring down the established leadership and rule in its place."

"So far, we agree," said Toth, smiling.

"I would lie to the people, blame You for what has happened, bring forth dissenters to testify against The Law, and make promises about a new life with technology. I would do anything necessary to obtain their sympathy. Failing to do that I would use force and those who refused to cooperate would be publicly executed. I would establish a military dictatorship, Lord, and our people would quickly yield, for they have been treated gently and with respect under Your Rule. Their love for You could not stand up to the possibility of their families being murdered. All of this could be taking place even now, Lord, we should move quickly!" Jezrul's voice quivered, and there were tears in his eyes.

He shows real fear for the people, thought Rudy. *Is it possible I'm wrong about his intentions?*

"Calmly, Jezrul," said Toth. "We are speculating here. Now, you say it is necessary to overthrow the existing order. How do we do that?"

"By military action, Lord, even though as Queal I'm aware of weapons powerful enough to destroy my ship. I'm also aware that such weapons are relatively immobile and difficult to bring to bear on a small, highly maneuverable fighting force. I would use a scattered flotilla of boats to find the source of those weapons and destroy it by ground action."

Now Jezrul smiled slyly. "But where to find these weapons? In the new sanctuary of Lord Toth, far out to sea? The people know that much, Lord. And where might that be? Well, there is one piece of land they see on occasion, a long range of mountains far out on the horizon."

"The big island!" said Rudy.

"Yes. I would organize my force, cross the barrier and attack the island."

"What about the Charni?"

"A minor problem with my firepower. I've seen what their weapons can do, Rudy."

"They will find few people on the island, and none who will oppose them."

"They will be allies if I blame Our Lord for the fighting in the village, and remind them of their history. I will recruit them to increase my numbers, use their boats and whatever technology they have, disguise them as villagers and use them as shields. The islanders know where we are, and also the wanderings of the barrier. I can get here from the big island without crossing the barrier, a frontal diversion with the major force coming in from the south."

"We've seen no advanced technology on the island. At best they're an iron-age people with simple weapons," said Rudy.

"Once I reach this rock my own technology is sufficient to get inside, and then it will be hand-to-hand. My people are well trained and seasoned, and here is my real advantage, although I don't know it yet. If I can scatter my forces and get within five hundred meters of my objective the laser cannon emplacements cannot harm me, cannot be brought to bear within that range because of their height above the water. That is our vulnerability, Lord; we cannot let them get close. Once they get inside, despite their small numbers, we could be lost. Our best tactic is to intercept them at the big island

and destroy them there. I suggest we send our forces to the island this very hour."

"You think they will move this quickly?" said Toth. "They might still have hope for the safety of their ship, and await reinforcements from it."

"It's possible," said Jezrul. "Queal struck me as a cautious man, but he will move against the big island, I'm sure. We take the island today, wait for his forces and destroy them in the water. Retaking the village should then be a simple matter."

"For the most part you have read my mind, Jezrul," said Toth. "Rudy, you have seen *no* signs of boats at sea?"

"None, Lord, but at sea level the range of our scanners barely reaches to the western tip of the island. If they landed on the south shore we would never see them."

"Unlikely," said Jezrul. "I would move as quickly as possible, and make a frontal assault. Let me send a fifty-man force this hour, Lord. I will lead them."

Toth smiled. "No, Jezrul, I will not risk your life, not now. I need you here. But I agree with your plan. You will send the men in three boats, two to the north, and one to the south. See to it, and tell me when they have left."

"Yes, Lord Toth!" Jezrul walked quickly from the room, leaving Rudy standing in the glow of the throne. Toth slumped wearily there.

"He is a man of thought and action, Rudy. He will lead the people when I am gone."

"Lord, You will be here long after I'm dead! The people need You!"

"Dear Rudy, you've cared well for me, but we both know I'm not immortal. How well you would know this if you beheld me the way I really am, floating in this darkness behind your panels and machines. No, it is Jezrul who will lead the people, and soon. I'd hoped it would be Diego, but then he—"

Toth clutched at his chest. "Rudy, the pain!"

Rudy rushed to a control panel, typed in a command, another injection of Beta-Choline streaming into the life-support system. "Done, My Lord!"

Toth stared at him glumly when Rudy returned to the throne. "These attacks—now coming so close together—I dare not feel emotion. I cannot *feel*. I cannot be human. See to Jezrul; watch over him, for he is still young and impetuous. But be loyal to him; he thinks only of the people."

"I hear your words and obey, Lord." *But I'm not sure I agree with you.*

"I must rest now. Awaken me when Jezrul returns." The hologram faded as Toth spoke, and the throne was empty again. Rudy went to a terminal, and accessed a routine to monitor Toth's finger movements, for they were closely associated with his bouts of pain, and he interfaced it with the Beta-Choline supply package for automatic injection. Beyond the panel he faced, perhaps a meter away, His Lord dwelled in darkness, alone in transfigured isolation. Only four screws and a centimeter of metal separated him from the man he had served for years without direct contact. What was he like? What *was* the transfigured state of Lord Toth?

Rudy forced the question deep into his mind, left the room to find Jezrul, and found him in the launching bay.

Fifty armored and visored troops were clambering into three boats and the door to the sea had been raised. Jezrul was talking to three officers, but broke off the conversation as Rudy approached. "When you return," he said, slapping the men on their backs and shaking hands warmly. "Good hunting."

One loaded boat was already being lowered by elevator pad to the sea. "A quick response," said Rudy.

"I have anticipated Our Lord's wishes. The men were alerted before we spoke to Him." Jezrul waved an arm and the other two boats moved into position, a roar from outside as the first sped out to sea. In two minutes they were alone in the bay and the big door was closing. Jezrul put an around Rudy's shoulders. "They are good men. Your training and discipline has been thorough, Rudy. I congratulate you. Despite your youth, the men respect you, and that is a real accomplishment."

"My appearance is deceiving, since I haven't spent so many days at sea as you, Jezrul. There are only a few years between us."

"Your apprenticeship began early, Rudy. Our Lord saw good things in you even as a boy and that is why you have been closest to Him these many years. He places His very life in your hands, and his choice has been a wise one." Jezrul patted him affectionately on the shoulder.

"Thank you, Jezrul," said Rudy, flattered.

"Let us look in on our guests quickly before returning to Toth. Come with me." They left the bay and walked a long corridor to the staircase. "I am concerned with something, and your close working with Lord Toth makes you the person I must direct a question to. I hope it is a foolish question, but I'm deeply troubled, and my instincts may be wrong."

155

"What is it?"

"Since coming here this time I've detected a kind of lethargy in Our Lord, a fatigue that comes and goes, yet at times he's the man I've known for years. I'm concerned about his health. Is he ill?"

Rudy hesitated, a deep instinct he could not define rising to caution him about a response.

Jezrul looked at him. "When I first arrived today, He seemed exhausted and in pain. You know as I do that His image is a reflection of His true Self: emotions, feelings, mental and physical. It is a fundamental part of our communication interface to His transfigured being. I am First Counselor, and my life belongs to Toth, and right now I—I fear for him."

Rudy's cautioning instinct died at the sight of tears in Jezrul's eyes. "There have been problems," he said.

Jezrul stopped him on the staircase, put hands on his shoulders. "What? Please, tell me!"

"Attacks of some kind, and they're growing more frequent. Pain—it comes and goes, for years now, but since the starship came it is daily, sometimes twice in a day, and severe. It must be stress, and I've been using Beta-Choline continuously now for the past two days. It helps, but the pain is still there. I can see it in his face. Jezrul, I don't know what else to do!"

Jezrul closed his eyes, a tear resting on a cheekbone. "Oh, Dear Toth, Lord of my life, is suffering in silence when I am here to serve Him. Why didn't He tell me?"

Rudy felt tears in his own eyes. "He seems resigned, Jezrul, He feels the hour of his final breath is approaching. This very hour, when you had left us, he said that—that you would lead the people. He said I was to look after you when His hour had come."

Jezrul burst into tears.

He buried his face in Rudy's shoulder, and cried like a little boy.

Rudy put his arms around the bigger man and comforted him, ignoring his own tears.

"How can I do it, how can I take the place of Our Lord? I am only a man with faults, weaknesses. We must do everything to save Him, Rudy, everything!"

Jezrul grasped Rudy by the shoulders, his tear-stained face close. "The hour may come when there will be fighting here. You are first to be protected, Rudy, for Toth's life depends on it. But if something happens to you, what do I do? How do I preserve the life of Our Lord? Show me what to do!"

156

"I will, Jezrul, I will."

"Quickly, then, we'll check on our guests. After that, you will instruct me," Jezrul said breathlessly.

They went to Diego's room first, and found him sleeping, his breathing slow and regular. "He recovers," said Jezrul, closing the door softly.

"What will become of him?"

"He will live out his days right here and away from the people. He can no longer be trusted, but Toth again shows His mercy. Once he was Our Lord's Prime, a man of strength and character who could make the hardest of decisions without hesitation, including the sacrifice of his own family. Did you know that?"

"Yes. Toth has told me."

"For me, he was more than First Counselor. He became my tutor, my mentor when my parents were concerned only with their own lives, and I was a boy not yet old enough for apprenticeship. I revered him. He was like a father to me. His neglect of the people, his breaking of The Law, the yielding to those who would destroy our society, all these were terrible disappointments to me. I stand in his place, yet I grieve for him. He was a good man."

Rudy was moved by the sorrow in Jezrul's voice.

They came to the woman's room, and Jezrul knocked softly three times. No answer, so he opened the door. The woman was in bed, looking fearful, bare arms pulling the covers up to her chin. "Are you comfortable?" said Jezrul.

"Yes," she said. "When can I leave the room again?"

"Perhaps this evening. I'll return for you then, and food and wine is coming for you. Rest yourself in the meantime."

He closed the door, locked it and they started towards the staircase again.

"She doesn't know," said Rudy.

"Know what?"

"She doesn't know she will die when the fighting is over."

"Toth has not condemned her to death," said Jezrul softly.

"He said she's to be eliminated along with the others. All the un-baptized are to be eliminated. Isn't that death?"

"For the entire unbaptized, yes. They are not The Chosen."

"I feel badly about her, she's no threat to us, and she's a scientist, a botanist. She could be useful here."

"I agree," said Jezrul, "but Toth has spoken and I obey his words."

"You will kill her, then. How?"

"The Law forbids me to raise my hand against her, but a sleeping drug in her wine, casting her adrift along the barrier; I will leave her to the appetites of the Charni. She will feel nothing."

"A difficult decision that a First Counselor must make, one I could not make. She seems so innocent."

"Again I agree. She is a pawn used by those who destroyed the village and seek to destroy us. Your logic is strong, Rudy. If she were baptized, Our Lord might feel otherwise about her. Perhaps you could make a plea for her on the basis of her usefulness as a scientist? I would support you, of course, for she has been placed in my care. Would you do this for her?"

"Yes, of course I will, and soon."

"For the good of our world."

"And to continue the work of Our Lord," said Rudy.

"Excellent," said Jezrul, and put a warm hand on his shoulder. "Now, take me below and show me what I must do to preserve Toth's life if anything should prevent you from doing it."

Rudy took Jezrul to Toth's throne room—and showed him everything.

* * * * * * *

Nathan Feld stood at the bow of the speeding boat, and stared fixedly at the sea so the men would not see his own fear. Captain of the lead boat, he had not experienced a single day of combat in his life, and yet here he was, leading fifty men into what could become a war. The third boat had already split off from the other two to make a wide sweep around the south side of the island before joining them at the approximate site of the settlement along the north shore. His first concern was the dead time in their communication while the island was between them. His second was the possibility the visitors had already occupied the island, and were there waiting for them. Laser rifles bristled behind him, but not one had ever been used in battle. The troops were mere boys trained for island defense, and without drill in aggressive tactics. Their leader was no better off, but with one difference. He was aware of his ignorance, and they weren't. In the final hour of his life, Nathan Feld stood at the bow of his charging vessel, the spray in his face, and thought of the command Jezrul had promised him, a command over all the island forces when Jezrul was in control, and Toth, an ancient relic of a man incapable of other than electronic control, was gone forever.

The big island loomed ahead and the two boats sped towards it in echelon formation, crossing the snaking barrier with the great transponder below the hull sending forth The Pleasures to the Charni, and lulling them to listlessness. No sails were in sight in any direction, and Nathan had reason for hope. Alone, the islanders could offer little if any resistance against their weapons. He'd seen them from afar, a ragged lot on the edge of survival. He would place his forces in the trees above the beach coming into view and catch the visitors while they were still in the barrier. What his laser fire didn't do the Charni would quickly finish.

Several people were on the beach, and they ran for the trees in fear. "Straight in!" he shouted, "right up on the beach!" His men readied their weapons, pulled their visors down as they came within a hundred meters of the sand at full speed.

Flame belched from the trees in a dozen places, concentrated laser fire coming from a gully running back from the beach. The roar reached Nathan's ears as the armor-piercing projectile of an M-34 assault rifle struck him in the chest and exploded his heart, and all around him were the screams of dying men.

CHAPTER SEVENTEEN

Michael and Derald talked for two hours that first day on the island. Osen sat quietly, radio protruding from one ear. Eves left after a few minutes, and returned with three plates of food: small potatoes and a thin slab of Lonia meat, sweet and rich. Derald told the details of their expulsion from the mainland: growing disbelief in a leader who appeared only as a hologram, strict rule of the counselors, rigid laws against technological advancement, and the people facing a future of menial labor. Derald was an inventor and tinkerer, and he knew how to read, a skill discouraged by Toth for all except the counselors who received their education in the sanctuary under close supervision. Derald had taught Diego how to read at age four, and by the time the boy was twelve and beginning his apprenticeship his knowledge of nature, the stars and technology had been far beyond that of the adult counselors. He had been a bright, ambitious boy, quickly coming to the attention of Toth.

Diego had served four years in the new sanctuary of Toth before he was eighteen, and when he returned home at age twenty one he was a changed man: strong minded, decisive, a zealot in enforcing The Law, a young person who had faced Toth and been chosen as His right hand. The Law would be enforced. It would be obeyed. The previous First Counselor had disappeared the night before Diego's return.

All dissenters were expelled within the month, including his own parents, but even in this first, decisive act Diego had broken The Law. He had disobeyed Toth by providing the means of safe passage through the barrier. For this, Derald had long ago forgiven his son's ambition and sought only to create a new society on the island, a society without The Law, without Toth.

"When we first arrived I thought we would soon perish. There was nothing here but trees and rocks, but the island is rich in natural resources, and we quickly discovered the shellfish that cover the rocks in shallow water along every shore. I will show you if you have the time."

"We have to reach Toth's island as quickly as possible. One of our people is there, and perhaps your own son," said Michael.

"Yes, of course, but if you simply rush in on the huge rock that is his sanctuary you will be obliterated in the water. In fear of our own safety we have watched the comings and goings of his people for many years and we know of an entrance. I can show you the location and give you routes that avoid the meanderings of the barrier. There's a narrow channel that guides a transponder signal to either calm or enrage the Charni. It is an adaptation of the transmitter used in a counselor's staff, like this."

Derald picked up a metal box smaller than his fist, and opened it. He showed Michael the small stack of circuit boards and chips. "It's a simple transmitter, highly amplified, with a single loop antenna in the tip of the staff. It resonates with a receiver placed in all of Toth's baptized near birth."

"At the base of the neck," said Michael. "I've seen a biochip used for the baptisms."

"It attaches itself to the spine in hours," said Derald, "even minutes, for a newly-born child. There are two frequencies, one for pleasure, and one for pain. We have forbidden both practices here by our own baptism of those baptized in Toth."

"How?"

"The chip itself is not deep, though the conducting tendrils that attach to the spine must never be disturbed. We expose the chip itself, and destroy it by the application of a single burning ember from a wood fire. It is quite vulnerable to such heat. The operation itself is quite simple, and was our first symbolic act of separation from Toth."

"He must know you've survived," said Michael. "Why hasn't he occupied this island?"

"We were no threat to him. Why bother? Now, I'm not so sure. His boats appear regularly. They're watching us."

"I have special glasses that can see heat. There is a great plume of heat over this island and it can be seen from the mainland. Toth must also be able to see this, and it's a signature one expects to see when heavy industry is present. If I were Toth, I would want to see what you're up to."

"I will show you," said Derald. "There *is* industry here, but most of what he sees is geological in origin. There is great power beneath this island, Major Queal, and we have taken advantage of it.

Please, let me show you, and then we will talk about a plan for you to reach Toth. His island is only a few sailing hours east of here."

"We could use the time, Major," said Osen. "Remember that Nik thought he heard something from *Belsus*. We might get a flyer down here yet."

"Okay," said Michael, "we'll take a quick tour, but I want Krisha to have her people on full alert."

"On it, sir," said Osen, and he left the room before Michael could reply.

Derald showed him the designs and models representing only a part of his forty-year life on the island. There was the little glass diving boat used to harvest the Lonia, and a large boat with multiple glass cabins that would take them far out to sea. Michael picked up the models, fingered the metal parts. "Is this steel?"

"Iron," said Derald. "There is rich ore on the southern slopes, but the mining has been by hand, and our production is limited. There's much coal here near the summits, and pure veins of it set afire by natural causes in ancient times. These have aided us in our smelting operations, and also in the manufacture of glass. I can show you some of this today if we leave now."

Derald led him up a steep, narrow trail along the edge of the canyon. Below them a wider path was laced with parallel logs and periodic wooden structures housing heavy block and tackle for moving heavy loads down to the settlement. Whiffs of sulfur came to them and as the wind shifted Michael could feel blasts of hot air coming down from the mountains. Derald climbed slowly, but steadily, Michael huffing and puffing to keep up with him until they suddenly stopped. "Listen," said Derald. "You can hear the fires."

A low, steady roar came down from the rocky peaks above and west of them, like the sound of a gas furnace. The air was now foul with the smell of sulfur, and something sharper. They moved on, around a cornice, and ahead the trail steepened. A slope there sparkled in sunlight, green, red and yellow, two thick iron cables appearing from a black maw in rock and descending towards the southern shore of the island. One cable moved, vibrated, and a wooden crate appeared, attached to the cable, rising to the maw where two men now stood. They grabbed the crate, slid it into darkness and a moment later another crate appeared, moving downwards on the second cable. "We use sand from the northern beaches because it is purer there, and finer. Our artisans have become quite particular about this. Would you like to rest here? The last climb is steep."

"I can use a break," said Michael, gasping. The old man wasn't even breathing hard. *He must be ninety and I can't keep up with him. How am I going to fight a war?* They rested a moment near the summits, and to the south Michael could see the edge of the ocean separating the island from the great southern continent a thousand miles away. He pointed and said; "There's a huge body of land far out to sea. We saw it from our ship."

"Someday we'll go there," said Derald. "We have only begun to settle this planet, Major Queal, but we will do it in time if all constraints are removed from us. If Toth moves on this island, it will have to be sooner. That model I showed you, the big boat? It is no longer a model; the full-scale version is nearly completed and is hidden in a bay a little west of us on the southern shore. It will carry forty people, and the supplies they need for a long crossing."

"You would take that chance?"

"If we must. We will never again live under Toth's rule, that much is certain. We will die first. Are you rested now?"

"Yes." Michael smiled wanly and they made a final climb up a scree-covered trail to the opening in the rock from which hot air was streaming. Michael coughed at the smell of it. "It will be better inside. The tunnel here acts as a vent for the fumes," said Derald.

The roar was loud and steady, the tunnel dimly lit by an intense light ahead. A crate passed them, heading down the mountain, followed by two sweating men with shovels. They nodded to Derald, looked curiously at Michael and went their way.

When they came out of the tunnel it was as if they had entered a blast furnace. Swirling heat rushed towards them from a terraced pit, five levels carved from rock, and on the bottom of the pit lay a treasure of glass in neat stacks. Carts were being filled, and moved into three tunnels heading north and south, slabs of every color, globes, drinking glasses, huge torpedo shapes of blown, clear material, dinnerware of all kinds. On the second level a stone slab was pushed aside, fierce light spilling from a fiery interior from which workers using long tongs withdrew iron drawers filled with molten material, and poured it into molds. Others with long tubes withdrew smaller samples. The men blew into the tubes, and before Michael's eyes globes and finely shaped goblets of colorful glass were born.

"These are the burning coal veins," said Derald. We've closed them off except for three places on each level, and added drafts from the outside so we can control the heat. There is more, two other caverns such as this, but further west. It is there we process our metal ores, mostly iron, but some lead and even copper, which appears in pure form here. The copper has been most difficult for us to process.

163

There is also some fine quartz west of here, large crystals that I have been experimenting with. They produce small amounts of electricity when put under pressure, but so far I've found no practical use for them."

Michael was clearly awed. "You dug this out by hand?"

"It was a natural cavern, but we removed a lot of rock and dirt to make room for temporary storage, and then there were the tunnels to dig. It was a labor of twelve years."

"This glass you make here would be priceless on many planets, even Arkon, the federation capital."

"We make what we need," said Derald, "but there is a surplus growing and our artisans in recent years have been producing some wonderful things you might find interesting. Their shop is back in the canyon, near mine. We passed it on the way up. You are our first contact with other worlds, Major Queal. I would be glad to show you what they're doing."

"Yes, of course. The products I see here would be valuable trade goods for other planets if we could arrange it."

Derald laughed. "We have been on this planet three centuries and you are the first to visit us. I think such trade would be a very slow process, even if Toth would allow it, which he won't. He has attacked your ship and he will attack any other that comes here."

"I intend to deal with that," said Michael, "and once his dictatorship is ended we can arrange regular arrival of merchant ships within a few years. They follow our survey ships wherever they go and there is certainly one not far from here now. It is only one jump between here and Brown's Planet and once the flow starts, say in five years, the trade can be regular. Anything you want, Derald: produce, high technology—"

"—Heavy machinery and electrical generators?" said Derald.

"Anything."

"This other planet you say is one 'jump' away?"

Michael smiled. "I'll explain it later. What is that sharp odor?"

"The coal," said Derald. "It has high sulfur content."

"It makes me dizzy."

"That and the heat. The men work here in three-hour shifts twice a day. It is a hard, but fulfilling life for them. I think a few minutes have been enough for you, Major Queal. Let's go outside again, and breathe some fresh air."

Michael did not object, and they went back through the tunnel as two workmen wrestled still another crate of sand inside. He sucked in cool air near the tunnel entrance, his clothing soaked with perspiration. Below him the cliffs were covered with a rainbow of color, broken slag from the glass works. "We could have ridden a cart down to the village through the north tunnel, but then we would have to climb again. You'll find it easier going down."

Michael laughed. "I think you're in the same shape I was in when I was a thirty-year-old combat marine, Derald. How old are you?"

"I am eighty-five," said Derald, "I've made this climb every day for the last thirty years. That is the difference between us. Now, let me show you the artisans' shop before we talk further about Toth. I think you have good intentions, but you underestimate his power, and what you wish to do can cost your life and the lives of many others unless you plan carefully. Even then, I have doubts about your success, but your thoughts about trade with other worlds are very appealing to me. We will do what we can to help you."

"That's a good start," said Michael, "and we will do what we can to rid you of Toth."

He followed Derald back down the trail. *An easy promise to make, but Derald is right. How am I going to go up against laser cannon in a bunch of wooden sailboats?* The sun was now low in the west and the cliffs were turning orange. Derald spoke over his shoulder, his feet moving without the guidance of sight over a trail walked for many years. "In four days I could show you the entire island: our potato farms on the eastern point, the magma lake in a high-vaulted cavern in the western mountains. There are hot springs on that end of the island and they feed our Lonia beds to produce some extraordinarily large animals. We cultivate them there."

"That's where we saw the little glass boat?" Michael grimaced. His breath came easy, but now his knees were complaining about the downhill walk.

"The crawler, yes. It is all-mechanical, peddled from inside, and a hand-driven pump to pressurize the floaters. I've designed an alcohol motor, but our metals are too soft, and corrode quickly in the sea air. Good metals are another thing we would be happy to have."

He sees the benefits we can provide. He's thinking about the possibilities.

"You can trade with the mainlanders too, Derald. They have many foodstuffs you don't have here."

"Not while Toth is around," said Derald.

They reached the artisans' shop in half an hour of painful walking for Michael, and Derald introduced him to Chelli Fyhrie and Ardie Hoal, the two master craftsmen who supervised the several apprentices working there, and did all the designing and composition

165

work. They were cleaning up the shop when Derald and Michael arrived, but were proud to show their wares: multiple-paned windows and table-tops in every color, food containers, glassware, plates that could only be described as exquisite on any planet, even eating implements out of clear, heavy glass. They lectured him on the additives used for each color, techniques learned over two dozen years, and were flattered by the obvious delight he had in seeing everything they showed him. For those few moments, Michael was able to forget the danger he would encounter in the next few days, the possibility of his own death, as he handled the beautiful things they had created.

It was growing dark in the canyon, and there were no lights in the shop, so their visit was cut short. They walked down to the settlement, where odors of cooking shellfish filled the air. Few people were visible, the amphitheatre empty except for Osen and Krisha, who stood waiting for them. Michael introduced them to Derald, and told about the marvelous things he'd seen. This obviously pleased the old man, but both Osen and Krisha remained stony-faced, and shifted nervously from one foot to another. Finally, Osen said, "Major, can we have a word with you in private?"

Derald was gracious. "I take my meals in the house with the red windows," he said, pointing. "When you're finished, I would be pleased if the three of you would join me there and we will talk about your plans."

"Thank you, Derald," said Michael, and the old man walked away from them.

"What's up?"

"Funny message from Nik, sir. He was on the radio for five seconds and didn't even wait for a reply. He has to know I'm on the radio all the time."

"This seems to be true. What did he say?"

"Just this, sir: 'Tell Mike that mother is concerned, and sends her greetings. Listen quietly.' I started to acknowledge, but he was gone."

"Mother? The ship?"

"Could be, but he doesn't want us transmitting anything for now."

"Okay, but keep the plug in your ear. Krisha, how're we doing for security?"

"Everyone's in place, sir, all along the shore with crossfire over the beach. The rocks give us a lot of good cover. Where is Toth, sir?"

"To the east of us a few hours, a small island from what I've heard. Derald is aware of one entrance to it; these people have been watching the place for years."

"Will they help us, sir? We have to get a move on."

"They'll do what they can, Krisha; I haven't seen anything that will help much, but they know the island and the placement of the barrier, and that's important to us. We'll still have to attack the place in boats."

"Not good, sir, not with those laser weapons. God, if we just had one flyer to take those things out!"

"How long can we wait, Major?" said Osen. "If Nik is right, and *Belsus* is still up there, we could get one or both of the Gulls down here for the attack."

"We move within forty eight hours. If Toth discovers we're here he'll hit the mainland and isolate us out here. That would be the best time to make our move, when his forces are divided. If he's using standard optical scanners we might get in close at night, without sails, and jump him before dawn. Derald will give us the details on the island, so let's have a talk with him. Anything you need, Krisha?"

Krisha smiled wryly. "I have thirty people in the rocks, our ammo is limited, the laser rifles are maybe half-charged and a third of those people have never fired in combat. Other than that, sir, everything's fine."

Michael laughed, and slapped her on the shoulder. "I hear you, Captain, now let's go eat."

Derald met them at the doorway and ushered them inside where three coal lamps were burning, and painted the interior in dull red. He introduced them to Adah and Sabine Agbayekhai, perhaps in their seventies, two old friends with whom he took his meals. They had lost a son and daughter in the crossing forty years earlier, he explained, and welcomed those who might rid them of Toth. They remembered Davos as a young man and had had a nice visit with him earlier in the day, but Davos was standing guard with his son and would not be joining them.

They sat on iron-grill benches around a table with a top of glass in panes of red and green and Sabine served them slabs of Lonia and new potatoes and smaller shellfish that had been steamed to be eaten right out of the shell. This they washed down with highly mineralized water from the springs in the west and tiny glasses of *Fiero*, a potent brew that Derald explained was nearly pure potato alcohol with a few herb additives. Before the evening was over their heads were buzzing, even though they had sipped slowly.

When the meal was over Adah and Sabine excused themselves, and Derald brought forth a thin wooden sheet and a crayon cut from coal, saw their curious looks and said; "It is bark from the softwood trees here, boiled and then pressed. Now, let me show you where we are and where you plan to go."

He drew a map on the bark: the mainland, the island, a smaller island east like a small mountain rising from the sea, a dark line coming from it to run a meandering course west to just beyond the western tip of the big island. "This is the barrier, a channel perhaps a hundred meters deep. We have seen it from the edge in our crawler. Both the Charni and Yellowfin run deep there for food, but Toth has a device that sends vibrations through the water to calm or excite the fish. When excited, the Yellowfin rise from the deep and the Charni follow. Some even leave the barrier if the water is turbulent, usually during a storm, but not on calm days. You can reach Toth by staying south of the barrier all the way. It is a giant rock and his fortress is inside it. The one entrance we know of is here, on the east side. We have seen his boats enter there, a door that looks like rock but is metal. You must go in there."

"Where are the big weapons?" asked Michael.

"We haven't seen them. So far our boats have been left alone. I would put big weapons at the top of the rock where coverage of the sea and sky is greatest. They could be anywhere, on any side, I don't know. But if you get inside their big weapons will be useless. Your vulnerability will be on the approach."

They talked for two hours, and a plan evolved. A few scattered boats with small crews would sail east from the north and south shores of the big island, rowing in on Toth's stronghold from the west and south under cover of darkness with sails and masts down. The main force would sail from the south shore to a point well east of the stronghold and then charge in to blow the entrance on the east side. There was no easy way. Many casualties were expected. They would make their move in only twenty-eight hours.

Adah and Sabine graciously offered Michael a spare bed for the night, while Osen and Krisha returned to the little band of defenders hunkered down in the rocks above the beach. Michael went to bed with an M-34 within reach, and quickly fell asleep, but sometime in early morning he awoke from a dream, sweating. He was in the forward observation bubble of a Gull and below him a mountain rose from the sea. As he flew over it the top of the mountain opened up and laser beams probed to greet him, a gigawatt of optical power coming straight up between his legs as the Gull roared in evasive maneuver. Awake, he still heard the roar, but decided after a moment that it was only the faint sound of burning coal veins high in the mountains, and then he went back to sleep again.

* * * * * * *

Michael awoke well after sunrise, and his legs were stiff and sore from the previous day's climb. Adah, age seventy two, had already left for the day, riding a cart up a steep tunnel in the west to put in a four hour shift in the iron smelter Michael had not yet seen. Everyone, regardless of age, worked hard on the island. It was the reason they had survived.

Sabine served him a breakfast of potato cakes and water, then took her digging stick and headed towards the beach in search of small mollusks that supplemented their diet. Derald had arisen before dawn, and was in his shop. He'd asked that Michael join him there, said Sabine.

Michael walked to the rocks above the beach where Krisha had placed her little force of marines and villagers, and he found them all awake and alert in dugouts from which they peered out to sea between massive boulders. Osen and Krisha were together in one hole, with assault rifles, Osen plugged into his radio. "Any sleep last night?" asked Michael.

"A little," said Krisha, looking like it had been very little, if any. "Did you hear anything last night?"

"No. I slept pretty sound."

"We thought we did, early this morning, a low rumbling sound and then it was gone. Didn't see anything, but it was pitch black out there."

"Anything from Nik?"

"Nothing," said Osen. "We're ready when you are, sir. Some of the people were up before dawn to pick up boats from the south side. They're bringing them around late this morning. Looks like we'll have ten boats to work with."

"Load three and make sure the masts can come down. The rest of the boats will be diversionary. Krisha, keep everyone in place until we're ready to sail. Toth might sit out there and wait for us, or he might try to hit us here first. Have you seen any boats at sea?"

"Nothing, sir."

"Okay, I'll be with Derald until mid-afternoon. If Nik calls, I'd like to hear about it. I don't know about you, but I've the feeling *Belsus* is still up there and we might be getting some backup soon. Let me know."

169

Michael made the climb to Derald's shop again, and found him at his cluttered table scribbling on a piece of bark. "How are you feeling today?" said the old man. "The trail we were on yesterday continues around the mountain to our foundry. Would you like to see it?"

"I need to be back with my people by mid-afternoon," said Michael.

"There is time, then, and I can show you the large vessel we've nearly finished. The walk is flat just beyond where we stopped yesterday."

"That's good news," said Michael, smiling.

They made the steep, tedious climb again, more slowly this time, yet it seemed they climbed faster than the day before, and the slag-covered cliff was soon before them. They passed the entrance to the burning coal veins and made a precarious traverse along the cliff, the faint trail wandering crookedly through skree and past small trees clinging tenaciously to cracks in the rock. Up to their right a ruby-red peak thrust up at the center of the island. "The mines are up there, in a bowl-shaped depression below the peak. Fortunately for us, the ore is very rich, and there are also black nodules that are nearly pure metal, mostly iron, but some lead."

It was another hour before they reached the foundry, a second cavern with still another burning coal vein where men were tempering cast implements and rods of iron. In the floor of the cavern were large shafts going down to a magma lake where crushed ore was melted repeatedly in large pumice pots and brought up to skim off impurities, producing a low-grade iron that served their purposes. The heat was incredible. The men walked the floor with slabs of pumice tied to their feet, and retired every few minutes to cool themselves in two short tunnels leading to natural balconies on the cliff face. "The work is slow," said Derald, "and we must make things over and over again. The sea air is very corrosive. I've tried several coatings with little success. This is something else we need."

They remained there only a few minutes. Derald took him outside, and pointed down to a bay surrounded by trees, where a huge platform of woven iron with four enormous pontoons of glass lay hidden, visible only from above. "There it is," said Derald. "It is a square twenty meters on a side. Now we work on the life modules, large versions of what you saw on the crawler. The masts are wooden, and there will be three sails. It has taken us seven years to get this far."

Michael sighed. Another sailboat, only bigger and heavier. These people had indeed come far in only forty years, but their technology remained simple. Derald seemed to sense his mood. "You see why I said there is little we can offer to help you fight Toth?"

"You've offered boats and people, Derald. I am very grateful for that. My hope is that we will succeed for you, as well as for ourselves."

Derald smiled and began to walk back on the trail, and stopped when he realized Michael wasn't following. Instead, he was standing there, shielding his eyes with one hand to block sunlight, looking out to sea. A boat was there, moving very fast towards the west, getting closer to shore and producing a considerable wake stretching far behind it. Derald followed his gaze. "It's one of Toth's boats," he said. "They're usually further out than this one."

Michael cursed himself silently for leaving his night glasses behind, but the boat was coming in fast, turning about two hundred meters out to run a parallel course along the shore. He could see the boat was filled with men. Light reflected from the visors pulled down over their faces. All were armed. "I don't like the looks of this. I don't like it at all. We've got to get back to the beach, and quick!"

They hurried back along the trail as the boat sped west. They shouted ahead: "A boat from Toth is close to the island, coming around from the west end! Stay inside!" Men were shouting ahead of them as they passed the slag dump and came around the cornice at canyon's edge where they had a clear view of the sea north of them. Two more boats were charging in from the east, white wakes trailing. "Invasion! They're coming in from west and east!" shouted Michael, and he heard his warning being relayed down the canyon. Helpless, he could only scramble as quickly as he could down the slippery, skree-covered trail as the boats drew closer and closer to shore, passing from his view behind trees.

He was past Derald's shop and halfway down the canyon when the roar of assault rifle fire struck his ears, a continuous thing that went on and on. An explosion, then another, grenades launched from rifles and when he reached the amphitheatre he could see streams of laser fire heading out to sea from the gully leading to the beach. Derald ran for a house. Michael ducked low, and rushed to the rocks where he'd seen Osen and Krisha. Both were firing, Osen screamed into the radio; "Nik, we're under attack! Under attack! Come in!"

A smoking pontoon boat lay only forty meters from the beach, engine growling. Bodies were draped over railings, and floating in the water. The second boat had turned, and was fleeing east, fire being directed at the third boat that had come in from the west and was now two hundred meters from shore. It dodged the geysers of water caused by grenades exploding near it. Tracers found the target, laser beams as well, but the boat kept going at high speed, chasing its surviving companion.

A cheer broke out among the marines and villagers at the shore. They shook their weapons at the fleeing invaders and hugged each other in victory. "They're getting away!" screamed Osen into the radio. "Two boats, heading east! The only thing out there. East of us, Nik, hurry!"

So what can Nik do about it? thought Michael, but then he looked out to sea and saw something that made his heart soar, the sight of a dark, flat shape moving towards them at incredible speed, meters above the sea. Tornados of water churned up from the vortices at the tips of droopy wings. It was a Gull, a flyer from *Belsus*. It turned east sharply as the marines screamed hysterically; "Get 'em, get 'em, get 'em!" They heard the roar of the engines, the crackle of a Gatling gun in the nose of the Gull, and then a tremendous explosion as an orange ball of fire rose from the sea. The Gull turned south, passed behind the island and instants later rushed straight over them, angling in for another kill. Cheering was drowned by the roar of the engines, and then suddenly stopped.

From the east came a flash of light like an exploding sun, and the wings of the Gull were sheared off, smoking and in flames. The pilot struggled for control, dropping near the water and somehow turning, lifting thrusters whining as another blast tore off a tail section. Nearly on the water, the crippled Gull came in slowly, smoke pouring from it, and plopped gently into the waves only meters beyond the anchored boats of the settlement. There it floated as a hatch popped open, white smoke gushing forth, the sound of men yelling and the smoke dissipating to a trickle. "All of you down to the water!" yelled Michael. "Get them out of there!"

Marines and villagers dropped their weapons and ran, splashing into the water and swimming as a figure emerged from the hatch and climbed three metal rungs down to stand on what little remained of the Gull's port wing. He was covered with soot and white foam from a fire extinguisher, but he grinned and gave the splashing rescuers a thumbs' up.

The man was Floyd Mootry.

CHAPTER EIGHTEEN

Jezrul was satisfied that Rudy Hoffman would not be an obstacle once Toth was dead. Toth himself had designated the future leader of the people, and Rudy was probably the only man left who maintained true loyalty to His Lord. He would obey the words of Toth as he would obey the command of a God. Once Toth was gone, Jezrul's position would be secure. It was only a question of timing, whether to wait or act soon. A battle was coming, a battle that could destroy all his plans. Quick decisions would have to be made without discussion with or groveling before the optical image of a man degenerating before their eyes, a man old beyond old who hid whatever remained of His true self behind panels in the throne room below.

Jezrul thought these things as he sat in lotus position on a boulder by the large pool in Toth's garden. He was lulled by the sound of the waterfall, yet aware of the few counselors watching him there. Even now they saw him as leader, and he would play the part, decisive, firm, a man of deep spirituality who took the time for quiet, thoughtful meditation. Rudy would arrive soon, and then the audience with Toth when he would plead the case for Kari. Regardless of Toth's decision he would have that woman, if only for a short time, baptize her, show her The Pleasures—The Pain. Especially the pain. The very thought of it made him tremble.

Rudy was late. He had gone to the gun crews and their scanners for an up-date on the big island where their troops should now be landing. So why the delay? Surely there would be no resistance, no armed response on the part of the islanders. They were primitives hanging on to barest survival.

His legs were cramped. He opened his eyes and stood up, folded his hands reverently together and walked the garden trail with growing impatience. Finally, he could stand it no longer, climbed the steps to the platform above the fishpond, and made his exit from the garden. He walked the curving passage towards the staircase, and suddenly stopped.

The lights had dimmed to near darkness and were now bright again. Again it happened. Lights flickered back to brightness as power returned. He knew the cause of such a power variation, had seen it before on the days of battle practice.

The laser cannon had just been fired—twice.

Jezrul ran. He took the stairs three at a time up the closed staircase, threw open a metal door to hear screaming and cheering coming from the gun crews. The smell of ozone was heavy in the air. The great domed turret was rotating as the gunners swept the sea in their sights, but there was no more firing. Rudy ran towards him, breathless and smiling. "We just shot down a landing vessel from the starship, hit it twice and watched it go down in flames! It came out of nowhere, Jezrul; it must have come in close to the sea! There was an explosion, and a ball of fire. The ship appeared suddenly, coming up from the sea and circling the island a few hundred meters up, and the crews locked on it instantly, firing as it was coming down again! We destroyed it, Jezrul! There's no way Queal can get his people back to the ship!"

The gun crews cheered when they saw Jezrul, and he shook a fist at them in victory, and then grabbed Rudy by his robe and pulled him close, scowling. "Have you forgotten there were *two* landing craft when they first arrived? Where is the other one? You celebrate a victory and forget that seeing even one means their starship has somehow survived our attack! It's *still* up there, with weaponry that can vaporize this island, and our fire has given them a target!"

"We've seen *nothing*, Jezrul!" said Rudy, his smile fading. "The ship isn't *up* there, I tell you. The attacking vessel was after our boats, I'm sure of it. That fireball we saw before we opened fire, I—I think it was one of our boats. We *had* to fire!"

Jezrul relaxed his grip. "All right, then, that much was correct, and I applaud it. I applaud the accuracy of your crews, but calm them *down*! Get them on the scanners and sweep the sky. If something moves up there, shoot it, and keep watch on the island for any other aircraft. Do it *now*!" He released him, and Rudy scrambled up to the gun decks, shouting orders until the cheering had stopped, and all men were back at their posts. Jezrul climbed up behind him, went to a screen showing an optical observation of the island, highly magnified. The first thing he saw was a column of black smoke curling up where the island met the sea. The second thing he saw was a boat heading towards them at high speed, skimming the waves with a load of armed men. His men. One boat.

Jezrul swallowed hard. "Hold your fire towards the sea, but search the skies! Our men are returning!"

Rudy looked at him in dismay, and scrambled down the ladder behind him.

They sprinted to the boat bay and the two remaining boats there, one of them filled with visored troops he had kept in readiness. "Open the door!" Jezrul shouted. "One of our boats is coming in!"

"One?" said Rudy. "ONLY ONE?"

"Quiet!" growled Jezrul, and Rudy recoiled from him.

They heard the boat slow outside, the clang as it locked onto the lifting platform and then it appeared before the door, sliding towards them. The men looked grim, and clung to their weapons. There were several holes drilled neatly amidships, two of them scorched. Renz Haegele leaped from the bow before the boat had docked, and came to Jezrul, who took him by the arm while giving an order to Rudy. "I want silence in the bay. No talking among the men." He took the boat commander aside as the bay door clanged shut, and talked to him in a near whisper.

"What happened out there? Where are the others?"

"Gone," said Renz, wiping his brow. "All gone, and I thought we were gone, too. When that aircraft came in for a second pass we were the target. I thought—"

"It's shot down, Renz, destroyed. It got the others?"

"One boat, with Shaun commanding. They'd come around the island, and were behind us. They went up in a single explosion, pieces coming down around us. I didn't know projectile weapons could do that, but the firing rate was incredible."

"What about Nathan's boat?"

"They hit us close to shore, projectiles and laser fire all along the rocks. His boat was nearly on the beach when they opened up. They focused on that first boat, Jezrul, and shot it to pieces in seconds! Why didn't we know the islanders had such defenses? I got out of there instantly; we wouldn't have had a chance!"

"Don't be a fool, Renz. Queal has managed to move all his forces to the island, and he was waiting for you. The error is mine in underestimating his quickness, but in doing so he has left the mainland unguarded, and we'll take advantage of that. His next move will be to come here, and then it will be his turn to become an easy target at sea. There are several strategies, and he might come in from any number of directions, but there will be things other than laser cannon awaiting him. I want a circle of boats surrounding this island, Renz, boats filled with villagers he left behind. If I know this man as I think I do he is more a diplomat than a soldier. He will not readily kill the villagers to get at us."

"You want us to go out again, to invade the mainland?" said Renz, looking horrified.

"Immediately. Two boats and you'll have an hour to reach the village and occupy it. With the firepower you described, Queal must have left only a few soldiers in the village. They cannot stand up to fifty if you have courage, Renz. If you don't have it I will send someone else. Loy, perhaps. He would happily lead if given the chance."

It was as if Renz had been slapped. "So, he's been talking to you, as I've been told. He's all thought and no action and the men see him as a boy. No, First Counselor, I will lead the attack on the village."

"Words I expected you to say, Renz. You'll come in from the southeast, close to shore. They can't see you until you're right at the beach. Kill whomever you have to, take women and children and tow them back here in at least six boats, skiffs, whatever you can find. I want to see a ring of hostages around this island by morning, because I think Queal must now make his next move quickly."

"The men are still shocked by what they've seen today," said Renz.

"You will convince them Queal's full force is on the island and the villagers are helpless. Keep their minds on the urgency of their action, the speed with which they must perform this task. Fire them up; remind them of their comrades! This is vengeance! Anything that resists, they kill! Lead them, Renz! Ptak's troops are loaded and ready. Bring him to me."

Renz walked past Rudy to reach the other boat where Kyle Ptak watched silently over his men. Rudy started to follow them coming back, but Jezrul waved him off curtly, and so the man stood sullenly watching a few meters from them while Ptak was briefed on the plan. The two commanders ran to their boats, both shouting for the door to be opened, and Renz's boat was already moving when Rudy rushed up to Jezrul.

"What's going on? You're sending them out again?"

"Yes."

"But where? Queal might attack by nightfall! We need our troops *here!*"

"Queal will not attack so quickly. He has an aircraft down, and there might be survivors, and he will now have renewed hope about his starship. There might be reinforcements coming, and we need all the advantage we can get. I'm sending these boats to take hostages on the mainland. They will be a shield against air attack and the starship will have to consider carefully before firing on us."

Rudy's face turned red. "The occupation of the village was to be later. Toth will not approve this action!"

"I'm not asking for his approval," said Jezrul, and before Rudy could react he seized the man by the throat, and pulled his face close. "There is no time for approval, no time for discussions in between fits or whatever he is suffering from, and no time for references to The Law or what plans He has for the future. I am First Counselor, and I deal with the present, which is this: the starship is alive because you did not kill it, a landing vessel has arrived, heavily armed, and the gun crews have prevented a catastrophe for you. This is only for the moment, since other vessels may be on their way. You see nothing in the skies? Of course not, the starship hides in orbit out of our view, its landing craft coming in low from the west where you can't see *them* either. There could be one, two, or several them. I will try to determine this from the woman, but truth from her is uncertain. Queal is on the island with his major force, hoping for reinforcement. We could be up against attack from air, sea and orbit within a day. Do you think our weapons can defend against this? Do you really *think* it?"

"I will defend Lord Toth to my death," said Rudy, struggling to breathe.

Jezrul squeezed harder. "In the next days we might all die in His defense. Does that make you wise? And is it wise to burden Our Lord with the bad news from the island when he is so seriously ill? Have you thought of that, Rudy? *Have you?* You could kill him, but I won't allow it! I will kill you by my own hand if necessary, unless you remain silent about this. I am responsible only to My Lord, and when the hostages are in place He will be informed, but only then. I will not allow Him to be without hope, even if I risk His displeasure over my decision. *My* decision, Rudy, I take full responsibility for it!"

Rudy relaxed and Jezrul eased the pressure on his throat. "He will ask about what has happened on the island. What can we tell Him?"

"A half-truth that will force his decision to invade the village. I will not mention the landing craft we shot down because the implications are too negative and are only speculations on our part. We are preparing to destroy the invaders at sea, as planned, and that's all He needs to hear. We still haven't seen the star craft, and if it ap-

177

pears again we are prepared to shoot it down. Positive news, Rudy, only positive. Do you understand me?"

"I'm to remain silent."

"No. When I'm finished, you will put forth our case for the woman, and I will support you. We will talk about the future to give Our Lord confidence. You must do this, for if you say anything that gives Toth pain I swear I will destroy you! He is everything to us!"

Rudy's face softened, and he looked away, and Jezrul knew he'd won. The zealous rage, the constant reference to the welfare of Toth had worked—for the moment. But Jezrul made another decision in that instant, sensing distrust. When Toth was gone, Rudy Hoffman would be gone with His Lord to whatever fate lay beyond death.

"I will do as you say," said Rudy. "I do it for Toth's safety."

"Your reason is mine. Thank you. Before we see Toth I must speak with the woman. Come with me."

While they had spoken the troop-laden boats had left and the door to the sea was now closed. They left the bay and went up the stairs to the woman's room where Jezrul knocked three times before unlocking the door. She was sitting on the bed, dressed in a robe and Rudy was once again struck by her loveliness: small hands folded in her lap, dark eyes looking up submissively and stirring in him a desire to care for her. A gentle person, innocent, unaware that she had been condemned to death.

"Wait here," said Jezrul and so Rudy stood in the doorway. Jezrul sat down beside the woman, but she looked at Rudy, studying him. "He's a friend," said Jezrul, "and very close to Toth. Kari, I only have a moment, so listen carefully. I don't want to give you false hope, but there's a chance your starship has survived, and is hidden in an orbit we can't see from here. Leader Queal has managed to reach an island not far from here, and he will likely attack us within a day or two."

Rudy saw her eyes widen and a flicker of a smile.

"If he comes at us from the sea we will almost certainly destroy Queal and all your companions before they even reach us, and this goes beyond everything we believe in. Rudy and I," he gestured towards the doorway, "have been talking, and we have a plan that might avoid all bloodshed, but only if your starship still exists. There are dissenters among our people, those who will not live under The Law, though they are not numerous. Still, they are loud and provocative, and we wish to be rid of them so the rest of our people can remain in peace. Rudy and I meet with Lord Toth in a few minutes, and I wish to propose the following: we propose a truce with Queal, release you and Diego to him, but with the provision that you leave immediately, and take all the dissenters with you at one time. That is perhaps thirty people, in addition to your own supplies and personnel. But it must be done in one trip, Kari. We want no further landings. Can it be done, Kari? How many landing craft are on your star craft?"

Kari looked straight at Rudy. "Yes, it can be done. *Belsus* has four Gulls for planet fall. Each one can carry twenty people. They're also heavily armed, so if *Belsus* is still up there, you're in deep trouble right now."

"So are you if they attack us, Kari, but we don't want that. There has been enough killing, and we want it to stop right here. We'll talk to Toth, and if he agrees we'll contact Queal and do all we can to reach your ship."

"If it's still there," said the woman.

"We've overheard radio conversation that leads us to believe that. Now we meet with Toth, and I'll return later. You must feel closed in by now; we'll take a walk in the gardens, if you like."

"That would be a nice change," she said, voice flat, still looking at Rudy.

"Good," said Jezrul, and he returned to Rudy, smiling as he locked the door again. "Four landing craft," he said.

"Perhaps. She might be lying."

"And spoil a plan to get her away from here? I think not. We go to see Toth, now, and remember what I told you."

"I will," said Rudy, remembering the death threat. *How smoothly you tell lies?*, he thought as they descended the staircase to Toth's throne room and sanctuary. *All that you say is a lie, to the woman, to me, to Our Lord. I should let it destroy you.*

He had seen her eyes as she'd spoken to Jezrul. *You lie so well you don't see it in others.* The woman had said four Gulls. They had seen two, and now Rudy was certain that only one remained.

He worried about that one.

And the audience with Toth did nothing to improve his day.

Toth was exhausted, his illness now progressing at a horrible rate. He appeared before them slumped in the throne, eyes sunken, His breath came in ragged gasps. "There is news?" he asked.

"Good and bad, My Lord," said Jezrul. "Queal has played into our hands. He has landed with full force on the island to the west, and fired on our troops. They wisely turned away with only a few casualties, and have just now returned. Lord, the mainland village has been left unguarded, and now is the best time to strike. Queal

179

will be isolated on the island if we control the mainland. He cannot run away, and will surely be forced to attack us with limited resources. We will destroy him on the water, Lord, if he cannot retreat. I ask that we send our troops to the mainland to occupy it and when Queal's attack begins they will move in behind him to cut off any retreat, then immediately take the island. In one move we will have destroyed the invaders and accomplished other elements of Your Plan."

Toth coughed, and sighed. "Do it, Jezrul, and then return to me. It is you who must preserve our society when I am gone, and there are things we must discuss."

Jezrul dropped to his knees before the throne. "Lord, you will be with us for many years. Rudy and I will see to that. Your Wisdom determines our future, but I am truly thankful for your confidence in me. The men will be on their way to the mainland within the hour. There is another matter, Lord, regarding the woman. Rudy will speak to this. Lord? LORD?"

Toth's head had dropped as if he were dozing. It jerked upwards and Toth sighed again. "Yes?"

"About the woman, Lord. Rudy has a suggestion to make."

Rudy stepped forward, and made his case for Kari: her use as a scientist, her innocence. Jezrul agreed. "It is logical, Lord, and she can atone for the actions of her comrades with a lifetime of service to You."

"She is not baptized, Jezrul. She is alien to us."

"You need only order her baptism, Lord, and I will see to it," said Jezrul. "You have placed her in my care."

Toth shook his head sadly. "I must remain firm on this, Jezrul. She is not one of The Chosen, and can never be. When the fighting is over there will be no aliens left among us, not even one. I trust you to take care of the woman, innocent as she is, in a way as painless as possible. Now, see to the men, and return here. We will talk about your responsibilities."

Jezrul's expression remained calm and passive. "Your Will is mine, Lord Toth. It will be done."

The image of an emaciated old man slumped in the throne flickered, and was gone.

"I'm sorry," said Rudy. "I'd hoped he would change His mind. The hour is near, Jezrul. He's dying."

Rudy went to a panel and increased the flow of Beta Choline to his beloved patient. Jezrul stood at his side, watching. "I can only ease His pain," he said sadly, and Jezrul put a hand on his shoulder.

180

"Your caring loyalty will not be forgotten, Rudy."

Tears flooded Rudy's eyes, and his body shuddered. "Please excuse me," he said, and then put his hands to his face as he turned and started towards the door. Jezrul hesitated one instant, then typed in a quick series of commands on the keyboard, watching with satisfaction as the Beta-Choline sensors showed a decrease in drug flow to a level far below what Rudy had programmed. He left the room to comfort Rudy, and took him to a room for a few moments of seclusion and rest.

Rudy had not slept for over two days and a night, and in moments he was snoring. Jezrul left him there and went to his own room where he retrieved some surgical tools, a syringe and a liquid-encased biochip. He went down the hall to Kari's room and unlocked the door without knocking. She was standing near it, had probably seen him coming, and there was fear in her eyes, a look that made him shiver in anticipation.

"What are those things you're holding?" she said.

"Something that will save your life. Now, take off your robe and lie face down on the bed. Do it!"

She complied, and Jezrul sat down besides her, concentrating hard to control the shaking of his hands. He ran his hands over her back, massaged her neck, and then shot a burst of anesthetic into her at a point just above the top of her spine. Her head was turned towards him as she tried to see what he was doing. "Turn your head the other way!" he ordered. "You've seen this done to a baby; it is painless and will only take a moment. It is necessary, Kari. Toth will have it no other way if you're to stay alive even another day."

Knife in one hand, the other reaching around to feel a breast, he leaned over to whisper in her ear; "Kari, even if you leave us, for a little while you will be one of us—and I will show you The Pleasures."

It was not The Pleasures he was thinking about as he cut into her, and he shivered at the sound of her muffled scream.

CHAPTER NINETEEN

The maw of the Gull opened wide and spit out two inflated rubber boats in a cloud of white smoke. Marines followed in full battle dress with laser rifles and power packs, tumbled into the boats and rowed to shore. One boat picked up Mootry from the remnants of the port wing. Mootry slogged the last few meters to where Osen stood knee-deep in water, smiling. They shook hands, embraced as Michael watched in bewilderment from the shore. "How you doin', boy? Taking care of the old man? Hi, Mike!"

Michael waved. "We'd just about given up on you, Floyd. Didn't see much to assure us you were still up there."

"We nearly weren't," said Mootry. He walked up to Michael, pumped his hand, and looked out at the crippled Gull. "Sure did a number on the lander. We're lucky to be alive. The battery must be right at the horizon, otherwise I don't see how they could have spotted us only a hundred meters up. Heavy laser cannon out there, Mike. Were you actually going after them in boats?"

"That's still the plan, with the Gull all shot up. Our hopes for air cover are still smoking out there."

"Fire's out," said Mootry. "Voltage surges when the wings were blown off, but the lifters weren't affected, thank God. I don't know *how* Muesl brought her in without any control surfaces, but he did. Thruster's okay, but she's a ruptured duck at this point."

The marines were coming to shore in relays, twenty-five men with rifles and field packs. A crowd had come down to the beach, marines exchanging obscenities, embracing. Krisha arrived and saluted smartly. "Colonel," she said, "glad you made it in, sir. We sure could have used that Gull."

"Captain," said Floyd, grinning. "Had yourself a little firefight?"

"Yes, sir, and we shot 'em up pretty good—with your help, sir."

"We'll get at them again. Gull Two is at your camp on the mainland. We were doing fine low to the water, but when we came in at two hundred meters those lasers out there opened up on us. I don't think they can see the beach from there. Where's the radio, Osen?"

"Right here, sir," said Osen, pulling it from his ear.

Floyd took it and called Nik, warning the other Gull to stay below thirty meters on any sortie it was called upon to fly, and to sit tight for the moment. He clicked off.

"Whoever fired at you might hear that," said Michael.

"I don't care," growled Floyd. "We're going after their ass just as soon as we're all dried out. What's your plan?"

Michael gave it to him in detail while the marines finished coming ashore. Islanders were now coming down to the beach, Derald with them. Michael introduced Floyd to the old man, and they shook hands. Derald looked out at the floating Gull. "It does not sink," said Derald.

"Airtight, but she'll never fly again."

"Is there other damage: the weapons, or the big engine?"

"Nope, only the flight control system, anything connected to the wings and tail. Muesl used the vernier vanes in the engine exhaust to get us turned around and that's okay for fine maneuvering in space, but down here we can't fly without wings. We'd be like a spinning plate."

Derald listened quietly, forehead wrinkled in thought. "You can lift off?" he finally said.

"Sure, a few meters, but with no flight control we'd take off like a kid's leaky balloon if we powered up. Look, forget about the Gull. We've got another one, but that's it, and I'm not taking any chances with stranding everyone here. We've got to use it right the first time."

"What about *Belsus*?" asked Michael.

"A little scarred up, but okay, considering how chewed up our reflective coating is after a hundred years of space dust. Blew one of the supplies pod all to hell and both aft turrets, which were fortunately empty at the time. We were dropping to a lower orbit when they fired; the feeler beam got intense a minute before that and we knew they were locked on. Another second earlier and *Belsus* would be no more. Sorry about the silence, Mike. We heard you calling, but didn't answer until we were ready to come down, and contact time is short anyway. We're in geosynch right at the southern horizon, and this island has been giving us reflections."

"We need to make a move soon, Floyd. Toth knows we're here now and the flyer is down. He'll be looking for the other one, and with us out here he might make a move against the mainland to cut us off."

"Gull's there, and twenty-five fresh marines," said Floyd. "He'll be in for a bad surprise unless he goes in with a big force."

"Not likely, not with us here and close to him. He'll only need a small force to take the village, and keep the rest to greet *us*. I'd feel better if Gull Two kept an eye out, but close to the water. If Toth's lasers can reach targets over our heads here they can get near the village and all they need is a target high enough to see at that range."

"You want it right now, Mike?"

"I'd like that, sir."

Mootry smiled. "You've got it, sir." He got on the radio again, and gave the order: sorties along the mainland every four hours, staying right on the water, no radio noise. "Now, you got anything to eat around here?"

"Please, come with me," said Derald, and they followed him from the beach. Behind them, Krisha barked orders at the new additions to her force. Osen tagged along behind, and Floyd looked over a shoulder to smile at him. "How's the boy doing for you, Mike?" he said quietly.

"Sticks to me like glue. You didn't tell me he was a seasoned professional."

"What?"

"A professional, with combat experience. Where'd a kid his age get that? On Brown's Planet? Or am I being followed around by someone who has a lot of deep-sleep time?" He told Floyd about the firefights, the night on the beach, the knife in the boot. "Who is he?"

They'd reached the Agbayekhai house and Sabine stood in the doorway, waiting to be introduced. "Later, Mike," said Floyd, and he held out his hand to the woman.

Derald was silent but attentive throughout the meal, and listened to Floyd's full story of the attack on *Belsus*, the dramatic rescue of two marines who had sealed themselves in a shuttle tube when the storage pod was blown away, and the long wait while they wondered if members of the planet fall crew were still alive. Osen sat next to Michael on one side of the table, Floyd on the other, and Michael couldn't help but feel much of the conversation was being directed at the boy and not the rest of them. There was a strong bond between the two of them, something beyond that of a Colonel and his orderly, a mystery Michael found disturbing. They reviewed the attack plan again. Floyd inserted the use of Gull Two coming in low from the northwest once the boats had drawn laser fire. The ship would take out the laser cannons, then hover at the island to drop a load of marines as a first wave of ground attack after taking out the door on the east side of Toth's stronghold. He reminded them of the risk; Gull Two was the last of the flyers, it was all they had to get back to *Belsus* and the skeleton crew now manning it.

"The risk can be reduced," said Derald, breaking his long silence. "It can even be eliminated if you use the ship that was shot down."

Floyd laughed. "How? It's an airship, not a boat."

"It could be used as a boat," said Derald. He got up from the table and returned quickly with a sheet of bark and crayon in his hand, pushing aside empty dishes to make room for the bark and then drawing on it. "You say the engine is operational, and there is some control over the direction of thrust."

"Yes."

"It can float, but is not designed to move on a water surface."

"Of course not, Derald, it's an aircraft."

"Pontoons?" said Michael, suddenly catching on.

"More than that," said Derald, scribbling furiously. "We mount the airship on a boat and use the engine at low power to propel it. I have such a boat." He held up the bark so they could see the picture he'd drawn, the picture of a Gull mounted on an enormous framework of iron sitting on torpedo-shaped pontoons.

Michael touched the bark, tapped it. "The boat you've hidden on the south side of the island," he said softly.

"Yes. It is nearly as broad as your aircraft.

"But it was meant to be a sailing vessel, Derald."

"True, but it is very strong and designed for rough seas. You've seen Toth's boats, how they skim the waves at high speed. This boat could do that, and more."

"A floating weapons platform," said Floyd. "You say this thing exists?"

"Yes. We can bring it here in a few hours, use the lifters on your aircraft to mount it. The problem is to make the mounting secure."

"It's an iron structure," said Michael, "fairly soft iron, mostly thick cable, and flexible. Is there a welding unit on the Gull?"

"A small one, but certainly enough for soft metal. Good Lord, it might work. Wire the Gull to this structure and make a speedboat out of it! We could let the sailboats draw fire, then come in with this thing and target the laser batteries!"

Derald jumped from the table. "I will have the boat brought over," he said, and rushed from the room as they sat staring at the picture he'd drawn.

"This will take time, sir," said Osen. "Do we have it?"

"I wanted to make our move early tomorrow," explained Michael. "If we wait, Toth could hit us here with everything he has, and I don't know what that is. That small force he sent had to be a token thing, because he wasn't expecting any resistance, and I'm worried about Kari. She's already been on that island for days."

"If she's alive now she'll be alive a day from now," said Floyd. "Her real danger will come when we attack, and the faster we move at that time the safer she'll be. I like this idea, so let's do it. We go in full-bore with what we can muster, and keep Gull Two in reserve. Use Gull One to take out the laser batteries and discharge a landing force by boat. And what about the boat Toth sent that's floating out there? Is it useable?"

"It's shot up pretty good. We haven't checked it out yet," said Michael.

"Let's do that now," said Floyd. "It could be used for a first landing. We'll need speed to get in under those lasers."

They excused themselves and went down to the beach. Derald stood watching two sailboats headed towards the west end of the island. He pointed at them and said; "it will be a few hours before they return. The load will be heavy."

"Plenty to do before then," said Mootry.

The next few hours saw a flurry of activity on the beach, Krisha's marines loaded packs and cleaned weapons, and a flotilla of skiffs moved back and forth between Gull One, the damaged boat from Toth, and the beach. The engine of the boat was pronounced sound, but the controls and one steering cable had been shot away. The boat was towed alongside Gull One and the flight crew set to work on the controls. Iron cable was brought down from the canyon and welded in place while the flight crew returned to the Gull to check out the weapons system and replace several blown relays. Islanders swarmed over the boat, patching holes with pitch and small squares of pressed bark, bringing down glass amphorae filled with alcohol that they emptied into the fuel tank. Near dusk the boat's engine coughed, sputtered, coughed again, and then roared into life as the people on the beach cheered. Derald himself took the controls and drove the boat in a tight circle beyond the Gull, making a sprint west, then back again. As he returned, they spotted the sails in the west, two small boats ponderously moving towards them and behind them the low silhouette of iron latticework floating on four enormous glass pontoons. People waved and shouted, and suddenly were silent.

A loud booming sound came from the mainland, a flash appearing at the northern horizon, then another boom. They looked out to sea, saw streams of light coming up from it, sweeping the sky as if searching for a target and ceasing at the sound of a third explosion. The horizon lit up in orange and red. Osen was on the radio with Nik again.

"Sir! Two speedboats attacking the mainland from the east! Gull Two is on it!" A moment later he smiled, looked at Michael and drew a finger across his own throat. "Got 'em, sir! Missiles at five hundred meters as the boats were coming in towards shore! Blew them to pieces, sir, not even scrap left. Gull Two requests permission to make an island flyby and look for a place to land."

"Denied!" yelled Mootry. "Tell them to get back to the plateau and stay ready to fly! Mike says there's no landing place for them out here. Get home and I'll call for them when we're ready."

Osen relayed the message. Out on the northern horizon, two puffs of black cloud rose from the sea. Two more boats gone, that plus two made four, filled with Toth's troops, perhaps eighty men. Marines cheered at the news; at least eighty people would not be shooting at them in the hours to come.

The two sailboats came in slowly, towing the huge flatboat behind them. They anchored it a few meters north of the Gull as Derald called for a skiff and rowed over to clamber aboard his creation. It was a boat meant to cross the great sea to the lands in the south, but now destined to become a weapon of war. He walked it from one end to the other, comparing its size with the Gull, pausing to doodle on a piece of bark, walking again, and balancing delicately on the multi-layered mesh of iron cable making up the structure. In a few minutes he was back on shore, handing out lists of materials to be brought down the canyon: sheets, angle iron, thirty-millimeter cable and clamps. Islanders scattered to their tasks while Michael and Mootry stood there, looking befuddled. Derald came up to them, enthusiastic.

"The breaks in the wings must be covered and iron eyehooks welded here, here, and here on the aircraft." He showed them the points on his drawing, an accurate rendition of the Gull.

"Iron to titanium alloy?" said Michael. "I don't think so."

"I'll get Sergeant Auk on this," said Mootry. "Maybe it can be brazed."

For the moment Michael felt useless, while around him the islanders and flight crewmembers were running in every direction. He went up to the edge of the beach and sat in the sand to watch. It was getting dark, and alcohol lanterns were brought down to illuminate the beach and Toth's attack boat. The Gull was lit up by a dozen hand lamps brought from its interior. Krisha came up to him an hour later, a bulky pack slung over her shoulder, and an M-34 in one hand. "Excuse me, Major, but are you going in with us?"

"What?"

"The attack on Toth's island, are you going in with the rest of us?"

The question made him angry. "You're damned right I am! Did you think I was going to sit here and wait for it to be over?"

"No, sir. You'll need these." She dropped the pack at his feet and laid the assault rifle across it.

Michael grabbed the rifle. "I'm still a marine, Captain," he mumbled.

"Yes, sir. Colonel said that about himself, too. Begging your pardon, Major, and no offence intended, but I think the high-ranking officers should go in with the second wave. We don't know what to expect out there."

"That includes you, Krisha? You're third in command here."

Krisha's eyes narrowed. "No, sir, I'm going in first. Do I have to explain why?"

Michael softened. "No, you don't. I want her safe and alive as much as you do, Krish. When you're looking for her, just keep an eye behind you. I don't want to lose you, either."

"Aye, aye, sir," she said, then walked away, leaving him there fondling a weapon he hadn't fired in over fifteen years. *I was a marine—once. Now I'm a military diplomat about to be mustered out. What then? Be a fisherman?*

It suddenly occurred to him that was not such a bad idea.

The work went on throughout the night. Michael hauled sheet metal for lining the cutouts in the flatboat frame spaced to fit the landing feet of the Gull. There were three circular plates, each a meter in diameter. For three hours he met with Floyd and Krisha in the Agbayekhai house, going over alternate plans for the attack: one with boats only, the second using the floating Gull, the third with Gull Two providing air cover. In each case the maximum danger was to those few brave men who would provide a diversion by piloting their little sailboats in from the west, and almost certainly drawing heavy laser fire from Toth's island. In seconds their boats could be smoking ruins and they could be in the water only tens of meters from the barrier and its den of Charni. The thought chilled them all, yet it was these men who had first volunteered, both villagers and islanders, to do the job. They did it to be rid of Toth.

The meeting broke up near midnight and Krisha returned to her troops, Michael and Mootry walked outside to sit in the amphitheatre, away from the lights and the noise near the beach. They sat close together, and Mootry laid back, hands behind his head, to look at the stars. "Not so pretty here," he said. "A lot of rock, and smelly air."

"It's beautiful on the mainland," said Michael. "Trees, flowers, as far as you can see, pretty much untouched. Even the seawater is crystal clear. When I see this, the idea of going back to Brown's Planet doesn't appeal to me at all."

"Doesn't seem we have any choice, Mike, and that assumes we come out of this alive. God, I never thought I'd be ending a career with a firefight, but here I am and here you are, two old marines with one more battle between the pasture and us. Now Krisha, the little snip, she doesn't think that's such a good idea. I'm too important, she says, and shouldn't go in until they're mopping up."

Michael laughed. "She tried the same thing with me. Hell, she's right. My wind is gone, my knees are gone, and I'd be in the way trying to go in first. I settled for second wave, and Krish seems to go along with that."

"Pissed me off," said Floyd. "I had two major wars behind me before she was out of diapers. How'd she do over there—with Toth's people?"

"Professional—a little brutal, maybe. She shot an unarmed prisoner in the leg when he didn't talk fast enough for her. Her marines are young and she's got them through their first and second firefights without a casualty. You won't hear any girly jokes about her; she's Captain Elg, and that's it."

"Think she's exec material?"

"Definitely."

"Not that I want to dwell on it, but if something happens to me you might want to use her as your number one on the way back to Brown's Planet when we're done here." Mootry didn't look at him, just stared up at the stars.

Michael's face flushed hot at his response, for it came from deep inside him, the articulation of a decision he'd made subconsciously sometime during the past two days. "There's only one problem with that idea, Floyd. I'm not going back to Brown's Planet. One way or another, I'm staying right here."

Mootry propped himself up on an elbow, looked at Michael closely. "I thought about that before the trouble started, but not anymore. You sure?"

"Yes," said Michael, stunned by his own words. "It's the first time I've said it aloud to myself or anyone else."

"What happened, you fall in love with the trees and flowers?"

Michael smiled. "Not just that. There's—something else."

Now Mootry was grinning. "Does it wear a skirt?"

"Yes."

"A villager?"

"Yes, a widow. She has a little boy who hasn't said more than two words to me. I think his father was murdered by Jezrul for questioning Toth's laws."

"My God," said Mootry, lying down again, "an old marine like you—trapped by a woman."

"Feels okay to me," said Michael.

"Yeah, I know. I know how it feels. Had a woman myself, once."

"You? When did *that* happen?"

"Oh, you were on the team, then. We were together about six months, and then it was time to ship out and I didn't look back, just left her there."

"Where?" said Michael.

Mootry sat up, turned to face Michael, very close. "Brown's Planet. You were in deep sleep when we finally went back, and I looked her up. Shouldn't have, but I did, and now I'm glad I did. I had a kid, Mike, born only months after I'd left her. A son. Good kid, smart, too smart for his own good. He'd got himself involved in the revolution, underground stuff, bombings, assassinations, and the works. Ran with the Torres gang, and even the Federation couldn't forgive some of the things they did. He was declared an outlaw after Arkon got rid of the Maester regime that had brought about the revolution in the first place. On the run, hiding out, but his mom knew where to find him. Tia, his mom, lost most of her farm to reparation, was barely making it by the time I got back. She'd given up, wouldn't eat, even when she saw me. I was holding her hand when she died."

"What happened to the boy?"

Mootry hesitated, looked down. "I took him on, called him a marine. God knows he had the training for it. He's an illegal, no papers, no records, nothing." He looked up as the dawn of realization hit Michael's eyes.

190

"Osen," said Michael.

"Yeah. You wanted to know about him, and there it is."

"Does he know? Does he know you're his father?"

"Yes. He's a good kid, Mike, no bitterness about the past, accepts things as they come, but I can't take him back with me, and he knows that too. I brought him on after the last crew audit, and he has to be gone before the next one. We talked earlier this evening; he's staying here too, like you say, one way or another. We had some time together, and it's best for both of us. I don't want to spend old age in a military prison. The house and what's left of the farm will keep me busy. My name's on the papers, and Harve Osen, well, he'll just disappear."

Michael shook his head. "All these years I've known you, and I never would have guessed this."

"You were asleep most of the time, Mike." Both of them laughed at that. "Anyway, it looks like Krisha is number one on the way back, and if something happens to me she's running the show. You still sure, Mike?"

"Yes."

They stood up, faced each other, Mootry putting a hand on Michael's shoulder. "One more firefight to go, Mike. Let's get at it."

They walked back down to the lights, and the noise on the beach.

* * * * * * *

It was early afternoon when Muesl rowed alone out to the Gull and powered it up. Derald and several other islanders stood at the corners of the barge, and the beach was crowded with onlookers. The boat captured from Toth had made several sprints back and forth along the shore earlier, running smoothly on alcohol fuel and pronounced ready by Derald. Now it sat meters from the barge, two men in it to help guide Muesl in placing the Gull's landing plates precisely in the receptacles made for them. Lifters whined and the Gull lifted two meters above the water as everyone held their breath. Fire shot from the main thruster, a short burst, and then another. The Gull rotated slowly, drifted over the barge, and descended a meter, the men on Toth's boat gesturing frantically. What seemed an eternity was five minutes of trial and error, lifters screaming, thruster spitting as Muesl maneuvered the Gull into position and finally plopped it one meter down onto the barge with a resounding clang. The onlookers cheered as Muesl appeared at the open hatch and bowed grandly to them. Workers swarmed over the aircraft, thread-

191

ing cable through eyehooks to secure it in place, winching and welding. The bizarre vessel bobbed on the waves, half-plane, half-boat, stubby remnants of wings sealed with iron sheet. The maw of the Gull opened, and above it the Gatling appeared from its recess, swiveling ominously as Muesl played with the controls.

The excitement lasted only minutes and the crowd dispersed. Marines assembled their kits, fitted armor, and the villagers and islanders struggled with metal collars and helmets that would shield them from Toth's electromagnetic control if it were used against them. Michael joined Mootry, Krisha, Nimri, and Davos in the Agbayekhai house and they went over the final assault plan, a plan that would keep Gull Two in reserve until the last possible moment. Derald joined them and Osen was right behind him, standing silently behind his father as the plan was reviewed one last time. Michael looked at the boy in a new way: dark, brooding eyes, and chiseled face. The boy did not resemble his father, but the mother must have been something, he thought.

Krisha oversaw the loading of the Gull, speedboat and four sailboats making up the nucleus of the attack force. Twelve other boats to be sailed by twelve brave men stood forlornly in a great semicircle beyond the Gull, sails down, and their futures dark and uncertain. Michael sat on the beach with Mootry, watching silently until Nimri approached them, dressed in a robe, a staff in his hand. "Leader Queal," he said stiffly, "I have a protest to make."

"What's the problem?" said Michael.

"Captain Elg insists that I be assigned to the second wave of the operation. This can not be allowed."

"Why not? The first wave is marines only and you've put yourself in the roll of emissary to Toth. You'll go in without a weapon, and that makes the rest of us responsible for your safety. You'll be in the second wave with me and the colonel here."

"I've heard your troops talking. They will shoot anything that moves, and Lord Toth must not be harmed. I must be there."

"You'll be there soon enough; we'll be right behind the first wave and you don't go *anywhere* without us," said Michael firmly. "Do you know the island?"

"No, I've never been there."

"Then we'll help you find Toth, and that means we don't let you out of our sight. Captain Elg's order stands. Understood?"

Nimri sighed. "Yes, Leader Queal, but if Toth is harmed, you are responsible." He turned, and in his haste to get away nearly walked into Osen, who was standing right behind him.

"Sir," said Osen, saluting them both, but looking at his father, "Captain Elg, at my request, has assigned me to second wave. Is this acceptable to you, sir?"

"It is if you want it that way, private," said Mootry, looking stern. "If you want first wave I can get it back for you. You're ready for that, and I'm proud to say it."

"Second wave, sir. I have my reasons."

"Then you watch our backsides when we get in there, son."

Osen's eyes widened in surprise and flicked towards Michael, who maintained a straight face as if nothing had been said.

"Yes, sir!" Osen saluted again, and marched away.

"Hell of a kid," said Mootry, "and I wasn't there for him, and now he wants to keep two creaky, old marines from getting their asses shot off. He deserves better."

Michael thought of his own aging son a thousand light years away. "He found his dad, Floyd, maybe that's all he really ever wanted, all he really needed, to know who he came from, the kind of man who fathered him."

Floyd slapped him on the shoulder. "For a combat marine you've become one hell of a diplomat, Mike. Thanks for that." He got up and followed his son.

Michael was left alone to sit on the sand—and think about Gini. He wanted to return alive from the coming battle. He wanted it desperately.

And he was afraid it might not happen.

CHAPTER TWENTY

Rudy dreamed Toth had summoned him. It startled him awake, but when he looked at the monitor in his room it was blank and silent. A clock next to the monitor showed it was near sunrise, and he'd slept nearly four hours. He leapt from his bed and left the room, walked quickly down an empty hall and up the twisting flights of stairs to the great dome housing the four laser batteries keeping watch over sky and sea. All men were at their posts, two of them on optical and infrared scanners. He went to the watch commander now standing behind the operator of the optical scanner. The man's eyes were rimmed with red from a lack of sleep, and he nodded curtly. "Good morning, Counselor."

"Anything new? Have the men returned from the mainland?"

"We've seen nothing, Counselor, not a single boat, and the starship has not appeared. The men should have been back by now. First Counselor is concerned about it. He finally went to his room about an hour ago for some sleep. He feels the attack will come soon, at night or early morning. We *have* to take some rest late this morning, and the scanners are only being manned in half-hour shifts. We're all exhausted."

Rudy grasped the man's arm warmly. "The blessings of Toth for you, Rustin, your vigilance will be rewarded."

His next thought was for the safety of Toth. He'd not been with him for nearly a day and had not been summoned. In the years he'd served on the island, never more than four hours had passed in his room before Toth had summoned him about some matter, large or small. He was suddenly worried, and took the stairs three at a time in his downward flight to the throne room.

The room was silent and empty, the throne dark and vacant, the only light coming from the terminals and monitor screens around the walls. He went to a terminal, typed in the coding that gave him private audience with His Lord, and then hurried to stand before the throne.

Nothing happened, no light, and the throne remained empty.

His heart pounded. He went back to the terminal and typed in the same command, and still there was no response. Sweat beaded on his forehead. He called up the display of the life-support system, checked the readings and gasped; "Can't be. It can't be!" The flow of Beta-Choline had been reduced to a trickle, an amount so small it could not relieve Toth's pain or perhaps even sustain His life. The supply of the drug was more than adequate, had hardly changed from the day before. Whatever had happened to the flow? Rudy typed furiously, hands shaking. He watched the flow-rate rise, brought it to a level even higher than he'd used previously. "Oh, Lord, what have I done to you? What have I *done*?"

He watched and waited long minutes, thinking; *this has never happened before. Never! A computer malfunction? Unlikely. Everything's fine now. No, the flow was reset, deliberate or accidentally, and I'm the only one who—*

The thought hammered him. No, there was one other who knew the procedure for controlling the flow of the drug. He had shown it to him only the day before. Jezrul. Jezrul had done this, and not by accident. He had knowingly done this to destroy Lord Toth!

Rudy waited, seething with fear and rage, and then the throne was suddenly illuminated and he remembered he had not cancelled the call to His Lord. The throne was illuminated and Toth appeared there, moaning, curled up in a fetal position and tearing at his own face with long, bony fingers.

"My Lord!" shouted Rudy.

Toth screamed a horrible thing that echoed from the walls, and filled Rudy with terror. He fell on his knees before the throne. "Forgive me, Lord! Forgive me for not coming sooner, but I could not know this had happened! Treachery, Lord! TREACHERY! Someone has attempted to take your life, Lord, and it is a person you have given your complete trust to! It is Jezrul, Lord! Only Jezrul could have done this! Please, Lord, speak to me, and hear me!"

Toth continued to claw at His face as Rudy repeated his claim, giving the details of how he'd shown Jezrul the procedures of the life support system only he had known until the day before. In fear for his life he blurted out his own suspicions of Jezrul, the things he'd seen and heard, the man's desire to baptize the woman, the sending of the men to the mainland before Toth had been coaxed into ordering it, and the fact that the men had not returned and were long overdue. The words streamed forth until he was babbling, arguing for his life, in terror of the possible wrath of the man who was now recovering before his eyes, no longer clawing at his face, un-

195

curling from his fetal position to sit normally on the throne, hands clutching the arm rests.

Rudy knelt, placed his forehead on the floor and waited for the worst to come.

"Rudy," gasped Toth. "Stop it now. Wait. Wait until I can breathe again. The drug—it's working—I can feel it!"

Rudy looked up. Toth's head was thrown back and he was panting. Rudy's eyes were clouded with tears. "Is it enough, Lord? Shall I increase the flow?"

"No. No, it is enough. I—Rudy—I think I was dead, and then—the pain—like never before, but now it goes away. Stand up; you've nothing to fear from me."

Rudy stood up, hands twisted together over his stomach. "I also fear Jezrul, Lord. The things I've said—Jezrul said he would kill me if I brought you disturbing news or told you what he'd done, and now I've said even more than that. If he finds out he will kill me, Lord, I know it."

Toth breathed heavily, but His eyes were now like green embers beneath the hood of his robe. "So, Rudy, he will *not* find out, just yet. If he inquires, you will say I'm resting and cannot be disturbed. You are concerned about this, but it is My Will. Change the access code to the life-support system, and if what you say is true, Jezrul will return to check on his handiwork, using the old code. I will then deal with him, but in the meantime his leadership is needed to rid us of the outsiders. If the battle is lost, all is lost. I must regain my strength before any confrontation, and as usual it is you I can depend on. Change the code, Rudy, do it *now*!"

The image on the throne flickered and disappeared. Rudy rushed to the terminal and performed the ordered task, but fear had not left him. Jezrul would expect His Lord to be dead by now, at best totally incapacitated. A careless word, a show of emotion or darting of the eyes on his part might show Jezrul his treachery had been uncovered and the result could be instant death. Rudy went back to his own room, retrieved a laser pistol and a fisherman's knife from his closet, and strapped both weapons to his sides beneath the robe. He opened the door and stepped out, then pulled back quickly.

Three doors down from him, Jezrul was coming out of the woman's room, staff in hand, and Rudy thought he heard sobbing before the door was closed.

He peeked, saw Jezrul walk away from him and enter the staircase at the end of the hall. He waited one minute, two, and then went to her door, fumbling to retrieve his own master key that gave him entrance anywhere in the sanctuary. He opened the door and stepped quickly inside, locking it behind him as the woman sobbed; "No! Leave me alone!"

He turned; saw her sitting up in bed, arms bare, the covers pulled up to her chin. Her face was streaked with tears and she was shivering convulsively, eyes wide with fear. "Don't come near me!" she said. "I'll scream!"

"What happened here?" said Rudy softly. "I saw Jezrul come out of your room and heard you crying. What has he done to you?"

"You don't *know*?" she sobbed. "Didn't he *tell* you what he was going to do? Doesn't *Toth* know? Is this what he does to *all* his chosen people?" She wrapped the bed cover tightly around her, lay down on her side and wept bitterly. A flash of white at the base of her neck and Rudy dared to approach the bed, sitting down slowly on its edge. "What's that on your neck? A bandage?"

His face flushed with the realization that a blasphemy had occurred. "Did Jezrul cut into you, did he?—"

"He said he *baptized* me," cried the woman. "I tried to tear it out after he left, but it *hurt*, and then he came back—last night—this morning—oh, I want to *die*! I want to DIE!"

Facing away from him, her body heaved under the covers.

"He had his staff with him. Has he used it to give you The Pleasures? Please, tell me. Such use of his staff is a perversion forbidden by Toth's Laws. Please." He reached over to touch her shoulder, but she jerked away.

"Don't touch me! *He* touched me, and at first—yes—it felt good, but then it HURT and *that's* what he wanted. He was all over me and covered my mouth so I couldn't scream, and the *pain* was all through me. He loves PAIN, even for himself! His eyes were wild and this thing he put in me—" Her hand scrabbled at the bandage on her neck, pulling at it, her back arching as she moaned; "It's like fire, and I can't even *touch* it without hurting awful, and he'll be back again and again!"

"No, no," said Rudy softly, and took her hand away from the bandage. "You can't get rid of what he's placed in you, but I can be sure he doesn't use you in this way again before your people come. Get up and get dressed. I'm taking you out of here."

"What?" she said, looking over her shoulder at him.

"Hurry *up*! We don't have time to discuss it. Your people will be attacking us any hour now. I'll hide you until then."

"But I thought—"

"Jezrul told you lies. There's no truce with Leader Queal, and you will either be saved by your people or die with them. That is Toth's Will, and what Jezrul has done is not. I cannot save your life, but I can prevent further blasphemies by Jezrul, so get dressed!"

The woman stood with the bed cover wrapped around her, and then dropped it, and Rudy watched her naked back as she slipped a robe over her head. "Follow me," he said, "and be quiet!"

He locked her door, took her hand in his and hurried along the hall and down two flights of stairs to the hallway encircling Toth's garden at sea. "There's only one place, outside, where you might be safe until the attack comes, but then you'll be in the line of fire from your own people and I take no responsibility for what happens to you. Can you swim?" They walked down the hall, footsteps echoing.

"Yes."

"The water is shallow, but nearly your height. It might be necessary. Here, we're coming to it."

It was the channel leading out to sea, the channel where the Yellowfin they fed on were collected, attracted by the signal from a transponder two meters beneath their feet.

Rudy went to a wall panel, opened it, and punched in a number sequence on the keys there. "There, the new signal will calm any fish, even a Charni which comes into the channel while you're there. When you reach the outside, climb up on the rocks and if your people get close they might see you. Get in and watch your head. The tunnel ceiling is close to the water."

The woman hesitated, eyes wide. The water was dark in the pit below. A railing surrounded it and there was no ladder or steps down to the water a meter below the edge. Rudy climbed over the railing, held out his hands. "Here, I will help you get down."

"I'm afraid," she said, shivering.

"It's only a few meters to the outside. You can see the light from here. Hurry, please, before Jezrul discovers you're missing."

She ducked under the railing and he grasped both her hands tightly, turned her back to the water. "Tell me when your feet are on the bottom." He pushed her backward, holding tight, her feet went over the edge and scrabbled at the wall until she felt him holding her up. "I've got you. Be calm. Now, down you go."

Her eyes were wide with terror and she gasped as her feet and legs hit the cold water. She was light, and the expression on her face gave him new strength. Rudy crouched and lowered her until her chin was nearly at the water, felt her feet hit bottom. "There," he said. "Now stay at either wall of the channel and go. Remember, no fish will hurt you, not even a Charni. You must not make a sound. See? The light is only a few meters away. Go!"

The woman finally let go of his hands, pressed against the far wall and inched along it. In moments she was in the tunnel, the rock ceiling centimeters above her head and Rudy crouched low to watch her progress.

She was halfway along the tunnel when the Charni arrived.

Rudy saw it first, the great dorsal fin slicing the water at the tunnel exit and drifting inside. The woman let out a muffled scream and pressed her back to the wall. "Quiet! It's lethargic by now, hypnotized by the signal. Be still!" he whispered.

She closed her eyes, chin touching the water, and sobbed. The dorsal fin drifted towards her, only its tip above water, came to her, slid past slowly. She gasped, voice barely controlled; "It's—it's touching me. It's squeezing me against the wall!"

"Stay calm! It's past you now. Go on, and remember to stay out of the water once you're outside! I'm turning on the barrier again as soon as you're safely outside." The huge Charni entered the pit, filling it, drifting until its horrible head was pressed to the screen behind which a transponder sang a tranquil song. The woman was moving again, more quickly now, and in seconds she was outside, looking left and right, then scrambling up out of sight to her right.

Rudy waited a moment, but she did not reappear. He climbed back over the railing again, went to the wall panel and punched in a new sequence, was startled by the thrashing sounds in the pit. The Charni was suddenly enraged, crashing against the walls, and water erupted out onto the floor. The ghastly animal arose from the water, twisting to snap at the railings before crashing down and streaking down the tunnel and out to sea. From outside there came a scream. Rudy froze, looked around, but the hallway was empty. He closed the panel and started back towards the staircase, thinking; *I have followed the will of My Lord. I have prevented further blasphemy by Jezrul and placed the woman where the Charni and her own people determine her fate. We are now rid of her. It is the Will of Toth.*

He climbed the staircase to the laser batteries, and found Jezrul there.

Jezrul looked grim, and worried as Rudy came up to him. "The men have not returned," he said. "They should have been back last night. Something has happened, but nothing has been seen. People are falling sleeping at their posts here."

"Everyone is exhausted, First Counselor, they've been without sleep for two days. I will stay with you to watch the scanners, but please let the others sleep the rest of the day. Queal would not dare to make a move in daylight, and we need our people fresh tonight.

"What people we have left, you mean. How many, forty? And that's counting the gun crews."

"We'll destroy them at sea, First Counselor, but the crews must be rested and alert to accomplish that."

"Then let them rest, but I want everyone back here by dusk. The attack will come tonight, I can feel it." Jezrul's voice quivered as if he perceived impending doom.

"They can be called back in an instant, and we are rested. You and I will be the eyes of Our Lord."

Jezrul grumbled something inaudible, perhaps a curse, and Rudy gave the orders to the crews. They tumbled gleefully from their positions and hurried from the great dome housing the batteries, nodding thanks to Rudy as they passed by him.

Jezrul glowered at Rudy. "Queal has somehow tricked me, or his starship is still alive and has sent reinforcements to the mainland, yet none of those fools have seen anything," he grumbled. "Some of our best troops were in those boats."

"And the best remain here," said Rudy. "These weapons will spread their ashes on the sea long before they can reach us." Rudy frowned, for there was fear in Jezrul's eyes, a dangerous fear that disturbed his own confidence in the power of the lasers to fend off an attack.

"They will come at us with support from the air, perhaps four of their aircraft with missiles and heavy projectile cannon. They can blow this rock to pieces."

"At most there will only be one aircraft and we will shoot it down the way we did the other. One burst will be enough."

"Kari said four," growled Jezrul.

"She lies, First Counselor. We saw only two, and one is gone. She will say anything to protect her own people, to give them an advantage. She is our enemy."

"I have other means of questioning her," said Jezrul, and there was a horrible glint in his eyes.

For an awful instant Rudy thought Jezrul might go to question the woman. "Not now, First Counselor, not when we must be here. Wait until the crews have returned. Please, I cannot operate both scanners at the same time and we really can't be certain when the attack will come. Please, Jezrul, not now."

Rudy's concern was genuine, and it showed in his voice and eyes. Jezrul looked at him carefully and shrugged his shoulders.

"Very well, it can wait. I will take the optical scanner first. I want you to do a complete IR scan of the sky from horizon to horizon and look for that *ship*!"

They went about their tasks in silence, sitting only a meter apart, and ignored each other for hours. Rudy searched and searched, looking for the signature of a thruster burn, and saw nothing. Above the island summits barely visible at this distance the plume he was familiar with glowed green, an anvil-shape formed by the wind. He had long ago decided the phenomenon had a natural origin, some kind of volcanic vent near the mountaintops. Finally Rudy sat back in his chair and rubbed his eyes.

"I see nothing to indicate a ship in orbit. If it's up there, the engines are shut down or it is indeed dead. Nothing at sea, either."

"Watch the sea, then, south and west," said Jezrul curtly. "A group of men in a boat could show up in IR before I see them. If the attack is to be this evening, they will already be moving. And look for *any* signs of aircraft."

Rudy returned to his careful observations of the monitor screen, but nothing was there, and when Jezrul spoke again a few minutes later Rudy was ready for it, his reply rehearsed.

"Has Toth been informed about our present status? Has he asked about the men we sent to the mainland?" Jezrul spoke without moving his head, his eyes fixed on the screen in front of him.

"Our Lord has chosen not to make himself available to us for the moment. When I called him this morning he did not appear, so I assume he's resting and does not wish to be disturbed. It has happened in the past."

"It's just as well, since we have no good news to bring him."

"Yes, the past days have weighed heavily on him, but I'm confident his strength will return quickly and he'll be there for us when we need him. I checked the life-support system this morning and all is well. A few more hours of quiet sleep should do the rest."

Jezrul's voice remained calm and his eyes never left the viewing screen. "Regardless of what happens to Our Lord, Rudy, your loyalty and care for Him will be remembered and rewarded."

"Thank you, Jezrul." Rudy stared at the screen in front of him, careful not to smile. The seed had been planted, a seed he hoped would soon bare fruit, but not too soon, for now Toth rested, gaining strength, and when the time was right, Rudy hoped he would be sent to fetch Jezrul for one final meeting with His Lord whom he had tried to murder.

He wanted to be there at the moment of Jezrul's death.

CHAPTER TWENTY-ONE

The sky was clear and filled with stars. A cluster only thousands of light years away illuminated the sea like a moon. The sailboats destined to be diversionary targets for Toth's weapons moved out first, spread out into an arc and headed east under half-sail. The Gull would follow quickly from behind them at the first sign of fire. The main attack force—speedboat and three sailing craft—headed west around the island, then south and east. When the eastern tip of the island was due north of them the speedboat shut down its engine and was towed by the others. Krisha commanded the speedboat, and it was filled with twenty marines she'd handpicked for the first wave, all of them people who'd seen action at the village. Michael, Mootry, Osen and Nimri were together in Davos's boat with a mixture of marines and villagers who'd been under fire on the island and considered themselves veterans. The boat running parallel to them was crammed with fresh marines from *Belsus* who were going into combat for the first time, but the two boats were intended to hit the island simultaneously as a second wave in the attack, coming in a hundred meters behind Krisha and her troops when the entrance to the stronghold was blown.

Michael felt the dread of approaching combat: sweaty palms, an aching hollow in his stomach, and the whirling visions of family, friends—Gini. He looked at Mootry and Osen, father and son standing silently next to him, eyes scanning the sea. What were they thinking? It was only a short time they'd had together, a time that might soon end with the violent death of one or both of them. Perhaps they thought of the woman they had both loved, and lost.

He worried about Krisha, her lover a captive for days, perhaps dead. She'd been unusually quiet during the loading that evening, her face painted black, a determined, dangerous-looking mask. Would she stick with her troops, or run off alone in search of Kari once they were inside? His instincts told him she would be professional and put the operation first in her mind. And if Kari were found injured or dead? Well, he wouldn't bet a dime on any of the lives of those who defended the stronghold, and that included Toth, whoever or whatever he was.

In some ways Michael felt empathy for Nimri. Here he was, without any weapon except his staff, careening towards a violent confrontation with a man he still believed in, a man he thought deceived by Jezrul and his followers and guilty only of defending a society and a world created by him, a father who sought to protect his chosen people from the evil influence of outsiders. Would he seek out Toth and try to reason with him, or would he, in the midst of battle, suddenly become an enemy? Somehow, Michael trusted him to do the right thing, though perhaps it was because the man was Davos's son, and Gini's brother.

Gini's face was as clear in his mind as if she was standing next to him, and his heart skipped a beat. She was waiting for him as she had waited for a husband to come back from the sea. 'You'll break her heart" Davos had said, but that was not his intention. He wanted to return whole and live out his life with her, thought of her standing on the beach, waiting, then a skiff rowing to shore, bearing his lifeless body, her cry of grief, the tears...

Michael was jolted back to reality; knuckles white from his strangle hold on the rifle. He suddenly wanted to talk to Davos, but the man was at the tiller and a tightly packed mass of people separated them.

Osen caught his eye. "You okay, Major?"

Michael wondered about what had prompted the question. His face? "Just thinking," he said.

"Now's the time," said Floyd, not looking at them, "then you put it aside and get the job done. You remember that, Mike? Nothing in your head except the present, and staying alive. That's how the kids with Krisha get to be old dogs like us."

"I remember, Floyd," said Michael, and patted the man on the shoulder.

They huddled shoulder to shoulder in the early morning cold, looked north and saw nothing but water. The big island was now a faint silhouette to the west and north as Davos forged ahead, navigating only by the stars, estimating his speed by sight, the speedboat following with Krisha a statue at its bow. Michael's anxiety grew, and his stomach knotted as they awaited the first hint of light at the horizon that would signal them to turn north.

An eternity later it appeared, and they turned north after shortening sail, and slowed to a crawl with the weight of the speedboat pulling back on them. Long oars appeared, six of them, and set between thole pins by the villagers who would soon man them. By Michael's watch they had sailed north for less than an hour when Davos shouted and the villagers leapt to haul down sail. Davos detached the stern line to the speedboat and Krisha hauled it in as they drifted slowly, and then slowed to a stop. Only now did the engine of the speedboat cough, then catch with a low growl. The boat eased up alongside them and Krisha gave them a thumb's up as they went past, moving out in front of the sailboats and idling west. Villagers jumped to the oars and rowed in unison as Krisha and her armored, visored marines pulled slowly away from them.

Toth's island would be directly ahead of them now. Michael squinted ahead in semi-darkness, looked for a shape, a reflection that might be a rock, a flash of light that could be a laser beam searching for them. This far out, without sail, the motor of the speedboat shielded by the hull, they should be invisible to Toth's scanners. He was encouraged by the layer of mist ahead, lying low to the water, an inversion layer to scatter Toth's signals, at least until they were within sight. Krisha's boat was fifty meters out, now, still pulling away as the villagers grunted and pulled on the oars.

A half-hour later the island appeared as a dark nipple rising from the mist dead ahead of them. It looked far away, but was *not* far away, for Derald had said it was little more than a monstrous boulder above sea level. The stars above were now fading and an orange glow had appeared at the eastern horizon. They rowed steadily, Krisha keeping her distance from a hundred meters out, and then suddenly the engine of her boat roared. The bow rose as she streaked away from them. Michael's heart jumped as he squinted, and saw colors flashing around the island, streams of color flickering in the mist.

Davos shouted, "Up sail!" and oars creaked as the men bent their backs. Laser fire. The island was firing at boats lying in mist on the southern side. The boat jumped as sails filled, and the men were pulling hard, faces glistening. Krisha's boat was far ahead, visible only by its wake and the island was larger now, a thumb of rock turning from black to ocher in the first, weak light of pre-dawn. To the south of it rose a curl of smoke from what had to be a burning boat. Light sparkled in mist again and there was more smoke, and a flash of fire. Michael thought of men in the water, their boats in ruins, struggling to stay afloat and waiting for a Charni to come, and then there was a terrible flash from the island summit, and for an instant he thought the lasers had found them in the east. He ducked instinctively and saw a second flash and then it seemed as if the south side of the island summit just disappeared, an eruption of rock and dust forming a plume drifting down to the sea. Seconds later the sound reached him, the hollow booms of explosions followed by the high-speed rattle of what had to be the Gatling gun of Gull One. Smoke poured from the south side of the island as the villagers broke into cheers.

"Gull coming in!" yelled Osen, and Michael thought he meant the floating weapons platform they'd wired together until he saw rapid movement north of them at sea level, a flat shape streaking east and turning, wings vertical, coming back at terrible speed right on the water and throwing up two long lines of geysers as it came. Gull Two came past them in a blur, releasing two missiles running parallel in white lines towards the base of the island and this time a flash of fire was instantly followed by the roar of an explosion that deafened them. The Gull veered north, turned to make another pass and now Michael could see the island was only hundreds of meters away, a black opening at its base and from the opening streamed laser fire, tiny figures scrambling around it, the crackle of assault rifles reaching him. Another explosion flashed at the base. A satchel charge. The Gull had just completed its turn for another pass and was coming in higher this time, releasing a missile before reaching them. The missile ran straight and level to strike the summit of the island, blowing it away with a white flash.

A hundred meters out they saw flashes as Krisha's troops filled the rock's interior with concussion and fragmentation grenades, saw them scrambling inside, heard rifles crackling on full-automatic, and then a single scream. Michael looked up and was amazed; a cloud of black, white, yellow, and red, a living cloud belched from the summit of the rock and flew crazily around it, coming low overhead. Birds of all descriptions, and butterflies, fluttering past them, the birds screeching in terror and then, obeying some instinct, circling the island and soaring out over the sea towards the mainland. Davos charged straight for the entrance where the speedboat laid half in and half out of the water, its bow resting on a platform partially raised. Oars were pulled in, sails crashing, and then villagers and marines alike were pressed behind Michael as he teetered on the bow. The adrenalin rush in his body was like fire as the bow crashed into the speedboat, and in one instant his instincts for survival, unused for over fifteen years, were suddenly there again.

Speed, speed, speed.

Michael leapt into the speedboat, bounced off a seat and onto the platform, and then swung up onto the rock where a marine lay with a single burn in his chest, eyes glazed over. Rifle fire roared from the dark cavern in front of him, and he darted left to the edge of the entrance where a marine crouched, frantically motioning for him to get down and stay left. One more burst of fire as he huddled against the marine and then a shout from inside; "Clear!"

An answering shout, deeper inside. "Clear! Going in!"

Krisha's voice.

A door clanged, and there was another burst of fire, the sound of boots pounding rock, and fading.

"Now!" said the marine and Michael followed him into the cavern, glancing over a shoulder to see Mootry right behind him, grinning crazily. The cavern was a docking bay, two bodies in the water, one a marine. Shattered bodies lay on the walkways and platforms around the bay, men dressed in black with visored helmets. Toth's troops. Beyond the bay was an open metal door. A marine stood there, beckoning. They trotted up to him.

"Captain says stay on this level! She's looking for a way up to the laser batteries! She says stay out of stairwells and elevators, but clean out and occupy this level!"

Michael peeked around the doorway and saw a hall curving to his right; empty except for two visored bodies sprawled there. He moved slowly down the hall, a sweaty back pressed against a wall, past three rooms, doors open, one splattered with debris and what was left of a man after a grenade explosion. Gunfire sounded from ahead, but distant. He came around the curve of the wall and saw a marine crouched ahead, waving him on. He trotted, saw a stairwell leading up and down, and heard scattered gunfire coming from above. "They went up here," said the marine. "You're to take the rest of this level, and watch yourselves! We saw people run that way, and you're on point from here on!"

Michael nodded, scooted along the wall and Mootry jumped to the wall opposite him. Osen stepped up between them, right in the center, rifle leveled at his waist as he shuffle-stepped ahead of them, swinging the muzzle back and forth. He came to a closed door, pounded on it, stepped back. No answer. He stepped back again and fired a burst, destroying lock and door. The room was empty, someone's living quarters.

"In front!" screamed Mootry, his rifle swinging around.

Two visored men jumped to the center of the hall meters in front of them, firing as they appeared. Three assault rifles roared in unison, splattering the men against the walls, Osen grunted, and behind them someone screamed. Michael looked back, saw a villager writhing on the floor and holding his leg. Osen's cheek had been seared by a near miss. He gritted his teeth, pulled out a grenade, tapped its base on the wall and flipped it back-handed down the corridor to ricochet off a wall and roll out of sight. Men screamed a split-second before the explosion belched rock and smoke and the remains of a laser rifle skittered up to Michael's feet. He charged, saw three men down, two obviously dead with blood-splattered visors, the third a robed counselor, sitting with his back against a wall, legs bloodied. As they approached, the man held up a buzzing staff and waved it at them ineffectively until a villager walked up grinning, jerked it from his hand and clubbed him over the head with it.

"Two of you take the wounded back to the bay," ordered Michael, and they obeyed. *The fewer villagers here, the better*, he thought, and they pressed on.

Mootry looked at Osen. "Nice scar you'll have there, boy," he said, making no effort to hide his pride. "Now, let's get the rest of them."

A scream came from ahead of them, high and shrill, then another scream. A woman's scream and a gurgling cry that was a different voice. *Kari!* "Go!" yelled Michael, and they charged down the center of the curving hall. A railing ahead to their left, two robed figures struggling there, a third sprawled on the floor in front of them.

One of the struggling figures was Jezrul.

The other was Kari.

The instant they came into view, Jezrul grabbed Kari by the hair and jerked her in front of him, his laser rifle coming up, and eyes crazy.

Trigger fingers relaxed for a split-second, Kari shielding her captor.

Jezrul fired a single burst that hit Floyd Mootry in the throat just above his armored vest. Mootry crashed to the floor on his back, blood gushing from his neck, eyes open.

Osen fired a long burst as another explosion rocked the hallway, but Jezrul had moved out of sight, Kari screamed again and again until cut off by the sound of a door clanging shut.

Michael stood frozen as Osen dropped to his knees at Mootry's side. Floyd gurgled once, his hand reaching up towards Osen's face, and then falling limply back to the floor. Osen sobbed, looked up at Michael.

"He's gone. We've got to get after Jezrul," said Michael, his heart aching.

"He was my father," said the boy.

"I know. He told me all about it. Now load and lock! We find Jezrul; you have the first shot at him. Come on!" Michael hated his own words, the coldness of them, the way they denied his own grief. He turned to the people who huddled behind him and now stood staring at Mootry's corpse. "Marines only from here on! Get the Colonel back to the bay and guard this corridor in case we're forced back! Move!"

Michael and Osen moved cautiously but quickly to the robed figure on the floor. The hall ended there at solid rock, but there was a heavy metal door. Left of them, beyond railings, was a concrete-lined pit filled with water. Water was on the floor all around the body of a young man on his back, arms outstretched, and next to one hand was a laser pistol. A single hole was burned in the front of his robe and his eyes were open, his face looking surprised at what had happened to him. A trail of water went to the door and as Michael turned to it he saw Cainen Nimri standing there, looking down at the body. "I said marines only, counselor," he growled, and the two marines who'd followed edged close to Nimri as if to take hold of him.

Nimri glared at all of them, pointed at the door. "He's gone through there, and we're wasting time. Jezrul has fled to Toth and I'm going with you. I won't be denied this," he said firmly.

Michael hesitated, then leaned over and picked up the laser pistol, handed it out to Nimri. "If you don't take this you're not going anywhere, and that's an order."

Nimri nodded and took the pistol. Osen had tried the door, but it was locked from inside. "Get around the corner," he said, then took out a grenade and jammed it between the door handle and the door as they all fled.

The explosion was terrific, reverberating from the door like a gong, leaving the thing buckled inwards and hanging on grimly to one cracked hinge. Michael and Osen hit it together in a unified shoulder block and sprawled forward as the door fell over. Plastic sheet fluttered before them and beyond it was bright light.

They pushed the sheet aside and stared at what had once been a beautiful garden.

The ceiling had been dome-shaped, but had been blown away during the attack and sunlight now streamed in onto a jungle of trees, ferns and flowers, many now crushed by fallen rock chunks, one the size of a Gull. Michael and Osen darted for cover in thick ferns by a pond filled with colorful fish, a bridge across it cracked in half by a single fallen boulder of yellow rock. Nimri and the two marines moved left and crouched at the base of a moss-covered tree, startling a bird that soared straight up to the mammoth hole in the ceiling and disappeared. The air above their heads was filled with butterflies, swirling, and rising towards the sky in escape from their ruined habitat. On the other side of the cavern what had once been a waterfall now was a trickle leaking into a green pond. Nothing moved ahead of them.

They moved forward in a crouch along a curving path to the green pool. Beyond the pool, once hidden by the waterfall, was a door in rock. Nimri and the two marines reached it first, and waited for Michael and Osen. Michael reached to open it, but Nimri put a hand on his. "Please, this door might lead to Toth, and you said I could speak to him."

"That depends on Toth, and on Jezrul. If they fire at us we'll do everything we have to do to defend ourselves. I want you in the middle of us when we go in. The pistol is for your own defense and the only reason I trust you with it is because you're Davos's son. If you even look like you're turning that pistol on one of us, I'll shoot you down myself," said Michael.

"I understand," said Nimri. "All I ask is that you not be too quick to shoot. I've come to speak with Toth, not to fight him."

"Fair enough. Now, stay together; here we go." Michael opened the door, and saw a tunnel running straight ahead into darkness. "Lights," he said. Osen and the two marines each produced small hand-lamps from their packs. They left the door open and entered the tunnel, Osen and a marine lighting the way, Michael and Nimri following, and the other marine brought up the rear with another lamp. The tunnel ran straight for ten meters, then curved right and ended at stone stairs snaking downwards steeply. The stairs had seen little use and were covered with fine dust, but a trail of water ran down them, water from the soaked garments of someone who had recently passed by.

The stairs were a descending helix and they tiptoed down them with warm air blowing in their faces. Gradually they began to hear voices from ahead, murmurs at first, then growing louder. The stairs ended and to their left a short tunnel led to a slat-gate through which green light streamed. Osen motioned to turn out the lamps. They crept forward towards the light, and one voice was suddenly familiar: Jezrul. He was arguing with someone, the other person's voice deep and hoarse and suddenly there was a buzzing sound beyond the gate and Jezrul began to laugh. "Come now and share my pleasure!" he shouted, and then a woman screamed.

Michael and Osen hit the gate simultaneously and burst into a room filled with green light. The first thing they saw was a stone throne, and the bizarre apparition that was sitting there.

CHAPTER TWENTY-TWO

The return of the gun crews to their stations near sunset was a welcome relief. Jezrul had spent hours staring at the monitor screen without really seeing it. His mind wandered again and again, returning to what Rudy had said. He had checked the life-support system. Everything seemed undisturbed and Lord Toth was resting peacefully. How? How could everything be as it should when the flow of Beta-Choline had been reduced to nothing? Jezrul went over the procedure in his mind again and again during that long watch: entry code, display access, the response of the readings, the command to store and lock, all done correctly. Could Rudy be lying? Had he discovered the sabotage, and made the necessary correction in time to save Toth's life? Or was Toth dead at this very moment, Rudy fearing blame from everyone and keeping the secret to himself?

Rudy had made his statement with a calm, passive expression and Jezrul knew him to be an emotional man with an intense, zealous passion for Lord Toth built by years of close, intimate association. It was his emotions that made him vulnerable to manipulation, a fact Jezrul had always counted on to sway the man and keep him off balance. No, if Toth were dead, Rudy would be incapable of hiding his grief, for without His Lord there was no life for him. But how would he react upon uncovering an attempt to kill His Lord? Anger? Yes. Righteous indignation and confrontation of the perpetrator? Yes. So where were these signs of discovery? Not in anything Rudy had said or done.

A sudden thought chilled him. Rudy's loyalty to Toth was absolute, his response to orders immediate and accurate. If he'd been ordered by *Toth* to cover up a murderous act, he would accomplish the task with perfection and if Toth *knew* Jezrul had committed the act, Rudy's performance—

He would proceed cautiously, stay away from Toth for the moment, and resist all temptation to check the life support system again. His excuse was simple, all his attentions needed to run the defense against imminent attack. The men were his, all of them. Toth had only Rudy. He, Jezrul, would deal with both of them, one at a time.

So when the gun crews were in their places again Jezrul was not surprised when Rudy said; "I'm going downstairs to see if Lord Toth is awake yet. He will want to know where we stand at the moment, and it's best if he hears it from His First Counselor. Will you come with me?"

Jezrul smiled, and shook his head. "Rudy, of all times, this is surely the worst for me to leave here for any reason. I will trust you to inform Our Lord. We are prepared for the attack, and await first sign of our targets. That's all there is to say, except to express my hope His strength is recovered. Please convey this to Him, and then hurry back. I must remain here."

Rudy nodded, and then left the dome. The expression on his face had said nothing.

Jezrul walked among the gun crews, murmured into each ear, hand warm on a shoulder, whispering; "Your alertness and accuracy will bring us victory. I'm counting on you, and the blessings of Toth are with you. Good hunting." A squeeze of his hand on each shoulder, then on to the next man.

Even as he did this, there was an awful hollow within him, a feeling of doom that had begun when the men failed to return from the mainland. The gun crewmembers numbered sixteen, his remaining troops and a handful of counselors only twenty-three, and in his mind he saw three aircraft and hundreds of fighters coming at them before dawn. He'd placed the bulk of his defense force in the docking bay, for it was the only real way inside. The laser batteries would be the primary targets, the entrance secondary, nearly all his force clustered at those two places. If the aircraft got through and hit those targets, it—well, it would be over, attackers swarming inside, hand-to-hand against the remaining few.

Jezrul sensed defeat, and was angered by it. He could die, and for what? A bunch of simple-minded people and a man who'd tricked him into believing He was invulnerable, a man who'd manipulated them all with ceremony, Pain and Pleasure, and then hid Himself from them. It was Toth who had conspired to throw out Diego Segur, yet Jezrul knew the people saw *him* as conspirator, not Toth. The murder of Lebyn had been by Toth's order, yet He'd forbidden such things by His Own Laws. It is fitting, thought Jezrul that Toth Himself has, or will die by my own hand, for he has used me to subvert The Law and maintain His power. And if I must now die, everything will go with me: Rudy, the men, Toth and our society. Everything will be gone.

He suddenly remembered Kari. She would go too, and if possible her own people would witness her death. He thought of her waiting for his return, the sight of his staff, knowing now what to expect. Her reaction to The Pain had been exquisite, driving him into frenzy. He wanted to do it again, one more time, even if it was a last time. He wanted to do it to her *now*.

No, that would have to wait until after Rudy returned, perhaps with new lies to tell about Lord Toth's health, a missive to boost the spirits of the men, something to remind them their leader was not yet Jezrul, but a specter that dwelled in the bowels of the island. Jezrul wiped sweaty palms on his robe and busied himself, but it was well after dark when the younger counselor finally returned.

Rudy's face was haggard, as if he had spent an entire day in argument. Jezrul was looking over the shoulder of the man on the optical scanner when Rudy walked up to him. "You're very late," said Jezrul. "I have other matters to look after, you know."

"One of them is Toth," said Rudy, plopping into a chair. "He's awake and wants to see you, so you'd better get right down there. I've just run up four flights of stairs to give you that message."

"I cannot see Our Lord right now," said Jezrul. "I expect to see boats any second, and our people in the docking bay are not yet under proper cover for an air attack. Tell Him that, Rudy."

"He asked for you, First Counselor, and he is waiting."

Was that a faint smile on Rudy's face? Was Toth *really* alive and waiting for him? It was not time for the final confrontation, not before he'd dealt with Rudy and the woman, and not before the battle had been fought. His heart pounded.

"I will not see Toth now, and I have explained why. What are you up to, Rudy? You seem pleased about something. Good news to share?" He could no longer hide his contempt for the man, or the mounting concern and anger inside him, and it must have shown in his face for Rudy suddenly backed up a step, his smirk disappearing.

"Toth commands your presence. You're refusing?"

"I am, and you may tell him that. I am in charge here, in charge of fending off an attack that can destroy us all. I have no time for quibbling, and neither do you." Jezrul spoke loudly, and all the men could hear him. They now looked stony-faced, not at him, but at Rudy. "You will stay here and keep watch while I see to the men in the loading bay. You will not leave here until I return!"

Rudy's mouth opened in protest, but he said nothing as Jezrul stalked past him in a huff of righteous indignation to flee from the dome, leaving the man there under the glaring eyes of the gun crews.

Jezrul *did* go to the docking bay and there he said words of encouragement to the handful of troops, placed them in sheltered positions around the bay before leaving. He walked the halls, rounded up the guards of Toth's sanctuary and Diego's room, peeking inside to see the former first counselor sitting on his bed, staring catatonically at a wall. He found two counselors "meditating"—hiding was more like it—in Toth's garden. He placed them along the hall and in two rooms near the loading bay, and then raced up the stairs to his own room, head pounding, and his palms sweating in anticipation. He took his staff from the closet, raced around the curve of the hall to Kari's room.

A guard was standing there, visor down, right in front of her door.

Jezrul could barely contain his fury. He stomped up to the guard and struck the floor hard with the base of his staff. "What are you doing here?" he asked sharply.

The guard's face was hidden behind his visor as he snapped to attention. "Guarding the prisoner as ordered, First Counselor."

"Guarding her from what? She's locked in her room. Who ordered this?"

"Counselor Hoffman, an hour ago. I'm to keep anyone from entering her room." The man was shaking.

"And does anyone include your First Counselor?" Jezrul's nose was nearly touching the man's visor.

The guard's voice was a squeak; "He *did* mention your name, First Counselor. He said he didn't want you listening to her lies or being otherwise distracted by her before the attack. He said..."

"Hoffman does *not* give the orders here! *I* do! And by listening to him, you've abandoned a defense post! Would you like a taste of my staff, or would you prefer to be shot for dereliction of duties?" Jezrul's spittle fell on the guard's visor.

"I—I received no orders for a defensive position, First Counselor."

There was a shout from the stairwell, someone calling his name. Jezrul stepped back in mock surprise. "Really? Well, that's a different matter, an oversight on my part. I can't have you standing here guarding a locked door, so get downstairs and place yourself in the hall by the door to the docking bay. Do it *now!*"

"Yes, First Counselor!" The guard fled to the stairwell and collided with a gun crewmember descending the stairs.

"First Counselor! Jezrul! You're needed upstairs immediately!"

"He's in there," said the guard.

Jezrul had his hand on the door handle. "First Counselor, come quickly! There's something on the scanners, boats heading towards us from west and south! Counselor Hoffman says the attack is coming! Please, I have to get back to my post!"

Jezrul wanted to scream his rage and frustration, but held it back. "I'm coming," he said, and followed the man back up the stairs to the laser batteries.

The room was cherry red in the lights used for night operations and the dome rumbled as it opened and rotated towards the west. Gun crews were scrambling to their seats high up in the dome and Jezrul heard the barely audible whistle of gigavolt capacitors charging in the power bay a few meters beneath his feet. The four huge laser cannon ascended on pedestals to maximum height in the room, their metal and glass snouts turning south and west, then downward slightly towards the sea.

Rudy stood at the IR scanner, frantically beckoning to him. He pointed to the screen as Jezrul arrived, his finger flitting from one faint dot to another on a field of blackness, specks of green in an arc around the southwest quadrant near the island. "Sails," he said, "coming in from west and south and moving steadily. They must have been sitting out there for hours with their sails down, but now they're coming in."

"How far out?" asked Jezrul, stepping over to the optical scanner.

"Three, maybe four kilometers, about where we usually see the islanders' boats."

Under high magnification they seemed to be the usual fishing craft, single-sail, no motors, spread out in an arc from west to south, and definitely converging on the island. "Too dark to see what they're carrying," said Jezrul, "but even if they appear empty there could be people in the holding tanks below deck."

"Should we fire a warning?" said Rudy.

"No, wait until they get much closer. There will be no warnings. Have you looked in all directions?"

"Yes. Nothing east or north, but we'll keep monitoring. Even before dawn the IR background will be too strong to see much in the east."

"What's the minimum range the cannon can be brought to bare?"

"Five hundred meters."

"Then open fire if and when they cross the one kilometer mark. Burn every boat and keep burning, even if they run away."

Rudy went to the crews to pass on the orders, and Jezrul settled himself at the optical scanner. The telescope itself sat at the very summit of the island and could see in all directions, while the IR unit had a twenty-degree shadow to the north. He set the telescope for continual rotation, and watched the screen as it went through one revolution, then another, and another. Each time the boats were closer, squeezing in on the island like a great claw.

At the two-kilometer mark they stopped.

Before Jezrul's eyes sails were coming down, one man working them in each boat. Jezrul's stomach crawled. One man in each boat? Not unusual, for when the islanders observed them it was usually two or three boats with a solitary man in each. But now it didn't seem right, and his suspicion returned that people were hidden in the catch tanks of each vessel. One shot amidships would take them out in a ball of fire. He yelled to the crews, "When we open fire, aim for the decks just aft of the mast, and if they turn, go for the hull amidships at water level!"

But now the boats just sat there at two kilometers out, watching. Waiting for what? He turned to Rudy; saw him frowning at the IR screen. "See something?"

"I thought so, but it's gone now, a flickering point far out. It was there for only a second."

Again the crawling uneasiness in his stomach, and Jezrul rotated the telescope east and west, and saw nothing. The first glow of coming sunrise was just appearing in the east, though the water was still black out there. Darkness in the north, where the IR scanner was blind. He held there for a moment, swept west. The boats had not moved. "What are you waiting for?" he growled at the screen. He wanted to open fire, to incinerate them all on the spot, but some instinct from within him prevented it. The boats had stopped simultaneously, a pre-planned move; yet far enough out that even a sudden charge would not allow them to escape destruction. Surely they knew that? Could they be moving people *underwater* at this very moment? Did they have such technology? He turned again to Rudy. "Anything in or around the boats?"

"Just one man in each. I can see them clearly, now."

Somehow this was part of a bigger plan, some pieces missing. "Turn the IR east and scan slowly, then the northern sector as much as you can."

Rudy obeyed, searched the screen for long, agonizing moments. Jezrul squirmed in his chair, wanting to scream at the man for a response. Finally, Rudy shook his head. "Nothing and it's getting difficult to see in the east. Sunrise is only an hour away and there's some mist forming."

Jezrul turned the telescope east, stared at the screen long and hard. Nothing. He sighed, flopped back in his chair and jabbed the controls with a finger. Something was missing, something the boats were waiting for, but where could it....

He jumped up from his chair as the telescope came around again, and he saw sails up, men stumbling to tillers, the prow waves of boats suddenly on the move, converging on him. "Stand ready!" he screamed, but the gun crews were alert, peering at the screens before them, bracketing their targets amidships as their weapons turned slowly to south and west. *Suicide*, he thought. *These people are committing suicide. And for what reason?*

The boats charged inwards, their pilots now standing at their tillers, alone. They moved fast, approaching the one and a half kilometer mark, and Jezrul could stand it no longer.

"Fire!" he screamed, "fire, FIRE!"

The huge guns fired simultaneously, dome lights dimming, a whine from below them. Three boats west and one to the south were neatly cut in half amidst a shower of wood shards, sinking like rocks, the heads of their pilots bobbing in the sea. Jezrul's blood was boiling. "Keep firing! Leave nothing!"

The cannon moved with ponderous delay, finding new targets and firing again, accurately, more boats flashing in flame. Six left, coming inside of a kilometer, cannon following them down, down, nearing the limit of maneuverability. "Hurry!" screamed Jezrul, and two boats south, and two in the west erupted in balls of fire. Two had escaped, were inside five hundred meters, veering to skirt the island, heading east and he turned the telescope to follow them. Suddenly the plan was clear, the reason for human sacrifice so obvious, for closing in on them from the east was one of their own boats filled with troops, and not their own, for standing in the bow was one who carried not a laser rifle, but a projectile weapon. He turned in his seat, grabbed up his rifle.

"Jezrul!" screamed Rudy. "Something white hot coming in from the west! It looks like a—"

The explosion was horrible, deafening, throwing the crews from their seats into a tangled pile on the metal deck and shattering the monitor screens of the scanners. They scrambled to their feet, heard a roar, and then the room was filled with a horrible heat and the light of a sun. Jezrul felt himself lifted from the floor and carried to a crash landing on the floor near the stairwell. He looked up dazed to see the dome hanging in shards, two laser cannon twisted ruins over the broken and bloody bodies of their crews. Four men scrambled to the remaining two cannon, tried vainly to maneuver them for a shot. "A ship!" one screamed, "It's firing at us! It's—"

A clattering of heavy bullets cut off his words, his body jerking and exploding in gore as the remaining lasers were cut to pieces. Shrapnel sprayed, and men screamed in agony. Rudy disappeared beneath the wreckage.

Jezrul thought only of death: his own, Rudy's, Kari's, the man who had brought this on them. Before he died, he would kill them all.

Jezrul ran. He stumbled into the stairwell and went up the stairs in a bound, holding his rifle in a numbed hand. No easy death for her, no pleasure before pain, he would start with her groin and work upwards. He ran to Kari's room and destroyed the lock with a single burst, kicked the door open.

The room was empty! He screamed a curse, threw open the closet, the bathing stall, looked under the bed. She was gone! *Rudy!* He thought. *If he's not dead, he soon will be!*

As he reached the door, another explosion slammed him against it and threw him on his face in the hall. Still <u>another</u> explosion, from below this time. No time. Where would she go? Where would Rudy have taken her? Was it the garden, with its trees and thick foliage, and the tunnel behind the waterfall? Or one of the rooms? No time. NO TIME! He sprinted to the stairwell, and held his breath against the swirling smoke and dust there. He plummeted down the stairs to sea level, collided with a frightened counselor blocking the exit, and knocked him to the floor.

Several troops were in the hall, backing towards him. Another explosion rocked them and he heard screams from the loading bay, quickly followed by the rattle of heavy gunfire. They had penetrated! Queal's people were inside!

Jezrul's mind whirled with singleness of purpose, a final objective. There was killing to be done. He left the few defenders where they were and sprinted to the door leading to Toth's garden. As he grasped the door handle another explosion shook everything around him and the door flew open, slamming him back against a wall. He darted inside, blinded at first by a cloud of dust and falling rock. The great domed ceiling of the garden was gone, fragments still falling, crushing trees and flowers. The waterfall was a trickle and a cloud

218

of hysterical birds circled the garden like a living tornado, lifting up into the early morning sky, thousands of butterflies moving with them. He ran around the path circling the garden, looking for a robed figure hiding or crushed under debris, finding nothing and returning to the door, rifle at the ready, hope fading.

He could not believe his luck when he heard her crying, the sobs coming from the pit housing the transponder for the barrier.

He stepped up to the railing surrounding it, and there she was, just coming out of the tunnel, half-wading, half-swimming, and from outside came the sound of rock tumbling into the sea. There was a bloody gash on her forehead and she thrashed her way into the pit, moaning, not seeing him until he reached down to grab her by the hair and wrench her screaming from the water. Her scream drove him wild as he pulled her soaked body over the railing, bent her over it and put the muzzle of the rifle under her chin, but then heavy fire erupted in the hallway behind him and people were running. He jerked her head, slammed her against a wall and her eyes clouded. "I will find a private place for you to die," he said, and then jumped at the sound of a voice behind him.

"Let her go, Jezrul, or I'll kill you where you stand."

Rudy stood two meters away from him, his head bloody, and aimed a laser pistol at him. "Our men are dying, and you run from the fighting. You are cursed, Jezrul."

Jezrul whirled as an explosion shook the hall. He jerked Kari in front of him as his rifle came up to fire a single burst into Rudy's chest. Kari screamed as the man flopped on his back, arms outstretched. Footsteps echoed in the hall, shadows on the walls as people approached, and he recognized Queal and Osen—and Nimri, a traitor who had joined them. He grabbed Kari by the hair again, fired wildly at Nimri with one hand, but the struggling woman spoiled his aim and he hit another man instead. He dragged her to the door, shut and locked it behind him as a fusillade of bullets tore up the walls around the pit. He half-carried her through the garden to the door leading to Toth's sanctuary, where he intended to complete his last murdering tasks.

Moments later he was in the sanctuary, shutting the gate behind him and looking around the room.

The throne was empty.

Jezrul deposited Kari on the floor before the throne, and put the rifle muzzle against her nose. "If you move I'll kill you slowly, starting with your feet." She was dazed, and collapsed on the floor, sobbing. He went to the terminal, punched his entrance to the life-support system and stared in dismay at the readings. *So Rudy wasn't lying.*

The throne lit up, and Toth was there, sitting tall and glowering at him.

"So, Rudy was correct. You tried to kill me, Jezrul; you, the one I would make leader of My People. And you've brought the woman with you. That's just as well, for now both of you will die together. Guards, take them! Rudy!"

Jezrul stood with Kari at his feet, grinning in the light of the throne. "There are no guards to help you, and Rudy is dead! The fortress has been invaded and they will be here any minute, oh great and mighty lord, but not before I've killed you!" He brandished his rifle at the hologram.

Toth grinned a horrible grin. "Then feel my wrath, Traitor!"

The Pain struck him like laser heat, coursing up and down his body with intensity he'd never imagined, a delicious thing, warming him, pleasing him at a level he'd only dreamed of. He screamed; "More, more! I want MORE!" He reached down, grabbed Kari by the hair. "Come, now, and share my Pleasure!"

Kari screamed in hysterical agony.

The gate to the tunnel burst open, spilling Michael Queal and his followers into the room.

CHAPTER TWENTY-THREE

The holographic image of an old man was perched on the throne. Michael saw a hooked nose on a withered face, and eyes that glowed like green coals. The throne was bathed in green light. A buzzing came from it and Jezrul was standing in the light, laughing, and holding Kari up against him as a shield. Jezrul's body was shaking, one arm around her neck, the other trying to level a rifle at them as Kari writhed in his grasp, screaming. There was no clear shot without risk to Kari, and Michael raised the muzzle of his rifle towards the ceiling as the others tumbled in behind him. "Give it up, Jezrul. There are a hundred marines right behind us. Whatever you're doing to her, stop it or we'll kill you right now!"

"But she's one of us, now!" screamed Jezrul. "She shares The Pain. Now watch her die! I have baptized her, Lord; see how she feels your wrath? My pleasure is her agony, but it isn't enough! More! Give us more!"

The buzzing sound intensified. Kari cried out hysterically, and then slumped unconscious in his grasp. "No! Stay awake!" yelled Jezrul, shaking her.

"She will die with you," growled the holographic man. "You are a fornicator, Jezrul, a devil, and I will be rid of you."

Jezrul shook, eyes rolling crazily, but still he laughed. "See the impotence of Toth! With all his power he cannot harm me!"

"He has betrayed you, Lord!" shouted Nimri from the darkness. "He has murdered in Your Name and spread lies about our visitors!"

Jezrul snapped off a single shot at the accusing voice. Nimri howled and went down as Jezrul pressed Kari to him, preventing retaliation.

"Stay together, behind me!" said Michael. "Don't give him another shot! Nimri?"

"My shoulder," said the counselor now lying in darkness at his feet. "It burns."

Michael aimed carefully. "If Kari is dying anyway I'll shoot right through her, Jezrul. Stop the pain or I'll fire right now!"

Jezrul believed him; Michael saw it in his eyes. He backed up two steps, and pointed his rifle at the throne base. "The Pain is our gift from Toth, from here, and here!" He fired twice at the base of the throne, shattering it in a double spray of stone fragments. The buzzing stopped.

"Jezrul!" screamed Toth, leaning forward.

"Our great and mighty Lord who hides from us there and there!" Jezrul twisted, still shielded by Kari and fired twice behind him at the panels above a computer terminal in the corner of the room.

Toth shrieked, a holo-man now writhing and kicking his legs in sudden agony as they all watched in amazement.

"I give you my pleasure and pain, Great Lord!" Jezrul fired again, and flame erupted from the panel. To the right there was a loud clang, and voices. Michael saw a door there, the main entrance to the room.

"It's locked!" yelled someone outside.

"Blow it!" Krisha's voice.

"They're here, Jezrul!" shouted Michael over the screams of Toth. "Let her go and you might live through this!"

"To live in your world? NEVER! Oh, Lord, do you feel it? Do you feel the loveliness of it? This is my gift to you!" Jezrul was backing up, dragging Kari towards the terminal. The door exploded inwards with a cloud of acrid smoke and marines poured into the room, Krisha in the middle of them, her visor up.

"Hold your fire, Krisha! She's alive!"

The marines spread out around the back of the room, but Krisha stood near the door, rifle leveled at Jezrul, the taut muscles and veins in her arms standing out in high relief.

Twenty-five rifles were aimed at Jezrul as he backed towards the corner. Toth still screamed, his image flickering in and out. Kari was slumped against Jezrul, his arm around her chest. Michael saw her head move, her eyes opening, blinking rapidly as Jezrul dragged her towards the corner. And when he was there, still holding her tightly in front of him, he raised his rifle and brought the butt of it crashing down on the computer and controls there, smashing everything to junk and laughing insanely as he did it. Toth let out one final, agonized scream and his image disappeared, the room suddenly in gloom. Jezrul twisted around, fired two quick shots at a panel which fell away, bright light issuing forth to momentarily blind them, but in making his move his grip on Kari had loosened and she suddenly came back to life, dropping straight to the floor and out of his grasp, rolling away from him as twenty five assault rifles on full-automatic roared their approval. Jezrul's body exploded, the impact of hundreds of bullets lifting him from the floor and smashing him into the panel opening where a figure danced grotesquely in a liquid-filled cylinder like an obscene puppet on strings, a living corpse connected to a thousand tubes and wires.

Shots missing Jezrul shattered the cylinder, spraying liquid, shattering bones of a living skeleton without muscle or flesh, covered only with a layer of tissue-like skin, a lump that was a beating heart protruding from a shriveled chest. Skeleton arms flailed wildly as the bullets struck, and the mouth of a huge, cadaverous medusa head was open in a silent scream. The heart exploded in a shower of sparks; arms and legs shattered and fell away. The horrible head jerked again and again, then slumped forward to stare down at Jezrul's ruined body as a sudden, terrible silence descended on the room. All stood in shock, magazines empty, staring at the cadaver that was Toth, wires and tubes stretching and relaxing in gentle rhythm, the connections to his world, the connections to his power now holding him in final death.

Kari sobbed and finally someone moved. Krisha rushed to her, swept her up in strong arms and carried her from the room as the others moved in to view the bodies.

"My God," said a young marine, "what *is* it?"

"This is Toth," said Michael, "Edward Tothman, a man who should have been dead a long time ago." He turned and saw Nimri standing there, one arm limp, a marine holding him up. The man's eyes were filled with tears.

"This is who you believed in, Counselor, this is who has been ruling your lives. Did you hear Jezrul? The things he did were by Toth's orders, the orders of an ancient, failing mind that felt control slipping away. He was responsible, Counselor, and Jezrul was a tool, a tool that in the end turned against the master. It's over, Nimri, they're both gone. What will you now say to the people?"

"I don't know," croaked Nimri. Tears streaked his face. "Take him back to the bay and do what you can for his shoulder," said Michael, and the marine holding Nimri half-carried him from the room.

There was a snap, then the sound of a rifle bolt slamming home. Osen stepped up to Michael's side, aimed his loaded rifle at Jezrul and looked at Michael for a response. His expression was emotionless, a deadly expression Michael had seen once before on a darkened beach.

"What the hell, boy, do it, but I don't want any further damage to Toth's body."

They all watched passively as Osen stepped up to point-blank range and they held their ears as he emptied the thirty-round magazine into Jezrul's pulpy remains.

He was still standing there, Michael's arm around his shoulders, when two marines returned with the body bags.

* * * * * *

The final count for marines, villagers, and islanders was twelve dead and several wounded. Four of the brave men who had sailed into Toth's laser fire had been found floating at sea, but Michael considered it fortunate no other islanders or villagers had been killed, and their four wounded would likely have complete recoveries. Of Toth's defenders, only three had survived, one of them a counselor. Bandaged, they huddled together in the loading bay as bodies were brought out, labeled and bagged. They feared for their lives, despite Nimri's quiet assurances that blame would not be placed on them, that their knowledge of the island would be vital in the societal reconstruction to come. One of them, a gun crew commander named Rustin Nolting had already helped them to power down the island, shutting off the barrier and putting the great fusion reactor beneath them on standby.

Osen sat by the bag containing the remains of Floyd Mootry, and Michael left him to his grief, walked outside and found Krisha sitting on a rock, embracing Kari. They were talking softly. Krisha's fingers caressed Kari's hair. Both had been crying and Michael left them alone in their private moment. He found Davos in his boat. Nimri was with him, and looked up as Michael hopped from the platform to the bow to join them.

"So, Michael, you've survived," said Davos, smiling. "I know at least one person who will be happy about that."

"Are you okay?"

"Oh yes. I stayed close to the boat most of the time. The only danger out here was all the falling rock, but it was enough."

"How about you, Counselor? I see they got you bandaged up."

Nimri's left arm was in a sling. "It missed the bone, but I'm told there might be numbness for a long time. I feel fortunate it isn't worse."

Michael sat down beside them. "You're taking this well, Counselor, about Toth, I mean. But I don't see how it could have been avoided. We're bringing his remains out pretty soon and returning them to our camp for study, but it won't be for long. I presume you'll want to bury him."

"Yes," said Nimri, "but not before the people see him and pay their last respects."

"You want them to *see* him? Do you think that's wise?"

"It will help them to understand," said Nimri. "Many thought of him as something other than a man, an immortal who could not be replaced, a God, if you will. With his death, our society is forever changed, and those changes must be according to the will of the people."

"I'm glad to hear you say that."

"You will do nothing to interfere with the process? My father has just told me about your intention to remain here, the relation between you—and my sister. Will you live according to the wishes of the people—help us to rebuild?"

"Yes, if I can be accepted here. Right now I'm concerned about that."

Nimri nodded his head. "We can only wait and see."

"Private Osen will be staying with me. Colonel Mootry was his father, and for political reasons he can't return with our starship. There will be two of us left behind."

"I can think of advantages to that. Our isolation is ended, and others will come now. We'll need you here to prepare for that, our connection to the other worlds. Yes, there are reasons for you remaining here, and I think the people will agree."

Nimri looked over Michael's shoulder then, eyes widening in surprise. "Ah. He wasn't killed after all, but he doesn't look well."

Michael turned; saw two marines escorting a tall, robed man between them, holding him up as he shuffled unsteadily across the rock.

It was Diego Segur.

His face was a blank, eyes unfocused, and there was dried blood on his chin. The marines brought him to the boat and Nimri jumped up to help the big man step into it, sitting him down carefully opposite Michael.

"We found him alone in a room, staring at a wall," said a marine. "He hasn't shown any reaction to us, hasn't said a word. The med-techs think he's been tortured. A piece of his tongue is gone, and they figure he bit it off while they were doing whatever they did to him. All locked up in his mind, now, catatonic."

"Diego? First Counselor? It's Nimri. Can you hear me?"

The man stared ahead, unmoving.

"No marks on him, other than the tongue," said the marine. "Physically he seems to be okay. There was a half-eaten plate of food in his room."

"Thank you," said Nimri. "We will take care of him now. We'll take care of you, Diego." Nimri put an arm around the man's shoulders, patted him. "So many dead and injured and now this. There's much hurt to undo. So much."

"What in hell did they do to him?" said Michael.

"Toth's Pain, and he is an old man, locked into himself to escape it. We'll bring him back to us, won't we? You'll come back to us, Diego, if you want to." He patted the man's shoulder again.

The Gull-boat had pulled up to the boat platform and all bodies, including Mootry's, were loaded into it. It was early evening before they finally pulled away from the island. The Gull raced ahead, the four remaining sailboats and speedboat following slowly. Here and there they passed the scorched boards of boats now at the bottom of the sea and Michael was reminded of the men and their families who'd made the ultimate sacrifice to spearhead the attack. Suddenly it all sickened him: the pain, death, and family losses of loved ones. War. This was the end of it for him. He would never willingly participate in it again. From this moment on, he was not a marine.

But the most poignant moment of the day came for him after they had reached the big island and taken skiffs to shore. He climbed the steps to the settlement and found everyone crammed in the amphitheatre, eating a hot meal. Osen was nowhere to be seen, but Krisha and Kari were there, pressed close together, and Davos joined them. Michael followed Nimri and Diego to the amphitheatre and found a space in a top row. Women served them a stew of Lonia and potatoes, and cups filled with warm Fiero. Nimri fed Diego with a glass spoon, and the man ate well, eyes blinking when the first sip of Fiero hit his stomach. Then the people around them were suddenly silent. Michael looked up and Derald was standing there, shaking, his eyes glistening with tears. He pressed past Michael, knelt at his son's feet and looked straight into the man's eyes. "Diego," he said, "my son, you're still alive. You're still alive." He put his hands on Diego's shoulders and squeezed hard.

Diego's mouth opened. Inside it his ruined tongue moved, thrusting out and in. It was as if a film had suddenly been lifted from his eyes. He made a strangled cry and reached out both hands to touch Derald's face.

"Faaah," he said.

226

* * * * * * *

There was no sleep for any of them that night. What started out as a simple dinner turned into a series of toasts, then a wake for those who had died. A boisterous party lasted until dawn when a year's supply of Fiero finally ran dry. Michael nursed two glasses of the strong drink until midnight, feeling a light buzz despite his caution, and then retired to the Agbayekhai house where Derald had taken his son for a night's rest. He found the old man at the lovely glass table there in the light of a lantern, scribbling furiously on bark. Derald looked up and smiled.

"How's Diego doing?"

"He sleeps. I can do nothing for his tongue, and his speech will be slurred, but otherwise I think he will do well. I never thought I'd see him again."

"Will you come with us to the mainland?"

"Not just yet. I'm working on some ideas here and I want to get them down while they're fresh. The reactor on Toth's island can give us unlimited power, you know. I see an underwater cable running to it if I can get the materials. Iron will not do; its electrical resistance is too high."

"Copper or silver," said Michael, "or you might convert the power to microwaves and beam it both here and to the mainland. The technology could be brought here within a few years."

Derald's eyes were bright with excitement. "So many possibilities, so many things to do."

"Yes, but I have a simpler matter to discuss and a request to make. While Kari was a prisoner on the island Jezrul implanted a biochip in her. You told me once that you had a simple procedure for deactivating it without major surgery, and I'd like you to do it for her. She's had the implant for only a couple of days."

"Of course," said Derald. "It will take only a few minutes, but you understand the chip must remain where it is. It will simply become inert."

"When can you do it?"

"In the morning, before you leave. Bring her here."

"I appreciate it, Derald. I'll go and tell her." Michael turned to leave.

Derald held up his hand. "One moment, Michael. I hear rumors that when your ship is gone you will remain here. Is that true?"

"Yes, if the people will allow it."

"And why would they *not* allow it?"

"The fighting. The dying. Some will continue to blame my people and I for what have happened, including Toth's death. He had his supporters right up to the end."

"On the mainland, perhaps, certainly not here. If you cannot live comfortably on the mainland there will always be a place for you here, Michael, I can assure you of that."

Michael felt gladness in his heart. "Thank you for saying that, Derald. I really *want* to stay, to help rebuild your society, and that's going to be several lifetimes of work. Mainlanders—islanders—you're really two different cultures now."

"Our histories and philosophies are different, yes, but we're all one people. You'll see some tearful reunions when several of our older people return to the mainland with you tomorrow. You will see we're only family members returning after an absence of forty years. Ah, a question: what will you do with the aircraft we mounted on my pontoon boat for the attack?"

"Leave it here, of course. It's useless as a flyer."

"Wonderful. You know, it ran nicely on alcohol, very efficiently. It will be only a twenty-minute trip to the mainland with it, and I'd like to begin some trade right away. I think we will come together as one people faster than you imagine, Michael, and you should be part of that happening."

* * * * * * *

The Gull left just after dawn, Osen having spent the night in it with the body of his father. The few remaining sailboats and the speedboat were loaded by noon, the delay caused by slow, painful awakenings of marines and islanders who'd participated in the previous night's revelry. Michael took Kari to meet Derald at the Agbayekhai house, then walked a very anxious Krisha down to the beach and sat down beside her in the sand.

"She'll be fine," he said. "It'll only take a few minutes, and we need to talk about something."

His voice tone was serious, and she looked at him expectantly. "Sir?"

Michael took a deep breath, and let it out. "I'm not going back with you, Krisha."

"You're staying on the island, Major? You want me to—"

"No, I'm staying on this planet, not going back to *Belsus*. I'm past due for mustering out and I'm preparing my separation papers as soon as we get back to the mainland. With Colonel Mootry dead, you're number two on *Belsus* and I want to appoint you commander. There'll be a field promotion to Major, and if you say yes, I can have the papers cut today."

Krisha was stunned, and swallowed hard. "Can you live here, Major? Will they let you do it?"

"It seems so. Osen's staying here too. I won't tell you why, but if you check the computer on *Belsus* I'm pretty sure you'll find out he doesn't exist. He's not a marine, Krisha, that's all I'll say. Osen stays with me.

"Maybe you want some time to think. You're the natural choice, third in rank and career military. I've seen your record; it's flawless, and I've watched you turn boys into hardened veterans in one week. They'll follow you anywhere, and so will the rest of the crew. What do you say?"

A faint smile was on her face. "Yes sir. I accept. It's an unexpected honor, Major. I'm surprised."

"It's done, then." Michael started to get up, but then Krisha startled *him* with a sudden insight of her own.

"Begging your pardon, sir, but if you're going to be staying here, I presume you'll be helping these people to rebuild their society and acting as some kind of liaison when the trading ships begin to arrive. You know they're right behind us, sir, it's only one jump to the closest freighter lane."

"Probably. I'll do what I can."

"Well, wouldn't it make sense to formalize it, to keep you here as a representative of the Federation? All we'd have to do is put you on active reserve status."

"I'm seventy-five *now*, Krish."

Now Krisha truly smiled. "You know deep-sleep isn't counted, sir. You can have ten more years of service, if you want it, maybe twenty if Arkon decides to give you a fancy title, and *that* could take twenty years."

Michael paused, scratched his chin. "Let me think about it and get back to you. We've got some fences to mend on the mainland before you fly away."

"I understand, sir. Can I get back to Kari, now?"

"Sure, and tell her I said that to be on the safe side she should stay away from the radio shack for awhile."

Krisha actually laughed, a smile spreading across her face as she got up. "I'll do that, sir." She walked away from him, still chuckling.

Four hours later he was standing at the bow of the speedboat, the village now visible and beyond it the rolling green hills of the mainland. He still thought about what Krisha had suggested, and remembered what Floyd had told him. *For an old combat marine, Mike, you've turned into a pretty good diplomat.* So maybe it wasn't such a bad idea: staying on reserve status, a formal representative of the Federation. Who could know what was coming, the problems they would have when the money people who operated the freighter lines discovered what was here? An Arkon presence could bring some security in dealing with them.

His thoughts snapped back to what was real and not conjecture, what was happening *now*. The beach was visible, and the sailboats that had started out ahead of them had just reached the surf. A crowd was waiting for them, and Michael's stomach churned with uncertainty about the reception. Nimri came up to stand at his side, the staff of his former office conspicuously absent from his hand. "It's good to be home again," he said.

Home? Could this place be home to him after all that had happened? Word must already have spread about the returning dead. What about the families who had lost loved ones and providers? What could he say to them to justify their loss? How could he ask to live out his life among them?

Michael's heart was pounding in anticipation as they hit the surf and coasted in with it. People were wading ashore and there were embraces, men and their families, old people peering uncertainly, then crying out and rushing forward at the sight of relatives cut off from them for over forty years. They stood in the surf, hugging, crying as Michael's boat slowed to a stop. Nimri jumped in and began wading to shore and a crowd was moving towards him.

It was at that instant he saw Gini. She'd been further down the beach and now she was running towards him at water's edge. He jumped in, waded to intercept her as she thrashed toward him in knee-deep water. She let out a little cry as she launched herself into his arms, hugging, kissing him over and over again, yet not a word passed between them until they were on the beach. People looked at them curiously as they came out of the water, hand-in-hand, and Michael caught Kari grinning at him. Davos had found his grandson, Uhli, and came up to them, the little boy in his arms.

"Here is Michael," said Davos.

The little boy looked solemnly at Michael, then down to where his hand joined Gini's.

And then his mouth curved into a shy, uncertain smile.

CHAPTER TWENTY-FOUR

Michael stood on the plateau, and the Gull was a black silhouette against the first light on the eastern horizon. Osen had declined to come with him, choosing instead to watch the departure from a point on the ridge overlooking the village and the sea. It was the place where they had buried his father three weeks before. A monument was to be erected over the grave, a slab of stone commemorating the man who lay there, and the event that had caused his death.

The viewing of Toth, alias Edward Tothman, had been a sobering occasion for the villagers, and showed them the real creature who had ruled their lives for centuries from his liquid bath at sea. The broken body had been partially hidden from view beneath the folds of a counselor's robe, the huge head visible and undamaged. Grumbles of disgust and muffled cries of horror had been heard during the viewing. There were still those who would remember him with quiet reverence, those who saw him as a man who'd prolonged his life too far to see to the needs of his people, a man victimized by his own counselors, notably Jezrul. They had buried Jezrul at sea, shrouded in white, along with the rest of their dead and those from the stars who had given their lives to begin a new order.

Mutual grief had brought them closer together: villagers, islanders and marines alike. The work to repair the damage to the obelisk had moved even further to form a bond between them. The night before, when the Gull had returned to begin its final loading, a crowd of people had come to the plateau with gifts for their departing 'cousins': fish, vegetables, sprays of flowers, an assortment of glass objects, including a wonderful window brought from the island. They'd presented their gifts to Krisha in their quiet, unemotional manner, and then gone away. Krisha was clearly moved, and Kari had wept without shame.

But now the moment was rapidly approaching when Michael's world would vanish into the sky, leaving him to an unknown future.

There had been no outcries against he and Osen remaining behind, and a few people had even given him words of welcome, but still he worried. In the end he'd said yes to Krisha's suggestion and so he was now Lieutenant Colonel Michael Queal, a member of Victoria's Marine Reserve assigned as Trade Liaison Officer to the planet Emerson, also known as Tothwelt. The move had been applauded by the islanders' council, which saw a future in trading with other worlds, while the villagers saw him as possible protection against unscrupulous visitors who might seek to exploit them in the future.

In only four weeks after Toth's death an infrastructure was beginning to develop. Derald had arrived with his council, met formally with Nimri and a group of villagers hand-picked by him to discuss future governance. Michael had felt it significant he'd been invited to attend. He answered questions about future problems they might face in dealing with other worlds, even the dangers they should be prepared for. It was agreed that mainlanders and islanders would maintain their separate councils by election, but meet together regularly in unified assembly. The technology on Toth's island would be kept intact, or repaired where possible, though the huge lasers there seemed unrepairable, at least in the immediate future. Existing weapons, in considerable supply, were to be stored under the supervision of the Assembly and used only to defend against off-world attack. Staffs of all former counselors were to be dismantled and the components used for peaceful purposes. So much accomplishment in a single four-hour meeting had given Michael much hope and optimism for the new society.

Michael smiled as he thought about Derald. The old man was a strategic thinker and the wonderful gifts he'd brought over for Krisha were a part of that thinking, some little things to show the merchants who wandered among the stars in search of profit. His list of trade items had included copper wire and paints and some machinery, including electrical generators and motors, but for the most part, somewhat surprising Michael, what he mostly desired was knowledge: books, tapes, discs, entire data banks on bio-computer, any form available on any subject, even including the history and cultures of the Federation. Did he really think he could absorb such vast knowledge during his remaining years? No, he'd answered, but he would teach others how to learn and apply that knowledge before he was gone. And they would be selective.

So now it was the morning of final departure and he was standing alone fifty meters from the Gull as the last few marines trotted up the ramp into its maw and disappeared inside. A moment later

Krisha and Kari came back down the ramp and over to him to say their goodbyes.

"Good morning, Commander."

"Colonel. We're ready to go, now. Anything we've missed?"

"Nothing I can see. You have a nice clear day for flying. Have a good trip."

"We will, sir, and thank you." Krisha put out her hand and shook his firmly. "You might be setting a precedent, sir. Now Nik is talking about coming back here to retire. By the time we get to Brown's Planet he'll be eligible for it."

"He could do a lot worse," said Michael, "and if he hurries I might even be around to greet him."

"You have a lot of years left, Mike," said Kari. "You going to start a new family here?"

"Maybe. I didn't do very well with the last one, so we'll see."

"Sorry we couldn't leave more, sir," said Krisha. "Osen has the radio, but Derald wanted the front-loader and the prefab shack real bad, and I had to turn him down. There's only so much I can explain away when headquarters asks about what happened here. We put a full load of munitions for the Gull back in the obelisk as you requested, and I can say that stuff got shot up in the fighting. Any messages to pass along?"

"Nope. Just try to get some merchant ships back here as soon as possible. These people have plans. I probably won't see you again, so have a good life—both of you."

Kari jumped up and kissed his cheek. "Don't forget us, Mike."

"How could I forget either one of you? Good luck in your career, Krish; I hope you go all the way."

"Thank you, sir. We'd better go."

"Yeah," said Michael.

He pumped Krisha's hand once again, and then they turned away from him, walked to the Gull and disappeared inside. The ramp retracted and the maw closed. Turbines whined and the lifters sprayed a cloud of fine dust as the Gull lifted slowly, hovered, then moved off over the cliff and out to sea, climbing more steeply. He saw the big thruster ignite before he heard the roar. The Gull disappeared rapidly, a speck trailing a line of mist, and he was standing there alone on the plateau in terrible silence, a deep hollow within him.

They were gone. His world was gone, and he was left—to what? He looked up at the ridge, but didn't see Osen there. What was *he* feeling right now? Michael walked to the edge of the cliff, looked out to sea. The sun without a name had risen and he felt its

233

warmth, smelled salt, his hair fluttering in the usual morning breeze. He stood there for a moment, and then walked across the plateau and up the trail to the village past trees and hanging moss and a profusion of flowers smelling sweetly. He heard a chirp and a rustling, looked up to see a redheaded bird sitting on a small tree branch, a twig in its mouth. The bird eyed him suspiciously, and then fluttered out of sight high in the tree. New life on the mainland, he thought. A final gift from Toth.

The obelisk loomed before him, the former sanctuary of a man-God that, at least according to Nimri, would now be a school, yet in a secret room within the hill were stored the weapons of war, and weapons that Michael sincerely hoped would rot in their place. But he was somehow comforted by their presence. *You never know when the need might arise.*

He walked the winding trail down to the village where people scurried about on their morning chores. He saw Osen and Deena, Davos's younger daughter, cross the trail ahead of him. They had just come down from the ridge and now they headed towards the beach. Michael followed them there, but when he arrived they were sitting close together on an overturned skiff, Deena waving her hands in animated conversation. The hollow in Michael's stomach seemed to get smaller when he saw them there. He left them alone and walked back to Davos's house.

The fisherman met him at the doorway, pointed north and said; "Someone is waiting impatiently for you at the waterfall. And when you return I'll show you how to toughen your hands for the fishing. We go out again in four days."

Michael waved, but said nothing, the hollow within him shrinking once again. He climbed the steep trail leading north and east from the village, his legs stronger than they'd been the time before, and his breathing was normal when he reached the gathering fields. The big island was a jagged shadow above the horizon and two birds came in from seaward to fly overhead, sailing north. Michael thought about what Kari had said, that there were other gardens like the one on the island, but scattered inland. Toth had set boundaries, and his obedient chosen had not crossed them in three hundred years, but now the boundaries were gone and they would explore their world. Why the boundaries, anyway? What had Toth been doing inland that he didn't want the people to see?

He strolled through the gathering fields and up the hillock below the pool, and again heard the tranquil sound of water falling over rock. His mind whirled with what there was to do: establishing order, rebuilding the fishing fleet, the school, relations with the islanders and still aloof planters, the adaptation of Toth's island technology, and then, someday soon, the arrival of visitors, people with their own agendas and desires. What then?

The whirl of problems was wiped from his mind in an instant as he topped the hillock and saw the pool—and Gini. She was swimming in the center of the pool and waved. "Come on in! It's just right!" She veered and dog-paddled towards him, a white shape beneath the clear water. A yellow butterfly fluttered above her head, then rushed away.

No time to be prudish. Michael took off his boots, stripped down to his shorts and paused, shivering.

Gini laughed. "Are those your bathing clothes?" She stood up in waist-deep water and held out her arms towards him.

Michael took one look at her, then pulled down his shorts and posed. "No, they are not."

"Ohhh," she said, giving him an appraising look and smiling at what she saw.

He waded into the water and it was *cold*, but in a few steps he had reached Gini and her arms were sliding around his neck, her warmth pouring into him.

His hands moved over her arms and back as her chin tilted up for a kiss, but he looked at her solemnly and said, "They're gone."

"I know," she said as their lips touched, "but you're here, and that's all that matters to me."